知識工場
Knowledge is everything！

知識工場
Knowledge is everything！

nowledge. 知識工場

Knowledge is everything！

知識工場
Knowledge is everything！

英語學習書暢銷第一名作者 **蘇秦** 著

考**公職**一定要會的

3000單字

MP3 + 題庫本

The 3000 vocabularies you must know in public service exam

輕輕鬆鬆捧得鐵飯碗，公職英文單字一次搞定！

3000個
高頻**公職**
必考**英單**

700題
歷屆**公職**
字彙題

英語**名師**
詳細**試題解析**

☑ **實力滿點**，**戰勝**考場**零失誤**

趕緊提升自己的超強英語力，
成為公職考場上的最終贏家。

1

MP3音軌標示

清楚註記MP3播放音軌，走到哪裡就聽到哪裡，輕鬆搞定英語聽力。

2

發音最正確

KK音標完整註記，善用本書重音提示，不懂單字發音也能標準又道地。

5

優質例句補充

隨單字附情境式造句，將單字融入句子中，背誦時易懂又上手。

A 🎧 001

0001 **abandon** [ə'bændən]　　　　v.　放棄　4th ★★★★★
Don't abandon yourself to destiny; everyone has the right to struggle for a better tomorrow.
別讓自己任憑命運擺佈，每個人都有權力為更好的明天奮鬥。

0002 **abbreviation** [ə,brivɪ'eʃən]　　n.　縮寫　4th ★★★★★
A common abbreviation for headquarters is HQ.
總部一般的縮寫是HQ。

0003 **ability** [ə'bɪlətɪ]　　　　　n.　能力　5th ★★★★★
What most distinguishes humans from other creatures is our ability to create and manipulate a wide variety of symbolic representations.
人類和其他生物最大的區別在於，我們有能力創造和使用各種語言文字。

0004 **abnormal** [æb'nɔrml]　　　adj.　反常的　4th ★★★★★
Paul's traumatic childhood experience has a great impact on his abnormal behavior.
保羅有創傷的童年經驗，大大影響他現在不正常的行為。

0005 **aborigine** [æbə'rɪdʒənɪ]　　n.　原住民　4th ★★★★★
Settlers overtook the land of the aborigines.
殖民者過份侵占原住民的土地。

0006 **abortion** [ə'bɔrʃən]　　　　n.　墮胎　4th ★★★★★
In America, abortion is still illegal in some states.
在美國某些州，墮胎仍是違法的。

0007 **abridge** [ə'brɪdʒ]　　　　　v.　摘要　4th ★★★★★
I did not have enough time to read the original version of the novel Bleak House, so I read an abridged one.
我沒時間看原版的《荒涼山莊》，所以改看了刪減版。

0008 **abroad** [ə'brɔd]　　　　　adv.　到國外　5th ★★★★★
Nowadays more people are going abroad for vacations, their favorite places being Japan and Thailand.
現在越來越多的人到國外度假，最受歡迎的地方包括日本和泰國。

A

6

字母A到Z排列

公職高頻3000單字依字母排序，方便搜尋查找，迅速增強應考實力。

0010 absent ['æbsənt]　　　**adv.** 缺席的　　**3rd** ★★★★★
The accounting assistant was absent from the weekly seminar.
會計助理沒有參加這次的每週研討會。

0011 absolutely ['æbsə,lutlɪ]　**adv.** 絕對地　　**4th** ★★★★★
That dessert looks absolutely delicious.
那道甜點看起來實在太美味了。

0012 absorb [əb'sɔrb]　　　**v.** 吸收　　**4th** ★★★★★
The function of the plant root is to absorb water and nutrients from the soil.
植物根部的功能是用來吸收土壤的水分和養分。

4

單字職等分析

以3rd、4th、5th代表三、四、五職等，標記該單字最容易出現的職等範圍。

0013 abstain [ab'sten]　　　**v.** 棄權　　**3rd** ★★★★★
Usually a contract involves a promise to perform an action or to abstain from some action.
一張合約通常涉及承諾執行一項行動，或放棄一些行動。

0014 abstract ['æbstrækt]　　**adj.** 抽象的　**4th** ★★★★★
I am fascinated by the artist's abstract painting.
這位畫家的抽象畫令我深深著迷。

0015 abundance [ə'bʌndəns]　**n.** 富裕　　**4th** ★★★★★
Kaohsiung is a port with an abundance of seafood; it also has popular dishes a the Liuho Night Market including fish ball soup and eel noodles.
高雄是盛產海鮮的港口，在六合夜市也有許多熱門小吃，像是魚丸湯和鱔魚麵。

0016 abundant [ə'bʌndənt]　　**adj.** 大量的　**4th** ★★★★★
The seas around Green Island are abundant with more than two hundred differer species of colorful coral.
綠島周圍的海洋蘊含超過兩百個品種的彩色珊瑚。

3

重要星等排序

善用80/20原則，依公職考常出頻率做星號標記，快速擷取關鍵標的。

0017 abuse [ə'bjuz]　　　**v.** 虐待　　**4th** ★★★★★
Retarded children are most vulnerable to physical abuses in a family.
發展遲緩的小孩最容易受到家庭的身體虐待。

0018 academic [,ækə'dɛmɪk]　**adj.** 學術的　**4th** ★★★★★
Because Tom had poor academic performance last year, his New Year's welfa

3000單字，
照亮考生的公職夢想！

如果說升學考試是考試領導教學的話，那公職考試就是考試領導學習！以英文科來說，堪稱台灣英文教育最灰暗的一角。由於許多考試的英文配分偏低，一些基礎不佳的考生率然放棄英文，向十多年的英文學習棄械投降！一些不願放棄的考生就開始找尋歷屆試題拼命猛K，其目的僅止於知道歷屆考試內容，多看多心安！於是坊間出版社便迎合考生需求，隨時印製一堆應景的公職英文書搶攻市場！然而，隨手翻閱其內容，不禁令人質疑這些未來的國家公職人員研讀英文的方法！還有，出版社提供給這些日後掌握國家競爭力的公職考生研讀的英文書籍的品質！

坊間公職英文書籍的普遍缺失有：
1. 教材內容不足，一本書涵蓋所有考試項目，讀者只能走馬看花，囫圇吞棗，無法充實提升英文能力。
2. 缺乏學習規劃，歷屆試題與答案解析並陳，考生只有單向記憶，毫無思考，剝奪應試思考訓練機會。
3. 版面印刷粗糙，錯誤頻仍，常見書中試題與考試項目不符，如高普考用書收錄國營事業試題。
一生中要背的單字何其多，況且字彙涵蓋的領域範圍這麼廣，若沒有切題、仔細撿選實用性質，眞的就白下一番苦功了！有鑑於此，本人應知識工場出版社之邀，規畫此公英文單字寶典，讓考生能輕易過關，其特點如下：

1. 從歷屆試題精心挑選三千單字，直擊公職英文核心字彙。
2. 首創題組字彙預習編排，培養讀者閱讀信心、累積經驗。
3. 收錄詳盡公職試題語料供考生研讀，並針對試題內容做詳盡解析，累積堅強考試實力。
4. 遵循認知學習原理，編排漸進式學習程序，協助讀者在緊迫的預備時間中，有效掌握命題重點。
5. 提供作者與讀者互動平台，即時解答讀者學習問題，提升學習效果。
6. 版型條理清晰，印刷質感精美，閱讀效果良好。

　　本人竭誠希冀因著《一考就上！考公職一定要會的3000單字》問世，能在公職英文這塊台灣英文教育的灰暗角落中發出一線亮光，照亮諸多埋首苦讀的考生的英文希望及公職夢想。

蘇秦

★目　　錄

CONTENTS

公職必考
英文單字3000

n 名詞
v 動詞
adj 形容詞
adv 副詞

The essential 3000
words in public
service exam

0001 abandon [ə'bændən]　　　　**v.**　放棄　　4th ★★★★★
Don't abandon yourself to destiny; everyone has the right to struggle for a better tomorrow.
別讓自己任憑命運擺佈，每個人都有權力為更好的明天奮鬥。

0002 abbreviation [ə‚brivɪ'eʃən]　　**n.**　縮寫　　4th ★★★★★
A common abbreviation for headquarters is HQ.
總部一般的縮寫是HQ。

0003 ability [ə'bɪlətɪ]　　　　**n.**　能力　　5th ★★★★★
What most distinguishes humans from other creatures is our ability to create and manipulate a wide variety of symbolic representations.
人類和其他生物最大的區別在於，我們有能力創造和使用各種語言文字。

0004 abnormal [æb'nɔrml]　　　**adj.**　反常的　　4th ★★★★★
Paul's traumatic childhood experience has a great impact on his abnormal behavior.
保羅有創傷的童年經驗，大大影響他現在不正常的行為。

0005 aborigine [æbə'rɪdʒɪne]　　**n.**　原住民　　4th ★★★★★
Settlers overtook the land of the aborigines.
殖民者過份侵占原住民的土地。

0006 abortion [ə'bɔrʃən]　　　**n.**　墮胎　　4th ★★★★★
In America, abortion is still illegal in some states.
在美國某些州，墮胎仍是違法的。

0007 abridge [ə'brɪdʒ]　　　　**v.**　摘要　　4th ★★★★★
I did not have enough time to read the original version of the novel Bleak House, so I read an abridged one.
我沒時間看原版的《荒涼山莊》，所以改看了摘要版。

0008 abroad [ə'brɔd]　　　　**adv.**　到國外　　5th ★★★★★
Nowadays more people are going abroad for vacations, their favorite places being Japan and Thailand.
現在越來越多的人到國外度假，最受歡迎的地方包括日本和泰國。

0009 absence ['æbsn̩s]　　　　**n.**　缺少　　5th ★★★★★
The man's absence of mind during driving led to a traffic accident.
駕駛因為開車時心不在焉而釀成車禍。

A

0010 absent ['æbsənt]   **adj.** 缺席的   3rd ★★★★★
The accounting assistant was absent from the weekly seminar.
會計助理沒有參加這次的每週研討會。

0011 absolutely ['æbsə,lutlɪ]   **adv.** 絕對地   4th ★★★★★
That dessert looks absolutely delicious.
那道甜點看起來實在太美味了。

0012 absorb [əb'sɔrb]   **v.** 吸收   4th ★★★★★
The function of the plant root is to absorb water and nutrients from the soil.
植物根部的功能是用來吸收土壤的水分和養分。

0013 abstain [ab'sten]   **v.** 棄權   3rd ★★★★★
Usually a contract involves a promise to perform an action or to abstain from some action.
一張合約通常涉及承諾執行一項行動，或放棄一些行動。

0014 abstract ['æbstrækt]   **adj.** 抽象的   4th ★★★★★
I am fascinated by the artist's abstract painting.
這位畫家的抽象畫令我深深著迷。

0015 abundance [ə'bʌndəns]   **n.** 富裕   4th ★★★★★
Kaohsiung is a port with an abundance of seafood; it also has popular dishes at the Liuho Night Market including fish ball soup and eel noodles.
高雄是盛產海鮮的港口，在六合夜市也有許多熱門小吃，像是魚丸湯和鱔魚麵。

0016 abundant [ə'bʌndənt]   **adj.** 大量的   4th ★★★★★
The seas around Green Island are abundant with more than two hundred different species of colorful coral.
綠島周圍的海洋蘊含超過兩百個品種的彩色珊瑚。

0017 abuse [ə'bjuz]   **v.** 虐待   4th ★★★★★
Retarded children are most vulnerable to physical abuses in a family.
發展遲緩的小孩最容易受到家庭的身體虐待。

0018 academic [,ækə'dɛmɪk]   **adj.** 學術的   4th ★★★★★
Because Tom had poor academic performance last year, his New Year's welfare is to work hard to keep up with his classmates.
湯姆去年課業表現太差，他的新年假期就是認真唸書，趕上同學。

0019 **accelerate** [æk'sɛlə,ret]　　v.　加速　　4th ★★★★★
To boost the economy, great efforts are being made to accelerate the development of science, technology, and education.
為了刺激經濟，必須加倍努力去加速科技與教育的發展。

0020 **accept** [ək'sɛpt]　　v.　接受　　4th ★★★★★
Thank you, but I cannot accept this gift. It is too expensive.
謝謝你，但我不能接受這份禮物。這太昂貴了。

0021 **access** ['æksɛs]　　n.　進入　　4th ★★★★★
Harry's police badge gave him access to the crime scene.
亨利的警徽，讓他得以進入犯罪現場。

0022 **accessible** [æk'sɛsəbl]　　adj.　可接近的　　4th ★★★★★
Music is the most ordinary and accessible of the arts.
音樂是最平凡可親的藝術。

0023 **accessory** [æk'sɛsərɪ]　　n.　配件　　4th ★★★★★
Equipped with accessories, the iPod music player can also function as an alarm clock, allowing you to wake up to your own songs.
iPod配有鬧鐘附屬功能，讓你能夠用自己的歌叫醒自己。

0024 **accident** ['æksədənt]　　n.　意外　　5th ★★★★★
When there is a heavy rain, you have to drive cautiously so as to avoid traffic accidents.
下大雨時你要小心開車，以防交通意外的發生。

0025 **accidentally** [,æksə'dɛntlɪ]　adv.　意外地　　5th ★★★★★
My wife accidentally dropped her wedding ring down the drain.
我妻子不小心把她的結婚戒指掉到排水管。

0026 **accommodate** [ə'kɑmə,det]　v.　容納　　4th ★★★★★
The suite can only accommodate one or two persons.
這間套房只能容納二到三人。

0027 **accommodation** [ə'kɑmə'deʃən]　n.　住宿　　4th ★★★★★
The fire forced the evacuation of 520 guests, most of who were forced to spend hours on the sidewalk due to a failure to provide alternative accommodation.
這場大火強制撤離五百二十名旅客，卻因未能提供暫時住宿而使大部分的人被迫在人行道上乾等好幾個小時。

0028 accompany [əˈkʌmpənɪ]　　**v.**　陪伴　　**4th** ★★★★★
The secretary accompanied her boss on his business trip.
秘書陪她老闆出差。

0029 accomplish [əˈkɑmplɪʃ]　　**v.**　完成　　**4th** ★★★★★
In order to accomplish the job independently, Sarah refused her brother's offer of help.
莎拉想要獨立完成工作，所以拒絕哥哥所提供的協助。

0030 accomplishment [əˈkɑmplɪʃmənt]　**n.**　完成　　**4th** ★★★★★
Many accomplishments would never be achieved without some risk being taken.
許多成就都需要冒些風險才能完成。

0031 accord [əˈkɔrd]　　**v.**　符合　　**5th** ★★★★★
According to the weather forecast, it will be colder tomorrow in Tokyo.
根據氣象報告的預測，明天東京會更冷。

0032 accordingly [əˈkɔrdɪŋlɪ]　　**adv.**　相應地　　**4th** ★★★★★
Keep these regulations in mind and act accordingly.
要牢牢記住這些規定，不要做出逾矩行為。

0033 account [əˈkaunt]　　**n.**　帳戶　　**5th** ★★★★★
There are no funds available in your bank account, which is why the check bounced.
你的銀行帳戶沒有任何存款，這就是為什麼支票會跳票的原因。

0034 accumulate [əˈkjumjəˌlet]　　**v.**　累積　　**4th** ★★★★★
Adults have usually accumulated a wealth of experience of life in general that can help them in learning.
成年人通常已經累積豐富的人生經驗，這些經驗能幫助自己學習。

0035 accuracy [ˈækjərəsɪ]　　**n.**　精確　　**4th** ★★★★★
The security analyst usually predicts market changes with accuracy.
證券分析師對於市場波動的預測通常很精準。

0036 accurate [ˈækjərɪt]　　**adj.**　準確的　　**4th** ★★★★★
We are looking forward to the witness's accurate statement.
我們期盼目擊證人提供準確的證詞。

0037 accusation [ˌækjəˈzeʃən]　　**n.**　指控　　**3rd** ★★★★★

The accusation that I cheated on the exam is false.
對於我考試作弊的這項指控是不實的。

0038 **accuse** [ə'kjuz]　　　　v.　控訴　　3rd ★★★★★
The Mayor of California was accused of dubious accounting practices.
加州市長因為帳目不實之嫌而遭到控訴。

0039 **accustomed** [ə'kʌstəmd]　adj.　習慣的　　4th ★★★★★
My brother was not accustomed to getting up early in the morning.
我哥哥不習慣早起。

0040 **achieve** [ə'tʃiv]　　　　v.　達成　　4th ★★★★★
The part-time workers have achieved all the tasks.
這些兼職員工完成所有的工作。

0041 **achievement** [ə'tʃivmənt]　　n.　成就　　4th ★★★★★
The professor was rewarded by the government for his academic achievement.
教授因他的學術成就而獲政府獎勵。

0042 **acronym** ['ækrənɪm]　　n.　頭字詞　　3rd ★★★★★
The acronym FIFA stands for Federation Internationale de Football Association.
頭字詞FIFA代表國際足球協會。

0043 **acid** ['æsɪd]　　　　n.　酸　　4th ★★★★★
Acid rain can do great damage to people, animals and plants.
酸雨對人類和動植物有害。

0044 **acknowledgment** [ək'nɔlidʒmənt] n.　回報　　4th ★★★★★
Brown applied for ten jobs three months ago. To his great disappointment he has only had one acknowledgment so far.
布朗三個月前陸續應徵十份工作，但令他失望的是，他到目前只收到一封回覆信。

0045 **acquire** [ə'kwaɪr]　　　v.　獲得　　4th ★★★★★
Culture is passed from one generation to another, acquired through learning.
文化一代傳一代，藉由學習獲得。

0046 **action** ['ækʃən]　　　n.　行動　　5th ★★★★★
The movie is very exciting because it has a lot of action.
這部電影很刺激，因為有很多動作場景。

A

0047 active ['æktɪv]   **adj.** 活潑的   5th ★★★★★

The exchange student is not very active and he usually stays at the dormitory.
這個交換學生不是很活潑，常常待在宿舍裡。

0048 activist ['æktəvɪst]   **n.** 活躍份子   3rd ★★★★★

Human rights activists say maybe millions of migrants are cheated by the criminal group each year.
人權活躍份子說，每年至少有上百萬的移民遭犯罪集團詐騙。

0049 activity [æk'tɪvətɪ]   **n.** 活動   5th ★★★★★

With the population increasing day by day, more and more space is needed for public activities.
隨著人口日益增加，公眾活動也需要越來越多的空間。

0050 actually ['æktʃuəlɪ]   **n.** 實際上   5th ★★★★★

No, that woman is not Ben's sister. Actually, she is his wife!
不，那個女人不是班的妹妹。實際上，她是他的老婆！

0051 acupuncturist [ˌækju'pʌŋktʃərɪst]   **n.** 針灸師   3rd ★★★★★

In all there are an estimated 10,000 acupuncturists in the country, but not all are certified one way or another.
這個國家估計總共有一萬名針灸師，卻不一定都持有執照。

0052 adapt [ə'dæpt]   **v.** 改編   4th ★★★★★

The musical is adapted from a famous European fairy tale.
這部歌劇是由歐洲著名的童話故事改編而成的。

0053 addition [ə'dɪʃən]   **n.** 附加   5th ★★★★★

The company John works for is very generous. In addition to a good salary, they give him a big car.
約翰待的這間公司對員工很大方，他除了有豐厚的薪水外，還得到一輛汽車。

0054 additional [ə'dɪʃənl]   **adj.** 附加的   5th ★★★★★

If you want to learn more about the activity, you can get additional information from the university homepage.
如果你想知道更多有關活動消息，可以上學校網站取得額外資訊。

0055 addict [ə'dɪkt]   **v.** 使沉溺   4th ★★★★★

The Internet is really appealing. Many students are addicted to playing games in Internet cafes.
網路真的太吸引人了，許多學生都沉溺於在網咖打電動。

0056 addiction [əˈdɪkʃən]　　　　**n.**　沉溺　　4th ★★★★★

Marie's doctor asks her not to drink too much and tells her that her poor health may be due to her addiction to the bottle.

瑪莉的醫生要求她不要喝太多酒，並說她健康欠佳就是因為喝酒成癮。

0057 additive [ˈædətɪv]　　　　**n.**　添加物　　4th ★★★★★

Many pure metals have little use because they are too soft, rust too easily, or have some other additives.

許多天然金屬很少拿來使用，因為質地太過柔軟，容易生鏽，或者含有許多其他添加物。

0058 adept [əˈdɛpt]　　　　**adj.**　熟練的　　4th ★★★★★

The vice mayor is adept in civil engineering.

副市長對土木工程很在行。

0059 adequate [ˈædəkwɪt]　　　　**adj.**　足夠的　　4th ★★★★★

The boss told Phil that he was doing an adequate job as a radio host.

老闆告訴菲爾，他足以勝任電臺主持人的工作。

0060 adjust [əˈdʒʌst]　　　　**v.**　調整　　4th ★★★★★

If it is too cold in this room, you can adjust the air conditioner to make yourself feel comfortable.

如果房間太冷，你可以調整一下冷氣讓自己舒服點。

0061 admit [ədˈmɪt]　　　　**v.**　承認　　4th ★★★★★

He admitted that he did something wrong and asked his parents for forgiveness.

他承認做錯事並請求父母親原諒。

0062 admission [ədˈmɪʃən]　　　　**n.**　入學許可　　4th ★★★★★

Having fully recognized Sandy's academic ability, Mr. Lin strongly recommended her for admission to the university.

林老師充分了解珊蒂的學業成績後，強烈推薦她到那間大學就讀。

0063 adolescent [ˌædlˈɛsn̩t]　　　　**n.**　青少年　　4th ★★★★★

Schoolwork and the benefits of extracurricular activities tend to be less important when adolescents work long hours.

青少年長時間打工之下，學校課業和課外活動對他們來說較不重要。

0064 adopt [əˈdɑpt]　　　　**v.**　採用　　4th ★★★★★

The Romans did not develop writing until the 7th century, when they adopted an

alphabet used by the Etruscans.
羅馬人一直到七世紀才開始發展文字，採用伊特魯裏亞人所使用的字母系統。

0065 adult [ə'dʌlt]　　　　　　**n.** 成人　　　5th ★★★★★

The girl is only twelve years old, but she acts like an adult.
這個女孩只有十二歲，但她的言行舉止像個小大人似的。

0066 advance [əd'væns]　　　　　**v.** 前進　　　4th ★★★★★

Because of the advanced medical technology, infant mortality has fallen in the past thirty years.
由於醫療技術的進步，嬰兒死亡率在過去三十年來已經下降。

0067 advantage [əd'væntɪdʒ]　　　**n.** 好處　　　4th ★★★★★

Using sunlight as a source of energy offers considerable advantages.
利用陽光作為能量來源有很多好處。

0068 adventure [əd'vɛntʃə]　　　　**n.** 冒險　　　4th ★★★★★

Most young people seem to be fond of adventure.
大部分的年輕人似乎都愛冒險。

0069 adverse [æd'vɝs]　　　　　　**adj.** 不利的　　3rd ★★★★★

Scholars have called for immediate government action to minimize the adverse impacts of lotto fever on society.
專家學者要求政府做出立即的行動，將社會上樂透熱潮所帶來的負面影響降到最低。

0070 advertise ['ædvə‚taɪz]　　　　**v.** 刊登廣告　4th ★★★★★

The French government plans to promote the program with an advertising campaign aimed at young readers and their parents.
法國政府將打算用廣告宣傳推廣一項計畫，目標群鎖定年輕讀者以及他們的父母。

0071 advertisement [‚ædvə'taɪzmənt]　**n.** 廣告　　5th ★★★★★

Advertisements for the beer are plastered all over the buses in this city.
城市所有的公車都貼滿了這則啤酒廣告。

0072 advice [əd'vaɪs]　　　　　　**n.** 忠告　　　5th ★★★★★

Zack asked his father for advice about how to solve the problem.
查克詢問他父親有關如何解決這問題的建議。

0073 advise [əd'vaɪz]　　　　　　**v.** 勸告　　　5th ★★★★★

The doctor advised my uncle not to drink excessively.
醫生建議舅舅不要飲酒過量。

0074 advisor [əd'vaɪzɚ]　　　　**n.**　顧問　　5th ★★★★★
My professor served as a special advisor to the mayor.
我的教授擔任市長的特別顧問。

0075 advocate ['ædvəkɪt]　　　　**n.**　擁護者　　4th ★★★★★
Peter was a strong advocate of free market policies and always argued against government interference.
彼得是自由市場政策的堅定擁護者，一向反對政府干預。

0076 affable ['æfəbl]　　　　**adj.**　和藹的　　3rd ★★★★★
The hostess had an affable smile on her face.
女主人臉上掛著和藹的微笑。

0077 affair [ə'fɛr]　　　　**n.**　事件　　4th ★★★★★
All Foreign Affairs police officers should try to improve their English communication skills.
所有外事警官都應該設法增進他們的英語溝通技巧。

0078 affect [ə'fɛkt]　　　　**v.**　影響　　4th ★★★★★
Many people wanted to help the families that were affected by the disaster.
很多人想幫助受災難影響的家庭。

0079 affection [ə'fɛkʃən]　　　　**n.**　喜愛　　4th ★★★★★
The boy's stepmother felt no affection for him.
男孩的繼母對他漠不關心。

0080 affectionate [ə'fɛkʃənɪt]　　　　**adj.**　有感情的　　4th ★★★★★
The man is still affectionate toward his ex-wife.
這男人對他前妻還存有感情。

0081 afford [ə'ford]　　　　**v.**　付得起　　4th ★★★★★
I'd love to go on vacation this summer, but I can't afford it.
我想在今年夏天去度個假，但是我負擔不起。

0082 Africa ['æfrɪkə]　　　　**n.**　非洲　　4th ★★★★★
Remains of Roman-built structures can still be seen in various parts of Africa and Europe today.
現今在非洲和歐洲的許多地方仍然可以看見羅馬時期所建的遺跡。

0083 afraid [ə'fred]　　　　**adj.**　害怕的　　5th ★★★★★

一考就上！
考公職一定要會的3000單字

William has been afraid of clowns since his childhood.
威廉從小就很怕小丑。

0084 afterwards [ˈæftəwədz]　　**adv.** 之後　　4th ★★★★★
Salmon are born in freshwater streams and soon afterwards journey down to the sea.
鮭魚在淡水的溪流裡出生，不久之後便會游向大海。

0085 against [əˈgɛnst]　　**prep.** 反對　　5th ★★★★★
Peter was against going skiing because it looked like it was going to rain.
彼得反對去滑雪，因為天空看起來快下雨了。

0086 age [edʒ]　　**n.** 時代　　5th ★★★★★
Noise pollution is the new side effect of our technological age.
噪音污染是科技時代的新興副作用。

0087 agency [ˈedʒənsɪ]　　**n.** 機構　　4th ★★★★★
Complaints of crime should be responded promptly by the law enforcement agencies.
執法機關應該對犯罪投訴做出及時的回應。

0088 agenda [əˈdʒɛndə]　　**n.** 議程　　4th ★★★★★
Optimizing production lines is the prioritized agenda in manufacturing industries.
完善的生產線是製造業的首要議程。

0089 aggression [əˈgrɛʃən]　　**n.** 侵略　　4th ★★★★★
The slogan was regarded as an act of aggression.
這標語被視為一種挑釁行為。

0090 aggressive [əˈgrɛsɪv]　　**adj.** 有進取心的　　4th ★★★★★
Paul's aggressive pursuit of knowledge is praised highly by his instructor.
保羅對知識的積極追求受到老師高度稱讚。

0091 agree [əˈgri]　　**v.** 同意　　5th ★★★★★
Most anthropologists agree that romantic love has probably always existed among humans.
大多數人類學家同意浪漫愛情可能只存在於人類之間。

0092 agreeable [əˈgriəbl]　　**adj.** 贊成的　　5th ★★★★★
Is the manager agreeable to the proposal?
經理贊成這提案嗎？

0093 ailing [ˈelɪŋ]　　　　　　　　　**adj.** 衰退的　　　3rd ★★★★★
The rise in overseas sales is good news for the ailing American economy.
海外業務的增加對衰退的美國經濟而言是一項好消息。

0094 agreement [əˈɡrimənt]　　　　**n.** 協議　　　5th ★★★★★
The two companies are trying their best to work out an agreement to reduce the cost of their products.
這兩間公司一直要達成一項降低他們產品成本的協議。

0095 agriculture [ˈæɡrɪˌkʌltʃə]　　　**n.** 農業　　　3rd ★★★★★
The two eastern countries suffered losses of NT$11.4 million to farms and local agriculture.
這兩個西方國家的當地農業損失了新台幣一千一百四十萬。

0096 ahead [əˈhɛd]　　　　　　　　　**adv.** 事先　　　5th ★★★★★
Go straight ahead and turn left. The travel section will be on your right.
先直走然後左轉，旅遊部門就在你右手邊。

0097 air-conditioner [ˈɛrkənˌdɪʃənə]　**n.** 空調　　　5th ★★★★★
The air-conditioner of our apartment broke down last night, so we didn't get much sleep because of the heat.
昨晚我們公寓的冷氣壞了，我們都熱到睡不好。

0098 airline [ˈɛrˌlaɪn]　　　　　　　**n.** 航空公司　　　5th ★★★★★
Please remember to call the airline directly to confirm your flight.
請記得直接打電話給航空公司確認你的班機。

0099 airport [ˈɛrˌport]　　　　　　　**n.** 機場　　　5th ★★★★★
The plane landed at the small airport on the islet.
飛機降落在這座島的小型機場。

0100 aisle [aɪl]　　　　　　　　　　　**n.** 走道　　　4th ★★★★★
Would you prefer an aisle seat or a window seat?
你較喜歡走道的位子還是靠窗的位子？

0101 alarm [əˈlɑrm]　　　　　　　　　**n.** 鬧鐘　　　5th ★★★★★
Grandpa is getting so forgetful! He couldn't remember what he set his alarm for.
爺爺變得好健忘！他想不起來設鬧鐘是為了什麼。

0102 album [ˈælbəm]　　　　　　　　　**n.** 專輯　　　5th ★★★★★

The release of his new album has brought the pop singer a huge fortune as well as worldwide fame.
這位流行歌手的新專輯推出之後，為他帶來了一大筆財富還有享譽世界的名氣。

0103 alcohol [ˈælkəˌhɔl]　　　　　**n.** 酒精飲料　　**4th** ★★★★★
No beer or wine for me, thank you. I never touch alcohol.
謝了，我不要啤酒也不要紅酒。我不碰酒精類飲料。

0104 alert [əˈlɜt]　　　　　**adj.** 警覺的　　**4th** ★★★★★
Being a guide dog requires the dog to be alert at all times, so dogs that are easily distracted are not suitable.
導盲犬必須隨時保持警覺，所以容易分心的狗狗不適合。

0105 alibi [ˈæləˌbaɪ]　　　　　**v.** 辯解　　**3rd** ★★★★★
The clerk alibied for not attending the morning meeting.
店員為缺席朝會而辯解。

0106 alien [ˈelɪən]　　　　　**adj.** 外國的　　**4th** ★★★★★
There are more and more alien friends visiting my hometown.
越來越多外國朋友前來造訪我家鄉。

0107 alienate [ˈeljənˌet]　　　　　**v.** 疏遠　　**3rd** ★★★★★
The widow has alienated herself from her old neighbors.
那位喪偶的婦人一直讓自己和老鄰居疏遠。

0108 alive [əˈlaɪv]　　　　　**adj.** 活著的　　**5th** ★★★★★
The rescue team checked to see if the victim of the accident was still alive.
救援隊仔細查看意外事故中的受害人是否還活著。

0109 allergy [ˈælədʒɪ]　　　　　**n.** 過敏　　**4th** ★★★★★
Stop taking this drug and call your doctor at the first sign of allergy or sensitivity.
若有過敏或敏感的症狀，要馬上停止服藥並致電給你的醫生。

0110 allow [əˈlaʊ]　　　　　**v.** 允許　　**5th** ★★★★★
Angela's parents didn't allow her to sleep over at her friend's house.
安琪拉的父母親不允許她在朋友家過夜。

0111 alone [əˈlon]　　　　　**adv.** 獨自地　　**5th** ★★★★★
Mary wasn't allowed to travel alone because she was too young to do that.
瑪麗年紀太小了，不能一個人單獨旅遊。

0112 along [ə'lɔŋ]　　　　　　**pre.** 沿著　　　5th ★★★★★
The Liuho Night Market is set up along two city blocks, and the street is closed to cars.
六合夜市沿著兩個街區而設，而且車輛禁止進入街道內。

0113 aloud [ə'laud]　　　　　　**adv.** 大聲地　　　5th ★★★★★
Reading aloud is especially important for young readers.
大聲朗讀對年輕讀者來說特別重要。

0114 already [ɔl'rɛdɪ]　　　　　**adv.** 已經　　　5th ★★★★★
Because the performance was cancelled without any notice, everyone who already bought a ticket for it got their money back.
表演在預警情況下取消，所以已買票的人可以取回他們的金錢。

0115 alternate ['ɔltənɪt]　　　　**adj.** 輪流的　　3rd ★★★★★
The twin brothers do the work on alternate days.
這對雙胞胎兄弟輪天工作。

0116 alternative [ɔl'tɜnətɪv]　　**adj.** 替代的　　3rd ★★★★★
Some years ago, scientists started to consider an alternative source of electrical energy — sunlight.
幾年前，科學家開始考慮尋找電能的替代來源，那就是太陽能。

0117 alternatively [ɔl'tɜnətɪvlɪ]　　**adv.** 擇一地　　3rd ★★★★★
We could go to the Japanese restaurant, or alternatively we could try that Korean restaurant.
我們可以到日本餐廳吃飯，或是韓式餐廳作為另一選擇。

0118 although [ɔl'ðo]　　　　　　**conj.** 雖然　　　5th ★★★★★
Although the woman is rich, she is not happy.
儘管這位婦人家財萬貫，她卻不快樂。

0119 altitude ['æltə,tjud]　　　　**adj.** 高度　　　4th ★★★★★
Oxygen becomes thinner at higher altitudes.
氧氣在越高的地方變得越稀薄。

0120 aluminum [ə'lumɪnəm]　　　**adj.** 鋁　　　　4th ★★★★★
Aluminum weighs less by volume than most other metals.
鋁的重量比其他同體積的金屬都還輕。

0121 amateur [ˈæməˌtʃur] **adj.** 業餘的 **4th** ★★★★★
We did not expect any amateur players to win the contest. After all, most of the contestants were professional.
我們不期待任何業餘選手贏得比賽。畢竟，大多數參賽者都是職業水準。

0122 amazing [əˈmezɪŋ] **adj.** 令人驚異的 **4th** ★★★★★
The view from the top of Mt. Alps is amazing.
阿爾卑斯山上的風景真的太令人驚艷了。

0123 ambiguity [ˌæmbɪˈgjuətɪ] **n.** 歧異 **4th** ★★★★★
They are trying to remove all the ambiguities concerning the issue.
他們試圖消除所有關於這項議題的歧異。

0124 ambiguous [æmˈbɪgjuəs] **adj.** 模擬兩可的 **4th** ★★★★★
The government seems to be ambiguous on the issue of the death penalty.
對於死刑的議題，政府的立場似乎模擬兩可。

0125 ambition [æmˈbɪʃən] **n.** 雄心 **4th** ★★★★★
A salesperson who is filled with ambition works hard all the time.
心懷抱負的銷售員一直努力工作。

0126 ambitious [æmˈbɪʃəs] **adj.** 有抱負的 **4th** ★★★★★
Mr. Smith is ambitious to set up his own firm and get to the top before he is thirty.
史密斯先生想在三十歲以前建立自己的公司並登上巔峰，他野心真大。

0127 ambivalent [æmˈbɪvələnt] **adj.** 矛盾的 **3rd** ★★★★★
The girl has fairly ambivalent feelings towards her divorced mother.
小女孩對離婚的母親有著相當矛盾的情感。

0128 ambulance [ˈæmbjələns] **n.** 救護車 **5th** ★★★★★
My neighbor Kelly called an ambulance to send her mom to the hospital last night.
昨晚我的鄰居凱莉叫了一輛救護車，把她媽媽送到醫院。

0129 amend [əˈmɛnd] **n.** 改正 **3rd** ★★★★★
John used to be very rude, but he's amending his ways.
約翰以前很沒有禮貌，但他現在已有所改變。

0130 amicable [ˈæmɪkəbl] **adj.** 親切的 **3rd** ★★★★★
They never settle their dispute in an amicable way.
他們從未友善解決彼此的紛爭。

0131 amount [ə'maunt]　　　　n.　總和　　4th ★★★★★
Mass production results in lower prices chiefly because a large amount of material is used.
大量生產促使價格降低，主要是因為使用大量的材料。

0132 amusement [ə'mjuzmənt]　　n.　消遣　　5th ★★★★★
The first thing that a student should bear in mind is that a book ought not to be read merely for amusement.
學生首先要記住的是，書不該僅是讀著消遣。

0133 analysis [ə'næləsɪs]　　　n.　分析　　4th ★★★★★
The genetic analysis reveals that the tiger began evolving 3.2 million years ago.
基因分析顯示，老虎從三百二十萬年前就開始演化。

0134 ancestor ['ænsɛstɚ]　　　n.　祖先　　4th ★★★★★
Everyone should respect his ancestors.
每個人都應該尊敬自己的祖先。

0135 ancient ['enʃənt]　　　　adj.　古早的　　4th ★★★★★
Ancient people used the sundial to keep trace of time.
古代人利用日晷計時。

0136 anecdote ['ænɪk‚dot]　　　n.　軼事　　4th ★★★★★
My uncle told several amusing anecdotes about his years as a detective.
舅舅說了幾則他當偵探時的一些驚奇軼事。

0137 anesthetize [ə'nɛsθə‚taɪz]　　v.　使麻醉　　3rd ★★★★★
Alcohol is able to anesthetize the brain of animals.
酒精會麻痺動物的腦部活動。

0138 angel ['endʒl]　　　　n.　天使　　4th ★★★★★
Both angel and devil exist.
天使與魔鬼同時存在。

0139 anger ['æŋɡɚ]　　　　n.　生氣　　4th ★★★★★
"Get out of here!", said the lady in anger.
這位小姐生氣地說：「滾開！」

0140 angle ['æŋɡl]　　　　n.　角度　　4th ★★★★★
The sum of the angles of a triangle is 180.
三角形的角度和是一百八十度。

0141 angry [ˈæŋgrɪ]　　　　**adj.** 生氣的　　5th ★★★★★

Stella was really angry at her brother after he broke her Barbie doll.
史黛拉非常生哥哥的氣，因為他弄壞了她的芭比娃娃。

0142 annex [ˈænɛks]　　　　**v.** 併吞　　3rd ★★★★★

The territory had been annexed to England.
該領土被英國併吞。

0143 anniversary [ˌænəˈvɜsərɪ]　　**n.** 週年紀念日　　4th ★★★★★

I am so glad that they have invited me to take part in their anniversary celebration.
我很高興他們邀請我參加週年紀念慶祝活動。

0144 announce [əˈnauns]　　　　**v.** 宣布　　4th ★★★★★

The date for the final fixture of the World Cup will be announced soon.
世足賽開賽的日期近期就會公佈了。

0145 annoy [əˈnɔɪ]　　　　**v.** 打擾　　4th ★★★★★

The naughty boy annoyed his mother with his constant scream.
這頑皮的小男孩不停的尖叫打擾他的媽媽。

0146 annual [ˈænjuəl]　　　　**adj.** 每年的　　4th ★★★★★

There's no annual fee unless you use the credit card at least ten times a year.
除非你一年使用信用卡十次，否則你就要繳年費。

0147 antibiotic [ˌæntɪbaɪˈɑtɪk]　　**n.** 抗生素　　3rd ★★★★★

McDonald's ordered its considerable chain of meat suppliers to stop putting antibiotic growth promoters in its products.
麥當勞要求它的肉類供應商停止在肉品裡施打抗生素生長促進劑。

0148 answer [ˈænsə]　　　　**n.** 答案　　5th ★★★★★

Science is always on the move, providing answers to new questions and raising new questions on old issues.
科學一直不斷在進步，為新問題提供解答，也為舊議題提出新問題。

0149 anticipate [ænˈtɪsəˌpet]　　**v.** 期待　　4th ★★★★★

Every year, many migrant Asian labors go to a foreign country eagerly anticipating the lucrative jobs they have been promised.
每年有許多亞洲勞工移居國外，他們熱切期待別人承諾給予的報酬豐厚的工作。

0150 anticipation [ænˌtɪsəˈpeʃən]　　**n.** 期待　　4th ★★★★★

After three weeks' anticipation, we eventually reached the seaport.
歷時三週的期待，我們終於抵達海港。

0151 antipathy [æn'tɪpəθɪ]   **n.**   反感   3rd ★★★★★
The history of humankind details an ongoing antipathy and hostility toward those who are different.
歷史詳細記載人類彼此對於異己的反感和仇視。

0152 antique [æn'tik]   **n.**   古董   4th ★★★★★
The workers are thinking about how to exhume the antiques from the underground.
工人正思索著如何從地底挖掘古物。

0153 anxiety [æŋ'zaɪətɪ]   **n.**   憂鬱   4th ★★★★★
Tension and anxiety at test time may cause students to forget what they have read.
考試時壓力和焦慮會讓學生忘記他們讀過的東西。

0154 anxiously ['æŋkʃəslɪ]   **adv.**   焦慮地   4th ★★★★★
We were anxiously awaiting the results of the school's annual English drama contest.
我們焦慮等待著今年英文話劇比賽的結果。

0155 apartment [ə'pɑrtmənt]   **n.**   公寓   5th ★★★★★
Tom just moved into a new two-bedroom apartment across from the park.
湯姆才剛搬進一間位於公園對面的兩房新公寓。

0156 apathetic [ˌæpə'θɛtɪk]   **adj.**   冷漠的   3rd ★★★★★
Most rich business people in China remain apathetic about charity.
中國大多數的富商對於慈善事業表現冷淡。

0157 ape [ep]   **v.**   模仿   3rd ★★★★★
You are not supposed to ape the slow boy.
你不應該模仿遲緩兒。

0158 apologize [ə'pɑlə,dʒaɪz]   **v.**   道歉   4th ★★★★★
Leo apologized for breaking Ken's cell phone.
李奧為弄壞肯的手機道歉。

0159 apology [ə'pɑlədʒɪ]   **n.**   道歉   4th ★★★★★

Ms. Chen, I would like to make an apology for being late to class.
陳老師，我要為我上課遲到道歉。

0160 appall [ə'pɔl]　　　　v.　使恐懼　　3rd ★★★★★

The world was appalled when, on September 11, 2001, suicidal terrorists smashed the passenger airplanes they had hijacked into several important American buildings.
2001年九月十一日，恐怖份子劫機衝撞數棟美國重要建築物，震驚全世界。

0161 appalling [ə'pɔlɪŋ]　　　　adj.　低劣的　　3rd ★★★★★

To tell the truth, Mrs. Lin is an appalling cook.
說實話，林太太的烹飪功夫挺蹩腳的。

0162 apparent [ə'pærənt]　　　　adj.　顯然的　　4th ★★★★★

There have been a lot of apparent changes around the area these years.
近幾年來這地區四周已有很多明顯改變。

0163 appeal [ə'pil]　　　　v.　吸引　　4th ★★★★★

This tour package is very appealing, and that one looks equally attractive. I don't know which one to choose.
這個旅遊套裝行程很吸引人，另一個也是，我不知道該選哪一個。

0164 appear [ə'pɪr]　　　　v.　出現　　4th ★★★★★

Though Chris appears to be kind and friendly, he is actually very selfish.
雖然克里斯看起來親切且友善，但他其實很自私。

0165 appearance [ə'pɪrəns]　　　　n.　出現　　4th ★★★★★

The incumbent governor seems to be greatly interested in making a cameo appearance in blockbuster productions.
現任州長似乎對於在大螢幕上客串露面很有興趣。

0166 appetite ['æpə,taɪt]　　　　n.　胃口　　4th ★★★★★

Thanks to mankind's instinctive appetite for power and perks, there is always someone who wants to be the boss.
多虧人類與生俱來對權力及傲骨的愛好，總是有想要當老闆的人。

0167 applaud [ə'plɔd]　　　　v.　鼓掌　　4th ★★★★★

One difference between the theater and the movie is that the audiences applaud in the theater at the end of the performance.
戲劇和電影的不同點是表演結束後，觀眾會回以熱烈掌聲。

A
B C D E F G H I J K L M N O P Q R S T U V W X Y Z

The 3000 vocabularies you must know in public service exam

0168 **applause** [əˈplɔz]　　　　**n.** 掌聲　　5th ★★★★★
Kate's singing met with loud applause.
凱特的歌喉贏得熱烈掌聲。

0169 **architecture** [ˈɑrkəˌtɛktʃə]　　**n.** 建築　　5th ★★★★★
The lecture on modern architecture tonight is open to the public.
今晚的現代建築演講有對外開放。

0170 **applicant** [ˈæpləkənt]　　　　**n.** 應徵者　　4th ★★★★★
The applicant must be trained in English for the first year of employment.
應徵者雇用的第一年要以英文受訓。

0171 **appointment** [əˈpɔɪntmənt]　　**n.** 約診，約會　　5th ★★★★★
I have already made an appointment with my dentist.
我已經和牙醫約好看診的時間。

0172 **appreciate** [əˈpriʃɪˌet]　　　**v.** 欣賞，感謝　　4th ★★★★★
We appreciated the beauty of the scenery along the coast.
我們欣賞著海岸邊美麗的風景。

0173 **appreciation** [əˌpriʃɪˈeʃən]　　**n.** 感謝，欣賞　　4th ★★★★★
The children showed their appreciation by giving their mother a gift.
孩子送媽媽一份禮物，表達他們的感謝。

0174 **appreciative** [əˌpriʃɪˈetɪv]　　**adj.** 有欣賞力的　　4th ★★★★★
After his superb performance, the musician received a big round of applause from the appreciative audience.
結束精采表演之後，音樂家受到有鑑賞力的觀眾的熱烈掌聲。

0175 **apprehend** [ˌæprɪˈhɛnd]　　　**v.** 逮捕　　3rd ★★★★★
A felon escaped from the military jail was apprehended by the police yesterday.
一個從軍事監獄逃出來的重刑犯，昨日在台北遭警方逮捕。

0176 **approach** [əˈprotʃ]　　　　　**v.** 靠近　　4th ★★★★★
Snowmen melt as the spring approaches.
雪人在春天到來時融化了。

0177 **appropriate** [əˈproprɪˌet]　　　**adj.** 適當的　　4th ★★★★★
Opinions are strongly divided about the type of clothing being appropriate for worship.
講到穿什麼衣服去做禮拜比較適當，大家意見相當分歧。

0178 approximately [ə'prɑksəmɪtlɪ] **adv.** 近似地　4th ★★★★★
Venice is so popular that it hosts approximately 19 million tourists annually.
威尼斯非常熱門，一年將近有一千九百萬名觀光客湧入。

0179 approve [ə'pruv]　　　　**v.** 批准　3rd ★★★★★
Despite the financial difficulties, the committee finally approved the proposal.
即便財務吃緊，委員會最終還是通過提案。

0180 aptitude ['æptə,tjud]　　　**n.** 才能　4th ★★★★★
I am an accounting major, but I have no aptitude for accountancy. Maybe I should consider changing my career path.
我主修會計，但我沒有會計的資質，也許我該考慮改變我的職業生涯。

0181 arbitrary ['ɑrbə,trɛrɪ]　　**adj.** 武斷的　3rd ★★★★★
The party leader tends to make arbitrary decisions without thinking about the consequences.
黨主席完全沒有思考後果地下了一個武斷決定。

0182 archeologist [,ɑrkɪ'ɑlədʒɪst] **n.** 考古學家　3rd ★★★★★
The archeologist had bad luck after he opened the tomb. He received the mummy's curse.
考古學家打開棺木之後，運氣變得很差。他受到木乃伊的詛咒。

0183 architect ['ɑrkə,tɛkt]　　　**n.** 建築師　4th ★★★★★
The architectis working on a project to build a Cable-stayed bridge.
建築師正著手計畫建造一座斜弓長橋。

0184 area ['ɛrɪə]　　　　　　**n.** 地區　4th ★★★★★
The roads in rural areas are not well paved.
農村地區的道路鋪得不好。

0185 argument ['ɑrgjəmənt]　　**n.** 爭論　5th ★★★★★
Many quarrels result from arguments in which men become angry with the opinions others express.
許多爭吵都起源於一個人不滿另一個人所發表的意見。

0186 arid ['ærɪd]　　　　　　**adj.** 貧瘠的　3rd ★★★★★
A desert is an arid region with annual rainfall generally less than five inches.
沙漠一般指的是年降雨量少於五英寸的貧乏之地。

0187 arrange [ə'rendʒ]　　　　v.　安排　　4th ★★★★★
To live an efficient life, we have to arrange the things to do in order of priority and start with the most important ones.
為了過有效率的生活，我們要安排待辦事項的優先順序，並從最重要的開始做起。

0188 around [ə'raʊnd]　　　　adv.　四處　　5th ★★★★★
Josh saved his money and spent four weeks traveling around.
喬許存了一筆錢，花了四個禮拜到處旅行。

0189 arrest [ə'rɛst]　　　　v.　逮捕　　4th ★★★★★
Customs officers arrested the man who tried to leave the country on a copied passport.
海關官員逮捕持假護照出國的男子。

0190 arrive [ə'raɪv]　　　　v.　抵達　　5th ★★★★★
Gina has received many acts of kindness since she arrived in Taiwan.
吉娜抵達台灣後一直受到和善對待。

0191 arrogant ['ærəgənt]　　　　adj.　自大的　　3rd ★★★★★
More and more people found the newcomer a little arrogant.
越來越多的人發現這位新人有些自大。

0192 arson ['ɑrsn]　　　　n.　縱火　　3rd ★★★★★
Arson is the crime of setting fire to a building on purpose.
縱火是故意放火燒建築物的一種罪行。

0193 article ['ɑrtɪkl]　　　　n.　文章　　5th ★★★★★
Because this article contains numerous unknown words, it is difficult for beginning learners to understand.
文章裡充斥著不知道的字，對初學者而言難以理解。

0194 artificial [,ɑrtə'fɪʃəl]　　　　adj.　人工的　　4th ★★★★★
The ship was foundered to create an artificial reef.
這艘船被拆解做成人造魚礁。

0195 artist ['ɑrtɪst]　　　　n.　藝術家　　5th ★★★★★
Many pedestrians stopped to watch the street artist draw a portrait of a young lady.
許多行人停下腳步，看街頭藝術家畫一位年輕女子的肖像。

A

0196 **ascertain** [ˌæsəˈten]　　**v.**　確定　　4th ★★★★★
The plumber wants to ascertain that whether the showerhead works well.
水管工人想確定蓮蓬頭是否功能正常。

0197 **ashamed** [əˈʃemd]　　**adj.**　慚愧的　　5th ★★★★★
Many of the test questions are so difficult that no student should feel ashamed of not knowing the answers.
許多考試裡的題目都太難了，若學生不知道答案也不必感到慚愧。

0198 **aspect** [ˈæspɛkt]　　**n.**　方面　　4th ★★★★★
Climate and weather affect every aspect of our lives.
氣候和天氣影響我們生活的各個層面。

0199 **aspiration** [ˌæspəˈreʃən]　　**n.**　抱負　　3rd ★★★★★
Some politics majors have never had any political aspirations.
有些主修政治學的人從未懷有任何政治抱負。

0200 **assault** [əˈsɔlt]　　**v.**　攻擊　　3rd ★★★★★
The terrorists intend to assault the subway station.
恐怖份子打算襲擊地鐵站。

0201 **assemble** [əˈsɛmbl̩]　　**v.**　組合　　4th ★★★★★
The production procedure should be simplified for reducing errors on the assembly line.
生產程序應該簡化，以減少生產線上的錯誤。

0202 **asset** [ˈæsɛt]　　**n.**　資產　　3rd ★★★★★
The special committee investigating the inside trading had accidentally unearthed evidence of asset stripping.
調查內線交易的特別委員會意外發掘資產爭奪的證據。

0203 **assign** [əˈsaɪn]　　**v.**　指定　　4th ★★★★★
Our math teacher assigned ten problems for homework.
我們數學老師指派十個問題作為家庭作業。

0204 **assignment** [əˈsaɪnmənt]　　**n.**　作業　　4th ★★★★★
Our first assignment in school this year was to write an essay about our summer.
今年我們在學校的第一份作業是寫一篇有關暑假生活的短文。

0205 **assistance** [əˈsɪstəns]　　**n.**　協助　　4th ★★★★★

ABCDEFGHIJKLMNOPQRSTUVWXYZ

The 3000 vocabularies you must know in public service exam

029

Heather managed to put the puzzle together without any assistance from anyone.
希瑟試著在沒有任何人協助下完成拼圖。

0206 associate [ə'soʃɪˌet]　　　**v.**　聯想　　4th ★★★★★
Superstitions are also closely associated with healing and medicine.
迷信也和治癒及藥物息息相關。

0207 association [əˌsosɪ'eʃən]　　**n.**　關聯　　4th ★★★★★
A brand brings a set of associations in the mind of the consumer and one of these
is the country of origin.
一個品牌可以在消費者腦中帶來一連串的聯想，其中一個就是品牌的國家起源地。

0208 assume [ə'sjum]　　　　**v.**　臆測　　4th ★★★★★
The instructor assumed that the picnic would be cancelled for the sake of the rain.
指導員猜想野餐會因大雨緣故而取消。

0209 assumption [ə'sʌmpʃən]　　**n.**　臆測　　4th ★★★★★
It was always in my assumption that the had a happy relationship.
我以前總以為我父母擁有快樂的婚姻關係。

0210 assurance [ə'ʃʊrəns]　　　**n.**　保證　　4th ★★★★★
Producing a safe, high-quality food product requires a quality assurance system.
生產安全和高品質的食品需要品質保證系統。

0211 assure [ə'ʃʊr]　　　　　**v.**　保證　　4th ★★★★★
We can assure you that any information supplied by your company will be
regarded as strictly confidential.
我們保證將貴公司所提供的任何資訊視為最高機密。

0212 astonishment [ə'stɑnɪʃmənt] **n.**　驚訝　　4th ★★★★★
To my astonishment, the forest near my university had been burned down when I
revisited it.
令我驚訝的是，當我重返我大學附近的森林時，那裡已經被燒毀了。

0213 astrology [ə'strɑlədʒɪ]　　**n.**　占星術　　4th ★★★★★
Astrology has always been a hot topic. It is said that people of certain signs have
certain personalities.
星座一直是個熱門話題，據說某種星座的人會有某種的個性。

0214 astronaut ['æstrəˌnɔt]　　**n.**　太空人　　4th ★★★★★
Astronauts often work sixteen hours a day on the space shuttle in order to

complete all the missions.
太空人一天要在太空梭裡工作十六小時，以完成所有任務。

0215 asylum [ə'saɪləm]　　　　　　**n.** 庇護　　　3rd ★★★★★
A dissident strove to seek political asylum upon his arrival at the United States.
一名異議人士抵達美國後，就極力尋求政治庇護。

0216 athlete ['æθlit]　　　　　　**n.** 運動員　　　5th ★★★★★
Athletes who are going to be active for a long time often eat large amounts of carbohydrates before competing.
需要長時間活動的運動員通常在比賽前會攝取大量的碳水化合物。

0217 athletic [æθ'lɛtɪk]　　　　　　**adj.** 運動的　　　5th ★★★★★
Regardless of the weather, the athletic meetings will be held on time.
儘管天候不佳，運動會還是會準時舉行。

0218 atmosphere ['ætməsˌfɪr]　　　　　　**n.** 氣氛　　　4th ★★★★★
The key to a successful school environment does not lie in having a smaller class size, but in creating a pleasant atmosphere of the school.
成功的學校環境，關鍵不在於擁有較小的班級規模，而在於創造愉快的校園氣氛。

0219 attach [ə'tætʃ]　　　　　　**v.** 依附　　　4th ★★★★★
The mother attaches great hopes to her son.
母親對兒子抱有很大期望。

0220 attack [ə'tæk]　　　　　　**n.** 攻擊　　　5th ★★★★★
The old janitor died of a heart attack last year.
那個老管理員去年因心臟病發過世。

0221 attain [ə'ten]　　　　　　**v.** 獲得　　　4th ★★★★★
Many millionaires attain their status by being frugal with their money.
許多百萬富翁是靠節約用錢致富。

0222 attempt [ə'tɛmpt]　　　　　　**v.** 嘗試　　　4th ★★★★★
The lifeguard's attempt to save the drowning woman was not in vain.
救生員挽救溺水的女人的嘗試總算沒有白費。

0223 attend [ə'tɛnd]　　　　　　**v.** 出席　　　4th ★★★★★
Judy does not like to attend Bill's birthday party, so she asked me to go in place of her.
朱莉不想出席比爾的生日派對，所以她要求我代替她去。

0224 **attendance** [ə'tɛndəns]　　n.　出席　　4th ★★★★★
The former president's attendance escaped the chairperson's notice.
主席沒注意到前總統的出席。

0225 **attendant** [ə'tɛndənt]　　n.　隨從　　4th ★★★★★
The general was followed by a group of attendants.
將軍身邊跟著一群隨從。

0226 **attention** [ə'tɛnʃən]　　n.　注意　　4th ★★★★★
Miss Lin punished the student because he wasn't paying attention.
林老師懲罰那位學生，因為他上課不專心。

0227 **attitude** ['ætətjud]　　n.　態度　　4th ★★★★★
All gypsies share special traditions and attitudes, a society and culture of their own.
吉普賽人擁有獨特的傳統和生活態度，是一個屬於他們自己文化與社會。

0228 **attorney** [ə'tɝnɪ]　　n.　辯護律師　　3rd ★★★★★
The poor boy became a prominent attorney when he grew up.
貧窮小男孩長大後成為著名的辯護律師。

0229 **attraction** [ə'trækʃən]　　n.　吸引　　4th ★★★★★
The exhibition doesn't have any attraction toward me.
這場展示會一點都不吸引我。

0230 **attractive** [ə'træktɪv]　　adj.　吸引人的　　4th ★★★★★
The city essentially owes its fame and beauty to the aborigines who transform it into an attractive landscape.
這座城市的名氣和美麗要歸功於原住民，是他們將這裡改造成吸引人的風景區。

0231 **attribute** [ə'trɪbjut]　　v.　歸因於　　4th ★★★★★
Do you think it proper to attribute weakness to women?
你認為將軟弱歸因於女人適當嗎？

0232 **audible** ['ɔdəbḷ]　　adj.　聽得見的　　4th ★★★★★
The reporter spoke so quietly that she was hardly audible at the back of the room.
報告者講話聲音很小，坐在教室後面的人幾乎聽不見。

0233 **audience** ['ɔdɪəns]　　n.　聽眾　　4th ★★★★★
The audience stood up and cheered for the outstanding performance.
觀眾站起來為傑出的表演歡呼喝采。

A

0234 audio [ˈɔdɪˌo]　　　　**adj.** 有聲的　　　4th ★★★★★
One can even add pictures or audio files to improve a blog's attractiveness.
加上圖片或是聲音檔能夠增加部落格的吸引力。

0235 auditorium [ˌɔdəˈtorɪəm]　　**n.** 禮堂　　　4th ★★★★★
No smoking or eating in the auditorium.
不准在禮堂吸煙或飲食。

0236 auspicious [ɔˈspɪʃəs]　　　**adj.** 吉利的　　4th ★★★★★
Red is an auspicious color in Chinese culture.
紅色在中國文化裡是吉利顏色。

0237 author [ˈɔθɚ]　　　　　　**n.** 作者　　　4th ★★★★★
J. K. Rowling is the author of the famous Harry Potter books, which have been
published in twenty-eight languages.
J. K.羅琳是著名小說《哈利波特》的作者，系列叢書已經翻成二十八種語言出版了。

0238 authority [əˈθɔrətɪ]　　　**n.** 權威　　　5th ★★★★★
He is a leading authority in economics. His opinions are widely respected and
followed.
他是經濟學的領導權威，他的意見備受尊崇及效法。

0239 authorization [ˌɔθərəˈzeʃən]　**n.** 批准　　　4th ★★★★★
You can not make the information public without authorization from the minister.
你不能沒有部長的批准就將訊息公開。

0240 autograph [ˈɔtəˌgræf]　　　**n.** 親筆簽名　4th ★★★★★
The famous actress autographed her new book to promote it.
知名女演員在她的新書裡簽名作為宣傳。

0241 automatic [ˌɔtəˈmætɪk]　　**adj.** 自動的　　4th ★★★★★
I want to buy an automatic camera. Please show the newest model you have.
我想要買一台傻瓜相機，請給我看看你們的最新機型。

0242 automatically [ˌɔtəˈmætɪkḷɪ]　**adv.** 自動地　　4th ★★★★★
The doors of these department stores slide open automatically when you
approach them.
你一靠近這些百貨公司的大門，它們就會自動打開。

0243 automobile [ˈɔtəməˌbɪl]　　**n.** 汽車　　　4th ★★★★★

Automobiles changed the world during the 20th century, especially in the States and some industrialized countries.
汽車在二十世紀改變世界，尤其是在美國和一些工業化國家。

0244 autonomic [ˌɔtəˈnɑmɪk]　　　adj. 自律的　　　5th ★★★★★
Red has been found to stimulate the autonomic nervous system.
紅色證實可以刺激自律神經系統。

0245 available [əˈveləbl]　　　adj. 可獲得的　　　4th ★★★★★
Do you have any of the new magazines available?
你這裡有賣任何最新雜誌嗎？

0246 average [ˈævərɪdʒ]　　　adj. 平均　　　4th ★★★★★
On average, approximately one acre of the world's prime rainforest is lost every second.
世界主要的雨林平均每秒鐘少掉一英畝。

0247 averse [əˈvɝs]　　　adj. 反對的　　　5th ★★★★★
Some investors are risk averse. High-return investment tools are not what they desire.
一些投資者不願意承擔風險，高報酬的投資工具並不是他們想要的。

0248 aviation [ˌevɪˈeʃən]　　　n. 飛行　　　3rd ★★★★★
Aviation was in its infancy during World War I, which was the first war in which airplane played a significant part.
飛機在一次世界大戰時開始發展，這也是飛機第一次在戰爭中扮演重要的角色。

0249 avoid [əˈvɔɪd]　　　v. 避免　　　5th ★★★★★
We should have stopped avoiding the problem at that time.
我們當時應該要避免問題發生的！

0250 aware [əˈwɛr]　　　adj. 知道的　　　5th ★★★★★
Fashion designer Tommy Hilfiger was fully aware of the power of youth culture.
服裝設計師湯米·希爾費格完全明白年輕文化的力量。

0251 babble [ˈbæbl]　　　v. 嘮叨　　　3rd ★★★★★
Judy felt upset when her mom kept on babbling.
朱蒂母親不停的叨唸感到心煩意亂。

0252 background [ˈbækˌɡraund]　　　n. 背景　　　4th ★★★★★
In this course, the economic background of labor legislation will not be mentioned,

nor will trade unionism be dealt with.
本課程不會提到勞工立法的經濟背景，也不會探討工會制度。

0253 backyard [ˈbækjɑrd]　　　**n.**　後院　　　5th ★★★★★
Dad is used to weeding in the backyard in the late afternoon.
爸爸習慣在傍晚時在後院除草。

0254 badge [bædʒ]　　　**n.**　徽章　　　3rd ★★★★★
The boy scout had several badges on his cap.
男童軍的帽子上有數枚徽章。

0255 badminton [ˈbædmɪntən]　　　**n.**　羽毛球　　　5th ★★★★★
The contestant was skillful to receive the badminton accurately.
這位羽球選手接發球很到位，也很有技巧。

0256 baffle [ˈbæfl]　　　**v.**　使困惑　　　4th ★★★★★
I can't figure out the answer to this problem. It baffles me.
我想不出這問題的答案，我好困惑。

0257 bait [bet]　　　**v.**　引誘；釣餌　　　4th ★★★★★
Nothing can bait the old man.
這個老人不受任何誘惑。

0258 ban [bæn]　　　**n.**　禁止　　　4th ★★★★★
The congressmen have reached a consensus that smoking should be banned within thirty feet from the entrance of a building.
國會議員達成了一項共識，在任何建築物門口前三十英尺禁止吸煙。

0259 bake [bek]　　　**v.**　烘烤　　　5th ★★★★★
The hostess was baking some rice cakes in a pan.
女主人用平底鍋烤些年糕。

0260 balance [ˈbæləns]　　　**n.**　結餘　　　4th ★★★★★
Joanne has a US$100,000 balance in her savings account.
喬安的存款帳戶有十萬美元結餘。

0261 balcony [ˈbælkənɪ]　　　**n.**　陽台　　　5th ★★★★★
My new apartment has a balcony that faces a pond.
我的新公寓有一個面對池塘的陽台。

B 🎧 015

0262 balloon [bə'lun]　　　　　n.　氣球　　5th ★★★★★
The children blew up more than two hundred balloons for the party.
孩子們為派對吹了兩百多枚氣球。

0263 bandage ['bændɪdʒ]　　　　n.　繃帶　　4th ★★★★★
Everyone thought that Linda got hurt because she was wearing a big bandage.
每個人都認為琳達受傷了，因為她包著一大片繃帶。

0264 barbecue ['bɑrbɪkju]　　　　n.　烤肉　　4th ★★★★★
The couple invited some relatives to their house to have a barbecue in their backyard.
這對夫妻邀請一些親戚到他們家後院烤肉。

0265 barber ['bɑrbɚ]　　　　　n.　理髮師　　5th ★★★★★
The man was angry because the barber cut his hair too short.
那個男士很生氣，因為理髮師把他的頭髮剪得太短。

0266 barely ['bɛrlɪ]　　　　　adv.　幾乎不　　4th ★★★★★
The ship was barely invisible through the dense fog.
這艘船在濃霧中幾乎看不見。

0267 bargain ['bɑrgɪn]　　　　n.　廉價品　　4th ★★★★★
Night markets in Taiwan are often the best places for a bargain because you can find many things you like at low prices.
台灣的夜市常是撿便宜的最佳去處，因為你可以找到許多價格低廉的東西。

0268 barren ['bærən]　　　　　adj.　貧瘠　　4th ★★★★★
The moon's surface is barren, airless and waterless, so nothing can live there.
月球地表荒涼，沒有空氣和水，所以沒有任何東西可以在那裡生存。

0269 base [bes]　　　　　　n.　基地　　5th ★★★★★
To enter this military base, you must have a document.
要進入軍事基地，你必須要有文件證明。

0270 basically ['besɪkl̩ɪ]　　　　adv.　基本上　　4th ★★★★★
Our bodies need basically four types of nutrients from food: proteins, carbohydrates, fats, and vitamins and minerals.
人體基本上需要四種來自食物的營養：蛋白質、碳水化合物、脂肪以及維他命和礦物質。

一考就上！考公職一定要會的3000單字

0271 basis ['besɪs]　　　　　　**n.** 基礎　　　★★★★★

We cannot judge a person simply on the basis of his education.
我們不可以光憑學歷就對一個人妄下評論。

0272 bat [bæt]　　　　　　**n.** 球棒；蝙蝠　　★★★★★

The baseball player's bat broke when he hit the ball.
棒球員的球棒在擊球後斷了。

0273 batter ['bætɚ]　　　　　**n.** 攻擊；打擊手　★★★★★

By enforcing the anti-domestic violence act, the police play an active role to assist battered wives.
藉由實施反家暴法案，警方在協助受虐婦女方面扮演了重要的角色。

0274 battery ['bætərɪ]　　　　**n.** 電池　　　　★★★★★

My flashlight isn't working; it probably needs a new battery.
我的手電筒不亮了，可能需要換新電池。

0275 battle ['bætl̩]　　　　　**n.** 戰役　　　　★★★★★

This battle is over, but the war is not.
這場戰役結束了，但戰爭還沒有。

0276 bean [bin]　　　　　　**n.** 豆子　　　　★★★★★

Cacao beans, from which chocolate is made, were brought to Spain from Central America in the 16th century.
可可豆，巧克力的原料，在十六世紀時從中美洲傳入西班牙。

0277 bear [bɛr]　　　　　　**v.** 承擔；出生　★★★★★

Who will bear the cost of repair if the car is damaged?
如果車子受損了，誰要負擔修理費用？

0278 beat [bit]　　　　　　**v.** 打擊　　　　★★★★★

The younger team doesn't have a prayer of beating the older boys.
年輕球隊不奢望能打敗那些年紀較長的男孩。

0279 beginning [bɪ'gɪnɪŋ]　　　**n.** 開始　　　　★★★★★

Since the beginning of this year, our government has a ban on the use of plastic bags, so supermarkets will no longer provide them to customers.
自今年初開始，政府明令禁止使用塑膠袋，所以超市不再提供塑膠袋給顧客。

0280 behalf [bɪ'hæf]　　　　**n.** 代表　　　　★★★★★

I am Dr. Lin's lawyer. I am calling on behalf of him, who wishes to complain about the car he bought from you last month.
我是林博士的律師。我代表他致電申訴上個月在貴公司買的一輛車。

0281 **behave** [bɪ'hev]　　　　**v.**　　表現　　4th ★★★★★
After being deprived of interaction for a long time, children will behave abnormally.
孩童長時間缺乏人際互動會造成行為表現異常。

0282 **behavior** [bɪ'hevjə]　　　**n.**　　態度　　4th ★★★★★
His behavior always makes one feel welcome.
他的態度總是讓人感到賓至如歸。

0283 **believe** [bɪ'liv]　　　　**v.**　　相信　　5th ★★★★★
The former CEO of Highhills Inc. was believed to have committed a suicide.
一般相信高嶺有限公司的前執行長已經自殺了。

0284 **belong** [bə'lɔŋ]　　　　**v.**　　屬於　　5th ★★★★★
Jack doesn't belong in this class right now, which is too difficult for him.
傑克目前不適合這項課程，這對他而言太困難了。

0285 **belongings** [bə'lɔŋɪŋz]　　**n.**　　行李　　5th ★★★★★
During the accident, the boat sank so fast that we were unable to save any of our personal belongings.
意外發生時，船實在沉得太快，我們都沒辦法搶救任何一件私人行李。

0286 **beneath** [bɪ'niθ]　　　　**pre.**　　下面　　5th ★★★★★
They found the missing key buried beneath a pile of pillows.
他們在一堆枕頭底下找到不見的鑰匙。

0287 **benefactor** ['bɛnə,fæktə]　**n.**　　資助者　　4th ★★★★★
During my college years, Aunt Chen served as my benefactor. She helped to pay my tuition.
陳阿姨是我大學時代的資助者，她幫我付學費。

0288 **beneficial** [,bɛnə'fɪʃəl]　**adj.**　有益的　　3rd ★★★★★
Are you aware of any of the beneficial effects on employee performance due to the practice of our suitable policy?
員工表現因為合宜政策的實行而發揮良好效應，你有發現嗎？

0289 **benefit** ['bɛnəfɪt]　　　**n.**　　利益　　3rd ★★★★★
A career in health care has many benefits.
保健事業有許多好處。

B

0290 benevolent [bəˈnɛvələnt]   **adj.** 慈善的   4th ★★★★★
As human beings, we often vacillate between selfish and benevolent desires.
身為人類的我們，經常在自私和仁慈的慾望之間搖擺不定。

0291 besides [bɪˈsaɪdz]   **adv.** 此外   5th ★★★★★
William doesn't know who will go to KTV besides two of his classmates.
除了兩位同學之外，威廉不知道還有誰會來唱KTV。

0292 best seller   **n.** 暢銷書   3rd ★★★★★
Most books that reach the typical best seller list have been sold at least 50,000 copies.
大部分榮登暢銷書榜的書籍都賣了超過五萬本。

0293 between [bɪˈtwin]   **pre.** 兩者間   5th ★★★★★
A fair agreement has been reached between labor and management.
勞工和管理階層之間已經達成一項公平的協議。

0294 beverage [ˈbɛvərɪdʒ]   **n.** 飲料   4th ★★★★★
Tea was the first brewed beverage.
茶是第一種沖泡式飲料。

0295 beware [bɪˈwɛr]   **adj.** 當心   4th ★★★★★
Beware of pickpockets when you get inside a crowded MRT train carriage.
進入擁擠的捷運車廂時要當心扒手。

0296 beyond [bɪˈjɑnd]   **pre.** 超過   5th ★★★★★
One reason why the card debtors often live beyond their means is that they are prone to obsessive shopping and compulsive spending.
卡債族常入不敷出，因為他們有沉迷購物和衝動消費的傾向。

0297 bias [ˈbaɪəs]   **n.** 偏見   3rd ★★★★★
The age-old bias for boys has produced the largest, the highest, and the longest gender imbalance in the world.
重男輕女這由來已久的偏見，產生世界上最為深遠的性別不平衡。

0298 bibliography [ˌbɪblɪˈɑgrəfɪ]   **n.** 參考書目   3rd ★★★★★
It's important to include a bibliography, citing all referenced works, as part of your research project.
要將參考書目和所有參考資料包含在你研究計畫的一部分，這是很重要的。

A B C D E F G H I J K L M N O P Q R S T U V W X Y Z

The 3000 vocabularies you must know in public service exam

0299 bid [bɪd]   **v.** 投標   3rd ★★★★★

The government has actively invited bids for construction projects to improve the investment environment.

政府已經積極徵求建設計畫的投標以改善投資環境。

0300 bill [bɪl]   **n.** 帳單   5th ★★★★★

Mr. Li wants to buy a new cellular phone that can take pictures, do e-mail, pay bills and so on.

林先生想要買一支可以照相、收發電子郵件和付帳的新手機。

0301 billion [ˈbɪljən]   **n.** 十億   4th ★★★★★

More than 2.7 billion people will face severe shortages of fresh water by 2025.

到2025年，全球超過二十七億的人口將會面臨嚴重的淡水短缺問題。

0302 bilingual [baɪˈlɪŋgwəl]   **adj.** 雙語的   3rd ★★★★★

Stephen is bilingual in English and French. He has an excellent command of both languages.

史帝夫是英法雙語，這兩種語言他都十分流利。

0303 bind [baɪnd]   **v.** 裝訂   4th ★★★★★

E-books cannot provide the physical feel of the cover, paper, and binding of the original printed work.

電子書不能提供封面和紙張的實際觸感，以及原始印刷品的裝訂感覺。

0304 biography [baɪˈɑgrəfɪ]   **n.** 傳記   4th ★★★★★

I just read a very good biography of Dr. Sun Yet-Sen.

我剛剛讀了一本非常棒的孫中山自傳。

0305 biology [baɪˈɑlədʒɪ]   **n.** 生物學   4th ★★★★★

Julia takes interest in biology and performs quite well in her biology class.

茱莉亞對生物有很大的興趣，而且在生物學的課堂上表現很不錯。

0306 birth [bɝθ]   **n.** 出生   5th ★★★★★

We are in the company of other humans from the time of our birth to our death.

我們從出生到死亡都有其他人的陪伴。

0307 blame [blem]   **v.** 責備   4th ★★★★★

Tony, the architect who had designed the bridge, was to blame for its collapse during the earthquake.

設計這座橋的建築師東尼，因為橋在地震中坍塌遭到撻伐。

B

0308 blend [blɛnd]   **v.** 混合   4th ★★★★★
Be careful not to blend these raw materials together.
小心不要將這些原物料混在一起。

0309 blind [blaɪnd]   **adj.** 盲的   5th ★★★★★
The man became blind in one eye after the accident.
這個男人在事故之後變成單眼失明。

0310 blink [blɪŋk]   **v.** 眨眼睛   3rd ★★★★★
She blinks several times to try to get the dust out of her eyes.
她眨了幾次眼睛，想弄掉眼睛裡的灰塵。

0311 block [blɑk]   **n.** 街區   5th ★★★★★
Leo's apartment is only three blocks away from his office.
李歐的公寓和他的辦公室只隔了三條街。

0312 blog [blɑg]   **n.** 部落格   5th ★★★★★
A blog is interactive in the sense that readers can respond with comments in just a few steps.
部落格是互動式的，讀者只需要幾個步驟就可以發表評論。

0313 blood [blʌd]   **n.** 血液   5th ★★★★★
The doctor tested my blood to find the kidney problem.
醫生幫我驗血，以找出腎臟的問題。

0314 blow [blo]   **v.** 吹   5th ★★★★★
The instant noodles were too hot so Tom blew on it first.
泡麵太燙了，所以湯姆先吹一吹。

0315 blush [blʌʃ]   **v.** 害臊   5th ★★★★★
When I am forced to speak up in class, I begin to blush, and my heart begins to pound faster and faster.
當我被迫在課堂上發言，臉就漲紅起來，心臟也越跳越快。

0316 board [bord]   **n.** 董事會；板子   4th ★★★★★
The board of directors promised its employees a raise of salary by 3% yearly.
董事會承諾員工每年將會有百分之三的薪資調漲。

0317 boast [bost]   **n. v.** 誇耀   4th ★★★★★
One of the most famous cities in America, San Francisco boasts of the greatest

public transportation system in the world.
舊金山是美國知名的城市之一，以擁有全球最浩大的交通運輸系統自豪。

0318 boat [bot]　　　　　　**n.** 小船　　　　5th ★★★★★
The couple took a boat trip from Taipei to Penghu.
這對夫妻從台北坐船到澎湖旅遊。

0319 boil [bɔɪl]　　　　　　**v.** 煮沸　　　　4th ★★★★★
Mrs. Chen boiled some water to make coffee.
陳太太煮些開水來泡咖啡。

0320 bold [bold]　　　　　　**adj.** 大膽的　　　4th ★★★★★
Most girl students are not bold enough to walk through the yard alone at night.
大部份的女學生都不敢在晚上獨自走過庭院。

0321 bombard [bam'bard]　　**v.** 不斷提問題　4th ★★★★★
Like any curious 3-year-old child, Tina bombarded her parents with all sorts of funny questions.
蒂娜像任何好奇的三歲孩子一樣，用各種好笑的問題轟炸她的父母。

0322 bonus ['bonəs]　　　　**n.** 紅利　　　　3rd ★★★★★
The listed company will give discretionary bonus payments.
上市公司會酌量發放紅利。

0323 book [bʊk]　　　　　　**v.** 訂票　　　　5th ★★★★★
Cindy booked a ticket to the opera show last night.
辛蒂昨晚訂了一張歌劇的票。

0324 boredom ['bordəm]　　**n.** 無聊　　　　5th ★★★★★
More than three generations ago, Swedish adults, struggling with the boredom of the endless cold nights, began forming "study circles."
三個世代以前，瑞典成年人在無盡寒冷的夜晚苦悶地掙扎著，因此開始形成了「讀書會」。

0325 boring ['borɪŋ]　　　　**adj.** 枯燥的　　5th ★★★★★
The movie was so boring that Tom fell asleep twenty minutes after it started.
電影非常枯燥，湯姆在開演二十分鐘後就睡著了。

0326 borrow ['baro]　　　　**v.** 借入　　　　5th ★★★★★
Nicole borrowed NT$1,000 from her friend the day before yesterday.
妮可前天向她朋友借了一千塊錢。

B

0327 boss [bɔs] n. 老闆 5th ★★★★★
A lot of bosses are likely to be in a bad mood at work because of too little sleep.
很多老闆會因為睡眠不足而在工作時心情不佳。

0328 bother [ˈbɑðɚ] v. 打擾 5th ★★★★★
I'm sorry to bother you, but could you please do me a favor?
很抱歉打擾你，可以幫我一個忙嗎？

0329 bottle [ˈbɑtḷ] v. 使瓶裝 5th ★★★★★
Bottled water is mostly sold in plastic bottles and that's why it is potentially health threatening.
瓶裝水大部分都是以塑膠瓶子出售，這就是為什麼瓶裝水可能對健康有害的原因。

0330 bottom [ˈbɑtəm] n. 底部 5th ★★★★★
When Mike said he loved me, I really believed he said it from the bottom of his heart.
當麥克說他愛我時，我相信他是發自內心說這句話的。

0331 bounty [ˈbauntɪ] n. 慷慨 4th ★★★★★
Dispense bounty and do not seek reward.
慷慨施捨不求回報。

0332 boutique [buˈtik] n. 服飾店 4th ★★★★★
The advertisement says there's 50% off everything at Yvonne's boutique.
廣告上說伊娃服飾店的所有商品半價出售。

0333 boycott [ˈbɔɪˌkɑt] v. 抵制 3rd ★★★★★
The farm workers' union urged consumers to boycott imported fruit.
農業工會呼籲消費者抵制進口水果

0334 branch [bræntʃ] n. 支派；分公司 4th ★★★★★
Ecology is becoming one of the most important branches of biology.
生態學逐漸成為生物學裡最重要的一個分支。

0335 brand [brænd] n. 商標 5th ★★★★★
Without big brand names, these shirts wash well and have superior quality.
這些T恤雖然不是大品牌，但是容易清洗且品質一流。

0336 brave [brev] adj. 勇敢的 5th ★★★★★
Firefighters must be very brave because they have to get into burning buildings.
消防隊員一定要很勇敢，因為他們必須進入熊熊燃燒的建築物裡。

A B C D E F G H I J K L M N O P Q R S T U V W X Y Z

The 3000 vocabularies you must know in public service exam

0337 break [brek]　　　　v. n.　打破；煞車　5th ★★★★★
He broke his glasses while playing basketball.
他打籃球時摔破眼鏡。

0338 breakdown ['brek͵daʊn]　　n.　故障　4th ★★★★
Many of the problems were caused by a breakdown in communications.
許多問題是由於溝通不良所引發的。

0339 breakfast ['brɛkfəst]　　n.　早餐　5th ★★★★★
The pan caught on fire while my mother was making breakfast.
媽媽做早餐時，平底鍋著火了。

0340 breathe [brið]　　　　v.　呼吸　5th ★★★★★
She worked and worked until she breathed her last.
直到她斷氣前，她仍不停地工作。

0341 breed [brid]　　　　v.　養育；繁殖　4th ★★★★★
Most animals breed in the spring.
大多數動物在春天繁殖。

0342 breeze [briz]　　　　n.　微風　5th ★★★★★
Milton lay in the hammock watching the palm trees sway in the breeze.
密爾頓躺在吊床上看著棕櫚樹在微風中搖擺。

0343 bribe [braɪb]　　　　n.　賄賂　3rd ★★★★★
It is essential that officials at all levels of government refuse to accept bribe from business interests.
各階層的政府官員必須拒絕商業利益的賄賂，這件事非常重要。

0344 brick [brɪk]　　　　n.　磚頭　5th ★★★★★
The old man was walking on a road made of yellow bricks.
老先生走在黃色磚塊鋪成的路上。

0345 bridge [brɪdʒ]　　　　n.　橋樑　5th ★★★★★
A bridge is actually a little bit longer in the summer than in the winter.
橋在夏天的時候比冬天略長。

0346 bright [braɪt]　　　　adj.　明亮的　5th ★★★★★
People have similar emotional responses to specific colors, and in general, the brighter the color, the stronger the response.
人們對某些特定的顏色會有相似的情緒反應，總括來說，顏色越明亮，反應越強烈。

0347 brilliant ['brɪljənt]　　　　**adj.** 卓越的　　4th ★★★★★

Nicole is a brilliant language learner. Within a short period of time, she has developed a good command of Chinese and Japanese.

妮可是聰明的語言學習者，在很短的時間內，她的中文和日文就可以掌握地很好。

0348 broadcast ['brɔd,kæst]　　　　**v.** 播送；廣播　　4th ★★★★★

The TV is broadcasting the president's speech.

電視正在播放總統的演說。

0349 Buddhist ['budɪst]　　　　**adj.** 佛陀的　　3rd ★★★★★

Traffic controls were forced on several major streets in Taipei due to the arrival of a treasured Buddhist finger relic.

因為珍貴的佛指舍利抵達，台北市在幾條主要街道進行強制交通管制。

0350 bubble ['bʌbl]　　　　**n.** 泡沫　　5th ★★★★★

My grandmother drinks soda because she likes the bubbles.

我祖母喝汽水是因為她喜歡汽泡。

0351 budget ['bʌdʒɪt]　　　　**n.** 預算　　4th ★★★★★

As the project depends on what happens at the federal level, the city and county may have to wait until the budget cutting ends.

由於計畫經費必須仰賴聯邦政府，市和郡必須一直等到預算刪減結束。

0352 building ['bɪldɪŋ]　　　　**n.** 建築物　　5th ★★★★★

This type of building is peculiar to this area, and it is not often seen in other parts of the world.

這款建築樣式是此區特有的，在世界其他地方並不常見。

0353 bullet ['bulɪt]　　　　**n.** 子彈　　4th ★★★★★

Gunshot wounds occur when a bullet enters a human body.

子彈一穿進人體就會產生槍傷。

0354 bulletin ['bulətɪn]　　　　**n.** 公佈欄　　5th ★★★★★

I saw a bulletin for free guitar lessons this weekend.

我看到一則本週末有一個免費吉他課程的公告。

0355 bump [bʌmp]　　　　**v.** 碰撞　　4th ★★★★★

Candy cried out when she saw a motorcycle bumping into her cat.

凱蒂看見一輛摩托車撞到她的貓，她頓時哭了出來。

0356 burden [ˈbɝdn̩]　　　　　**n.**　負擔　　　4th ★★★★★
The government will need to shoulder the burden of providing services that families can no longer afford.
政府必須肩負提供許多家庭不再負擔得起的社會福利重擔。

0357 bureau [ˈbjuro]　　　　　**n.**　局；署　　　4th ★★★★★
The well-known abbreviation FBI stands for Federal Bureau of Investigation.
眾所皆知的FBI代表聯邦調查局。

0358 bureaucracy [bjuˈrɑkrəsɪ]　　**n.**　官僚主義　　4th ★★★★★
The new president of the university strives for efficiency and democracy. His plan is to eliminate unnecessary bureaucracy on campus.
大學的新任校長努力想要提升效率和民主氛圍。他計劃消除校園裡不必要的官僚主義。

0359 burglar [ˈbɝglɚ]　　　　　**n.**　竊賊　　　4th ★★★★★
The burglar felt embarrassed when he couldn't get into his own house.
竊賊覺得很尷尬，因為他無法進入自己的房子。

0360 burn [bɝn]　　　　　　　**v.**　燃燒　　　4th ★★★★★
If a factory burns less fuel, then it will put fewer unhealthy chemicals in the air and water.
如果工廠使用較少燃料，就會釋出較少的有害化學物質到空氣和水中。

0361 bury [ˈbɛrɪ]　　　　　　　**v.**　埋葬　　　4th ★★★★★
Less than three percent of the world's water is fresh, and most of it is trapped in polar ice or buried underground in springs too deep to reach.
全球的淡水含量不到百分之三，而且大部分都存在於極地的冰原或是埋在深不可及的地底溫泉中。

0362 bush [buʃ]　　　　　　　**n.**　灌木叢　　4th ★★★★★
The kids couldn't find the ball that fell into the bush.
孩子找不到掉進灌木叢裡的球。

0363 business [ˈbɪznɪs]　　　　**n.**　商務　　　5th ★★★★★
Many countries and businesses pledged to combat global climate change.
許多國家和企業承諾要對抗全球氣候變化。

0364 busy [ˈbɪzɪ]　　　　　　　**adj.**　忙碌的　　5th ★★★★★
Although the United States has one of the safest and busiest commercial airline systems in the world, the system is not without its problems.
雖然美國有全世界其中一套最安全、忙碌的商業航班系統，但不表示沒有任何問題。

0365 butter ['bʌtɚ]　　　　n.　奶油　　5th ★★★★★
Mom asked me not to plaster too much butter on bread.
媽媽要我別抹太多奶油在麵包上。

0366 butterfly ['bʌtɚˌflaɪ]　　　　n.　蝴蝶　　5th ★★★★★
My family went butterfly watching in Miaoli last Sunday.
我家人上星期日到苗栗賞蝴蝶。

0367 by-product ['baɪˌprɑdəkt]　　　　n.　副產品　　4th ★★★★★
Whey is the by-product in the manufacturing of cheese.
乳清是製造奶酪時所產生的副產品。

0368 cabinet ['kæbənɪt]　　　　n.　機艙　　4th ★★★★★
An economy cabinet has been organized.
經濟艙已經整理好了。

0369 cable ['kebl̩]　　　　n.　電纜　　4th ★★★★★
According to a survey, about 80% of television viewers here subscribe to cable television.
根據調查，這裡大約百分之八十的觀眾訂閱有線電視。

0370 cafeteria [ˌkæfə'tɪrɪə]　　　　n.　自助餐廳　　4th ★★★★★
Cafeterias and food stands offer cheap, quick meals in surroundings that are simple but great for people watching.
自助餐廳和攤販提供便宜快速的餐點，雖然簡陋但很引人注意。

0371 calculate ['kælkjəˌlet]　　　　v.　計算　　4th ★★★★★
Only trade, production and service within Taiwan's borders are used to calculate Taiwan's GDP.
只有台灣境內的交易、生產和服務才能計算到台灣的GDP值。

0372 calendar ['kæləndɚ]　　　　n.　日曆　　5th ★★★★★
Dad tore away a page of the calendar after looking at it.
爸爸看了一下日曆後，就把上面一頁撕掉。

0373 calm [kɑm]　　　　adj.　冷靜的　　5th ★★★★★
My homeroom teacher is always calm and relaxed. I have never seen him when he is angry.
我的導師總是冷靜和輕鬆，我從來沒有看過他生氣。

0374 calorie [ˈkælərɪ]　　　**n.**　卡路里　　4th ★★★★★

The amount of heat required to raise the temperature of one gram of water by one degree Celsius is called one gram calorie.

一克的水溫度上升攝氏一度時所需的熱量就叫一卡路里。

0375 camera [ˈkæmərə]　　　**n.**　照相機　　5th ★★★★★

I can't figure out how to operate this camera because it's too complex.

我不知道如何操作這台相機，它太複雜了。

0376 camp [kæmp]　　　**n.**　營隊　　5th ★★★★★

Summer camp offers a variety of activities for children and teenagers in the United States.

美國的夏令營提供孩童和青少年各式各樣的活動。

0377 campaign [kæmˈpen]　　　**n.**　競選活動　　4th ★★★★★

The aim of the campaign is to remind people of the damage the deadly weed does to their body.

活動的主要目的是要提醒民眾大麻對人體的危害。

0378 campus [ˈkæmpəs]　　　**n.**　校園　　4th ★★★★★

Staying in a hostel during our vacation reminded me of living in a dormitory on campus.

我們假期間住的旅舍讓我想起住在校園宿舍的歲月。

0379 cancel [ˈkænsḷ]　　　**v.**　取消　　4th ★★★★★

All the flights to and from Kaohsiung were cancelled because of the heavy thunderstorm.

因為暴風雨的關係，所有往返高雄的班機都取消了。

0380 candidate [ˈkændədet]　　　**n.**　候選人　　4th ★★★★★

The candidate gave a series of impressive campaign speeches and was; therefore; elected by a unanimous vote.

候選人發表一系列令人印象深刻的競選演說，因而贏得全體一致的推選。

0381 canyon [ˈkænjən]　　　**n.**　峽谷　　5th ★★★★★

We camped in the canyon and it was very cold at night.

我們在峽谷中露營，那兒晚上非常冷。

0382 capable [ˈkepəbḷ]　　　**adj.**　有能力的　　5th ★★★★★

The exchange student is capable of writing specific computer programs.

交換學生有能力編寫特定的電腦程式。

0383 capacity [kəˈpæsətɪ]　　n. 職位　　4th ★★★★★
An officer fully understands the criminal statutes in his capacity as a law enforcement officer.
警官身為執法者十分了解刑法法條和規章。

0384 capital [ˈkæpətl]　　n. 首都　　4th ★★★★★
Prague, the capital of the Czech Republic, is a very beautiful city.
捷克的首都布拉格是一個非常美麗的城市。

0385 capitalist [ˈkæpətlɪst]　　n. 資本家　　4th ★★★★★
The capitalist tries not to pill his workers and treats them kindly.
這位資本家設法不去剝削員工權利，並親切對待他們。

0386 captivate [ˈkæptə͵vet]　　v. 使著迷　　3rd ★★★★★
The audience is completely captivated by the movie. It is so exciting that they can't take their eyes off the screen.
觀眾對這部電影完全著迷。劇情如此刺激，他們的眼睛都無法離開螢幕。

0387 capture [ˈkæptʃɚ]　　v. 擄獲　　4th ★★★★★
Many Allied airmen captured in World War II escaped from German prison camps successfully.
許多遭德軍俘虜的二次大戰聯盟空軍成功逃離集中營。

0388 carbon dioxide　　n. 二氧化碳　　3rd ★★★★★
Among greenhouse gases, carbon dioxide is the main reason for climate change and natural disasters.
所有溫室氣體當中，二氧化碳是氣候變化和自然災害的主要原因。

0389 career [kəˈrɪr]　　n. 職業　　4th ★★★★★
To a politician, a single error of judgment can be tantamount to career suicide.
對政治人物來說，一個小小的判斷錯誤都可能毀掉自己的政治生涯。

0390 carefully [ˈkɛrfəlɪ]　　adv. 仔細地　　5th ★★★★★
The world carefully watches what the Korean crafts are doing as they sail on the sea.
全世界都在密切觀察韓國船舶在海上航行時舉動。

0391 cargo [ˈkɑrgo]　　n. 船貨　　4th ★★★★★
With current resources, we are able to examine only 15% of the cargo coming in.
靠著目前的人力資源，我們只能檢驗百分之十五的進口貨櫃。

0392 carol [ˈkærəl]   **n.** 聖歌   4th ★★★★★
The children sang Christmas carols in school in December.
孩子們十二月在學校唱聖誕頌歌。

0393 carpenter [ˈkɑrpəntɚ]   **n.** 木匠   4th ★★★★★
The carpenter made the log into a vivid figure statue.
木匠用原木做出栩栩如生的人物雕像。

0394 carriage [ˈkærɪdʒ]   **n.** 嬰兒車   4th ★★★★★
Mother pushed her baby around in an old fashioned black carriage.
母親用老式黑色嬰兒車推著她的嬰兒到處逛。

0395 carry [ˈkærɪ]   **v.** 攜帶   5th ★★★★★
You always forget your address, so you should write it down and carry it with you.
你總是忘記你家住址，你應該要把它抄下來隨身攜帶。

0396 carve [kɑrv]   **v.** 雕刻   4th ★★★★★
Ben used this knife to carve his name into the tree.
班用一把刀把他的名字刻到樹上。

0397 cash [kæʃ]   **n.** 現金   5th ★★★★★
Customers may pay cash or use a credit card in major department stores.
顧客可以在大多數的百貨公司用現金或信用卡付款。

0398 cashier [kæˈʃɪr]   **n.** 出納員   5th ★★★★★
Please go to Window Eight. The cashier there can help you.
請到八號窗口，那裡的出納員會為您服務。

0399 casino [kəˈsino]   **n.** 賭場   5th ★★★★★
Andy struck it rich at the casino.
安迪在賭場發了橫財。

0400 castle [ˈkæsl̩]   **n.** 城堡   5th ★★★★★
The elegant castle belongs to a rich business man now.
這座典雅的城堡現在屬於一名富商所有。

0401 casual [ˈkæʒuəl]   **adj.** 隨意的   5th ★★★★★
The host of the meeting said a casual remark, which made him embarrassed.
這個會議主持人脫口而出的一句話，讓他很尷尬。

0402 catalogue ['kætəlɔg]　　n.　目錄　　4th ★★★★★
Lucy enjoys shopping for the promotional products on the catalogue.
露西喜歡買目錄上的促銷商品。

0403 catastrophic [ˌkætə'strɑfɪk]　adj.　災難的　3rd ★★★★★
Conservationists assert that the wildlife losses have been severe and in some cases catastrophic.
保育人士呼籲，野生動物減少的問題非常嚴重，甚至會是場災難。

0404 cater ['ketə]　　v.　承辦宴席　3rd ★★★★★
The chef's job is to cater weddings and banquets.
主廚的工作是承辦婚禮和宴會酒席。

0405 category ['kætəˌgorɪ]　　n.　種類　4th ★★★★★
Onions can be divided into two categories: fresh onions and storage onions.
洋蔥可分為兩種：新鮮洋蔥和庫存洋蔥。

0406 cause [kɔz]　　n.　原因　5th ★★★★★
Labor dispute was the main cause of the strike. Workers threatened not to go back to work unless the working condition was improved.
勞資糾紛是罷工的主因。勞工威脅除非工作環境改善，不然不會回到工作崗位。

0407 caution ['kɔʃən]　　n.　小心　5th ★★★★★
You should handle these vases with caution because they are fragile.
這些花瓶是易碎品，你應該要小心處理。

0408 cautiously ['kɔʃəslɪ]　　adv.　謹慎地　5th ★★★★★
You should think very cautiously before you make an important decision.
你在下重大決定之前，必須非常小心謹慎地思考。

0409 cavity ['kævətɪ]　　n.　洞；穴　3rd ★★★★★
No matter what a child eats, brushing after each meal is still the best way to fight cavities.
不管孩子吃什麼，每餐飯後刷牙仍是防止蛀牙的最佳辦法。

0410 cease [sis]　　n.　停止　4th ★★★★★
The peace talks have brought about a cease-fire.
和平談判奏效，雙方已經停火。

0411 celebrate ['sɛləˌbret]　　v.　慶祝　5th ★★★★★

The football team celebrated its victory in a tumultuous fashion.
足球隊歡聲雷動地慶祝勝利。

0412 celebration [ˌsɛləˈbreʃən]　　**n.**　慶祝　　5th　★★★★★
The 100th Double tenth celebration will be very huge.
建國百年的雙十國慶將很盛大。

0413 celebrated [ˈsɛləˌbretɪd]　　**adj.**　有名的　　4th　★★★★★
Jin Yung is a celebrated Chinese martial arts writer, whose novels are widely published throughout the world.
金庸是知名的中國武俠小說作者，他的著作在全世界廣泛發行。

0414 celebrity [sɪˈlɛbrətɪ]　　**n.**　名人　　4th　★★★★★
The reason we find celebrities fascinating is chiefly due to our craving for becoming a peeping Tom.
我們對名人著迷，是因為我們想滿足自己偷窺的渴望。

0415 central [ˈsɛntrəl]　　**adj.**　中央的　　5th　★★★★★
The top two freshmen admitted to the Central Police University this year are aborigines from Hualian.
今年中央警察學校入學成績最高的前兩名新鮮人是來自花蓮的原住民。

0416 century [ˈsɛntʃurɪ]　　**n.**　世紀　　4th　★★★★★
Average global temperature has increased by almost 1°F over the past century.
過去一世紀間，全球平均氣溫上升了將近華氏一度。

0417 cereal [ˈsɪrɪəl]　　**n.**　穀片　　5th　★★★★★
In response to consumer demand, cereals will now be packaged in wax bags instead of cardboard cartons.
因應消費者需求，麥片將改為蠟袋包裝，而非硬紙盒。

0418 ceremony [ˈsɛrəˌmonɪ]　　**n.**　典禮　　3rd　★★★★★
She was disappointed that her best friend did not attend her wedding ceremony.
她很失望，因為她最好的朋友沒有出席她的結婚典禮。

0419 certain [ˈsɝtən]　　**adj.**　確定的　　4th　★★★★★
In fact, a certain amount of stress is necessary.
事實上，某種程度的壓力是必要的。

0420 certificate [səˈtɪfəkɪt]　　**v.**　證明　　4th　★★★★★
Nowadays people have to pass various tests for professional certificates so that

they can be qualified for a well-paying job.
當今人們必須通過各種專業證照考試才有資格得到薪水優渥的工作。

0421 challenge ['tʃælɪndʒ]　　　　n.　挑戰　　4th ★★★★★
Her work is a challenge to her. It keeps her busy and creative.
她的工作對她是一個挑戰，讓她一直忙碌有創意。

0422 champion ['tʃæmpɪən]　　　　n.　冠軍　　4th ★★★★★
Wayne is a champion because he keeps on fighting until the end.
維恩是冠軍，因為他不斷戰鬥直到最後。

0423 chance [tʃæns]　　　　n.　機會　　5th ★★★★★
Everybody is talented. What we need is a chance to develop our potentials.
每個人都有天份，我們需要發揮潛力的機會。

0424 change [tʃendʒ]　　　　v.　更換　　5th ★★★★★
I tried to change the tires. But I couldn't. I need to find a mechanic to do it for me.
我想換輪胎卻心有餘而力不足，我必須找一個技師來幫我。

0425 channel ['tʃænl]　　　　n.　海峽　　4th ★★★★★
Over 200 people have successfully swum solo across the channel from England to France.
已經有超過兩百人成功泳渡英國和法國之間的海峽。

0426 chapter ['tʃæptə]　　　　n.　章節　　4th ★★★★★
Anxiety can cause students to forget chapters that they may have read, to "go blank" at quiz time.
焦慮會導致學生忘記他們讀過的篇章，在考試時腦袋變得一片空白。

0427 character ['kærɪktə]　　　　n.　角色；性格　　4th ★★★★★
In the video game, the characters collect charms and use them for magic.
在電玩裡，各種人物都彙集咒語來施展魔法。

0428 characteristic [ˌkærəktə'rɪstɪk]　adj.　特有的　　4th ★★★★★
Anxiety is expressed by certain kinds of behavior and is accompanied by characteristic physiologic changes.
焦慮會由某些行為表現出來，且伴隨特有的生理變化。

0429 characterize ['kærəktə͵raɪz]　v.　以…為特性　　4th ★★★★★
A kind of natural disaster caused by earthquakes under the ocean and characterized by a sudden surge of giant and massive wave is known as tsunami.
大家都知道，海嘯是一種由海底地震所引發的天然災難，其特徵為突如其來的巨浪。

0430 charge [tʃɑrdʒ]　　　　　**v.** 索費；負責　✔✔ ★★★★★
Lawyers usually charge by the hour; therefore, it takes a big sum of money to go about a lawsuit.
律師通常以時計費，所以打一場官司得花上一大筆錢。

0431 charity [ˈtʃærətɪ]　　　　　**n.** 慈善　4th ★★★★★
The corporation began sponsoring charity events so that its public image would be enhanced.
這間公司開始主辦一些大型慈善晚會，藉此增加他們的公眾形象。

0432 charm [tʃɑrm]　　　　　**n.** 魅力　4th ★★★★★
The charm of living in the country soon wore off when the problems set in.
問題一發生，鄉村生活的種種魅力很快就消失了。

0433 chase [tʃes]　　　　　**v.** 追逐　5th ★★★★★
Two policemen were chasing the robber along the back street.
兩名警察沿著小巷追捕搶匪。

0434 chat [tʃæt]　　　　　**v.** 聊天　5th ★★★★★
The couple usually expanded their chat into an argument.
這對夫妻閒聊到一半通常會擴大為爭執。

0435 cheap [tʃip]　　　　　**adj.** 便宜的　5th ★★★★★
The man never wants to be a cheap worker.
這個男人不希望自己成為廉價勞工。

0436 cheat [tʃit]　　　　　**v.** 欺騙　5th ★★★★★
This information came from a very reliable source, so you don't have to worry about being cheated.
這個消息的來源非常可靠，你不用擔心被騙。

0437 check [tʃɛk]　　　　　**n.** 檢查　5th ★★★★★
The police are conducting a road check over there.
警察正在道路臨檢。

0438 chemical [ˈkɛmɪkl]　　　　　**n.** 化學物質　4th ★★★★★
This fresh produce is organic. No chemicals are used.
這些新鮮蔬果是有機的，沒有添加化學物質。

0439 chemistry [ˈkɛmɪstrɪ]　　　　　**n.** 化學　4th ★★★★★

Those five careless mistakes kept Tom from passing the midterm exam in chemistry.
湯姆犯的那五個粗心錯誤害得他化學期中考沒有過。

0440 cherish [ˈtʃɛrɪʃ]　　　　**v.**　珍惜　　4th ★★★★★
Susan tried to cherish every moment she had together with her husband.
莎拉珍惜每一個與丈夫相處的時刻。

0441 chief [tʃif]　　　　**adj.**　主要的　　4th ★★★★★
Economics was one of my chief courses in college.
經濟學是我大學的必修課之一。

0442 child [tʃaɪld]　　　　**n.**　小孩　　5th ★★★★★
This campus accident raises concerns about children's safety.
這件校園意外讓大眾開始憂心孩童的安全。

0443 chilling [ˈtʃɪlɪŋ]　　　　**adj.**　寒冷的　　4th ★★★★★
The weather will be chilling tonight so you should wear a jacket.
今晚會很冷，你應該穿一件夾克。

0444 chip [tʃɪp]　　　　**n.**　晶片　　4th ★★★★★
Implanted chips are to dogs what ID cards are to people.
狗狗的植入式晶片就等同人類的身分證一樣。

0445 choice [tʃɔɪs]　　　　**n.**　選擇　　4th ★★★★★
That is a very good choice for you to make.
你做了一個非常好的選擇。

0446 chronic [ˈkrɑnɪk]　　　　**adj.**　慢性的　　3rd ★★★★★
Chronic cough, which usually lasts a long time, is dangerous and harmful.
慢性咳嗽很危險且對身體有害，通常會持續很長一段時間。

0447 chronological [ˌkrɑnəˈlɑdʒɪk]]　**adj.**　按時序的　　3rd ★★★★★
The chronological format in your resume is organized according to time: the most recent experience is given first, and so on to the earliest.
你的履歷表形式應該是照時間排序的：先列出最近的工作經歷，再一路寫到最早的工作。

0448 cigarette [ˌsɪgəˈrɛt]　　　　**n.**　香菸　　3rd ★★★★★
The representatives, with cigarettes in their hands, were negotiating over a few details when suddenly smoke detector set off the fire alarm.
代表們手上拿著香菸，正在商討一些細節，突然間煙霧探測器啟動了火警。

0449 circle [ˈsɝkl̩]　　　　n.　圓圈　　5th ★★★★★
The heart consists of several layers of muscles arranged in circles and spirals.
心臟是由多層圓圈狀和螺旋狀的肌肉組成。

0450 circulation [ˌsɝkjəˈleʃən]　　n.　循環　　4th ★★★★★
More oxygen means better circulation.
氧氣越多代表循環越好。

0451 citizen [ˈsɪtəzn]　　　　n.　市民　　4th ★★★★★
To avoid the possible loss of human life caused by floods, citizens in this city have been transported to safer locations.
為了避免洪水導致人命傷亡，這座城市的市民已經轉移到較安全的地區了。

0452 city [ˈsɪtɪ]　　　　　　n.　城市　　5th ★★★★★
An earthquake destroyed much of the city. Many patients were sent to the only hospital in the area.
一場地震毀了城市大部分的區域，許多病患被送往該區唯一的醫院。

0453 civilian [sɪˈvɪljən]　　　n.　平民　　3rd ★★★★★
After being in the military for a decade, I decided to leave the army and become a civilian again.
在軍中待了十年之後，我決定退伍，重新當一個老百姓。

0454 civilization [ˌsɪvl̩əˈzeʃən]　　n.　文明　　4th ★★★★★
In Western civilization, kissing has been accepted for many thousands of years.
在西方文明中，親吻是大家千年下來所接受的行為。

0455 claim [klem]　　　　　v.　聲稱　　4th ★★★★★
Some Irish people claim that they bleed green.
某些愛爾蘭人聲稱他們流的是純愛爾蘭人血統。

0456 clandestine [klænˈdɛstɪn]　　adj.　暗中的　　3rd ★★★★★
That group was excellent at handling clandestine operations.
該小組善於從事秘密行動。

0457 clarify [ˈklærəˌfaɪ]　　　v.　闡明　　4th ★★★★★
When the teacher saw that the students did not understand, he tried to clarify.
老師看到學生不理解，便試著闡明清楚。

0458 clash [klæʃ]　　　　　n.　不協調　　4th ★★★★★

The red wall clashes with the blue door.
紅色牆壁與藍色大門不協調。

0459 classical ['klæsɪkl]　　　　**adj.** 古典的　　5th ★★★★★
Joe is interested in learning a classical language.
喬對學習古典語言有興趣。

0460 client ['klaɪənt]　　　　**n.** 客戶　　5th ★★★★★
Chris brought his client out to dinner to thank him for his business.
克里斯帶客戶上館子，感謝他在業務上的幫忙。

0461 climate ['klaɪmɪt]　　　　**n.** 氣候　　4th ★★★★★
The climate has a lot of influence on the agriculture.
氣候對農業有很大的影響。

0462 cling [klɪŋ]　　　　**v.** 堅持　　4th ★★★★★
After the big flood, the area was mostly deserted, with only one or two homes still clinging to their last relics.
這個地區在洪水肆虐後大多廢棄了，只有一兩戶人家堅守著這些最後的殘跡。

0463 clinic ['klɪnɪk]　　　　**n.** 診所　　4th ★★★★★
The clinic offered the couple an 80% chance of ensuring they will have a girl.
診所告知這對夫妻，他們有百分之八十的機率會生女兒。

0464 clink [klɪŋk]　　　　**v.** 叮噹作響　　5th ★★★★★
They clinked glasses and drank to each other's health.
他們相互乾杯，祝福彼此身體健康。

0465 clone [klon]　　　　**v.** 複製　　4th ★★★★★
The government now allows food made from cloned animals to be sold to the public.
政府現在准許由複製動物所做成的食品在市場上販售。

0466 clothes [kloz]　　　　**n.** 衣服　　4th ★★★★★
The type of clothes people wear tells others a lot about who they are.
人們身上穿的衣服款式，向別人說明了他們是怎麼樣的人。

0467 clue [klu]　　　　**n.** 線索　　4th ★★★★★
Few years later, a group of explorers found a clue to the mystery.
一群探險家在幾年後發現了一條關於這個祕密的線索。

0468 clumsy [ˈklʌmzɪ]　　　　**adj.** 粗魯的　　4th ★★★★★

Sue is so clumsy that she always breaks something when she is shopping at a store.
蘇笨手笨腳的，她在商店逛街的時候常常打破東西。

0469 clutter [ˈklʌtə]　　　　**v.** 亂堆　　3rd ★★★★★

Tom's desk was so cluttered with papers that it was hard to find anything.
湯姆的書桌堆滿了紙張，找什麼東西都很困難。

0470 coach [kotʃ]　　　　**n.** 教練　　5th ★★★★★

The basketball coach devises a new play to help his team win.
籃球教練設計一個新的打法幫助球隊獲勝。

0471 coal [kol]　　　　**n.** 煤炭　　5th ★★★★★

The firewalkers of Fiji, Hawaii, and the Cook Islands walk over blazing hot coals without flinching.
來自斐濟、夏威夷、庫克群島的火行者毫無畏懼的走過熾熱的炭火。

0472 coast [kost]　　　　**n.** 沿海地區　　5th ★★★★★

On the coast there are picturesque fishing villages and manufacturing towns.
這一帶沿海地區有許多風景如畫的漁村和製造業重鎮。

0473 cognize [ˈkɑɡˌnaɪz]　　　　**v.** 認知　　3rd ★★★★★

The boy's writing is not easy to cognize at all.
這個男孩的筆跡根本就不容易被認出。

0474 cohesive [koˈhisɪv]　　　　**adj.** 凝聚性的　　3rd ★★★★★

Teenagers are always regarded as a cohesive group.
青少年總是被視為有凝聚力的群體。

0475 coin [kɔɪn]　　　　**n.** 錢幣　　5th ★★★★★

Old coins are not necessarily valuable. For example, some old coins are very common.
古錢幣不一定值錢，舉例來說，有些古錢幣就十分常見。

0476 coincident [koˈɪnsədnt]　　　　**adj.** 同時發生的　　4th ★★★★★

Mrs. Lee's death was coincident with her husband's birth.
李太太去世那天剛好是她先生的生日。

0477 collaborative [kəˈlæbərˌetɪv]　**adj.** 合作的　　3rd ★★★★★

Community policing is a collaborative effort between the police and community to solve the root cause of crime.
社區警務是警察和社區之間共同努力合作，以解決犯罪的根源。

0478 collapse [kə'læps]   **v.**   衰退   4th ★★★★★
Continual overwork led to the collapse of the woman's health.
持續過度工作造成那女人的健康衰退。

0479 colleague ['kɑlig]   **n.**   同事   3rd ★★★★★
My colleagues and I like to have a drink at the pub after work.
我和同事下班後喜歡到酒吧喝杯酒。

0480 collect [kə'lɛkt]   **v.**   收集   5th ★★★★★
Our neighbor's house has solar panels on the roof to collect the energy from the sun.
我們鄰居家的屋頂上有太陽能電池板可聚集太陽能。

0481 collection [kə'lɛkʃən]   **n.**   收集   5th ★★★★★
The museum is famous for its abundant collection of Chinese paintings.
這間博物館因為收藏大量的中國書畫而聞名。

0482 college ['kɑlɪdʒ]   **n.**   大學   5th ★★★★★
Downloading music over the Internet is pretty common among high school and college students.
從網路下載音樂在高中生和大學生之間十分常見。

0483 collision [kə'lɪʒən]   **n.**   碰撞   3rd ★★★★★
By slamming on the brakes in time, the bus driver was able to avoid a collision with the train.
公車司機及時踩煞車，避免與火車相撞。

0484 column ['kɑləm]   **n.**   圓柱   4th ★★★★★
Can you see Matt standing beside the column?
你有看到麥特嗎？他站在圓柱旁邊。

0485 combat ['kɑmbæt]   **v.**   對抗   3rd ★★★★★
The government may require individuals to limit the carbon dioxide they produce to combat global warming.
政府需要限制每個人製造的二氧化碳，以對抗全球暖化。

0486 combine [kəm'baɪn]   **v.**   結合   4th ★★★★★

Disasters and starvation combine to kill tens of thousands.
災害加上飢荒使數萬人喪命。

0487 comedy [ˈkɑmədɪ]   **n.** 喜劇   ~~4th~~ ★★★★★
William could not see the comedy in his bad fortune.
威廉沉浸在他的不幸中，看不見任何開心的事。

0488 comfortable [ˈkʌmfətəbl]   **adj.** 舒適的   ~~5th~~ ★★★★★
I need a pad for this chair to make it more comfortable.
我要在這張椅子上加個墊子，坐起來才會更舒適。

0489 command [kəˈmænd]   **n.** 眺望   ~~4th~~ ★★★★★
Located on the top of the mountain, the house commands a very good view of the meadow.
這棟房子座落在山頂上，可以眺望一大片綠油油的美景。

0490 commemorate [kəˈmɛməˌret]   **v.** 慶祝   ~~3rd~~ ★★★★★
Dr.Chen delivered a speech in which he commemorated the Institute's achievements.
陳博士發表了講話，慶祝研究所的成就。

0491 commence [kəˈmɛns]   **v.** 開始   ~~3rd~~ ★★★★★
Leo and Nancy's relationship commenced several years ago.
李奧和南西幾年前開始戀愛。

0492 commencement [kəˈmɛnsmənt]   **n.** 畢業典禮   ~~3rd~~ ★★★★★
All his family members attended the commencement because they wanted to congratulate him on obtaining a college diploma in person.
他全家都出席了畢業典禮，因為他們想親自恭喜他拿到了大學文憑。

0493 commercial [kəˈmɝʃəl]   **n.** 商業   ~~4th~~ ★★★★★
A lot of trees were felled and burned for commercial reasons.
許多樹木因為商業理由遭砍伐和燒毀。

0494 commission [kəˈmɪʃən]   **n.** 佣金   ~~4th~~ ★★★★★
The price is net price, without any commission.
這價格是淨價，不含手續費。

0495 commit [kəˈmɪt]   **v.** 犯罪   ~~4th~~ ★★★★★
We all think that man committed the crime, but he won't confess.
我們都認為那個人有罪，但他不會承認。

0496 committee [kə'mɪtɪ]　　　**n.** 委員會　　4th ★★★★★

To have a full discussion of the issue, the committee spent a whole hour exchanging their ideas at the meeting.
為了讓這項議題有完整的討論，委員會在會議上花了整整一個鐘頭交換意見。

0497 commodity [kə'mɑdətɪ]　　**n.** 日用品　　4th ★★★★★

With the lack of harvest on some grains, the prices on several basic commodities such as bread in the global market have been greatly increased.
由於一些穀物的歉收，許多基本商品的價格如麵包已在全球市場大幅上漲。

0498 commonly ['kɑmənlɪ]　　**adv.** 普通地　　5th ★★★★★

Near-sightedness is commonly corrected with contacts and glasses.
用隱形眼鏡和眼鏡矯正近視非常普遍。

0499 commonplace ['kɑmən,ples]　**adj.** 平凡的　　3rd ★★★★★

The cell phone is a commonplace nowadays.
手機是時下很平常的東西。

0500 communicate [kə'mjunə,ket]　**v.** 溝通　　4th ★★★★★

Rapid changes in technology have transformed the way society communicates.
科技的快速變遷改變了社會溝通的方式。

0501 communication [kə,mjunə'keʃən]　**n.** 溝通　　4th ★★★★★

Many of the problems were caused by a breakdown in communications.
許多問題的產生都是因為溝通破裂導致。

0502 communicative [kə,mjunə'ketɪv]　**adj.** 暢談的　4th ★★★★★

The spokesman is quite communicative.
這位發言人相當健談。

0503 communism ['kɑmju,nɪzəm]　**n.** 共產主義　　3rd ★★★★★

Some communism countries are considering the possibilities of privatizing their state-run enterprises. Then the ownership will belong to the shareholders, not the government.
一些共產國家正考慮將國營企業私有化的可能性，所有權將進而屬於股東，而非政府。

0504 community [kə'mjunətɪ]　　**n.** 社區　　4th ★★★★★

John was quite rude; almost everyone in the community tried to put up with his behavior.
約翰很沒禮貌，社區裡幾乎每一個人都得忍受他的惡行。

0505 commuter [kə'mjutɚ]　　**n.** 通勤者　4th ★★★★★
Major commuter arteries were choked with stalled traffic.
主要交通幹線都擠滿了堵塞的車輛。

0506 companion [kəm'pænjən]　　**n.** 同伴　4th ★★★★★
You would go far to find a companion as agreeable as Catherine, always pleasant and humorous, smiling and helpful.
你應該去找一位像凱薩琳那樣隨和的同伴，她總是親切、幽默，時常面帶微笑也會主動幫忙。

0507 company ['kʌmpənɪ]　　**n.** 公司　4th ★★★★★
Mike has worked as an assistant manager for more than ten years at the company.
麥克擔任公司副理已經超過十年了。

0508 comparative [kəm'pærətɪv]　**adj.** 比較的　4th ★★★★★
Professor Li is teaching Comparative Literature at a college.
李教授在大學教比較文學。

0509 compare [kəm'pɛr]　　**v.** 比較　4th ★★★★★
Craig's story about his sneakers was pretty tame compared to his brother's story about the bear.
克雷格的運動鞋故事比他哥哥熊的故事還乏味。

0510 compassion [kəm'pæʃən]　　**n.** 同情　4th ★★★★★
The enterpriser was filled with compassion for the flood victim.
企業家非常同情水災罹難者。

0511 compassionate [kəm'pæʃənɪt] **adj.** 富同情心的　4th ★★★★★
The compassionate and generous woman donated a large amount of money to the charity.
這位富有同情心又慷慨大方的女人捐了一大筆錢給慈善團體。

0512 compatible [kəm'pætəbl̩]　　**adj.** 相容的　4th ★★★★★
Luckily, the antivirus software is compatible with my computer.
幸好這個反毒軟體適用於我的電腦。

0513 compel [kəm'pɛl]　　**v.** 強迫　4th ★★★★★
The cyclists are compelled to wear a helmet based on the traffic regulations.
根據交通法規，單車騎士須強制配戴安全帽。

0514 **compendium** [kəmˈpɛndɪəm] **n.** 摘要 **3rd** ★★★★★
John is doing translation for the compendium of his essay from Chinese to English.
約翰正為他的文章摘要中翻英。

0515 **compensation** [ˌkɑmpənˈseʃən] **n.** 補償 **4th** ★★★★★
The worker received NT $ 10000 in compensation for the loss of one of his fingers.
這個工人因為失去一根手指，而得到台幣一萬元的賠償金。

0516 **compete** [kəmˈpit] **v.** 競爭 **4th** ★★★★★
In the Olympic Games, the best athletes from all over the world try their best to compete with one another.
來自世界各地的運動好手在奧運上都拿出他們的看家本領相互競爭。

0517 **competent** [ˈkɑmpətənt] **adj.** 能幹的 **4th** ★★★★★
My uncle is a competent basketball coach.
我叔叔是一位稱職的籃球教練。

0518 **competitive** [kəmˈpɛtətɪv] **adj.** 競爭的 **4th** ★★★★★
You need to struggle all the time in the highly competitive society.
在這個高度競爭的社會，你要一直努力奮鬥。

0519 **competition** [ˌkɑmpəˈtɪʃən] **n.** 比賽 **4th** ★★★★★
A lot of people braved the chilly weather to watch the ski competition.
許多人不畏寒風刺骨，堅持去看滑雪比賽。

0520 **complain** [kəmˈplen] **v.** 抱怨 **4th** ★★★★★
Mrs. Lin likes to complain about her husband all the time. It seems that she cannot find anything good about him.
林太太一天到晚喜歡抱怨她的丈夫，她似乎從他身上找不出一絲優點。

0521 **complaint** [kəmˈplent] **n. v.** 抱怨 **4th** ★★★★★
Harry's restaurant received several complaints about their poor service.
哈利的餐館收到幾則關於他們服務不佳的抱怨。

0522 **complement** [ˈkɑmpləmənt] **n.** 配對物 **4th** ★★★★★
The music played by the band is a complement to the party.
樂隊演奏的音樂很適合這場派對。

0523 **complete** [kəmˈplit] **v.** 完成 **4th** ★★★★★
The teacher gave us a handout to complete in class.
老師發給我們一份要在課堂上完成的講義。

0524 complex ['kamplɛks] **adj.** 複雜的；合成的 3rd ★★★★★
Kopi Lowak is reported to have a character in taste unlike any other coffee, complex with caramel undertones and an earthy or gamey flavor.
印尼的麝香貓咖啡據說和其他咖啡喝起來很不一樣，混合著淡淡的焦糖、泥土和天然生物的野味。

0525 complexity [kəm'plɛksətɪ] **n.** 複雜 4th ★★★★★
The chief must understand the task assigned to his team. It's not an easy task this time.
長官務必要對指派小組的任務有所了解，因為這次的任務並不輕鬆。

0526 complicate ['kamplə,ket] **v.** 使複雜 4th ★★★★★
It will only complicate the situation if we invite her ex-boyfriend as well.
如果我們也邀請她前男友，只會讓情況複雜。

0527 complication [,kamplə'keʃən] **n.** 併發症 4th ★★★★★
The patient will recover soon if no complication sets in.
如果沒有出現任何併發症，病人很快就會復原。

0528 compliment ['kampləmənt] **v.** 恭維 4th ★★★★★
Most of us are flattered when we receive someone's compliment.
當我們得到某人的恭維時，大多會覺得很榮幸。

0529 comply [kəm'plaɪ] **v.** 順從 4th ★★★★★
The manager complied with the employees' demands.
經理應允員工的要求。

0530 compose [kəm'poz] **v.** 組成 4th ★★★★★
The population of Taiwan is composed of four distinct ethnic groups, each of which has its own language.
台灣的人口由四個不同的民族組成，擁有各自的語言。

0531 composition [,kampə'zɪʃən] **n.** 作文 4th ★★★★★
Students were asked to revise or rewrite their compositions based on the teacher's comments.
學生要根據老師給的評論修改或重寫他們的文章。

0532 comprehend [,kamprɪ'hɛnd] **v.** 理解 4th ★★★★★
Most of the students couldn't comprehend the sentences because they were too complicated.
因為這些句子太複雜了，大多數學生都無法理解。

0533 comprehensive [ˌkɑmprɪˈhɛnsɪv] **adj.** 廣泛的 4th ★★★★★
The girl has a comprehensive knowledge of Taiwanese literature.
這個女孩對台灣文學有全面的認識。

0534 compromise [ˈkɑmprəˌmaɪz] **v.** 妥協 3rd ★★★★★
The drunk driver should have compromised with the injured on the accident.
這位酒醉駕駛應該向事故中的傷者妥協。

0535 compulsive [kəmˈpʌlsɪv] **adj.** 強迫的 3rd ★★★★★
Oniomania is the technical term for the compulsive desire to shop, more commonly referred to as compulsive shopping or shopping addiction.
購物狂是專業術語，指的是有強迫性的購買慾，更普遍稱作強迫性購物或購物成癮。

0536 conceal [kənˈsil] **v.** 隱藏 3rd ★★★★★
The newcomer tried to conceal his background.
這位新人試圖隱瞞他的背景。

0537 conceit [kənˈsit] **n.** 自負 3rd ★★★★★
The student who is full of conceit never gets well along with his classmates.
這個驕傲自大的學生從來無法和同學好好相處。

0538 concentrate [ˈkɑnsɛnˌtret] **v.** 專注 3rd ★★★★★
Miguel was so angry at the news that he was unable to concentrate on his project.
米格爾對那則新聞感到很生氣，害他無法專注在他的企畫上。

0539 concept [ˈkɑnsɛpt] **n.** 概念 4th ★★★★★
She is familiar with the concept that where there is a will, there is a way.
她熟知有志者事竟成的道理。

0540 conception [kənˈsɛpʃən] **n.** 觀念 4th ★★★★★
Soldiers should have a clear conception of their obligations.
士兵應該要清楚了解自己的義務。

0541 concern [kənˈsɜn] **n.** 關心 4th ★★★★★
Parents can air their concerns for their children at PTA.
家長在教師座談會上可以說出他們對孩子的關心和擔憂。

0542 concierge [ˌkɑnsɪˈɛrʒ] **n.** 門房 3rd ★★★★★
The amicable concierge always wears a sweet smile on her face.
這位門房的臉上總是掛著甜美的微笑。

030

0543 concise [kən'saɪs]　　　　　**adj.** 簡潔的　　**3rd** ★★★★★
Remember to make your presentation concise and to the point.
記得要讓你的演講簡明扼要，並點出重點。

0544 conclusion [kən'kluʒən]　　　**n.** 結論　　**4th** ★★★★★
I would like to postpone the conference call until both analyses have sent us their conclusions.
我想延後電話會議，直到兩份分析結果送來再開始。

0545 concrete ['kɑnkrit]　　　　　**n.** 水泥　　**4th** ★★★★★
Everywhere there is color, from the blue sky to the green grass, from the gray concrete in a city to the black of a moonless night.
那裡到處都是顏色，從藍色的天空到翠綠的青草，從城市灰色的水泥牆到沒有月亮的黑夜。

0546 condemn [kən'dɛm]　　　　　**v.** 判罪　　**3rd** ★★★★★
The coach is right to condemn his players for lack of sportsmanship.
教練譴責球員缺乏運動家精神是對的。

0547 condense [kən'dɛns]　　　　　**v.** 壓縮　　**4th** ★★★★★
The students are learning how to condense gas in the laboratory.
學生正在實驗室學習如何凝結氣體。

0548 condition [kən'dɪʃən]　　　　**n.** 狀況　　**4th** ★★★★★
Because our landlord will not maintain the property and keep it in good condition, we are withholding our rent.
因為房東不將房子維持良好狀態，所以我們拒付房租。

0549 conduce [kən'djus]　　　　　**v.** 導致　　**3rd** ★★★★★
Resistence conduces to success.
阻力有助成功。

0550 conducive [kən'djusɪv]　　　　**adj.** 有助於　　**4th** ★★★★★
The pitcher's excellent performance is conducive to the team's victory.
投手出色的表現有助於球隊獲勝。

0551 conduct [kən'dʌkt]　　　　　**n.** 舉動　　**4th** ★★★★★
Such conduct might give rise to antagonism.
這種舉動可能會引起對立。

0552 conductor [kən'dʌktə]　　n.　指揮　　4th ★★★★★
The new conductor of the orchestra comes from England.
新的樂隊指揮來自英國。

0553 conduit ['kɑnduɪt]　　n.　溝渠　　3rd ★★★★★
There was something wrong with the conduit system this morning.
今早排水系統出了點問題。

0554 conference ['kɑnfərəns]　　n.　會議　　3rd ★★★★★
Many scholars and experts from all over the world will be invited to attend this yearly conference on drug control.
這次的年度會議邀請了世界各地的專家學者出席，一同討論藥物管制的議題。

0555 confession [kən'fɛʃən]　　n.　承認　　3rd ★★★★★
The boy finally made a confession that he used my password and posted those photos.
男孩終於承認他盜用我的密碼張貼這些照片。

0556 confidence ['kɑnfədəns]　　n.　信心　　4th ★★★★★
Doing exercise helps us not only strengthen the body but also increase confidence.
運動不但可以強健體魄，還可以增加自信心。

0557 confidential [ˌkɑnfə'dɛnʃəl]　　adj.　機密的　　3rd ★★★★★
This document is highly confidential, inaccessible to anyone except the Minister of Foreign Affairs himself.
這份文件是高度機密，除了外交部長本人之外，任何人都拿不到。

0558 configuration [kən,fɪgjə'reʃən]　　n.　結構　　3rd ★★★★★
The configuration of the mountain changed after the earthquake.
地震改變了山的結構。

0559 confinement [kən'faɪnmənt]　　n.　限制　　3rd ★★★★★
The prisoner was sentenced to two years' confinement.
這個囚犯被判兩年監禁。

0560 confirm [kən'fɝm]　　v.　確認　　4th ★★★★★
The newspaper confirmed the winner of the election.
報紙證實了選舉的贏家。

0561 confirmation [ˌkɑnfə'meʃən]　　n.　確認　　4th ★★★★★

031

We have a confirmation that the manager will be transformed to China.
我們確定經理將會轉調到中國。

0562 conflict [ˈkɑnflɪkt]　　n.　衝突　　4th ★★★★★
I had to decline Jack's invitation to the party because it conflicted with an important business meeting.
我得拒絕傑克的派對邀請，因為派對和一個重要的商務會議撞期了。

0563 conform [kənˈfɔrm]　　v.　遵照　　4th ★★★★★
He tried to conform his tastes to those of his girlfriend's.
他試著順應女朋友的愛好。

0564 confront [kənˈfrʌnt]　　v.　面對　　3rd ★★★★★
Too often are we confronted with difficult circumstances in life that we fail to pull through?
是不是在我們人生中總會面臨自己無法渡過的難關？

0565 confusion [kənˈfjuʒən]　　n.　混亂　　5th ★★★★★
The unexpected event threw the staff into confusion.
這起突發事件使工作人員陷入慌亂。

0566 congestion [kənˈdʒestʃən]　　n.　混亂　　4th ★★★★★
Many experts were invited to tackle the problem of traffic congestion during rush hours.
許多專家受邀處理尖峰時間的交通混亂問題。

0567 congress [ˈkɑŋgrəs]　　n.　會議　　4th ★★★★★
A medical congress will be held in Taipei in late November.
醫學大會在十一月下旬於台北舉行。

0568 connect [kəˈnɛkt]　　v.　連結　　5th ★★★★★
Compared with Westerners, the Japanese are more connected with packaging as a symbol of love and care.
比起西方人，日本人更懂得用包裝來象徵愛與關懷。

0569 connection [kəˈnɛkʃən]　　n.　連結　　5th ★★★★★
When Jason failed to pay his bill, the network company cut off his Internet connection.
傑森沒有繳網路費，網路公司便切斷他的網路連線。

0570 conscientious [ˌkɑnʃɪˈɛnʃəs]　　adj.　認真的　　3rd ★★★★★

She is a conscientious person. She always works hard, has excellent self-control, and takes great care to follow moral goodness.
她很認真，總是努力工作，非常自愛也認真遵從道德善行。

0571 **conscious** ['kɑnʃəs]　　　adj. 有意識的　　4th ★★★★★
The injured was still conscious when the accident happened.
意外發生時傷患還有意識。

0572 **consciousness** ['kɑnʃəsnɪs]　n. 意識　　4th ★★★★★
It was about twenty hours before the mountain climber came to consciousness.
這位登山客大約過了二十個小時才恢復意識。

0573 **consecutive** [kən'sɛkjutɪv]　adj. 連續的　　3rd ★★★★★
Our school soccer team has have three consecutive victories so far.
我們的足球校隊目前已取得三連勝了。

0574 **consensus** [kən'sɛnsəs]　　n. 共識　　4th ★★★★★
The congressmen have reached a consensus that smoking should be banned within thirty feet from the entrance of a building.
議員達成共識，大樓門口的三十英尺內禁止吸煙。

0575 **consent** [kən'sɛnt]　　　n. 同意　　4th ★★★★★
All teenagers under the age of sixteen must have the consent of their parents to drive a car.
十六歲以下的青少年必須得到父母的同意才可以開車。

0576 **consequence** ['kɑnsə,kwɛns] n. 結果　　4th ★★★★★
The assurance of a good job is one of the consequences of finishing one's studies and getting a degree.
完成學業、取得文憑的其中一項結果，就是能確保有一份好工作。

0577 **consequently** ['kɑnsə,kwɛntlɪ]　adv. 結果　　4th ★★★★★
Henry put off doing all his biology assignments; consequently, he failed the course.
亨利的生物作業全都遲交，結果被當。

0578 **conservative** [kən'sɜvətɪv]　adj. 保守的　　4th ★★★★★
Many conservative voters live in this district.
許多保守派選民住在這個行政區。

0579 **conserve** [kən'sɜv]　　　v. 保存　　4th ★★★★★

Using the sun's heat makes sense to most people to produce and to conserve energy.
對大部份的人來說,使用太陽熱能有辦法生產和節約能源。

0580 consider [kən'sɪdə]   **v.** 認為   **4th** ★★★★★
Millions of people are using cell phones today. In fact, in many places it is actually considered unusual not to use one.
現今數百萬人都在使用手機,事實上,沒有手機在許多地方才是不尋常的。

0581 considerable [kən'sɪdərəbl]   **adj.** 相當的   **4th** ★★★★★
For more than 30 years, the outstanding success of the Taiwan experience has had considerable impact on mainland China.
台灣經驗的卓越成就,對中國造成的巨大影響已超過三十年。

0582 considerate [kən'sɪdərɪt]   **adj.** 體貼的   **4th** ★★★★★
It was considerate of you not to disturb us.
你不想打擾我們真的是很體貼。

0583 consist [kən'sɪst]   **v.** 包括   **3rd** ★★★★★
A dream usually consists of various visual images that tell a story.
夢通常包括各種視覺影像,以組成一個故事。

0584 consistent [kən'sɪstənt]   **adj.** 一致的   **3rd** ★★★★★
A good phonetic transcription system is consistent and unambiguous.
一個好的音標系統是一致且明確的。

0585 consolidation [kən,sɑlə'deʃən]   **n.** 合併   **3rd** ★★★★★
The two businesses formed a large one by consolidation.
這兩家企業合併成一家大公司。

0586 consonant ['kɑnsənənt]   **adj.** 一致的   **3rd** ★★★★★
The young man's behavior is always consonant with his words.
這個年輕人向來都是言行一致。

0587 constantly ['kɑnstəntlɪ]   **adv.** 不斷地   **4th** ★★★★★
The weather changes so constantly that no one can accurately predict what it will be like the next day.
天氣如此變化多端,沒有人可以精確預測明天將會如何。

0588 constraint [kən'strent]   **n.** 限制   **3rd** ★★★★★
In an online school, students can do most of their work at their convenience—

without the time constraints of regularly scheduled classes.
在線上學校，學生可以利用方便的時候做大部分的作業，不會因為固定的教學排程而有時間限制。

0589 construction [kən'strʌkʃən]　　n.　建造　　　3rd　★★★★★
The traffic was crawling because of the construction on Main Street.
交通像蝸牛一樣緩慢，因為主幹道正在施工。

0590 consult [kən'sʌlt]　　　　　　v.　諮詢　　　4th　★★★★★
It is wise to consult a dictionary when you come across a word you don't know.
當你遇到不認識的字時，查閱字典是明智的。

0591 consumer [kən'sjumɚ]　　　n.　消費者　　4th　★★★★★
The British are the biggest consumers of chocolate; each person, on average, eats nearly 10 kilograms per year.
英國是巧克力的最大消費國，平均每個人一年可以吃掉十公斤的巧克力。

0592 consumption [kən'sʌmpʃən]　n.　消費　　　4th　★★★★★
China contributed almost 30 % of global consumption growth, more than the G3 and almost doubled that of the US.
全球消費增長，中國貢獻將近百分之三十，超越世界三大經濟體，而且幾乎是美國的兩倍。

0593 contact ['kɑntækt]　　　　　v.　聯絡　　　4th　★★★★★
The head of the department will soon contact you for a follow-up interview.
部門的負責人將會盡快與你連絡接下來的面試時間。

0594 contagious [kən'tedʒəs]　　adj.　傳染性的　3rd　★★★★★
The infection is highly contagious, so don't use public towels at restaurants or spas.
傳染病具高度傳染性，所以不要在餐廳或SPA使用公共毛巾。

0595 contain [kən'ten]　　　　　　v.　包含　　　4th　★★★★★
Lacking teeth, whales gather food by gulping the seawater that contains it.
鯨魚沒有牙齒，牠們進食的方法是把食物連著海水一起吞下肚。

0596 container [kən'tenɚ]　　　　n.　容器　　　4th　★★★★★
If you recycle glass and aluminum containers, then factories won't have to burn so much fuel to make new containers.
如果你回收玻璃和鋁製容器，工廠就不用燃燒過多的燃料製作新容器。

0597 contaminate [kən'tæmə,net]　**v.**　污染　　**3rd** ★★★★★
This river has been badly contaminated. No fish can live in it because it is so dirty.
這條河川受到嚴重汙染，因為太髒了沒有魚可以存活。

0598 contemporary [kən'tɛmpə,rɛrɪ]　**adj.** 當代的　**3rd** ★★★★★
The contemporary history of football spans more than 100 years.
當代足球的歷史橫跨了一百多年。

0599 content [kən'tɛnt]　　　**v.**　使開心　　**3rd** ★★★★★
For all his riches, he is not contented.
雖然他很有錢，但他並不開心。

0600 contest ['kɑntɛst]　　　**n.**　比賽　　**4th** ★★★★★
From the many speech contests she has won so far, Mary has gained a fresh impetus to prepare for the national one next week.
瑪莉目前為止已贏得諸多演講比賽，並從中獲得強勁的動力來準備下週的全國比賽。

0601 continual [kən'tɪnjʊəl]　　**adj.** 連續的　　**4th** ★★★★★
We don't like Tom; his continual complaints make us upset.
我們不喜歡湯姆，他總是不停的抱怨，害我們心情低落。

0602 continue [kən'tɪnju]　　　**v.**　繼續　　**4th** ★★★★★
Taiwan's exports and imports continued expanding in June.
台灣的進出口在六月持續擴張。

0603 continuously [kən'tɪnjuəslɪ]　**adv.** 持續地　**4th** ★★★★★
Traditional Chinese brush painting has developed continuously over a period of more than six thousand years.
傳統的中國山水畫已經持續發展超過六千年了。

0604 contract ['kɑntrækt]　　　**n.**　合約　　**3rd** ★★★★★
The contract will be in force for two years from the date it is signed.
合約從簽訂日起兩年有效。

0605 contrary ['kɑntrɛrɪ]　　　**adj.** 相反的　**3rd** ★★★★★
Though George and Mary are happily married, they cast contrary votes in almost every election.
雖然喬治和瑪麗的婚姻很美滿，但他們幾乎在每場選舉中都投相反票。

0606 contribute [kən'trɪbjut]　　**v.**　貢獻　　**3rd** ★★★★★

Many factors may explain why people are addicted to the Internet. One factor contributing to this phenomenon is the easy access to the Net.
人們對網路成癮有許多因素，其中一個要歸咎於上網的管道太便利了。

0607 contribution [ˌkɑntrəˈbjuʃən]　**n.** 貢獻　**3rd** ★★★★★
Tourism has no doubt made vital contribution to the local economy.
旅遊業無疑已為當地經濟做出重大貢獻。

0608 control [kənˈtrol]　**n.** 控制　**4th** ★★★★★
The Center for Disease Control reminded citizens traveling overseas during the holidays to be on guard against contagious diseases.
疾病管制中心提醒民眾，假日出國旅行時要特別注意傳染性疾病。

0609 controversial [ˌkɑntrəˈvɝʃəl]　**adj.** 有爭議的　**3rd** ★★★★★
The controversial singer must fulfill 100 hours of community service for altering the age on his ID card.
這位備受爭議的歌手必須做滿一百個小時的社會勞動，因為他竄改了身分證上的年紀。

0610 convenience [kənˈvinjəns]　**n.** 便利　**5th** ★★★★★
I'm going to the convenience store. You can come along with me if you'd like.
我要去便利商店一趟，你如果想跟的話可以一起來。

0611 conversation [ˌkɑnvəˈseʃən]　**n.** 會話　**4th** ★★★★★
E-mail eliminates face-to-face conversation and everything that goes with it.
電子郵件消弭了面對面的談話互動以及其他相關的情況。

0612 convert [kənˈvɝt]　**v.** 轉變　**5th** ★★★★★
Traffic is being converted from the main road while it's under repair.
主要道路維修期間，車輛已改道行駛。

0613 convey [kənˈve]　**v.** 傳遞　**4th** ★★★★★
In tonal languages such as Chinese, meaning is conveyed not only by the sound of a word but also by its pitch.
有聲調的語言像是中文，語意的傳達不僅是靠字的發音，音調也很重要。

0614 convince [kənˈvɪns]　**v.** 說服　**4th** ★★★★★
You must convince him that it is wrong to take drugs.
你一定得說服他，讓他知道吸毒是錯的。

0615 colonist [ˈkɑlənɪst]　**n.** 殖民者　**3rd** ★★★★★
Many great colonists made an impact on American history.
許多偉大的殖民者都對美國歷史有很大的影響。

0616 console [kən'sol]　　　v.　安慰　　　4th ★★★★★
The Dalai Lama arrived in Taiwan to console victims of Typhoon Morakot.
達賴喇嘛到台灣來撫慰莫拉克颱風的受害者。

0617 cooperate [ko'ɑpəˌret]　　　v.　合作　　　4th ★★★★★
Perhaps by that time, we will have learned that it is better to cooperate than to fight.
也許到那個時候，我們會了解到合作勝於爭鬥。

0618 cooperation [koˌɑpə'reʃən]　　　n.　合作　　　4th ★★★★★
I'd like to take advantage of this opportunity to thank you all for your co-operation.
我想要利用這個機會謝謝你們的合作。

0619 copyright ['kɑpɪˌraɪt]　　　n.　版權　　　3rd ★★★★★
When students download and share copyrighted music without permission, they are violating the law.
學生若沒有經過同意下載音樂並分享版權，他們就是觸法了。

0620 corner ['kɔrnə]　　　n.　角落　　　5th ★★★★★
The bakery is on the corner of the First Street and Park Road.
這家麵包店位於第一街和公園路的轉角。

0621 corporal ['kɔrpərəl]　　　adj.　身體的　　　3rd ★★★★★
The bottom line is that corporal punishment does not make students become better-behaved.
體罰結果並不會使學生的表現更好。

0622 corporation [ˌkɔrpə'reʃən]　　　n.　公司　　　4th ★★★★★
Company gifts are given to commemorate the anniversary of a corporation's founding or the opening of a new building.
公司禮品是用來紀念一間公司的成立或一棟新大樓的開幕。

0623 correct [kə'rɛkt]　　　adj.　正確的　　　4th ★★★★★
This is such a difficult question that few students got the correct answer.
這個題目非常困難，沒有幾個學生可以寫出正確答案。

0624 corruption [kə'rʌpʃən]　　　n.　墮落　　　3rd ★★★★★
A documentary film won the Oscar Award last year for its explicit exposure of corruption in our society.
一部深度探索社會墮落的記錄片去年贏得奧斯卡獎。

0625 cosmetics [kɑz'mɛtɪks]　　n.　化妝品　　3rd ★★★★★

To protect consumers from the threat of mad cow disease, the government has decided to put a ban on European cosmetics.
政府為了保護消費者免受狂牛症威脅，決定禁止進口歐洲化妝品。

0626 cosmopolitan [ˌkɑzmə'pɑlətn]　adj.　世界的　　4th ★★★★★

As an experienced globe-trotter, Louisa has a cosmopolitan outlook of life. She is certainly the best spokesperson for the United Nations.
露西亞周遊列國、見多識廣，有著四海一家的人生觀，的確是聯合國最佳代言人。

0627 cost [kɔst]　　v.　犧牲　　5th ★★★★★

John never realizes that his unhealthy eating habit could cost his life.
約翰並不了解他這種病態的飲食習慣會害他送命。

0628 costume ['kɑstjum]　　n.　服裝　　5th ★★★★★

Dressed in wild, colorful costumes, a crowd of the singer's fans awaited her arrival in eager silence.
一大群穿著大膽、色彩鮮豔的歌迷，屏息等待歌手的到來。

0629 cotton ['kɑtn]　　n.　棉花　　4th ★★★★★

Except for a few wrinkles and a head of silvery, cotton-ball hair, Bennet doesn't look particularly old.
班納特除了有少許的皺紋，以及一頭棉花球般的白髮之外，看起來並沒有特別老。

0630 counselor ['kaunsḷɚ]　　n.　輔導員　　3rd ★★★★★

In most camps, there are counselors who guide the young campers during activities and ensure the safety of the campers.
大部分的營隊都有輔導員，他們在活動中帶領上營的小朋友，並確保他們的安全。

0631 couple ['kʌpḷ]　　n.　夫妻　　5th ★★★★★

After years of trying, the couple has finally come to terms with the fact that they will never have their own children. They decided to adopt one.
經過多年嘗試，這對夫妻終於面對現實，了解他們永遠無法有自己的小孩而決定領養。

0632 course [kors]　　n.　課程　　4th ★★★★★

He learned English in a three-month crash course.
他上了三個月的速成英語課程。

0633 court [kort]　　n.　法院　　4th ★★★★★

When the court was in session, the judge would not permit entrance by anyone.
開庭時，法官不允許任何人進入。

0634 courtesy [ˈkɝtəsɪ]　　　　n.　禮貌　　　3rd ★★★★★
When you enter a building, be sure to look behind you and hold the door open for someone coming through the same door. It is a common courtesy in many cultures.
當你進入大樓時，要注意替後來進門的人扶著門，這在許多文化裡都是基本禮貌。

0635 cover [ˈkʌvɚ]　　　　v.　覆蓋　　　5th ★★★★★
Cover your mouth when you cough or sneeze.
咳嗽或打噴嚏時，要摀住你的嘴巴。

0636 co-worker [ˈkoˌwɝkɚ]　　　　n.　同事　　　3rd ★★★★★
Both Danny and I are police officers from the same police station, so we are co-workers.
我和丹尼是同一間警察局的警員，我們是同事。

0637 crack [kræk]　　　　v.　使破裂　　　4th ★★★★★
The parrot used its strong beak to crack open the nuts.
那隻鸚鵡用堅硬的喙啄破堅果。

0638 crackdown [ˈkrækˌdaʊn]　　　　n.　痛擊　　　4th ★★★★★
There will be a crackdown on wasteful government spending.
將會有一個打擊政府浪費公帑的運動。

0639 cradle [ˈkredl]　　　　n.　搖籃　　　4th ★★★★★
The baby slept peacefully in the cradle.
嬰兒安詳睡在搖籃裡。

0640 craft [kræft]　　　　n.　工藝　　　4th ★★★★★
The National Palace Museum collects, preserves, and promotes the essence of Chinese art and crafts.
故宮博物院收集、保存並推廣中國藝術與工藝的菁華。

0641 crash [kræʃ]　　　　v.　撞壞　　　4th ★★★★★
The lamp fell off the table and crashed on the floor.
燈從桌上掉下來摔毀在地上。

0642 crawl [krɔl]　　　　v.　緩慢移動　　　4th ★★★★★
The traffic was crawling because of the construction on Main Street.
交通緩慢前進，因為主幹道正在施工。

0643 create [krɪˈet]　　　　v.　創造　　　4th ★★★★★

The latest technology has created a new society and a new sub-culture.
新科技創造了一個新社會和新興的次文化。

0644 creative [krɪ'etɪv]　　adj. 有創意的　　4th ★★★★★
She's very creative; for example, she designed the stage set for the community opera last month.
她非常有創意，舉例來說，她上個月就替社區的歌劇表演設計舞台。

0645 creativity [ˌkrie'tɪvətɪ]　　n. 創意　　4th ★★★★★
Experts say that creativity by definition means going against the tradition and breaking the rules.
專家解釋，創造力的定義在於不依循傳統和打破常規。

0646 creature ['kritʃə]　　n. 生物　　4th ★★★★★
Owls are nocturnal creatures, for they can hardly be seen during the day.
貓頭鷹是夜間生物，因為在白天幾乎都看不到牠們。

0647 credit ['krɛdɪt]　　n. 信用　　4th ★★★★★
Massive credit card debt is a late-twentieth-century phenomena.
龐大的信用卡債，是二十世紀末的主要現象。

0648 crime [kraɪm]　　n. 犯罪　　4th ★★★★★
I think Brian committed the crime, but I don't have any concrete evidence.
我認為布萊恩犯罪，但我沒有任何具體證據。

0649 criminal ['krɪmən]]　　n. 罪犯　　4th ★★★★★
A criminal is someone who has committed a crime.
罪犯指的就是犯罪的人。

0650 cripple ['krɪp]]　　n. 殘廢者　　4th ★★★★★
When you see a cripple, you should be kind to him. Never laugh at him.
看到身障人士，應該要體諒他們，千萬不要嘲笑他們。

0651 criterion [kraɪ'tɪrɪən]　　n. 標準　　4th ★★★★★
Little is known about the criteria, by which the committee selects the final winners.
大家對標準所知甚少，而最後的贏家也由委員會選定。

0652 critic ['krɪtɪk]　　n. 評論家　　4th ★★★★★
Critics have suggested that the Wenshan-Neihu MRT line be closed down during the 21st Summer Deaflympics in Taipei.
台北舉辦第二十屆聽障奧運的期間，評論家認為應全面停駛捷運文湖線。

0653 critical [ˈkrɪtɪk!]　　　　adj. 決定性的　　4th ★★★★★
The most critical of all investigative operations is the search at the scene.
調查行動最關鍵的一環就是搜查案發現場。

0654 criticize [krɪtɪˌsaɪz]　　　　v. 批評　　4th ★★★★★
When John was criticizing his boss, his boss was just standing behind him.
約翰批評他老闆時，他老闆正好站在他後面。

0655 crowd [kraud]　　　　n. 群眾　　5th ★★★★★
A few political extremists incited the crowd to attack the police.
一些政治極端份子煽動群眾攻擊警察。

0656 crowded [ˈkraudɪd]　　　　adj. 擁擠的　　5th ★★★★★
The highways are usually crowded before and after long holidays.
高速公路在長假前後通常很擁擠。

0657 crucial [ˈkruʃəl]　　　　adj. 重要的　　4th ★★★★★
It is crucial to clean your mouth with water after meals to flush any displaced debris.
飯後用水清潔嘴巴很重要，可以沖掉多餘的殘渣。

0658 crush [krʌʃ]　　　　v. 壓碎　　4th ★★★★★
Roxy has a major crush on Jet Li.
羅克西非常迷戀李連杰。

0659 crystal [ˈkrɪst!]　　　　n. 水晶　　4th ★★★★★
The wedding was held in an elegant hall with the glitter of the crystal chandelier that hung from the ceiling.
婚禮在一個高雅的大廳舉辦，大廳的天花板上吊掛著閃爍的水晶吊燈。

0660 cuisine [kwɪˈzin]　　　　n. 菜餚　　4th ★★★★★
There are different kinds of restaurants along the street, ranging from haute cuisine in five-star hotels to inexpensive stands selling traditional Taiwanese food.
沿街有不同種類的餐廳，從五星級飯店的高檔佳餚到台灣傳統的平價攤販都有。

0661 cultivate [ˈkʌltəˌvet]　　　　v. 培養　　4th ★★★★★
A good education should help children to cultivate a positive attitude toward life.
良好的教育應該要幫助孩子培養對人生的積極態度。

0662 cure [kjur]　　　　n. 治療　　4th ★★★★★
Experiments in genetic engineering have created important breakthroughs to find

cures for many cancers.
基因工程的實驗已經獲得重大突破，找到許多治療癌症的方法。

0663 curfew [ˈkɝfju]　　　n. 宵禁　　　5th ★★★★★

Despite their apparent success in reducing teen crime, curfews have been criticized by teens.
儘管他們在降低青少年犯罪有顯著成功，宵禁政策還是遭許多年輕人批評。

0664 curiosity [ˌkjurɪˈɑsətɪ]　　n. 好奇　　　5th ★★★★★

Driven by curiosity, Rick decided to visit the old man.
瑞可在好奇心的驅使下，決定去拜訪那位老人。

0665 curly [ˈkɝlɪ]　　　adj. 捲的　　　5th ★★★★★

Long curly hair has always been popular since ancient times.
從古至今，長捲髮一直都很流行。

0666 currency [ˈkɝənsɪ]　　　n. 貨幣　　　4th ★★★★★

The dollar will remain the key reserve currency for the foreseeable future.
在可預知的未來，美元仍是主流的儲備貨幣。

0667 current [ˈkɝənt]　　　adj. 現在的　　　4th ★★★★★

Languages change all the time. Many words that were found in Shakespeare's works are no longer in current use.
語言一直在變。過去許多在莎士比亞作品裡找到的文字，如今都不再使用了。

0668 curriculum [kəˈrɪkjələm]　　n. 課程　　　4th ★★★★★

The proposed nine-year curriculum integration will have profound impact on Taiwan's education.
九年一貫將對台灣教育帶來深遠的影響。

0669 cushion [ˈkuʃən]　　　n. 坐墊　　　4th ★★★★★

I bought an extra cushion to sit on when I'm at the computer.
我額外買了一個坐墊讓我打電腦時可以坐。

0670 custody [ˈkʌstədɪ]　　　n. 監護　　　3rd ★★★★★

The term "cultural genocide" has been sued to refer to situations in which whites are given custody of minority children.
「文化滅絕」這個詞用來形容少數民族兒童的監護權大多判給白人的情形。

0671 custom [ˈkʌstəm]　　　n. 風俗　　　5th ★★★★★

In Taiwan, setting off sky lanterns is now considered a custom at Lantern Festival.
放天燈已然成為台灣元宵節的一個風俗習慣。

0672 customer [ˈkʌstəmə]　　　n.　顧客　　5th ★★★★★
A menu serves to inform customers about the varieties and prices of the dishes offered by the restaurant.
菜單提供顧客餐廳裡菜餚的種類和價錢。

0673 cutting [ˈkʌtɪŋ]　　　adj.　尖銳的　　5th ★★★★★
Thanks to cutting-edge technology, communications are made far more efficient.
多虧尖端科技，讓通訊更有效率。

0674 cycle [ˈsaɪkl]　　　n.　循環　　3rd ★★★★★
The twelve months repeat in a cycle every year.
每年以十二個月重複一個循環。

0675 daily [ˈdelɪ]　　　adj.　日常的　　5th ★★★★★
Due to overweight, we are advised to pay close attention to our daily diet.
由於體重過重，我們應該密切注意日常生活飲食。

0676 damage [ˈdæmɪdʒ]　　　n.　損害　　4th ★★★★★
The court ruled that the company must pay for the damage.
法院判決這間公司必須要賠償損害。

0677 damp [dæmp]　　　adj.　沮喪的　　3rd ★★★★★
The damp weather will decay the wood and make people sick.
潮濕的天氣使木材容易腐壞，人們也容易生病。

0678 danger [ˈdendʒə]　　　n.　危險　　5th ★★★★★
Don't worry. Your father is in no danger now. In fact, the rescue team has rushed to help him out.
別擔心，你的父親現在沒有危險，搜救隊已經趕去幫忙了。

0679 dark [dɑrk]　　　adj.　黑暗的　　5th ★★★★★
Outside her window, Jennie could only see the dark figure of a man.
珍妮只能從窗外看見一個男子的黑暗身影。

0680 dawn [dɔn]　　　n.　黎明　　5th ★★★★★
The engineer works from dawn till dusk every day.
工程師每天從早忙到晚。

D

0681 dead [dɛd]　　　　　　adj.　死亡的　　　3rd　★★★★★
The ancient Hebrews regarded the body of a dead person as something unclean and not to be touched.
古代希伯來人視死者的身體為一種不潔的東西，而且不能碰觸。

0682 deadline ['dɛd͵laɪn]　　　n.　截止日　　　4th　★★★★★
As the deadline was approaching, he worked hard on the project around the clock.
隨著截止日期的逼近，他日以繼夜努力做那份計畫。

0683 dealer ['dilɚ]　　　　　　n.　商人　　　4th　★★★★★
The drug dealer was arrested by the police while he was selling cocaine to a high school student.
毒販向高中生販賣毒品時，遭警察逮捕。

0684 debate [dɪ'bet]　　　　　n.　爭論　　　4th　★★★★★
Euthanasia is an issue causing heated debate.
安樂死是一個引起熱烈爭論的議題。

0685 debris [də'bri]　　　　　n.　碎片　　　3rd　★★★★★
A lot of debris has been left at the site of explosion for quite a while.
爆炸現場有許多碎片遺留了好一段時間。

0686 debt [dɛt]　　　　　　　n.　債務　　　4th　★★★★★
The debt that I owe is my own burden to bear.
我要承擔自己欠下的債。

0687 decade ['dɛked]　　　　　n.　十年　　　4th　★★★★★
The world changes a lot each decade.
世界每十年就有大變化。

0688 decay [dɪ'ke]　　　　　　v.　腐爛　　　4th　★★★★★
Some fruit decays very quickly in room temperature.
有些水果在室溫下很快就腐爛了。

0689 deceive [dɪ'siv]　　　　　v.　欺騙　　　4th　★★★★★
Never judge a person by his appearance because it is deceiving.
永遠不要以貌取人，因為這只是騙人的假象。

0690 decent ['disnt]　　　　　adj.　像樣　　　4th　★★★★★
Tom has got a decent job in a chemical factory.
湯姆在一間化學工廠有份不錯的工作。

0691 deceptive [dɪ'sɛptɪv]   adj. 虛偽的   4th ★★★★★
Appearances are deceptive with ease.
外表很容易騙人。

0692 decide [dɪ'saɪd]   v. 決定   5th ★★★★★
Both sides of the battle decided to cease fire for Christmas. So people could go shopping and visit families without danger to their lives.
戰爭雙方都決定了聖誕節停火。因此人民可以無生命危險地去逛街及探視親友。

0693 decision [dɪ'sɪʒən]   n. 決定   5th ★★★★★
The British Parliament often has arguments over the decisions they will make.
英國國會對他們將作的決定經常有許多辯論。

0694 deck [dɛk]   n. 甲板   4th ★★★★★
It is not easy to keep your balance on the deck of a violent boat.
站在搖晃的船甲板上，要保持平衡很不容易。

0695 declaration [ˌdɛklə'reʃən]   n. 公告   4th ★★★★★
Could you show me your customs declaration form, please?
可以請你讓我看看你的海關申報表嗎？

0696 decline [dɪ'klaɪn]   v. 下降   4th ★★★★★
Income typically rises gradually from young adulthood through the middle years, but usually declines after retirement.
個人收入一般從成年早期到中年逐漸攀升，但退休之後就會下滑。

0697 decorate ['dɛkə,ret]   v. 裝飾   5th ★★★★★
The walls in my sister's room are decorated with white panels.
我妹妹房間的牆壁以白色的壁板裝飾。

0698 decrease [dɪ'kris]   v. 減少   4th ★★★★★
A research result shows that drinking a lot of water can help decrease the risk of developing kidney stones.
研究結果顯示，多喝水有助於降低腎結石的風險。

0699 dedicate ['dɛdə,ket]   v. 貢獻   4th ★★★★★
The old man has dedicated his time to serving as a volunteer for a local charity for years.
這位老人多年來為當地的慈善機構奉獻自己時間擔任志工。

0700 deduce [dɪ'djus]　　　v.　推論　　3rd ★★★★★
The research team deduced a conclusion from all the data.
研究小組從所有的數據中推出結論。

0701 deduct [dɪ'dʌkt]　　　v.　扣除　　3rd ★★★★★
This compensation will be deducted automatically from your salary.
這筆賠償會自動從你的工資中扣除。

0702 deduction [dɪ'dʌkʃən]　　n.　扣除　　3rd ★★★★★
There is a deduction of five hundred dollars for health insurance.
有一筆可以扣除五百元的健保。

0703 deep [dip]　　　adj.　深深的　　5th ★★★★★
Beauty is only skin deep.
外在美是膚淺的。

0704 defeat [dɪ'fit]　　　v.　打敗　　4th ★★★★★
The really good football team is hard to defeat.
真正優秀的足球隊是難以擊敗的。

0705 deficit ['dɛfɪsɪt]　　　n.　赤字　　3rd ★★★★★
Instead of governing in peace and prosperity, President Bush dealt with war and deficits.
布希總統不管理國家的和平與繁榮，而是去處理戰爭和經濟赤字。

0706 define [dɪ'faɪn]　　　v.　下定義　　4th ★★★★★
Culture, which can be defined as a system of beliefs, knowledge, and patterns of behavior, is learned.
文化是透過經驗獲得，可以定義為一個信仰、知識和行為模式的體系。

0707 defense [dɪ'fɛns]　　　n.　防禦　　4th ★★★★★
Police patrol is the first line of defense against crime.
巡邏員警是對抗犯罪的第一道防線。

0708 defensive [dɪ'fɛnsɪv]　　adj.　防禦的　　4th ★★★★★
Ruth is a very defensive person. She cannot take any criticism and always finds excuses to justify herself.
露絲的防備心很重，她無法接受批評，總是找藉口替自己辯駁。

0709 deficiency [dɪ'fɪʃənsɪ]　　n.　短缺　　3rd ★★★★★

Medical findings show that colorblindness, or more especially color vision deficiency, mostly affects men.
醫學研究成果發現，色盲或其他相關的視覺色彩缺陷好發於男性。

0710 define [dɪ'faɪn]　　v.　下定義　　4th ★★★★★
This company has a rigid hierarchy and every worker has strictly defined duties.
這間公司的階級制度很嚴苛，清楚劃分每位員工的職責。

0711 deflate [dɪ'flet]　　v.　緊縮通貨　　3rd ★★★★★
The government had better deflate its ranks from now on.
政府最好從現在就開始緊縮通貨層級。

0712 degree [dɪ'gri]　　n.　度數　　4th ★★★★★
Grandfather feels nice when the weather is above thirty degrees.
祖父覺得三十度以上的天氣很宜人。

0713 delay [dɪ'le]　　v.　延遲　　4th ★★★★★
Trying to do everything perfectly can often cause these students to delay doing any work at all.
凡事追求完美常常導致這些學生乾脆什麼都不做。

0714 delegate ['dɛləgɪt]　　v.　委派　　3rd ★★★★★
He was delegated to perform a task.
他受指派要執行一項任務。

0715 delete [dɪ'lit]　　v.　刪除　　4th ★★★★★
I hit a wrong button on my computer and accidentally deleted all the important information.
我不小心按錯鍵，把電腦上所有重要的資料都刪除了。

0716 deliberate [dɪ'lɪbərɪt]　　adj.　蓄意的　　4th ★★★★★
The car crash wasn't an accident; it was a deliberate attempt to kill him.
這場車禍不是意外，而是一場企圖殺害他、經過深思熟慮的計畫。

0717 delicate ['dɛləkət]　　adj.　易碎的　　4th ★★★★★
Hold the items very carefully because they are delicate.
拿這些物品時要小心，這些是易碎品。

0718 delicious [dɪ'lɪʃəs]　　adj.　美味的　　5th ★★★★★
The restaurant has superb business because it serves delicious and healthy food.
這間餐廳生意興隆，因為他們的食物好吃又健康。

D

0719 delegation [ˌdɛlə'geʃən]   n. 訪問團   3rd ★★★★★
With a good command of both Chinese and English, Miss Lin was assigned the task of oral interpretation for the visiting American delegation.
林小姐精通中英文，她受命為美國訪問團的口譯員。

0720 deleterious [ˌdɛlə'tɪrɪəs]   adj. 有害的   3rd ★★★★★
Excessive anxiety not only makes person unhappy but also has a deleterious effect on his performance.
過度焦慮讓人不開心，也會對表現造成不良影響。

0721 deliver [dɪ'lɪvə]   v. 遞送   5th ★★★★★
The customer complained that the lamps had not been delivered yet.
顧客抱怨羊肉還沒送到。

0722 delivery [dɪ'lɪvərɪ]   n. 運送   5th ★★★★★
Steve wasn't home this afternoon, so he couldn't receive the delivery.
史提夫今天下午不在家，所以他無法收郵件。

0723 demand [dɪ'mænd]   n. 需求   4th ★★★★★
The actress demanded an apology from the newspaper for an untrue report about her personal life.
女演員要求報社道歉，因為報紙刊登了一篇關於她私生活的不實報導。

0724 demanding [dɪ'mændɪŋ]   adj. 苛求的   4th ★★★★★
This math class is very demanding; I have to spend at least two hours every day doing the assignments.
數學課的要求很嚴格，我每天至少要花上二小時做作業。

0725 democracy [dɪ'mɑkrəsɪ]   n. 民主制度   4th ★★★★★
As democracy is becoming so widespread, we might expect it to be working in a highly successful way.
因為民主制度的普及，我們可以預期它能成功落實下去。

0726 demonstration [ˌdɛmən'streʃən] n. 示威   4th ★★★★★
There was a demonstration by the workers to request for a higher pay.
工人辦了一場示威遊行，要求更高的薪水。

0727 denomination [dɪˌnɑmə'neʃən] n. 面額   3rd ★★★★★
Postage stamps in five-and ten-cent denominations were first approved by the US Congress in 1847.
五分美元和十分美元面額的郵票，於一八四七年首次獲得美國國會通過。

0728 dense [dɛns]　　　　**adj.** 密集的　　4th ★★★★★
Howler monkeys are the loudest land animal and their howls can be heard three miles away through dense forests.
「吼猴」是聲音最大的陸地動物，牠們的叫聲能穿過濃密的森林，三英里外都能聽見。

0729 dentist ['dɛntɪst]　　　　**n.** 牙醫師　　5th ★★★★★
The dentist did a lot of work in my mouth, which made me feel awful.
牙醫在我牙齒上做了很多修整，讓我感覺很不舒服。

0730 deny [dɪ'naɪ]　　　　**v.** 否認　　4th ★★★★★
The committee denied the residents' petitions.
委員會拒絕居民的請求。

0731 depart [de'pɑrt]　　　　**v.** 起飛　　4th ★★★★★
The train to Hualien will depart in five minutes.
往花蓮的列車將在五分後出發。

0732 department [dɪ'pɑrtmənt]　　**n.** 部門　　5th ★★★★★
Bill works in the HR department of a large Wall Street finance firm.
比爾在華爾街一家大型金融公司的人事部門上班。

0733 departure [dɪ'pɑrtʃɚ]　　　**n.** 離開　　5th ★★★★★
A work schedule is an alternative to the traditional 9 to 5 workday, and it allows employees to choose their flexible time of arrival and departure.
工作時制代替了傳統朝九晚五的工作時間，讓員工能彈性選擇自己的上下班時間。

0734 depend [dɪ'pɛnd]　　　　**v.** 依賴　　3rd ★★★★★
Whether you will pass the exam or not depends more on your efforts than on your luck.
你的考試是否會過關，靠的是努力而不是運氣。

0735 dependent [dɪ'pɛndənt]　　**adj.** 依賴的　　3rd ★★★★★
Though Jack has moved out of his parents' house, he is financially dependent on them still.
雖然傑克已經搬出父母親的房子，他在經濟上仍依賴他們。

0736 depict [dɪ'pɪkt]　　　　**v.** 描述　　3rd ★★★★★
One of the most important decisions a company must make is how to depict the company in its advertisements through photographs, graphic design, or other means.
一間公司要做的主要決定之一，就是如何透過照片、平面設計或其他廣告手法來描述公司。

D

0737 depose [dɪˈpoz]　　　　　v.　罷黜　　　3rd ★★★★★
A lot of groups intend to depose those judges who are partial to the particular team during the competition.
許多團體計畫罷黜這些不公的裁判，因為他們在比賽中特別偏袒某隊。

0738 deposit [dɪˈpɑzɪt]　　　　　n.　押金　　　3rd ★★★★★
The dealer asked us to pay a deposit in order to reserve the car.
汽車交易員要我們支付押金才能保留車子。

0739 depreciation [dɪˌpriʃɪˈeʃən]　　n.　貶值　　　3rd ★★★★★
Falling greenbacks used to induce economic panic. Now, it seems the dollar's depreciation may actually be a good thing for America and the rest of the world.
鈔票貶值以往都會引發經濟恐慌，現在，美元貶值對於美國和世界其他地區而言，實際上可能是一件好事。

0740 depress [dɪˈprɛs]　　　　　v.　沮喪　　　4th ★★★★★
The long dark days and lack of a job made Mike feel depressed.
陰暗的天氣加上失業，讓麥克整個人感到非常沮喪。

0741 depression [dɪˈprɛʃən]　　　n.　蕭條　　　4th ★★★★★
A lot of people lost their job during the worldwide economic depression.
全球經濟蕭條期間有很多人失業。

0742 deprive [dɪˈpraɪv]　　　　　v.　剝奪　　　4th ★★★★★
Most people think that we cannot be deprived of the right to know whether the imported beef is edible or not.
大部份人認為我們必須了解進口牛肉是否可食用，這項權利是不能被剝奪的。

0743 derive [dɪˈraɪv]　　　　　v.　衍生　　　3rd ★★★★★
We should derive the conclusion from facts but not from assumption.
我們應該從事實推出結論而不是假設。

0744 descend [dɪˈsɛnd]　　　　　v.　下降　　　4th ★★★★★
The passengers were told to fasten their seat belts as the plane began descending.
飛機開始降落時，機長通知乘客繫緊安全帶。

0745 descendant [dɪˈsɛndənt]　　　n.　子孫　　　4th ★★★★★
The first immigrants to America came across the Bering Strait in small bands, and their descendants traveled farther south.
第一批美國移民聚集成群越過白令海峽，而他們的後代前往更遠的南方。

0746 describe [dɪ'skraɪb]　　　　v.　描述　　4th ★★★★★
Anxiety is primarily a conscious subjective state, variously described as an emotion, affect, or feeling.
焦慮主要是一種有意識的主觀狀態，被說成一種情緒或愛好，抑或是一種感受。

0747 description [dɪ'skrɪpʃən]　　n.　描述　　4th ★★★★★
Steve's description of the place was so vivid that I could almost picture it in my mind.
史帝夫對那個地方的描述非常生動，我幾乎可以在腦海中想像出來。

0748 desert ['dɛzət]　　　　n.　沙漠　　4th ★★★★★
Death Valley in California received its name because of its desolate desert.
加州的死亡谷之所以會有此稱號是因為其荒涼的沙漠。

0749 deserve [dɪ'zɜv]　　　　v.　值得　　4th ★★★★★
All dogs deserve to look and feel their best.
所有的狗狗都值得讓自己看起來最好，也感覺自己是最好的。

0750 design [dɪ'zaɪn]　　　　n.　設計　　5th ★★★★★
The design of the rich man's villa looks very elegant.
這位有錢人的別墅設計得很典雅。

0751 designate ['dɛzɪg,net]　　v.　指定　　4th ★★★★★
The president has designated Mr. Wu as the next general manager.
董事長指名吳先生為下任總經理人選。

0752 desirable [dɪ'zaɪrəbl]　　adj.　理想的　　4th ★★★★★
The houses in highly desirable areas are extremely expensive.
搶手地區的房子非常昂貴。

0753 desire [dɪ'zaɪr]　　　　n.　慾望　　4th ★★★★★
Jane usually buys things on impulse. Her purchases seem to be driven by some sudden force or desire.
珍常衝動買東西，她似乎是受突如其來的力量或慾望驅使而購買。

0754 desolate ['dɛslɪt]　　　adj.　荒蕪的　　4th ★★★★★
Death Valley in California received its name because of its desolate desert.
加州的死亡谷因為其荒蕪的沙漠而得到它的名字。

0755 desperately ['dɛspərɪtlɪ]　　adv.　拼命地　　3rd ★★★★★

The old woman at the street corner must be lost. She is looking around desperately for someone to help her.
街角的那位老太太一定是迷路了，她拼命環顧四周想找人幫她。

0756 despite [dɪ'spaɪt]　　prep. 儘管　　4th ★★★★★
I still want to buy a ticket for the concert despite the high price.
儘管演唱會的票價很高，我還是想去買票。

0757 dessert [dɪ'zɝt]　　n. 甜點　　5th ★★★★★
The professor first ate beans for dessert after he came to Taipei.
這位教授來台北之後，頭一次把豆子當點心吃。

0758 destination [ˌdɛstə'neʃən]　　n. 目的地　　4th ★★★★★
Phuket used to be a very popular tourist destination before the tsunami disaster.
普吉島在海嘯釀成災害前曾是一個非常受歡迎的觀光地點。

0759 destine ['dɛstɪn]　　v. 注定　　4th ★★★★★
The twin brothers are destined to never meet again.
這對雙胞胎兄弟注定從此不再相見。

0760 destiny ['dɛstənɪ]　　n. 命運　　4th ★★★★★
It's believed that marriage goes by destiny.
據說婚姻是天注定的。

0761 destroy [dɪ'strɔɪ]　　v. 摧毀　　4th ★★★★★
The failure on her performance seemed to have totally destroyed her confidence in playing the piano.
演出失敗似乎已完全摧毀她彈鋼琴的信心。

0762 destruction [dɪ'strʌkʃən]　　n. 破壞　　4th ★★★★★
It's important for everyone to decrease the environmental destruction.
減少環境的破壞對每個人來說都很重要。

0763 detail ['ditel]　　n. 細節　　4th ★★★★★
The major points of your plan are clear, but the details are still hazy to me.
我對你計畫的主要重點都很清楚，但是細節方面還是有點模糊。

0764 detain [dɪ'ten]　　v. 耽擱　　3rd ★★★★★
The police decided to detain the young man as a suspect.
警方決定以嫌疑犯拘留這個年輕人。

0765 detect [dɪ'tɛkt]　　　v.　發現　　4th ★★★★★
Although the thief was very quiet, my home alarm system detected him and notified the police.
雖然小偷很安靜，但我家的警報系統還是偵測到他並通知警方。

0766 deter [dɪ'tɜ]　　　v.　阻止　　3rd ★★★★★
The extreme cold deterred the man form going surfing.
嚴寒的氣溫打消了這男人衝浪的念頭。

0767 detergent [dɪ'tɜdʒənt]　　n.　清潔劑　　3rd ★★★★★
Wash your dress with cold water and detergents.
你的洋裝要用冷水加洗衣粉來洗。

0768 determine [dɪ'tɜmɪn]　　v.　決定　　4th ★★★★★
The exact cause of that woman's death couldn't be determined.
那個女人死亡的實際原因尚未確定。

0769 determination [dɪ,tɜmə'neʃən]　n.　決心　　4th ★★★★★
With hard work and determination, Britney Spears has built a successful career in show business.
小甜甜布蘭妮靠著努力和決心，在演藝圈闖出了一番成功的事業。

0770 detrimental [dɛtrə'mɛntl]　adj.　有害的　　3rd ★★★★★
Lack of sleep is detrimental to your health.
睡眠不足對你的健康有害。

0771 devastate ['dɛvəs,tet]　　v.　破壞　　3rd ★★★★★
On December 26, 2003, the worst earthquake in more than a decade devastated Bam, a historic city in Iran.
二千零三年十二月二十六日，一場十年來最慘烈的地震摧毀伊朗的歷史古城—巴姆城。

0772 develop [dɪ'vɛləp]　　v.　發展　　4th ★★★★★
The two companies made an agreement to develop software together.
這兩家公司簽訂一項合約，共同開發新軟體。

0773 development [dɪ'vɛləpmənt]　n.　發展　　4th ★★★★★
The child's development of scientific knowledge and understanding is a very disorderly and complex process.
孩子發展和了解科學知識的過程非常混亂且複雜。

D

0774 device [dɪ'vaɪs]   **n.** 設備   **4th** ★★★★★
The repairman knows how to fix many broken devices.
修理工知道如何修復損壞的設備。

0775 devote [dɪ'vot]   **v.** 致力於   **4th** ★★★★★
A wide body of recent research has been devoted to investigate the influence of attitudes towards the immune system.
最近有大量的研究致力於探討態度對免疫系統的影響。

0776 diabetes [ˌdaɪə'bitiz]   **n.** 糖尿病   **4th** ★★★★★
Drinking coffee cuts diabetes risk, but you may need to enjoy your java with lunch if you want to get any benefit.
喝咖啡幫助減低糖尿病的風險，但必須搭配午餐一起才有效。

0777 diagnose ['daɪəgnoz]   **v.** 診斷   **4th** ★★★★★
After spending much time carefully studying the patient's symptoms, the doctor finally made his diagnosis.
醫生花了很多時間仔細研究病人的症狀，最後才做出診斷。

0778 dial ['daɪəl]   **v.** 撥   **5th** ★★★★★
We can dial 110 in case we are in danger and need of help.
萬一遇到麻煩需要幫忙的時候，我們可以撥110。

0779 dictation [dɪk'teʃən]   **n.** 聽寫   **4th** ★★★★★
The assistant wrote from her supervisor's dictation.
助理按上司的口述寫下來。

0780 diet ['daɪət]   **n.** 飲食   **3rd** ★★★★★
Many people eat yogurt as a supplement to their regular diet because of its nutritional value.
許多人會吃優格補充平日飲食，因為優格含有很高的營養價值。

0781 different ['dɪfərənt]   **adj.** 不同的   **5th** ★★★★★
When traveling around the world, a person must get used to eating different types of food.
當一個人在世界各地旅行時，他必須習慣吃各式各樣的食物。

0782 difficult ['dɪfə,kəlt]   **adj.** 困難的   **5th** ★★★★★
Probably you have heard that grammar is difficult and dry. This is not true.
你也許常常聽到別人說文法很困難又無聊，但這並不是真的。

0783 difficulty [ˈdɪfəˌkʌltɪ]   n.   困難   5th ★★★★★
Meat-eaters often believe that meat is such an important source of protein and vitamins that vegetarians must have difficulty staying healthy.
食葷者認為肉類是蛋白質和維他命的重要來源，素食者一定很難維持健康。

0784 digest [daɪˈdʒɛst]   v.   消化   4th ★★★★★
Mary is suffering from a stomachache and needs to eat food which is easy to digest.
瑪莉胃痛，所以她必須吃一些容易消化的食物。

0785 digital [ˈdɪdʒɪtl]   adj.   數位的   5th ★★★★★
Teenagers and college students have an average of more than 800 illegally copied songs each on their digital music players.
每一個青少年和大學生的數位隨身聽裡，平均收錄超過八百首的盜版音樂。

0786 dignify [ˈdɪgnəˌfaɪ]   v.   使高貴   3rd ★★★★★
The suite is dignified by its elegant decorations.
這件套裝因為優雅的飾品而顯得高貴。

0787 diligence [ˈdɪlədʒəns]   n.   勤勉   4th ★★★★★
Diligence is the key to success.
勤勞是成功的關鍵。

0788 dilute [daɪˈlut]   v.   稀釋   3rd ★★★★★
Wine can be diluted by water.
葡萄酒可以用白開水稀釋。

0789 dim [dɪm]   v.   使暗淡   3rd ★★★★★
Old age will dim our skins.
年齡的老化會使我們的皮膚暗淡無光。

0790 diminish [dəˈmɪnɪʃ]   v.   減少   3rd ★★★★★
Most people with a serious depression will show weight loss with diminished appetite.
大部分心情沮喪的人，會出現體重降低和食慾減少的情況。

0791 diplomat [ˈdɪpləmæt]   n.   外交官   4th ★★★★★
As a diplomat, Helen always pays special attention to table manners and social etiquette in banquets and parties.
做為一名外交官，海倫總是特別注意在宴會或派對中的餐桌及社交禮儀。

D

0792 directly [dəˈrɛktlɪ]　　　adv.　直接地　　5th ★★★★★
We did not go directly to Singapore. On our way we traveled through Thailand.
我們不會直飛新加坡，旅途中會先經過泰國。

0793 direction [dəˈrɛkʃən]　　　n.　方向　　5th ★★★★★
A scooter rider asked a vendor for directions to the kite museum.
一位機車騎士向小販詢問去風箏博物館的路該怎麼走。

0794 directory [dəˈrɛktərɪ]　　　n.　姓名地址錄　　3rd ★★★★★
Because telephone directories contain printed pages, they are called books.
因為電話簿包含了印刷頁，所以也稱作書。

0795 disadvantage [ˌdɪsədˈvæntɪdʒ]　n.　不利　　4th ★★★★★
Every advantage has its disadvantage.
有利就有弊。

0796 disagree [ˌdɪsəˈgri]　　　v.　不適合　　4th ★★★★★
The climate here disagrees with the foreigner from Alaska.
這裡的氣候不適合來自阿拉斯加的外國人。

0797 disapprove [ˌdɪsəˈpruv]　　　v.　不贊成　　4th ★★★★★
Her parents disapproved of her marriage to Tom, but they went to the wedding after all.
她的父母不贊成她和湯姆結婚，但最後還是參加了他們的婚禮。

0798 disaster [dɪˈzæstɚ]　　　n.　災禍　　4th ★★★★★
Typhoon Morakot claimed more than six hundred lives in early August of 2009, making it the most serious natural disaster in Taiwan in recent decades.
莫拉克颱風在二千零九年八月初奪走逾六百條人命，成為台灣近幾十年來最嚴重的天災。

0799 disastrous [dɪzˈæstrəs]　　　adj.　悲慘的　　4th ★★★★★
It was disastrous that the floods were in the wake of the typhoon.
颱風過後緊跟著是水災，這真是一場災難。

0800 discard [dɪsˈkɑrd]　　　v.　放棄　　3rd ★★★★★
We should not discard old computers at random.
我們不應該隨意丟棄老舊電腦。

0801 discernible [dɪˈsɜnəbḷ]　　　adj.　可辨識的　　3rd ★★★★★
The peak of the mountain is discernible through the mist in the early morning.
早晨透過薄霧還是看的到山頂。

0802 discharge [dɪs'tʃɑrdʒ]　　v.　排出　　4th　★★★★★

The chemical factory discharged industrial water into the river nearby.
化學工廠排放工業廢水到附近的河流。

0803 disconnect [ˌdɪskə'nɛkt]　　v.　中斷　　4th　★★★★★

John had failed to pay his phone bills for months, so his telephone was disconnected last week.
約翰已經好幾個月沒有繳電話費了，所以他的電話上禮拜被停了。

0804 discount ['dɪskaunt]　　n.　折扣　　5th　★★★★★

People with a membership to this movie theater receive a discount when they watch a show.
這家電影院的會員看表演有優惠。

0805 discourage [dɪs'kɜɪdʒ]　　v.　勸阻　　4th　★★★★★

The teacher discouraged his students from staying at the Internet Café for a long while.
老師勸學生不要在網咖待太久。

0806 discourteous [dɪs'kɜtɪəs]　　adj.　無禮的　　4th　★★★★★

The discourteous clerk was laid off because of the complaints from a lot of customers.
這位無理的員工因為遭到許多顧客投訴而被解雇。

0807 discovery [dɪs'kʌvərɪ]　　n.　發現　　5th　★★★★★

New discoveries reveal alarming increases in jellyfish in the oceans, and the scientist suspect the causes could be overfishing and global warming.
新發現顯示海洋裡的水母數量驚人地向上攀升，科學家懷疑可能是漁撈過度和全球暖化造成的。

0808 discussion [dɪ'skʌʃən]　　n.　討論　　4th　★★★★★

With good language skills, Helen is always very articulate in class discussion.
有著良好語言技巧，海倫在班級討論時總是非常能言善道。

0809 disease [dɪ'ziz]　　n.　疾病　　4th　★★★★★

It is wise to treat a disease while it is still in its incipient stage.
發病初期就予以治療，才是明智的。

0810 disgruntled [dɪs'grʌntl̩d]　　adj.　不滿的　　3rd　★★★★★

Far from enjoying the economic recovery, millions of disgruntled workers in Europe are feeling squeezed, and their discontent is becoming the hottest social

and political issue of the day.
完全享受不到經濟復甦，數百萬名歐洲工人感覺被壓榨，他們的不滿逐漸成為當今最激烈的社會與政治議題。

0811 disguise [dɪsˈgaɪz]　　　v.　偽裝　　4th ★★★★★

Jacky escaped from prison by disguising himself as a priest.
傑克靠著假扮牧師成功越獄。

0812 disorder [dɪsˈɔrdə]　　　n.　失調　　3rd ★★★★★

For young women who suffer from eating disorder, body image is often their main concern.
對於那些患有飲食失調的年輕女孩來說，她們最擔心的就是身形。

0813 disparate [ˈdɪspərɪt]　　　adj.　不相干的　　4th ★★★★★

A merge takes place when two disparate computer companies become one.
兩家不相干的電腦公司合併了。

0814 dispatch [dɪˈspætʃ]　　　v.　派遣　　3rd ★★★★★

The rescue team was dispatched to the disaster area soon after the earthquake.
地震後，搜救小組馬上被派往災區。

0815 displace [dɪsˈples]　　　v.　迫使離開　　3rd ★★★★★

The Tsunami Disaster displaced millions of people in Southeast Asia. It might be several weeks before they could return to their homes.
大海嘯迫使數百萬的南亞居民離開家園，預計要好幾個禮拜後他們才可能重返家園。

0816 display [dɪˈsple]　　　v.　展現　　4th ★★★★★

This year, a big collection of photographs is displayed in the City Hall to commemorate the contributions made by honorary citizens.
今年市政府舉辦一場盛大的珍藏照片展示，以紀念榮譽市民所做的貢獻。

0817 disposal [dɪˈspozl]　　　n.　丟棄　　4th ★★★★★

Please use the green can for disposal of your cans and bottles. The blue one is for recycling paper.
請將你們的罐子和瓶子丟至綠色的垃圾桶，藍色的是給回收紙類用的。

0818 disposition [ˌdɪspəˈzɪʃən]　　　n.　氣質　　3rd ★★★★★

Patience is the key to raise a child with a benevolent disposition.
耐心是養育出一個有善良氣質的孩子關鍵。

0819 dispute [dɪˈspjut]　　　v.　爭論　　4th ★★★★★

Mary and Jane often fight over which radio station to listen to. Their dispute arises mainly from their different tastes in music.
瑪莉和珍時常為了要收聽哪一個電台吵架,她們的爭吵主要是因為音樂品味的不同。

0820 disrupt [dɪs'rʌpt]   v. 破壞   3rd ★★★★★
Traders worry that the conflict in the Middle East may disrupt supplies of oil.
貿易商擔心中東的衝突會破壞原油的供給。

0821 disruptive [dɪs'rʌptɪv]   adj. 破壞的   3rd ★★★★★
I enjoyed the concert last night. But someone's cell phone rang during the concert and it was disruptive.
我很享受昨晚的音樂會,但是中途有人的手機響了,有點掃興。

0822 dissolve [dɪ'zɑlv]   v. 消失   4th ★★★★★
His passion dissolved in the face of great challenges.
他的熱情在碰上巨大的挑戰後就消失了。

0823 dissuade [dɪ'swed]   v. 勸阻   3rd ★★★★★
The mother is trying to dissuade her son from playing computer games all day long.
母親正試著勸兒子不要打一整天的電動。

0824 distance ['dɪstəns]   n. 距離   4th ★★★★★
In the far distance was seen a lake surrounded by trees.
遠處有一面湖,湖的周圍環繞著樹木。

0825 distillation [ˌdɪstl'eʃən]   n. 蒸餾   3rd ★★★★★
Distillation, the process of separating the elements of a solution, is widely used in industry today.
現今在工業上廣泛使用蒸餾技術,蒸餾是一種將各種成分分開的過程。

0826 distinct [dɪ'stɪŋkt]   adj. 明顯的   4th ★★★★★
The tiger may be more ancient and distinct than we thought.
老虎可能比我們想像的還要古老和特別。

0827 distinguish [dɪ'stɪŋgwɪʃ]   v. 辨認   4th ★★★★★
The mother of the identical twins could always distinguish her sons.
雙胞胎的母親總是可以辨認出她的兒子。

0828 distort [dɪs'tɔrt]   v. 扭曲   3rd ★★★★★
The famous actress decided to sue the magazine for purposely distorted what she

actually said at the party.
知名的女演員決定要控告雜誌社，因為他們刻意扭曲她在派對上所說的話。

0829 distract [dɪˈstrækt]　　　　v.　使分心　　3rd　★★★★★

I don't want to distract you, but there is a phone call waiting for you at the front desk.
我不是有意打擾你，不過櫃檯有一通你的電話。

0830 distress [dɪˈstrɛs]　　　　n.　憂心　　4th　★★★★★

Sally's mother was in great distress when Sally said she was quitting school, and would work full-time in a restaurant.
當莎莉說她要輟學並去餐廳做全職工時，她的媽媽感到非常憂心。

0831 distributor [dɪˈstrɪbjətə]　　　n.　分配者　　3rd　★★★★★

In the new digital age, viewers themselves will become creators and distributors of their own video content.
在新的數位化時代，觀眾可以創造和分配屬於自己的電視節目。

0832 distrust [dɪsˈtrʌst]　　　　n.　不信任　　5th　★★★★★

My neighbors and I were anything but friendly, and for a long time we viewed each other with suspicion and distrust.
我和鄰居的關係很糟，我們有好長一段時間都在相互猜忌、彼此不信任。

0833 disturb [dɪsˈtɜb]　　　　v.　打擾　　4th　★★★★★

My cousin enjoys having a stable life. He hates to be disturbed by any change; even a small one may drive him crazy.
我表哥喜歡穩定的生活，他很討厭被任何異動打擾，即使是很小的事也會抓狂。

0834 disturbance [dɪsˈtɜbəns]　　　n.　打擾　　4th　★★★★★

Some students raised a disturbance at the restaurant.
有些學生在餐廳引起一陣騷動。

0835 dive [daɪv]　　　　v.　潛水　　5th　★★★★★

Natasha cannot join the swim team because she is afraid to dive.
娜塔莎不能加入游泳隊，因為她害怕潛水。

0836 diverse [daɪˈvɜs]　　　　adj.　分歧　　3rd　★★★★★

In a large and diverse society, customs may vary from area to area.
在如此大又變化多端的社會，風俗也因地區而各異。

0837 diversify [daɪˈvɜsəˌfaɪ]　　　v.　使多樣化　　3rd　★★★★★

046

How diversified are you when it comes to choosing friends?
你的交友類型有多麼多樣化呢？

0838 divide [də'vaɪd]　　　v.　除　　4th ★★★★★
If you divide seven by three you will end up with a fraction.
如果你用三去除七，結果會是除不盡的分數。

0839 dividend ['dɪvə,dɛnd]　　n.　紅利　　4th ★★★★★
Sales rose even faster, so the company raised its dividend 10%, the first increase since 1999.
該公司的銷售額增長快速，因此將股息提高百分之十，是自一九九九年以來的首次成長。

0840 division [də'vɪʒən]　　n.　分配　　4th ★★★★★
I'm sure it is a fair division of profits.
我相信分紅是公平的。

0841 divorce [də'vors]　　n.　離婚　　4th ★★★★★
The married couple was talking about getting a divorce.
這對夫婦正談論離婚。

0842 document ['dɑkjəmənt]　　n.　文件　　4th ★★★★★
Lift the lid of the photocopier and put the document you want to copy face down on the glass.
把影印機的蓋子打開，把你要影印的文件正面朝下放在玻璃平面上。

0843 dodge [dɑdʒ]　　v.　躲避　　4th ★★★★★
Superman could dodge bullets, but he doesn't need to.
超人可以躲開子彈，但他不需要這麼做。

0844 dolphin ['dɑlfɪn]　　n.　海豚　　5th ★★★★★
Dolphins are a lovely and friendly kind of animal that can be found in the sea around Taiwan.
海豚是種可愛又友善的動物，台灣附近的海域可以發現他們的行蹤。

0845 domestic [də'mɛstɪk]　　adj.　國內的　　4th ★★★★★
Indian companies, flush with cash from a booming domestic economy, are prowling for overseas acquisitions to expand their footprints.
印度公司充滿國內經濟活絡的現金，正尋覓海外收購以擴展他們的足跡。

0846 dominant ['dɑmənənt]　　adj.　支配的　　4th ★★★★★

The United States is the dominant world power, and with world power goes leadership of the currency.
美國是世界的主導強權，他們的貨幣也隨之成為強勢貨幣。

0847 donor ['donɚ]　　　　　n.　輸血者　　4th ★★★★★
The dean of our school is a regular blood donor.
我們學院的院長時常去捐血。

0848 downtown [ˌdaun'taun]　　　n.　市中心　　5th ★★★★★
Fire filled a major downtown hotel with smoke and gutted three of its restaurants early yesterday morning.
昨日一早，市區一間大飯店瀰漫著煙霧和大火，並燒毀了裡頭的三家餐廳。

0849 donate ['donet]　　　　　v.　捐贈　　4th ★★★★★
It is trendy that the very rich people donate their wealth to the charities instead of leaving it to their offspring.
富有的人捐贈財富給慈善機構，而非留給子孫，這是一個趨勢。

0850 dormitory ['dɔrməˌtɔrɪ]　　n.　宿舍　　4th ★★★★★
Brian's first year in college he lived in a male dormitory.
布萊恩大學一年級時住在男生宿舍。

0851 dosage ['dosɪdʒ]　　　　　n.　一劑　　4th ★★★★★
Children 6 years old to 12 years old take half of the adult dosage, not more than 6 spoonfuls per day.
六到十二歲的孩童攝取的劑量是成人的一半，一天不超過六匙。

0852 double ['dʌbl̩]　　　　　adj.　雙倍的　　3rd ★★★★★
We had to pay the driver a double fare for waiting so long.
因為司機等很久，所以我們必須付他雙倍車資。

0853 download ['daunˌlod]　　　v.　下載　　5th ★★★★★
All the space on Chris's computer is full, so he can't download anything.
克利斯電腦內所有儲存空間都滿了，所以他無法下載任何東西。

0854 downturn ['dauntɝn]　　　n.　衰退　　3rd ★★★★★
With the economic downturn, the company tried to cut down its annual budget.
隨著經濟衰退，公司試著縮減年度預算。

0855 doze [doz]　　　　　　v.　打瞌睡　　4th ★★★★★
Jason dozed off in the meeting. He must have stayed up all night partying again.
傑森在會議中打瞌睡，他一定又熬夜狂歡了整晚。

047

0856 draft [dræft]　　　　　　　**n.** 草稿　　**5th** ★★★★★
A good author writes many drafts before his work is ready.
一位好作家在作品完成之前會寫許多草稿。

0857 drag [dræg]　　　　　　　**n.** 麻煩事　**3rd** ★★★★★
It has been a drag for Tara to get up in the morning because she knew she and her husband would fight about the money problems at breakfast.
早上起床對泰拉來說是件麻煩事，因為她知道她和老公會在早餐時為錢的問題爭吵。

0858 drama ['drɑmə]　　　　　　**n.** 戲劇　　**5th** ★★★★★
The drama critic reviewed the second episode in the series to be the best.
戲劇評論家認為此系列的第二集最精采。

0859 drastic ['dræstɪk]　　　　**adj.** 激烈的　**3rd** ★★★★★
She takes a lot of drastic measures to lose her weight.
她採取很多激烈的方法減重。

0860 draw [drɔ]　　　　　　　　**v.** 畫　　　**5th** ★★★★★
The student drew a circle around the word on the board.
這位學生把黑板上的字圈起來。

0861 drill [drɪl]　　　　　　　　**v.** 鑽孔　　**4th** ★★★★★
Steve learned how to drill holes when he helped his dad build the shelf.
史帝夫幫父親做架子時，學會了如何鑽孔。

0862 drip [drɪp]　　　　　　　　**v.** 滴出　　**4th** ★★★★★
We need to fix the sink because it won't stop dripping.
我們需要修理洗臉槽，因為水槽不停在漏水。

0863 drive [dræɪv]　　　　　　　**v.** 駕駛　　**5th** ★★★★★
Although Maria drove very fast, the flight she planned to take had already taken off by the time she arrived at the airport.
儘管瑪利亞開車很快，她要搭的班機還是在她抵達機場時就起飛了。

0864 drizzle ['drɪzl]　　　　　　**v.** 下毛毛雨　**4th** ★★★★★
It's not raining cats and dogs; it's just drizzling.
這不是傾盆大雨，只是毛毛細雨罷了。

0865 drop [drɑp]　　　　　　　　**v.** 掉落　　**5th** ★★★★★
Please feel free to drop in and see me. Let's keep in touch.
歡迎隨時到我家坐坐，讓我們保持聯絡。

D

0866 drown [draun]　　　　v.　溺水　　4th ★★★★★

Wow, you look like a drowned rat! Didn't you know there's a thunderstorm today?
哇！你怎麼像個落湯雞一樣，你不知道今天會有暴風雨嗎？

0867 drug [drʌg]　　　　n.　藥品　　4th ★★★★★

The doctor gave Sally some drugs to help her get better.
醫生給莎莉一些藥物幫助她好轉。

0868 drunk [drʌŋk]　　　　adj.　醉的　　5th ★★★★★

All of the people coming out of the bar that just closed are very drunk.
所有從打烊的酒吧出來的人都是酩酊大醉。

0869 dry [draɪ]　　　　adj.　乾的　　5th ★★★★★

Dry snow avalanches move faster than wet snow - at over 100 miles per hour.
乾雪崩移動速度比溼雪還快，時速超過一百英里。

0870 due [dju]　　　　adj.　到期的　　4th ★★★★★

My dog just ate my homework. It's due in ten minutes!
我的狗剛剛吃掉我的作業，那份作業是我十分鐘後要交的！

0871 dull [dʌl]　　　　adj.　無趣的　　4th ★★★★★

Mike is a machine operator. His life in the factory is so dull that he often sings to entertain himself.
麥克是一名技工，他在工廠的生活十分無聊，所以常常唱歌娛樂自己。

0872 dumpling ['dʌmplɪŋ]　　　　n.　水餃　　5th ★★★★★

A food processor can chop up cabbages for making dumplings.
食物處理器可以用來切碎白菜做餃子。

0873 duplicate ['djupləkɪt]　　　　n.　複製品　　3rd ★★★★★

An exact duplicate of the Mayflower has been built in England and given to the people of the U.S. as a symbol of good will.
英國打造了一個五月花的完美複製品，並將它贈送給美國人民作為友好的象徵。

0874 duration [dju'reʃən]　　　　n.　期間　　4th ★★★★★

Whether anxiety is normal or abnormal depends on its intensity and duration and the circumstances that cause it.
無論焦慮正常或異常取決於其強度和持續時間，還有是在何種情況下發生的。

0875 dust [dʌst]　　　　v.　拂去灰塵　　4th ★★★★★

048

All bird bathing, however, is not in water; many birds prefer dusting.
所有鳥類都會洗澡，但不是在水裡，許多鳥類喜歡除去身上灰塵。

0876 duty ['djutɪ]　　　　　　　**n.**　職責　　　**4th** ★★★★★
All company employees are on duty at the exhibition to demonstrate the new software.
公司所有員工都要在展場值班，示範操作新的軟體。

0877 dwindle ['dwɪndl̩]　　　　　**v.**　漸漸減少　　**3rd** ★★★★★
The amount of open space has dwindled as more and more houses are built.
隨著房子越蓋越多，空地的數量也漸漸減少。

0878 dye [daɪ]　　　　　　　　**v.**　染　　　　**5th** ★★★★★
Vicky found an old white shirt and dyed it purple.
維琪找到一件舊的白襯衫把它染成紫色。

0879 dynamic [daɪ'næmɪk]　　　**adj.**　效率高的　　**4th** ★★★★★
The challenging job required a strong, successful, and dynamic candidate.
這個極具挑戰性的工作需要堅強、成功和高效率的應徵者。

0880 dynamics [daɪ'næmɪks]　　**n.**　動力學　　**3rd** ★★★★★
Nearly everyone yawns, but few understand the dynamics.
幾乎每個人都在打哈欠，卻沒幾個人了解動力學。

0881 each [itʃ]　　　　　　　　**adj.**　每一　　　**5th** ★★★★★
The kittens playfully tumbled over each other.
小貓開心地互相滾來滾去。

0882 eager ['igɚ]　　　　　　　**adj.**　渴望的　　**5th** ★★★★★
Toria was eager to get started on the new project.
托里亞渴望開始新的企劃。

0883 early ['ɝlɪ]　　　　　　　**adj.**　早先的　　**5th** ★★★★★
Ryan always takes a nap after his early class.
萊恩總是在早課後小睡一會兒。

0884 earn [ɝn]　　　　　　　　**v.**　賺得　　　**5th** ★★★★★
Leon is earning a lot more money at his new job.
李歐的新工作讓他賺更多錢。

E

0885 earth [ɝθ]   n.   地球   **5th** ★★★★★
In the movie, the UFOs had been on Earth since an immemorial time.
影片中，幽浮自遠古時代就已經存在於地球了。

0886 earthquake ['ɝθ,kwek]   n.   地震   **5th** ★★★★★
People in Taiwan feel earthquakes so often that it doesn't make them panic.
台灣人經常感覺到地震，所以地震時他們不會恐慌。

0887 easily ['izɪlɪ]   adv.   輕易地   **5th** ★★★★★
In the winter, people tend to eat too much and gain weight easily.
人們在冬天容易吃多而輕易讓體重增加。

0888 eccentric [ɪk'sɛntrɪk]   adj.   反常的   **3rd** ★★★★
The section chief looked a little eccentric this morning.
科長今早看起來有些反常。

0889 ecological [ˌɛkə'ladʒɪkəl]   adj.   生態的   **3rd** ★★★★★
The prime rainforests are vital link in the ecological chain.
原始森林是整個生態鏈的重要連結。

0890 economic [ˌikə'namɪk]   adj.   經濟的   **3rd** ★★★★★
Even as economic recovery spreads worldwide, workers are finding themselves not saving more money.
即使全球經濟復甦，工人發現自己並沒有存到更多錢。

0891 economical [ˌikə'namɪkl]   adj.   節約的   **4th** ★★★★★
Water power should be one of the most natural and at the same time most truly economical sources of energy.
水力發電是最天然的，同時也是真正經濟的能源。

0892 economist [i'kanəmɪst]   n.   經濟學家   **4th** ★★★★★
The economist believes the economic situation will recover from the recession soon.
經濟學家認為，經濟現況很快就會從衰退中復甦。

0893 economize [ɪ'kanə,maɪz]   v.   節約   **4th** ★★★★★
The couple need to economize on their budget.
這對夫妻需要節省他們的預算。

0894 economy [ɪ'kanəmɪ]   n.   經濟   **4th** ★★★★★

049

Because of the poor economy, reducing taxes has now become a necessity for the new government.
由於經濟不景氣，減稅已經成為新政府的一項必要課題了。

0895 edge [ɛdʒ]　　　　　　　**n.** 邊緣　　　**4th** ★★★★★
It's better to place your drink away from the edge of the desk.
最好把你的飲料放離桌邊遠一點。

0896 edible [ˈɛdəbl̩]　　　　　**adj.** 可食用的　　**4th** ★★★★★
For the Chinese people, all parts of a pig are edible.
對中國人來說，豬的所有部位都是可食用的。

0897 edit [ˈɛdɪt]　　　　　　　**v.** 編輯　　　**4th** ★★★★★
The teacher told Kevin that he needed to edit his papers better in the future.
老師告訴凱文以後他要把論文編輯得更好。

0898 educate [ˈɛdʒəˌket]　　　**v.** 教導　　　**5th** ★★★★★
A police officer came to educate the students about the dangers of drinking and driving.
一名警方人員來教育學生有關酒後駕車的危險。

0899 education [ˌɛdʒuˈkeʃən]　　**n.** 教育　　　**4th** ★★★★★
It may be said that the problem in adult education seems to be not the piling up of facts but practice in thinking.
成人教育的問題似乎不在於缺乏知識的傳授，而是欠缺了主動思考的能力。

0900 educational [ˌɛdʒuˈkeʃənl̩]　**adj.** 教育的　　**4th** ★★★★★
Most businessmen are more interested in the commercial success of their products than their educational values.
大部分的商人比起產品的教育意義，對其商業的成功更感興趣。

0901 effect [ɪˈfɛkt]　　　　　　**n.** 影響　　　**4th** ★★★★★
The farsighted woman was good at understanding the long-term effects of her actions.
有遠見的女人理解自身的行為會造成長遠的影響。

0902 effective [ɪˈfɛktɪv]　　　　**adj.** 有效的　　**4th** ★★★★★
As opposed to the hustle and bustle of the metropolitan city, the tranquility of rural life is indeed an effective prescription for one's peace of mind.
有別於大都會城市的喧鬧繁忙，恬靜的田園生活才是心靈平靜的一帖良方。

E

0903 efficiency [ɪˈfɪʃənsɪ]　　　n.　效率　　4th　★★★★★
The new supervisor wants to maximize work efficiency in the factory.
新的管理者想要將工廠的工作效率提升到最大。

0904 efficient [ɪˈfɪʃənt]　　　adj.　有效率的　　4th　★★★★★
Modern companies use efficient methods to keep their costs low.
現代的公司採行有效方法維持低成本。

0905 effort [ˈɛfət]　　　n.　努力　　4th　★★★★★
English is difficult for some people, but they still give it their best effort.
英文對某些人來說很困難，但他們仍盡最大的努力。

0906 elaborate [ɪˈlæbərɪt]　　　v.　闡述　　4th　★★★★★
The manager elaborated his project clearly in the seminar.
經理在研討會中清楚並詳細說明他的計畫。

0907 elastic [ɪˈlæstɪk]　　　adj.　有彈性的　　4th　★★★★★
It would be much better to make your plan elastic.
讓你的計畫多點彈性對你來說會比較好。

0908 elasticity [ɪˌlæsˈtɪsətɪ]　　　n.　靈活度　　4th　★★★★★
The specific socks have great elasticity.
特製短襪的彈性很好。

0909 elated [ɪˈletɪd]　　　adj.　興高采烈的　　3rd　★★★★★
My parents were elated at the news that I won the national contest.
爸媽聽到我贏得全國比賽時非常雀躍。

0910 elect [ɪˈlɛkt]　　　v.　選舉　　5th　★★★★★
I wonder whom the members will elect as director.
我很納悶這些成員誰會當選主管。

0911 election [ɪˈlɛkʃən]　　　n.　選舉　　5th　★★★★★
The president expected a favorable outcome in the election.
總統期待一個有利的選舉結果。

0912 electric [ɪˈlɛktrɪk]　　　adj.　電動的　　4th　★★★★★
An electric screwdriver works much faster than an old-fashioned one.
電動螺絲起子比舊式的工作起來快多了。

050

E

0913 electricity [ˌilɛkˈtrɪsətɪ]　　n.　電力　　4th ★★★★★
The generation of electricity can be achieved in several ways.
電力產生的方式可以分成好幾種。

0914 elegant [ˈɛləgənt]　　adj.　高雅的　　4th ★★★★★
Ken has an elegant style of handwriting that I try to imitate.
肯的筆跡風格高雅，我試著去模仿。

0915 elementary [ˌɛləˈmɛntərɪ]　　adj.　基礎的　　5th ★★★★★
The senior employee is less likely to make elementary errors.
資深員工不太可能會犯基本錯誤。

0916 elevate [ˈɛləˌvet]　　v.　提升　　4th ★★★★★
Music has the power to elevate our feelings and temporarily place us above the grinding concerns of everyday life.
音樂有力量提升我們的情緒，暫時讓我們忘卻日常生活中的煩惱。

0917 elevator [ɛləˌvetə]　　n.　電梯　　4th ★★★★★
The elevator is broken, so we'll take the stairs.
電梯壞了，所以我們要走樓梯。

0918 eligibility [ˌɛlɪdʒəˈbɪlətɪ]　　n.　資格　　3rd ★★★★★
They have decided to invite John to the head office for an interview regarding his eligibility for promotion.
公司決定邀請約翰到總公司面試，討論有關他升遷的資格。

0919 eligible [ˈɛlɪdʒəbl]　　adj.　合意的　　4th ★★★★★
Some single women may pursue their careers with such single-mindedness that they postpone marriage until the eligible men show up.
有些單身女郎在追求自己的事業時有這麼一個想法，她們晚點結婚，一直等到適合的男人出現再說。

0920 eliminate [ɪˈlɪməˌnet]　　v.　消除　　3rd ★★★★★
Grace practices her English every day to try to eliminate her mistakes.
葛雷斯每天練習英語來消除她英語上的錯誤。

0921 eloquent [ˈɛləkwənt]　　adj.　雄辯的　　3rd ★★★★★
The eloquent speaker moved us with his inspiring words and persuasive manner.
口才辨給的演說家用他振奮人心的字眼和具說服力的態度感動我們。

E

0922 elude [ɪ'lud]   v.   閃避   3rd ★★★★★
The Formosan pig eluded the hunter's grasp at last.
台灣山豬終於逃脫了獵人捕捉。

0923 elusive [ɪ'lusɪv]   adj.   難記的   3rd ★★★★★
The student has difficulty memorizing some elusive words.
學生記不住一些難記的單字。

0924 emanate ['ɛmə,net]   v.   起源   3rd ★★★★★
The creative idea emanated from a college student.
這個創新的想法出自一位大學生。

0925 embarrass [ɪm'bærəs]   v.   使窘困   4th ★★★★★
My mom embarrassed me by showing my baby photos.
我媽媽把我嬰兒時期的照片秀出來，搞得我很尷尬。

0926 embellish [ɪm'bɛlɪʃ]   v.   裝飾   3rd ★★★★★
The lady embellished her apartment with flowers and posters.
這位小姐用花和海報裝飾她的公寓。

0927 embrace [ɪm'bres]   v.   擁抱   4th ★★★★★
The mother embraced with her daughter at the airport.
母親和女兒在機場相擁。

0928 emerald ['ɛmərəld]   n.   綠寶石   3rd ★★★★★
The hostess is wearing an emerald ring.
女主人戴著一只綠寶石戒指。

0929 emerge [ɪ'mɜdʒ]   v.   出現   4th ★★★★★
Constructivism emerged as a prevailing paradigm only in the last part of the twentieth century.
建構主義是二十世紀末期才出現，成為普遍流行的藝術典範。

0930 emergency [ɪ'mɜdʒənsɪ]   n.   緊急   4th ★★★★★
In the cross-lake swimming race, a boat will be standing by in case of an emergency.
在泳渡湖泊比賽中，一旦出現緊急狀況，會有艘小船在旁待命。

0931 emission [ɪ'mɪʃən]   n.   排放物   3rd ★★★★★
People are making lifestyle choices to reduce greenhouse gas emissions globally.
為減少全球溫室效應氣體排放量，人們正對生活方式做出抉擇。

0932 emotional [ɪ'moʃənl̩]　　**adj.** 情緒的　　5th ★★★★★
The sad movie made Hilary feel very emotional.
那部悲傷的電影讓希拉蕊很感傷。

0933 emphasis ['ɛmfəsɪs]　　**n.** 強調　　4th ★★★★★
The country has put emphasis on improving its tourism.
該國把重點放在改善其觀光旅遊業。

0934 emphasize ['ɛmfə,saɪz]　　**v.** 強調　　4th ★★★★★
The benefits of vitamins and minerals are emphasized because they play an important role in maintaining good health.
維他命和礦物質的好處不斷被強調，因為他們在保持健康上有不可或缺的地位。

0935 empire ['ɛmpaɪr]　　**n.** 帝國　　4th ★★★★★
Italy enjoyed a highly developed and specialized civilization from about 264 B.C. until the fall of the Roman Empire.
在羅馬帝國衰亡以前，義大利從西元前兩百六十四年開始，一直是個高度發展和專業文明的地方。

0936 employee [,ɛmplɔɪ'i]　　**n.** 員工　　4th ★★★★★
More and more companies track their employees' computer activities.
越來越多的公司追蹤員工使用電腦的情形。

0937 employer [ɪm'plɔɪɚ]　　**n.** 僱主　　4th ★★★★★
Although work experience is important, a bachelor's degree is a prerequisite for most employers.
雖然說工作經驗很重要，但大學學歷還是許多雇主用人的一項必要條件。

0938 empty ['ɛmptɪ]　　**adj.** 空的　　5th ★★★★★
Empty vessels make the most sound.
「半瓶水，響叮噹」，不要因為一點小成就自鳴得意。

0939 enable [ɪn'ebl̩]　　**v.** 使…能夠　　5th ★★★★★
The young man's talent enabled him to hold the important position.
這個年輕人的才幹使他得以擔任要職。

0940 enclose [ɪn'kloz]　　**v.** 封入　　3rd ★★★★★
On Duncan's birthday, his grandmother gave him a birthday card with 100NT enclosed.
鄧肯的祖母在他生日時送他一張附有新台幣一百元的生日卡片。

0941 encounter [ɪnˈkaʊntɚ]   n.   相遇   4th ★★★★★
Megan had an interesting encounter with a stranger today.
今天梅根與一位陌生人有場很有趣的邂逅。

0942 encourage [ɪnˈkɝɪdʒ]   v.   鼓勵   4th ★★★★★
Many people worry that the computerized Public Welfare Lottery encourages gambling to become rich instead of working hard to make money.
許多人擔心電腦公益彩券變相鼓勵人們以賭致富，而非付出辛勞賺錢。

0943 endanger [ɪnˈdendʒɚ]   v.   危害   4th ★★★★★
Some bus drivers might feel sleepy while driving, which can endanger passengers on the bus.
有些公車司機開車時會昏昏欲睡，這樣會危害公車上的乘客。

0944 endorse [ɪnˈdɔrs]   v.   背書   4th ★★★★★
Many sports stars endorse products such as athletic shoes to make money.
許多運動明星為運動鞋等產品背書賺錢。

0945 endowment [ɪnˈdaʊmənt]   n.   基金   4th ★★★★★
The Gates Foundation is the largest foundation in the world, with an endowment of $29 billion.
蓋茲基金會是世界最大的基金會，擁有二百九十億美元的基金。

0946 endure [ɪnˈdjʊr]   v.   容忍   4th ★★★★★
In harsh dry habitats, plants endure great temperature extremes of scorching days and freezing nights.
植物在氣候乾燥惡劣的棲息地忍容極端的溫差，白天灼熱，夜晚則是凍寒。

0947 energetic [ˌɛnɚˈdʒɛtɪk]   adj.   精力充沛的   5th ★★★★★
The traveler looks energetic after a nice sleep.
旅者在一陣好眠後看起來精力充沛。

0948 energy [ˈɛnɚdʒɪ]   n.   能量   5th ★★★★★
Windmills spin as they collect natural energy.
風車為收集自然能源而旋轉。

0949 enforce [ɪnˈfors]   v.   實施   3rd ★★★★★
A police officer has to enforce the law of his country.
警察必須執行國家的法律。

0950 **engagement** [ɪn'ɡedʒmənt]　　n.　約會　　**5th** ★★★★★
I had a previous engagement with the lawyer.
我和律師有約在先。

0951 **engine** ['ɛndʒən]　　n.　引擎　　**5th** ★★★★★
We reached the plant and found that there was something wrong with the engine, and we must have it repaired.
我們到達工廠後發現引擎有點問題，所以我們必須修理。

0952 **engineer** [ˌɛndʒə'nɪr]　　n.　工程師　　**5th** ★★★★★
Uncle Bob has two sons. Both of them are engineers.
鮑伯叔叔有兩個兒子，他們兩個都是工程師。

0953 **engineering** [ˌɛndʒə'nɪrɪŋ]　　n.　工程　　**4th** ★★★★★
Genetic engineering deals with the DNA of living things.
基因工程負責處理生物的DNA。

0954 **enhance** [ɪn'hæns]　　v.　提高　　**3rd** ★★★★★
Community policing has a positive impact on reducing neighborhood crime, helping to reduce fear of crime and enhancing the quality of life.
社區警務工作對減少社區犯罪有正面影響，有助減少對犯罪活動的恐懼和提高生活品質。

0955 **enjoy** [ɪn'dʒɔɪ]　　v.　喜愛　　**5th** ★★★★★
My family likes to go up to the mountain to enjoy the fresh air there.
我的家人喜歡上山享受那裡的新鮮空氣。

0956 **enlighten** [ɪn'laɪtn]　　v.　啟發　　**4th** ★★★★★
Mr. Wang enlightened me on the difficult math question.
王老師啟發我解開困難的數學問題。

0957 **enliven** [ɪn'laɪvən]　　v.　使有活力　　**4th** ★★★★★
Warm sunshine enlivens all things on earth.
溫暖的陽光使地球上所有事物充滿生氣。

0958 **enormous** [ɪ'nɔrməs]　　adj.　巨大的　　**4th** ★★★★★
Near the shore, the waves were enormous. But as we rowed out into open water, they began to lapse.
海岸附近的浪很大，但當我們划向寬闊海域，浪花也逐漸消退。

0959 **enough** [ə'nʌf]　　　adj. 足夠的　　5th ★★★★★
The wind was strong enough to blow off the petals of the flower.
風力猛烈到足以吹掉花瓣。

0960 **enroll** [ɪn'rol]　　　v. 報名　　4th ★★★★★
Less than ten students were newly enrolled in the department.
只有不到十個新生註冊就讀這個系所。

0961 **ensure** [ɪn'ʃur]　　　v. 保證　　4th ★★★★★
He is one of the president's security guards by occupation. It is his responsibility to ensure the safety of the president.
他是總裁身邊的職業安全護衛之一，確保總裁安全是他的責任。

0962 **enterprise** ['ɛntə‚praɪz]　　　n. 企業　　4th ★★★★★
Taiwan's enterprises should be encouraged themselves at home, network throughout the Asia-Pacific region, and position themselves globally.
台灣的企業應該鼓勵自己在家，讓網絡遍及亞太地區，然後佈局全球。

0963 **entertain** [‚ɛntə'ten]　　　v. 娛樂　　4th ★★★★★
There was a singer at the wedding to entertain the guests.
婚禮中有歌手唱歌娛樂賓客。

0964 **enthusiasm** [ɪn'θjuzɪ‚æzəm]　　　n. 熱忱　　4th ★★★★★
Her enthusiasm for tennis is the main reason for her to become a world champion.
她對網球的熱忱是她成為世界冠軍的主要原因。

0965 **enthusiastic** [ɪn‚θjuzɪ'æstɪk]　　　adj. 熱忱的　　4th ★★★★★
She takes part in every activity. In fact, she is very enthusiastic about public affairs.
她參與了所有的活動，事實上她對公共事務非常有熱忱。

0966 **entire** [ɪn'taɪr]　　　adj. 全部的　　4th ★★★★★
In hopes of leading a stable life, his parents built a nest egg with the money earned during their entire life of toiling in the sweatshop.
他的父母在一家血汗工廠傾注一生辛勞，累積了一筆存款，就是希望過穩定的生活。

0967 **envious** ['ɛnvɪəs]　　　adj. 忌妒的　　5th ★★★★★
I don't think John is envious of you.
我不認為約翰忌妒你。

0968 **environment** [ɪn'vaɪrəmənt]　　　v. 環境　　4th ★★★★★

Throwing litter on the street does not help the environment.
在街上隨地亂丟垃圾會危害環境。

0969 epidemic [ˌɛpɪ'dɛmɪk]　　n.　流行　3rd ★★★★★
It is the season of an epidemic of influenza.
這是個流感疫情猖獗的季節。

0970 epitome [ɪ'pɪtəmɪ]　　n.　摘要　3rd ★★★★★
We did not have time to read the whole novel, so the teacher prepared an epitome for us.
我們沒有時間閱讀整部小說,所以老師為我們準備了摘要。

0971 equal ['ikwəl]　　adj.　相等的　5th ★★★★★
All man are created equal.
人生而平等。

0972 equip [ɪ'kwɪp]　　v.　配備　4th ★★★★★
Mastery of English equips us with a very important tool for acquiring knowledge and information.
精通英語等於在我們身上裝備了一項非常重要的工具,藉此獲得知識和資訊。

0973 equivalent [ɪ'kwɪvələnt]　　v.　同等物　3rd ★★★★★
These two sentences are equivalent in meaning.
這兩句話的意思一樣。

0974 era ['ɪrə]　　n.　年代　3rd ★★★★★
This is an era of greater access and convenience based upon instant communication, anytime, anywhere.
基於隨時隨地都可以即時通訊,這個年代人們有更多的通道和便利性相互聯絡。

0975 erase [ɪ'res]　　v.　擦拭　4th ★★★★★
Nathan likes to help the teacher by erasing the board.
內森喜歡幫老師擦黑板。

0976 erect [ɪ'rɛkt]　　v.　設立　4th ★★★★★
A group of scientists have started to erect a research station built on an ice block drifting in the Arctic Ocean because global warming is melting the ice early.
一群科學家在北極海漂流的冰塊上設立研究站,因為全球暖化正讓冰塊提早融化。

0977 err [ɝ]　　v.　犯錯　4th ★★★★★
If we had studied the plans carefully, we would not have erred so seriously.
如果我們仔細研究這些計劃,就不會犯下如此嚴重的錯誤了。

0978 escape [əˈskep]　　v. 逃跑　　3rd ★★★★★
The soldiers should have escaped before the bomb exploded.
軍人在炸彈爆炸前就應該要逃跑了。

0979 escort [ˈɛskɔrt]　　v. 護送　　5th ★★★★★
The gentleman escorted the lady to the door of her flat and kissed her good night.
紳士護送女士到她的公寓，並親吻她，和她道晚安。

0980 Eskimo [ˈɛskɪmo]　　n. 愛斯基摩人　　4th ★★★★★
The Eskimos have many different words to describe snow.
愛斯基摩人有許多不同的字來形容雪。

0981 especially [əˈspɛʃəlɪ]　　adv. 尤其　　5th ★★★★★
Always be careful when you are walking alone, especially at night.
你獨自行走時總要小心，尤其是夜晚。

0982 essential [ɪˈsɛnʃəl]　　adj. 必要的　　4th ★★★★★
It is essential to drink water every day.
每天喝水是必要的。

0983 establish [əˈstæblɪʃ]　　v. 設立　　4th ★★★★★
Zheng's voyages established Chinese diplomatic and trade relations throughout Asia and Africa.
鄭和下西洋建立了中國在整個亞洲和非洲間的外交和貿易往來。

0984 estimate [ˈɛstəˌmet]　　v. 估計　　4th ★★★★★
It is estimated that an average adult needs somewhere between 2,000 and 3,000 calories per day.
據估計，平均一個成年人每天大約需要攝取二千到三千卡路里。

0985 eternal [ɪˈtɝnl]　　adj. 永遠的　　4th ★★★★★
The car accident left an eternal scar on his face.
車禍在他臉上留下永久的疤痕。

0986 ethnic [ˈɛθnɪk]　　adj. 種族的　　4th ★★★★★
Africa is a land of many ethnic groups, but when Europeans carved Africa into colonies, they gave no consideration to the territories of African ethnic groups.
非洲為多元種族之地，但當歐洲人瓜分非洲為殖民地時，他們一點都沒考慮到這一點。

0987 ethical [ˈɛθɪkl]　　adj. 道德的　　4th ★★★★★

People for the Ethical Treatment of Animals believe that animals deserve the most basic rights— consideration of their own best interests regardless of whether they are useful to humans.
善待動物協會(PETA)相信動物應擁有最基本的權利—無論牠們是否對人類有益,都要從牠們本身的最佳利益做考量。

0988 ethnicity [εθ'nɪsɪtɪ]　　　**n.**　種族　　　**3rd** ★★★★★
The Red Cross provides international assistance to people of all races, ethnicities, religions, social classes, and political beliefs.
國際紅十字會提供援助給所有種族、民族、宗教、社會階層和政治信仰的人。

0989 Europe ['jurəp]　　　**n.**　歐洲　　　**3rd** ★★★★★
In Roman times sugar cane was known in Europe as a great luxury, and it was rare and expensive for many centuries after that.
羅馬時代,甘蔗在歐洲以高級奢侈品聞名,在那之後的幾世紀,仍十分罕見且昂貴。

0990 evacuate [ɪ'vækjuˌet]　　　**v.**　撤離　　　**3rd** ★★★★★
A fire started in this hotel so the guests had to evacuate immediately.
旅館發生了火災,所有的旅客都必須立刻撤離。

0991 evaluation [ɪˌvæljuˈeʃən]　　　**n.**　評估　　　**4th** ★★★★★
After meticulous evaluations of the pros and cons, the government agreed to give the green light to off-shore banking services.
經過縝密評估利弊得失之後,政府允許開放境外金融服務。

0992 event [ɪ'vɛnt]　　　**n.**　事件　　　**5th** ★★★★★
Henry didn't plan any events in New York; he just wanted to roam the streets.
亨利沒有計劃在紐約做任何事,他只是想在街上閒逛。

0993 eventually [ɪ'vɛntʃuəlɪ]　　　**adv.**　終於　　　**5th** ★★★★★
Eventually, she owned up.
她終於認錯了。

0994 evidence ['ɛvədəns]　　　**n.**　證據　　　**4th** ★★★★★
The evidence pointed out clearly that he stole the money.
證據清楚指出就是他偷了錢。

0995 evident ['ɛvədənt]　　　**adj.**　明顯的　　　**4th** ★★★★★
After the teacher's explanation, the answer to the math problem was evident.
經老師解釋之後,數學問題的答案變得顯而易見。

E

0996 **evil** ['ivl̩]   **adj.** 邪惡的   4th ★★★★★

The early American Indians shot arrows into the air to drive the evil spirits away.
早期的美國印地安人會將箭射向空中驅趕惡靈。

0997 **evolution** [ˌɛvəˈluʃən]   **n.** 進化   3rd ★★★★★

The Galápagos Islands are the Pacific island paradise where Darwin's theory of evolution was born.
加拉巴戈斯群島是太平洋島上的天堂，達爾文的進化論便是在那裡孕育出來的。

0998 **evolve** [ɪˈvɑlv]   **v.** 進化   3rd ★★★★★

In a world where standstills have become all too common, constant evolving is the key to business success.
停滯不前已極為普遍的社會，不斷進化是生意成功的關鍵。

0999 **exactitude** [ɪgˈzæktəˌtjud]   **n.** 正確   3rd ★★★★★

He described the scene with exactitude.
他精確地描述了那場事件。

1000 **exactly** [ɪgˈzæktlɪ]   **adv.** 準確地   4th ★★★★★

Robert was the only witness to the car accident. The police had to count on him to find out exactly how the accident happened.
羅伯特是車禍的唯一目擊者，警方必須靠他才能準確找出肇事原因。

1001 **exam** [ɪgˈzæm]   **n.** 考試   4th ★★★★★

If he had studied harder, he wouldn't have failed the exam.
如果他當初用功一點，考試就不會不及格了。

1002 **examine** [ɪgˈzæmɪn]   **v.** 檢查；檢驗   4th ★★★★★

Mastery of calculus and doing well on exams require active knowledge, the ability to solve problems without the aid of books.
精通運算及考出好成績需要活用的知識，就是沒有書本也能解決問題的能力。

1003 **example** [ɪgˈzæmpl̩]   **n.** 例子   5th ★★★★★

The essay is a fine example of how a writer's control of language and detail can re-create the point of view of a child.
作家對語言和細節的操控，對如何重塑孩子的觀點，本文是一個很好的例子。

1004 **excel** [ɪkˈsɛl]   **v.** 勝過   3rd ★★★★★

I am confident that I am able to excel the smart guy in the competition.
我有信心能在比賽中勝過這個聰明的傢伙。

1005 excellent ['ɛksḷənt]　　adj. 卓越的　　5th ★★★★★
Brave Tigers is a team which consists of twelve excellent players.
勇虎隊是由十二位優秀球員所組成。

1006 except [ɪk'sɛpt]　　prep. 除外　　5th ★★★★★
The police found no clues except for one fingerprint on the wall.
警察除了在牆上發現一枚指紋之外，找不到其他任何線索。

1007 exception [ɪk'sɛpʃən]　　n. 例外　　4th ★★★★★
From a historical perspective, successful intercultural communication has been an exception rather than a rule.
從歷史的觀點看來，成功的跨文化溝通是例外而非常規。

1008 excessively [ɪk'sɛsɪvlɪ]　　adv. 超過地　　4th ★★★★★
Obese or excessively overweight individuals are less likely to die in the 5 years after suffering a stroke than their normal-weight peers.
體重過重的人和體重正常的同儕比起來，中風後的五年內較不容易有身亡的危險。

1009 exchange [ɪks'tʃendʒ]　　v. 交換　　4th ★★★★★
Would you like to exchange this ring for a more stylish one?
你想要把這枚戒指換成更時髦的款式嗎？

1010 exciting [ɪk'saɪtɪŋ]　　adj. 令人興奮的　　5th ★★★★★
Eric told me about the many exciting events that happened on his trip.
艾瑞克告訴我許多在旅途中發生的趣事。

1011 exclaim [ɪks'klem]　　v. 呼喊　　4th ★★★★★
Everyone exclaimed in delight as soon as they heard the news.
每個人一聽到這個消息都高興地放聲大叫。

1012 exclude [ɪk'sklud]　　v. 排除　　4th ★★★★★
The Mexican immigrants were excluded from the membership.
墨西哥移民遭排除會員資格。

1013 exclusive [ɪk'sklusɪv]　　adj. 排他的　　3rd ★★★★★
There were ten of us in the lounge, exclusive of our homeroom teacher.
班導除外，我們有十個人待在貴賓室。

1014 excursion [ɪk'skɝʒən]　　n. 旅遊團　　3rd ★★★★★
Most excursion fares are for round-trip travel and have strict regulations and a

E

minimum and maximum length of stay.
大部份的團費是來回旅程，註有嚴格規定、還有停留的最長和最短時間。

1015 excursive [ɛk'skɜsɪv]　　　adj. 隨意的　　　3rd ★★★★★
I had an excursive conversation with a close friend of mine last night.
我昨晚和一位密友天南地北的閒聊。

1016 excuse [ɪk'skjuz]　　　n. 藉口　　　5th ★★★★★
If you ask students why they are late for class, their excuses will be very different.
如果你問學生上學遲到的理由，他們的藉口千奇百變。

1017 execute ['ɛksɪ,kjut]　　　v. 執行　　　4th ★★★★★
The soldiers' only choice is to execute the major's commands.
士兵的唯一選擇就是執行主將的命令。

1018 exercise ['ɛksə,saɪz]　　　n. 運動　　　4th ★★★★★
Exercise is also important in reducing stress and keeping the body healthy.
運動很重要，不但可以消除壓力，還可以保持身體健康。

1019 exhaust [ɪg'zɔst]　　　n. 廢氣　　　4th ★★★★★
Many countries have regulations which help control exhaust emission from motor vehicles.
許多國家都有法規來控管機車的廢氣排放量。

1020 exhibit [ɪg'zɪbɪt]　　　n. 展覽品　　　4th ★★★★★
The duties of the museum volunteers will include screening films, answering visitors' questions, and watching over the exhibits.
博物館志工的職責包括播放影片、回答參觀者的提問，以及看守展示品。

1021 exhibition [,ɛksə'bɪʃən]　　　n. 展覽　　　4th ★★★★★
Many exhibitions are held each year in Taiwan as the island is one of the world's largest manufacturers of computers.
台灣是世界的電腦主要生產國，每年都會舉辦許多展覽。

1022 exist [ɪg'zɪst]　　　v. 生存　　　4th ★★★★★
Freedom and rule by law must exist side by side.
自由和法律必須是共存的。

1023 existence [ɪg'zɪstəns]　　　n. 存在　　　4th ★★★★★
Although stories about aliens have never been officially confirmed, their existence has been widely speculated upon.
儘管官方從來不曾證實有關外星人的故事，但大家還是推測他們確實存在。

1024 exit ['ɛksɪt]　　　　　　n.　出口　　4th　★★★★★
You are now standing in front of the MRT station by the 2nd Street exit.
你現在站在捷運站第二街出口的前面。

1025 exotic [ɛg'zɑtɪk]　　　　　adj.　異國的　　3rd　★★★★★
This remote island, so beautiful and rich in culture, is just like an exotic paradise for tourists.
這座偏僻的島嶼，如此美麗又富含文化，對觀光客而言就像一個異國天堂。

1026 expand [ɪk'spænd]　　　　v.　擴展　　4th　★★★★★
Ms. Li's business expanded very quickly. She opened her first store two years ago; now she has fifty stores all over the country.
李太太的生意擴展很快，她兩年前開了第一家店，現在她在全國已經有五十家分店。

1027 expanse [ɪk'spæns]　　　　n.　廣闊　　4th　★★★★★
The cloudless sky was an expanse of blue.
無雲的天空是一片廣闊的藍。

1028 expatriate [ɛks'petrɪˌet]　　n.　移居國外者　3rd　★★★★★
A trip to another country is an opportunity to sample other cultures, but having to live away from home as an expatriate can make you feel sad.
到他國旅行是體驗異國文化的機會，但必須像移民者一樣遠離家鄉又很令人傷心。

1029 expect [ɪk'spɛkt]　　　　v.　期待　　4th　★★★★★
As lots of victims have moved into our district after the disaster, we expect a shortage of water very soon.
因為災後有很多難民搬入我們這一區，預計很快就會缺水。

1030 expectancy [ɪk'spɛktənsɪ]　　n.　預期　　4th　★★★★★
The phenomenon of population aging is a result of higher life expectancy and lower birth rate.
人口老化的現象是平均壽命延長和低生育率所造成的結果。

1031 expectation [ˌɛkspɛk'teʃən]　n.　期待　　4th　★★★★★
They say that the fear of not living up to unrealistic expectations is to blame.
人們認為不該為了無法達成不切實際的理想而害怕。

1032 expel [ɪk'spɛl]　　　　v.　開除　　4th　★★★★★
Some students might be expelled from schools for misusing their computers, such as illegal downloads.
有些學生可能會因為濫用電腦遭學校開除，像是非法下載。

1033 expenditure [ɪk'spɛndɪtʃə]　　n.　經費　　4th ★★★★★

Public education expenditures would need to be increased for small-size classes, teacher training programs and new E-learning facilities.
為了縮小班級規模、培訓教師和新的電子學習設備，需要增加公共教育支出。

1034 expense [ɪk'spɛns]　　n.　開銷　　4th ★★★★★

I'm not sure exactly how much scholarship you'll receive, but it will roughly cover your major expenses.
我不確定你會拿到多少獎學金，但是大致上可以支付你的主要開銷。

1035 expensive [ɪk'spɛnsɪv]　　adj.　昂貴的　　5th ★★★★★

This toy car is too expensive. Please give me a cheaper one.
這部玩具車太貴了，請給我便宜一點的。

1036 experience [ɪk'spɪrɪəns]　　n.　經驗　　5th ★★★★★

Visiting Walt Disney World was a magical experience for our whole family.
參觀迪斯尼世界對我們全家是一個神奇的經驗。

1037 experiment [ɪk'spɛrəmənt]　　n.　實驗　　4th ★★★★★

Building a digital city is a grand experiment in which wireless communications make it easier to find friends, keep abreast of local events, and build a warm community.
建造數位化城市是一項偉大的實驗，透過無線通訊聯絡朋友更加容易，也能及時了解當地大小事，建立一個溫暖的社會。

1038 expert ['ɛkspət]　　n.　專家　　4th ★★★★★

Mark is an expert on environmental problems.
馬克是解決環境問題的專家。

1039 expire [ɪk'spaɪr]　　v.　到期　　4th ★★★★★

The foreigner's passport was expired and he was forced to return to his country.
這位外國人的護照過期了，所以他遭強制遣返回國。

1040 explain [ɪk'splen]　　v.　解釋　　4th ★★★★★

Many UFO sightings can't be explained easily because most of the time people don't know exactly what they have seen.
許多關於幽浮的目擊都無法輕易解釋清楚，因為多數情況下，人們無法確定自己看到了什麼。

1041 explanation [ˌɛksplə'neʃən]　　n.　解釋　　4th ★★★★★

Instead of making things clear, Jane's explanation baffled me.
珍的解釋並沒有把事情說清楚，反而使我更困惑。

1042 explicit [ɪk'splɪsɪt]　　　　**adj.** 明確的　　**3rd** ★★★★★
With the worsening of global economic conditions, it seems wiser and more explicit to keep cash in the bank rather than to invest in the stock market.
隨著全球經濟惡化,與其投資股票市場,把錢存入銀行似乎更為明確和明智。

1043 explode [ɪk'splod]　　　　**v.** 爆炸　　**4th** ★★★★★
The passengers narrowly escaped death when a bomb exploded in the subway station, killing sixty people.
一枚炸彈在地鐵站爆炸,有六十人死亡,其餘乘客僥倖逃過一劫。

1044 exploration [ˌɛksplə'reʃən]　　**n.** 探索　　**4th** ★★★★★
Children's encounters with poetry should include three types of response—enjoyment, exploration, and deepening understanding.
兒童與詩學的接觸應包含三種反應:享受、探索和深度了解。

1045 explore [ɪk'splor]　　　　**v.** 探索　　**4th** ★★★★★
One of the best ways to explore Venice, a great city in Europe, is on foot.
探索威尼斯的最佳方法之一就是步行,那是歐洲一個很棒的城市。

1046 explosion [ɪk'sploʒən]　　　**n.** 爆炸　　**4th** ★★★★★
By the late seventeenth century, the Mainland was experiencing a population explosion.
十七世紀後期,中國大陸發生了一次人口爆炸的現象。

1047 export [ɪks'port]　　　　**v.** 出口　　**4th** ★★★★★
Though Taiwan exports an enormous quantity of machines, its natural resources are very limited.
儘管台灣出口了大量的機器設備,但其天然資源十分有限。

1048 expose [ɪk'spoz]　　　　**v.** 曝露　　**4th** ★★★★★
On high peaks, plants are exposed to fierce winds, heavy snow, intense sunlight, and extremely low nighttime temperatures.
高聳山頂上的植物暴露於狂風、大雪、強烈的陽光,和夜間極低氣溫之中。

1049 exposure [ɪk'spoʒə]　　　　**n.** 曝露　　**4th** ★★★★★
Long exposure to the sun may result in skin cancer.
在陽光下長時間曝曬可能會導致皮膚癌。

1050 express [ɪk'sprɛs]　　　　**v.** 表達　　**4th** ★★★★★
Thoughts can be expressed by means of words.
想法可以藉由文字表達。

1051 **expression** [ɪk'sprɛʃən]　　n.　表達　　**4th** ★★★★★
Almost every language has a topic that especially rich in vocabulary and idiomatic expressions.
幾乎每一種語言在某個主題上都會有特別豐富的字彙和慣用語表達。

1052 **exquisite** ['ɛkskwɪzɪt]　　adj.　精緻的　　**4th** ★★★★★
This piece of jewelry costs over a million dollars because it is made with exquisite craftsmanship.
這件珠寶價值超過一百萬元，因為它是由精細技術製成的。

1053 **extend** [ɪk'stɛnd]　　v.　延長　　**4th** ★★★★★
One week is not long enough for us to finish the work. Can you extend the deadline by three more days?
一個星期不夠長，我們無法完成這項工作，你可以把期限延長三天嗎？

1054 **extent** [ɪk'stɛnt]　　n.　程度　　**4th** ★★★★★
The government itself has little information on the extent of industrial pollution.
政府本身對於工業污染程度的資訊少之又少。

1055 **exterior** [ɪk'stɪrɪə]　　adj.　外部的　　**4th** ★★★★★
The exterior of Tina's apartment has an exceptionally large balcony.
蒂娜的公寓外部有一個非常寬大的陽台。

1056 **externally** [ɪk'stɜnlɪ]　　adv.　外觀上　　**4th** ★★★★★
One can generally judge the quality of eggs with the naked eye. Externally, good eggs must be clean, free of cracks, and smooth-shelled.
人可以用肉眼判斷雞蛋的品質。從外觀上來看，品質好的雞蛋一定要乾淨、無裂痕，而且外殼要光滑。

1057 **extinct** [ɪk'stɪŋkt]　　adj.　絕種的　　**4th** ★★★★★
Tropical rainforests are home to about one million plant and animal species. If the rainforests disappear, many of these species will become extinct.
熱帶雨林大約是一百萬種動植物的棲息地，如果熱帶雨林消失了，許多物種也會跟著絕種。

1058 **extra** ['ɛkstrə]　　adj.　額外的　　**5th** ★★★★★
The mayor promised to give his city an extra day off from work this year.
市長答應今年給他的市民額外休息一天不用工作。

1059 **extract** [ɪk'strækt]　　v.　吸取　　**4th** ★★★★★
Reading is an activity in which the reader extracts information from print.
閱讀是讀者從印刷字體裡吸取訊息的一項消遣。

1060 extraordinary [ɪk'strɔrdn͵ɛrɪ] **adj.** 特別的 **5th** ★★★★★
Last winter's snowstorms and freezing temperatures were quite extraordinary for this region where warm and short winters are typical.
這個地區冬季通常很短,而且是暖冬;去年冬天的暴風雪和嚴寒低溫顯得相當異常。

1061 extreme [ɪk'strim] **adj.** 極端的 **4th** ★★★★★
Randy will never go to the circus because of his extreme fear of clowns.
藍迪絕不去看馬戲團表演,因為他極度恐懼小丑。

1062 facilitate [fə'sɪlə͵tet] **v.** 促進 **3rd** ★★★★★
The newly-built airport will facilitate the development of tourism.
新建機場可望促進旅遊業的發展。

1063 facilitation [fə͵sɪlə'teʃən] **n.** 促進 **3rd** ★★★★★
Risk management is viewed as a method by which customs administrations can enhance trade facilitation.
海關當局可以藉由風險管理的方法,加強貿易便利化。

1064 facility [fə'sɪlətɪ] **n.** 設施 **4th** ★★★★★
The rest area has a bathroom and a shower facility.
休息區有一間浴室和淋浴設施。

1065 fact [fækt] **n.** 事實 **5th** ★★★★★
To avoid being misled by news reports, we should learn to distinguish between facts and opinions.
為了避免新聞媒體的誤導,我們必須學習分辨事實與個人意見的不同。

1066 factor ['fæktə] **n.** 因素 **4th** ★★★★★
Face is an important factor in Chinese negotiating style.
中國人在談判時,表情是一項重要因素。

1067 factory ['fæktərɪ] **n.** 工廠 **5th** ★★★★★
Large amounts of dangerous waste released by factories into the sea seriously harmed a lot of birds and animals.
大量的有害廢物從工廠排入大海,嚴重危害許多鳥類和動物。

1068 faculty ['fæk]tɪ] **n.** 教職員 **4th** ★★★★★
The online school itself has no need to maintain classrooms, faculty offices, and other expensive facilities.
線上學校本身不需要維護教室、教職員辦公室和其他昂貴的設施。

F

1069 fade [fed]   **v.**   褪色   **4th** ★★★★★
After the sun set, the sky faded to black.
太陽下山後，天空褪成黑色。

1070 fail [fel]   **v.**   失敗   **5th** ★★★★★
Michelle failed her driving test because she drove over a cone.
蜜雪兒駕駛考試失敗了，因為她輾過一個錐形路標。

1071 failure ['feljə]   **n.**   失敗   **5th** ★★★★★
You might fail in pursuit of your goals, but the lessons you learn from each failure will help you to eventually succeed.
追求目標時你可能會遭遇失敗，但在失敗中學到的經驗最終可以幫助你成功。

1072 faint [fent]   **adj.**   微弱的   **3rd** ★★★★★
There is a faint smell of pizza from yesterday's dinner.
還有一點點昨天晚餐留下的披薩氣味。

1073 fair [fɛr]   **n.**   展覽會   **5th** ★★★★★
They want to rent two floors from a very popular department store to hold the mid-summer fair there.
他們想向一家熱門的百貨公司租二層樓舉辦仲夏特賣會。

1074 faithful ['feθfəl]   **adj.**   忠誠的   **4th** ★★★★★
An honest person is faithful to his promise. Once he makes a commitment, he will not go back on his own word.
誠實的人言出必行，一旦做出承諾就不會反悔。

1075 fake [fek]   **adj.**   冒充的   **4th** ★★★★★
It is illegal to use fake credit cards.
使用偽造信用卡是違法的。

1076 false [fɔls]   **adj.**   假的   **4th** ★★★★★
Dentists often use porcelain to make false teeth.
牙醫經常使用陶瓷做假牙。

1077 falter ['fɔltə]   **v.**   動搖   **3rd** ★★★★★
A plan or project may falter, even if it finally succeeds.
一個最終成功的計劃或項目，在途中也可能會動搖。

1078 familiar [fə'mɪljə]   **adj.**   熟悉的   **5th** ★★★★★

ABCDEFGHIJKLMNOPQRSTUVWXYZ

The **3000 vocabularies you must know in public service exam**

Familiar fables can be narrated differently or extended in interesting and humorous ways.
我們熟悉的寓言可以用不同方式闡述，或者是擴展成有趣又幽默的故事內容。

1079 family [ˈfæməlɪ]   **n.**   家人   **5th** ★★★★★
Almost all Americans are taught to drive by an older family member; driving schools are not common in America.
幾乎所有美國人的開車技術都是由家中成員所教，駕訓班在美國不流行。

1080 famine [ˈfæmɪn]   **n.**   飢餓   **4th** ★★★★★
Starting from 1989, World Vision Taiwan 30-Hour Famine has been helping people victimized by man-made conflicts and disasters.
自一九八九年起，台灣世界展望會飢餓三十的活動幫助受天災人禍之苦的人們。

1081 famous [ˈfeməs]   **adj.**   知名的   **5th** ★★★★★
The boy wants to be a famous actor when he grows up.
那個男孩長大後想成為知名的演員。

1082 fantastic [fænˈtæstɪk]   **adj.**   美妙的   **4th** ★★★★★
You can enjoy a fantastic view of the sunset from the top of the mountain.
你可以從山頂上享受美好的夕陽景觀。

1083 fantasy [ˈfæntəsɪ]   **n.**   幻想   **4th** ★★★★★
Many people's fantasy is to win the lottery and never need to work anymore.
許多人都幻想中樂透，然後就永遠不需要工作了。

1084 fare [fɛr]   **n.**   交通費   **5th** ★★★★★
Robert had to pay the fare before getting on the bus.
羅伯特在上公車前必須支付車費。

1085 fascinated [ˈfæsn͵etɪd]   **adj.**   著迷的   **4th** ★★★★★
He is so fascinated by this movie that he saw it four times.
他對這部電影非常著迷，總共看了四遍。

1086 fashion [ˈfæʃən]   **n.**   時裝   **4th** ★★★★★
I like window shopping the fashion stores in the area.
我喜歡在這區的時裝店逛街。

1087 fashionable [ˈfæʃənəbl̩]   **adj.**   時尚的   **4th** ★★★★★
Made from a lightweight fabric that dries quickly, 'Xprit' sportswear is functional and fashionable.
Xprit的運動服材質輕巧易乾，兼具實用和流行。

1088 fatal ['fetl̩]　　　　adj.　致命的　　4th ★★★★★

On my way to the office, I saw a car collided with a truck; there were several fatal.
我在前往辦公室的途中，看到一輛轎車和卡車相撞，是一起致命交通事故。

1089 fatigue [fə'tig]　　　　n.　疲勞　　3rd ★★★★★

The heavy schoolbag with a lot of books fatigues each young student.
厚重的書包裡裝了一大堆書，讓每一位年輕學子感到疲累。

1090 fault [fɔlt]　　　　n.　錯誤　　5th ★★★★★

Everyone has his merits and faults.
每個人都有各自的優缺點。

1091 faulty ['fɔltɪ]　　　　adj.　有過失　　5th ★★★★★

If you argue that, "Socrates is wise and just. X is wise; therefore, X is just.", you have a syllogism that is faulty.
你若說：「蘇格拉底睿智且正義。X是睿智，因此，X是正義。」，這個推論方法是錯的。

1092 favor ['fevɚ]　　　　n.　恩惠　　5th ★★★★★

May I ask a favor of you?
可以請你幫個忙嗎？

1093 favorite ['fevərɪt]　　　　adj.　最喜愛的　　5th ★★★★★

My favorite season is fall because the weather is very comfortable.
我最喜歡秋天，因為天氣很舒服。

1094 fear [fɪr]　　　　n.　恐懼　　5th ★★★★★

You need to prepare your speech thoroughly if you want to avoid stage fear.
如果想要避免怯場，你需要充分準備你的講稿。

1095 feasible ['fizəbl̩]　　　　adj.　可行的　　4th ★★★★★

I wonder if it is feasible to complete the project by the end of September.
我不確定到九月底前是不是可以完成這項計畫。

1096 feast [fist]　　　　n.　宴會　　4th ★★★★★

Many families gather for a feast during the Moon Festival.
許多家庭在中秋節期間團聚吃大餐。

1097 feat [fit]　　　　n.　壯舉　　4th ★★★★★

It's really quite a feat for a child to swim across the strait.
對一個小孩來說，能泳渡海峽實是一大壯舉。

060

1098 feather [ˈfɛðɚ]　　　　n.　羽毛　　　5th ★★★★★
Birds of a feather flock together.
物以類聚，人以群分。

1099 feature [fitʃɚ]　　　　v.　由…主演　　4th ★★★★★
A movie featuring Jackie Chan is coming up soon.
成龍主演的電影快要上映了。

1100 fecundity [fɪˈkʌndətɪ]　　n.　豐饒　　　4th ★★★★★
All the staff appreciated the conductor's fecundity of imagination.
全體員工都很佩服領導人豐富的想像力。

1101 federation [ˌfɛdəˈreʃən]　n.　聯邦政府　4th ★★★★★
The U. S. is a federation of fifty states.
美國是一個由五十州組成的聯邦政府。

1102 fee [fi]　　　　　　　n.　費用　　　5th ★★★★★
The club demands a membership fee of NT$1,000 a year.
這個俱樂部要求一年的會員費用是台幣一千元。

1103 feed [fid]　　　　　　v.　餵食　　　4th ★★★★★
Attracting and feeding wild birds are pastimes long enjoyed by people all over the world.
招引和飼養野生鳥類是全球的人類長期以來的消遣。

1104 feedback [ˈfidˌbæk]　　n.　回饋　　　4th ★★★★★
By writing on blogs, people can get feedback from other audiences all over cyberspace.
人們藉由在部落格上寫作，可以得到來自各個網路空間的讀者回應。

1105 feeling [ˈfilɪŋ]　　　　n.　感覺　　　5th ★★★★★
The player had no feeling in her right leg after the game.
比賽結束之後，球員的左腳失去了知覺。

1106 felicity [fəˈlɪsətɪ]　　　n.　幸福　　　4th ★★★★★
Many people are jealous of Susan's marital felicity.
許多人羨慕蘇珊幸福美滿的婚姻。

1107 fence [fɛns]　　　　　n.　圍籬　　　5th ★★★★★
There used to be wooden fences around the barn.
穀倉周圍曾經有木柵欄環繞。

F

1108 fertile [ˈfɜtl̩]　　　　adj.　肥沃的　　4th　★★★★★
The southern district of the island is fertile in barley.
這座島的南部地區盛產大麥。

1109 fertilizer [ˈfɜtl̩ˌaɪzə]　　n.　肥料　　4th　★★★★★
Oil is essential for modern life. Apart from its use in transportation, it is also used in making fertilizers, plastics, and many other products.
石油在現代生活是不可或缺的，除了用在運輸工具外，也用於製造肥料、塑膠和其他產品。

1110 festivity [fɛsˈtɪvətɪ]　　n.　節慶活動　　5th　★★★★★
There are many festivities over the holiday.
假期間有許多慶祝活動。

1111 fetch [fɛtʃ]　　　　v.　去取回　　4th　★★★★★
Could you please fetch the trash can for me?
可以請你拿垃圾桶給我嗎？

1112 fever [ˈfivə]　　　　n.　發燒　　5th　★★★★★
David's mother had a fever yesterday so he sent her to the hospital.
大衛母親昨天發燒所以大衛送她去醫院。

1113 field [fild]　　　　n.　領域　　5th　★★★★★
Workers in the health care field have to respond to emergencies almost every day.
在醫學領域工作的人幾乎每天都得應付突發事件。

1114 fierce [fɪrs]　　　　adj.　激烈的　　4th　★★★★★
He made a fierce effort to catch up with his classmate after he got well.
他病癒後努力用功，以趕上同學的進度。

1115 fight [faɪt]　　　　n.　打架　　5th　★★★★★
The young guys armed themselves with many snowballs for the snowball fight.
這些年輕小夥子為了打雪仗，準備了很多雪球。

1116 figure [ˈfɪgjə]　　　　v.　認為　　4th　★★★★★
It is already 6:00. I figure we will have to go home real soon if we don't want to make mom angry.
已經六點了，如果不想讓媽媽生氣，我認為我們必須立刻回家。

1117 file [faɪl]　　　　n.　檔案　　5th　★★★★★

061

You should save the computer file on a disk.
你應該儲存電腦檔案到磁碟裡。

1118 film [fɪlm]　　　　　　　　　**n.**　電影　　**5th** ★★★★★
Fred liked the beginning of the movie, but he didn't like the ending.
佛雷德喜歡這部電影的開頭，但他不喜歡結局。

1119 final [ˈfaɪnl̩]　　　　　　　　**adj.**　最後的　　**4th** ★★★★★
Final exams put a lot of pressure on students. They have to study very hard.
期末考給學生的壓力很大，他們必須非常用功唸書。

1120 finally [ˈfaɪnl̩ɪ]　　　　　　　**adv.**　最後　　**4th** ★★★★★
Jack's aunt kept offering him cake; finally, he gave in and took a small piece even though he was not hungry.
傑克的阿姨不斷拿蛋糕給他，雖然他不餓，最後也屈服拿了一小塊。

1121 financial [faɪˈnænʃəl]　　　　　**adj.**　財務的　　**4th** ★★★★★
There has been a strong backlash against the government for its financial policy.
政府的金融政策遭到強烈反對。

1122 find [faɪnd]　　　　　　　　　**v.**　發現　　**5th** ★★★★★
You'll find great happiness if you pursue your dreams.
如果你追求夢想，你將會找到美好的幸福。

1123 fine [faɪn]　　　　　　　　　　**n.**　罰款　　**5th** ★★★★★
Nancy got a ticket for driving too fast. She has to pay a fine of $3000 for speeding.
南西因為開快車拿到一張罰單。她因為超速必須付三千元罰款。

1124 finger [ˈfɪŋgɚ]　　　　　　　　**n.**　手指　　**5th** ★★★★★
The worker sliced his finger while he was making my sandwich.
工作人員在幫我做三明治時切到手指。

1125 finish [ˈfɪnɪʃ]　　　　　　　　**v.**　完成　　**5th** ★★★★★
Because Carl already finished his homework, his parents let him watch cartoons.
卡爾的作業寫完了，所以他的爸媽准許他看卡通。

1126 firm [fɝm]　　　　　　　　　　**adj.**　堅固的　　**4th** ★★★★★
Melissa had a firm understanding of what was going on in math class.
美麗莎對數學課程的內容有實質的理解。

F

1127 firefighter [ˈfaɪrˌfaɪtə]   **n.**   消防員   5th ★★★★★
Don't worry and stay where you are. Firefighters are doing everything possible to get you out.
留在原地別擔心，消防人員正盡一切努力要把你救出來。

1128 firework [ˈfaɪrˌwɜk]   **n.**   煙火   4th ★★★★★
The first time I went to the Yenshui Fireworks Festival was in 2003.
我第一次去鹽水蜂炮是在2003年的時候。

1129 fiscal [ˈfɪskl̩]   **adj.**   財政的   3rd ★★★★★
The corporation is going to expand next fiscal year to include several new products.
下一個財政年度公司將拓展事業，包含七個新產品的上市。

1130 fit [fɪt]   **adj.**   健康的   5th ★★★★★
Susan managed to stay fit taking exercise in the gym five days a week.
蘇珊為了保持身材，她一個禮拜花五天去健身房運動。

1131 fix [fɪks]   **v.**   修理   5th ★★★★★
Should you fix the mosquito net before going to bed?
你不是應該在睡前把蚊帳修好嗎？

1132 fixed [fɪkst]   **adj.**   固定的   5th ★★★★★
Mr. Chen just paid off a fixed loan last month.
陳先生上個月才剛付清定期貸款。

1133 flash [flæʃ]   **n.**   一瞬間   5th ★★★★★
He felt a brief flash of jealousy.
他短暫的妒忌心一閃而過。

1134 flat [flæt]   **adj.**   扁的   5th ★★★★★
I can't drive my car because I have a flat tire.
我無法開我的車，因為有一個輪胎沒氣了。

1135 flavor [ˈflevə]   **n.**   口味   4th ★★★★★
Matthew's favorite flavor of ice cream is chocolate.
馬修最愛巧克力口味的冰淇淋。

1136 flawless [ˈflɔlɪs]   **adj.**   無瑕疵的   4th ★★★★★
Because his speech was flawless, the audience gave him a big hand.
他的演講無懈可擊，觀眾回以熱烈的掌聲。

1137 flee [fli]　　　　　　　　　　v.　逃避　　　　4th　★★★★★
The mailman fled from the fierce dog.
郵差逃離了兇猛的狗。

1138 flex [flɛks]　　　　　　　　v.　彎曲　　　　4th　★★★★★
The runner took off his sneakers and flexed his toes.
賽跑者脫下球鞋，讓自己腳趾彎曲活動。

1139 flexible [ˈflɛksəbl]　　　　adj.　靈活的　　4th　★★★★★
Many new cell phones are equipped with software that is flexible enough for
several functions.
許多新型手機所配備的軟體，靈活適用於許多功能。

1140 flexibility [ˌflɛksəˈbɪlətɪ]　　n.　彈性　　　4th　★★★★★
Choosing a weight loss or fitness program is not easy. You want convenience,
flexibility and motivation...but most of all, you want result.
選擇減肥或健身計畫並不容易，你想要方便、夠彈性，還要能激勵你⋯，但最重要的
是，你要看到成果。

1141 flight [flaɪt]　　　　　　　　n.　班機　　　　5th　★★★★★
I think the rescue team's flight arrived at about eight this morning.
我想救援隊的班機大約是在今早八點的時候抵達。

1142 flinch [flɪntʃ]　　　　　　　v.　畏懼　　　　3rd　★★★★★
The firewalkers of Fiji, Hawaii, and the Cook Islands walk over blazing hot coals
without flinching.
來自斐濟、夏威夷和庫克群島的火行者，走過炙熱的煤炭時毫不畏懼。

1143 flirtation [flɝˈteʃən]　　　　n.　挑逗　　　　3rd　★★★★★
She had a little flirtation with that man at the party.
她在派對上和那位男子有點似有若無的調情。

1144 flirtatious [flɝˈteʃəs]　　adj.　輕佻的　　3rd　★★★★★
The man kept giving the young lady flirtatious looks.
男人一直對年輕女士調情。

1145 flock [flɑk]　　　　　　　　n.　一群　　　　5th　★★★★★
A flock of customers were waiting for the store to open.
一群顧客等著商店開門。

1146 flood [flʌd]   n.   洪水   5th ★★★★★

The terrible flood washed away bridges, houses, and crops. The town soon disappeared.

可怕的洪水沖走了橋樑、房屋和作物，這小鎮一下子就不見了。

1147 floor [flor]   n.   樓層   5th ★★★★★

The janitor was sweeping the floor the moment I entered the building.

我進入大樓時，看門人正在掃地。

1148 flour [flaur]   n.   麵粉   5th ★★★★★

Most bread is made from flour.

大部分麵包是由麵粉做的。

1149 flow [flo]   n.   流動   5th ★★★★★

Yawning increases blood flow and helps maintain optimum levels of physical functioning.

打哈欠增加血液流動，幫助身體機能維持最佳狀態。

1150 flu [flu]   n.   流行性感冒   5th ★★★★★

At the outset of the New Year, Asia again faced a health scare after some seventy people died of bird flu.

新年的一開始，約有七十人死於禽流感，亞洲再度面臨健康恐慌。

1151 fluctuation [ˌflʌktʃuˈeʃən]   n.   波動   3rd ★★★★★

The violent fluctuation in prices has negative influence on people's daily lives.

價格劇烈波動對人們日常生活造成負面影響。

1152 fluently [ˈfluəntlɪ]   adv.   流利地   4th ★★★★★

Only if you speak both English and Chinese fluently will you be considered for that job.

只有當你中英文都說很很流利時，那份工作才可能屬於你。

1153 flunk [flʌŋk]   v.   不及格   4th ★★★★★

It is hardly surprising that Frank flunked English. He never paid any attention in class.

法蘭克的英文被當並不意外，他在課堂上從來沒有專心過。

1154 flush [flʌʃ]   v.   充溢   4th ★★★★★

Flush with cash, the mammoth multinational telecom company will intensively increase its investment at home in the coming years.

這家資本雄厚的跨國電訊大廠，會積極增加未來幾年在自己國家的投資。

063

1155 focus ['fokəs]   **v.** 專注於   4th ★★★★★
Ashley can focus on reading a book even when there are loud noises around her.
即使艾布莉的周圍有很大的噪音,她還是可以專心讀書。

1156 follow ['falo]   **v.** 跟隨   4th ★★★★★
He had to stop and pull over because the policeman was following him.
警察在後面跟著他,他只好將車子開到路邊停下來。

1157 fond [fand]   **adj.** 喜歡的   5th ★★★★★
Isabelle has always been fond writing. In fact, she likes writing so much that she has decided to be a writer.
依莎貝兒一直都很喜歡寫作,事實上,她因為太喜歡寫作了,所以決定當個作家。

1158 fool [ful]   **n.** 笨蛋   5th ★★★★★
He is not such a fool but he can tell a friend from a foe.
他不是一個笨蛋,但他卻敵友不分。

1159 foot [fut]   **n.** 英尺   5th ★★★★★
Colorado's 14,000-foot peaks are fairly easy to climb because they require no special climbing techniques.
科羅拉多州那座一萬四千英尺的山峰相當容易攀登,因為不需要特別的攀登技巧。

1160 force [fors]   **v.** 強迫   4th ★★★★★
I can work well under stress. In fact, pressure sometimes forces me to perform better.
我可以在壓力下做的很好。事實上,有時壓力會迫使我做的更好。

1161 forecast ['for͵kæst]   **n.** 預報   3rd ★★★★★
Today's forecast is calling for snow.
今天的天氣預測會下雪。

1162 foreign ['fɔrɪn]   **adj.** 外國的   5th ★★★★★
Throughout the lecture, not once did the speaker mention the subject of foreign aid.
演講者在整場演講中,完全沒有提到有關外國援助這個主題。

1163 foresee [for'si]   **v.** 預見   4th ★★★★★
We should foresee the difficulties on our way to start our own business.
我們在創業的過程中,應該要能預知各種困難。

F

1164 forest [ˈfɔrɪst]　　　　　n. 森林　　　5th ★★★★★
Forests are essential to the global environment.
森林是全球自然環境所不可或缺的。

1165 forget [fəˈgɛt]　　　　　v. 忘記　　　5th ★★★★★
We had a quarrel, I know. But let's just forgive and forget.
我知道我們之前有爭吵，但就讓我們既往不咎吧！

1166 form [fɔrm]　　　　　n. 形式　　　4th ★★★★★
Many people love to ride bicycles. It's a popular form of transportation.
許多人喜歡騎腳踏車，這種形式的交通工具很流行。

1167 formal [ˈfɔrml̩]　　　　adj. 正式的　　　4th ★★★★★
The high school prom is the first formal social event for most American teenagers.
高中舞會是大部分美國青少年第一個正式的社交晚會。

1168 former [ˈfɔrmɚ]　　　　adj. 先前的　　　4th ★★★★★
Guess who I ran into at Taipei Train Station last Sunday? It's my former boss!
猜猜看我上週日在台北火車站碰到誰，是我以前的老闆！

1169 formidable [ˈfɔrmɪdəbl̩]　　　adj. 傑出的　　　3rd ★★★★★
Professor Lee has a formidable knowledge of economics.
李教授擁有強大的經濟學知識。

1170 formulate [ˈfɔrmjəˌlet]　　　v. 配製　　　4th ★★★★★
This lotion is exclusively formulated with our unique, advanced ingredient that works naturally with your skin.
這款化妝水是由我們獨特先進的原料專門配製，能在你的肌膚上發揮天然的效用。

1171 forthcoming [ˌforθˈkʌmɪŋ]　　adj. 熱心的　　　4th ★★★★★
My niece is not a very forthcoming kind of girl.
我姪女不是個樂於助人的女孩。

1172 fortify [ˈfɔrtəˌfaɪ]　　　v. 堅定　　　3rd ★★★★★
Soldiers' spirits were fortified by their officer's fearlessness.
軍官的勇敢無畏堅定了士兵的士氣。

1173 fortunate [ˈfɔrtʃənɪt]　　　adj. 幸運的　　　4th ★★★★★
We are all very fortunate to have clean water in our homes.
我們很幸運在我們的家園有乾淨的水。

064

1174 fortunately ['fɔrtʃənɪtlɪ]   adv. 幸好   4th ★★★★★
Kyoto has changed a lot because of urban development; fortunately, some old cultural traditions are still preserved.
京都因為都市發展已經改變很多，幸好一些舊有文化傳統仍被保留下來。

1175 fortune ['fɔrtʃən]   n. 財富   4th ★★★★★
Playing the lottery is not a likely way to make a fortune.
玩樂透不是可能致富的方法。

1176 forum ['forəm]   n. 論壇   4th ★★★★★
Online forums can take place on any blog site.
任何博格網站都可開啟線上論壇。

1177 forward ['fɔrwəd]   adv. 向前   4th ★★★★★
After working for such a long time, I really look forward to taking a break.
工作了很長一段時間之後，我真的很期待可以休假。

1178 fossil ['fɑsl]   n. 化石   4th ★★★★★
The museum has a large collection of fossils.
博物館收藏很多化石。

1179 found [faund]   v. 創立   4th ★★★★★
This company was founded in the 60's and has been running successfully since.
這家公司創立於六零年代，從那時候起營運就很成功。

1180 foundation [faun'deʃən]   n. 基礎   4th ★★★★★
This course will provide students with a solid foundation for research. It is highly recommended for those who plan to go to graduate school.
這個課程提供學生紮實的研究基礎，強烈推薦給想唸研究所的學生。

1181 fountain ['fauntɪn]   n. 噴泉   4th ★★★★★
In some stores you can find a water fountain near the bathroom.
在某些商店裡，你可以在化妝室附近找到噴泉式飲水機。

1182 fragile ['frædʒəl]   adj. 易碎的   3rd ★★★★★
Crystal is fragile, but diamond isn't.
水晶易碎，但鑽石不會。

1183 fragment ['frægmənt]   n. 碎片   3rd ★★★★★
The vase dropped down and broke in fragments.
這只花瓶掉下來摔成碎片。

一考就上！考公職一定要會的3000單字

1184 fragrance [ˈfregrəns]　　n.　香味　　4th ★★★★★
Ann enjoyed going to the flower market. She believed that the fragrance of flowers refreshed her mind.
安喜歡逛花店，她覺得花香令她精神亢奮。

1185 framework [ˈfremˌwɝk]　　n.　架構　　4th ★★★★★
If you want to climb up that building you'll need a strong framework.
如果你想爬上那棟建築，你需要堅固的框架。

1186 freedom [ˈfridəm]　　n.　自由　　4th ★★★★★
For Mike, marriage means giving up his freedom.
對麥可而言，婚姻意味著放棄自由。

1187 freeze [friz]　　v.　冷凍　　4th ★★★★★
The policeman pointed a gun at the robber and shouted, "Freeze!"
警察拿槍對準搶匪然後大叫：「不許動！」

1188 frequent [ˈfrikwənt]　　adj.　經常的　　4th ★★★★★
An officer always tries to improve his patrol operation by making frequent stops and making contact with people.
官員藉由頻繁的拜訪以及和人民接觸來改善自己的視察績效。

1189 frequently [ˈfrikwəntlɪ]　　adv.　經常地　　4th ★★★★★
The most frequently used service on the Internet is electronic mail, which is fast and convenient.
網路上最常使用的是電子郵件，既快速又方便。

1190 fresh [frɛʃ]　　adj.　新鮮的　　5th ★★★★★
We couldn't put up with the smell, so we opened the windows to get some fresh air.
我們受不了那個味道，所以開窗想呼吸點新鮮空氣。

1191 friction [ˈfrɪkʃən]　　n.　摩擦　　4th ★★★★★
The mechanic put oil into the process to reduce the friction.
機械工在製造過程中放點油，以減少摩擦。

1192 friendly [ˈfrɛndlɪ]　　adj.　友善的　　5th ★★★★★
The new model of the cell phone is quite user-friendly.
新型手機非常簡單好用。

1193 frown [fraun]　　　　　　**n.** 皺眉　　　4th ★★★★★
We can talk to each other by a smile, a frown, a shrug, or a gesture with our hands.
我們可以藉由微笑、皺眉頭、聳肩或是手勢互相交談。

1194 fruit [frut]　　　　　　**n.** 水果　　　5th ★★★★★
The tropical weather in Taiwan makes it possible to grow various types of fruits such as watermelons, bananas, and pineapples.
台灣的熱帶氣候適合種植各種水果，像是西瓜、香蕉和鳳梨。

1195 frustrate ['frʌsˌtret]　　　　**v.** 挫折　　　4th ★★★★★
I feel so frustrated about not being able to use Japanese to talk to my Japanese friends even after six years of classes.
即使上了六年的課，我仍無法用日語和日本朋友交談，這讓我感到很挫敗。

1196 frustration [ˌfrʌsˈtreʃən]　　　**n.** 挫折　　　4th ★★★★★
A sense of frustration abraded the man who had failed the government tests many times.
這位先生考了很多次公職考試都沒能通過，挫折感使他精疲力竭。

1197 fuel ['fjuəl]　　　　　　**n.** 燃料　　　4th ★★★★★
Biofuels can help fight global warming by producing fewer greenhouse gases than gasoline fuels.
生物燃料可以幫助對抗全球暖化，因為和石油燃料相比，會產生較少的溫室氣體。

1198 fulfill [ful'fɪl]　　　　　**v.** 完成　　　4th ★★★★★
The construction team will fulfill the project ahead of time.
施工隊會提前完成這項工程。

1199 function ['fʌŋkʃən]　　　　**v.** 運作　　　4th ★★★★★
A balanced diet gives the body the nutrients it needs to function properly.
均衡飲食供給身體所需的營養，使身體正常運作。

1200 fund [fʌnd]　　　　　　**v.** 提供基金　　4th ★★★★★
Several alumni-funded scholarships are earmarked for underprivileged students.
這是幾位校友為了貧困學生，特別資助的獎學金。

1201 fundamental [ˌfʌndəˈmɛntḷ]　**adj.** 重要的　　4th ★★★★★
The fundamental principles of a country are usually stated in its constitution.
憲法中經常闡明該國的重要政策。

G

1202 funeral ['fjunərəl]　　　　**n.**　葬禮　　　3rd　★★★★★
No one could help but weep at the funeral.
葬禮上大家都忍不住哭了。

1203 furnish ['fɜnɪʃ]　　　　**v.**　供應　　　3rd　★★★★★
The apartment costs 7000NT per month and comes fully furnished.
公寓每月租金台幣七千元，含全套設備。

1204 furniture ['fɜnɪtʃə]　　　　**n.**　傢俱　　　4th　★★★★★
Maureen would like to go to the furniture store to look for a new couch.
莫林想去傢俱店找一張新的長沙發。

1205 further ['fɜðə]　　　　**adj.**　進一步的　　　5th　★★★★★
For further information, please contact Miss Liu by e-mail.
如需進一步的資訊，請透過電子郵件聯繫劉小姐。

1206 fuss [fʌs]　　　　**n.**　小題大作　　　4th　★★★★★
The newspaper made a big fuss over the news of her marriage.
報紙對她的婚姻報導太小題大作了。

1207 future ['fjutʃə]　　　　**n.**　未來　　　5th　★★★★★
Writing is a very useful skill for students. In the future, they can use it at different workplaces.
寫作對學生而言是非常實用的技能，未來他們可以運用在各種工作場合上。

1208 gain [gen]　　　　**v.**　獲得　　　5th　★★★★★
As a baseball pitcher, Wang Chien-ming gained his international reputation by having nineteen wins within a baseball season.
王建民是一名棒球選手，以一個球季十九勝享譽國際。

1209 gallery ['gælərɪ]　　　　**n.**　美術館　　　4th　★★★★★
Of all the paintings in the gallery, Picasso's work really caught my eye.
美術館所有的畫作中，畢卡索的作品最吸引我的目光。

1210 gangster ['gæŋstə]　　　　**n.**　幫派份子　　　4th　★★★★★
In spite of a very strict gun control law, gangsters still manage to smuggle weapons into Taiwan.
儘管台灣有非常嚴格的槍枝管制條例，幫派份子還是有辦法走私武器進來。

1211 garage [gə'rɑʒ]　　　　**n.**　修車廠　　　5th　★★★★★

My car broke down. I'll have to send it to the garage.
我的車子拋錨了，我得把車送去修車廠。

1212 garbage ['gɑrbɪdʒ]　　　n.　垃圾　　5th ★★★★★
The garbage thrown into the rivers has polluted them so badly that you can hardly find any fish now.
將垃圾丟進河裡使得河水污染相當嚴重，你現在幾乎找不到任何魚類了。

1213 gardening ['gɑrdnɪŋ]　　　n.　園藝　　4th ★★★★★
Not enough people signed up for the gardening class, so it had to be canceled.
報名園藝課程的人數不夠，所以只好取消課程。

1214 gas [gæs]　　　n.　氣體　　3rd ★★★★★
It is well known that the food system is responsible for at least 20 percent of greenhouse gases.
食物系統對於溫室氣體的產生要擔負至少百分之二十的責任，這是眾所皆知的事。

1215 gasp [gæsp]　　　v.　喘氣　　4th ★★★★★
Molly gasped when she found out that her favorite band will come to Taipei.
莫莉得知她最喜歡的樂隊將到台北時，驚訝地倒抽一口氣。

1216 gate [get]　　　n.　登機門　　5th ★★★★★
May I have your attention please? BR Flight 205 to Los Angeles is now boarding at Gate 86B.
各位旅客請注意，飛往洛杉磯的BR 205班機現在開始在86B登機門登機。

1217 gather ['gæðɚ]　　　v.　聚集　　4th ★★★★★
On Christmas Eve, lots of people gathered in the church, singing solemn hymns to pray for world peace.
平安夜裡，許多人聚集在教堂唱著莊嚴的聖歌，祈求世界和平。

1218 gender ['dʒɛndɚ]　　　n.　性別　　4th ★★★★★
Research about learning styles has identified gender differences.
研究顯示學習方式和性別差異有關。

1219 gene [dʒin]　　　n.　基因　　4th ★★★★★
Identical twins have almost all of their genes in common, so any variation between them is in large part due to the effects of the environment.
同卵雙胞胎幾乎擁有相同的基因，所以他們之間的任何差異絕大部分是環境造成的。

1220 generally ['dʒɛnərəlɪ]　　　adv.　一般地　　4th ★★★★★

Generally speaking, the whole family gather together at Chinese New Year's Eve.
一般說來，除夕夜這天全家人會聚在一起。

1221 generate [ˈdʒɛnəˌret]　　　**v.**　產生　　**4th** ★★★★★
An undersea earthquake in the Indian Ocean on December 26, 2006 generated a tsunami that killed over 250,000 people.
二千零六年十二月二十六日，印度洋的一個海底地震引發了海嘯，超過二十五萬人因此喪命。

1222 generation [ˌdʒɛnəˈreʃən]　　**n.**　世代　　**4th** ★★★★★
The next generation wants control over their media instead of being controlled by it.
下個世代的年輕人希望控制媒體，而不是受媒體控制。

1223 generous [ˈdʒɛnərəs]　　**adj.**　慷慨的　　**4th** ★★★★★
Our host for the evening was an extremely generous and caring person.
今晚的主人非常慷慨大方又善解人意。

1224 genetic [dʒəˈnɛtɪk]　　　**adj.**　基因的　　**3rd** ★★★★★
One question that is being debated these days is whether or not genetic engineering (GE) is a good thing.
基因工程是好或壞，最近常被拿來討論。

1225 genius [ˈdʒinjəs]　　　**n.**　天才　　**4th** ★★★★★
People speak very highly of you. It's said that you are a genius with a humble attitude and a great sense of responsibility.
大家都很讚賞你，說你是一位態度謙虛又具高度責任感的才子。

1226 gentle [ˈdʒɛntl̩]　　　**adj.**　溫柔的　　**5th** ★★★★★
The principal gave the poor child a gentle embrace.
校長給這個可憐的孩子一個溫柔的擁抱。

1227 geography [ˈdʒɪˈɑgrəfɪ]　　　**n.**　地理　　**5th** ★★★★★
Let us hope Mike doesn't become a sailor because he couldn't tell the difference between latitude and longitude in our geography class.
希望麥克不會成為一個水手，他上地理課時，連經度和緯度都搞不清楚。

1228 gesture [ˈdʒɛstʃə]　　　**v.**　做手勢　　**5th** ★★★★★
Gesturing is a form of nonverbal communication.
手勢是一種非語言的溝通方式。

1229 ghost [gost]　　　**n.**　鬼　　**5th** ★★★★★

067

Let's light some firecrackers to scare away the ghosts.
讓我們燃放一些鞭炮把鬼嚇跑。

1230 ghostwrite ['gost,raɪt]　　　**v.** 代寫　　~~3rd~~ ★★★★★
Ghostwriting is supposed to be an unfair and illegal action.
代寫是不公平且違法的行為。

1231 giant ['dʒaɪənt]　　　**adj.** 巨大的　　~~5th~~ ★★★★★
The dog dug a large ditch to bury the giant bone.
狗挖了一個大溝把大骨頭埋起來。

1232 gift [gɪft]　　　**n.** 禮物　　~~5th~~ ★★★★★
I never send gift copies to my friends.
我從來沒送過重複的禮物給朋友。

1233 give [gɪv]　　　**v.** 給予　　~~5th~~ ★★★★★
Last summer Lisa had a job in Hawaii giving surfing lessons.
去年夏天麗莎在夏威夷教衝浪。

1234 glance [glæns]　　　**v.** 一瞥　　~~4th~~ ★★★★★
I always glance at the headlines in the morning, but I rarely have time to read the whole newspaper.
早上起床後我總會瞄一眼頭版新聞，卻沒時間看完整份報紙。

1235 glacial ['gleʃəl]　　　**adj.** 冰河的　　~~3rd~~ ★★★★★
In west-central New York State there is a group of eleven long, narrow, glacial lakes known as the Finger Lakes.
中西部的紐約州有十一條又長又窄的冰河湖，即著名的指狀湖系。

1236 glimpse [glɪmps]　　　**n.** 一瞥　　~~3rd~~ ★★★★★
My father usually took a glimpse of the newspaper at breakfast.
我爸通常在早餐時會瞄一下報紙。

1237 global ['globl̩]　　　**adj.** 全球的　　~~4th~~ ★★★★★
Air pollution is a global problem.
空氣污染是個全球性問題。

1238 glory ['glorɪ]　　　**n.** 昌盛　　~~3rd~~ ★★★★★
The glory of the shopping district has considerably departed.
購物區的繁華已不復見。

1239 glow [glo]　　　　　　**v.** 發亮　　　4th ★★★★★
If you turn off the lights, you will be able to see my pen because it glows in the dark.
如果你把燈都關掉，你會看到我的筆，因為它在黑暗中會發光。

1240 glummer ['glʌmə]　　　**n.** 憂鬱者　　　3rd ★★★★★
The glummer committed suicide on a cold winter night.
那個憂鬱的人在寒冷的冬夜裏自殺了。

1241 goal [gol]　　　　　　**n.** 目標　　　5th ★★★★★
The problem of determining the policies that will meet the goals of the people is the greatest problem for every economic system.
每一個經濟體所面臨的最大困難就是要決定符合人民期望的政策。

1242 goods [gudz]　　　　　**n.** 貨物　　　5th ★★★★★
Bargain hunters are people who always look for low-priced goods and take five times as long to do their shopping.
喜歡買便宜貨的人總是尋求低價商品，多花五倍的時間採買。

1243 goodwill ['gud'wɪl]　　　**n.** 親善　　　4th ★★★★★
The famous model became a goodwill envoy for her government.
這位知名模特兒成為自己國家的親善大使。

1244 gorgeous ['gɔrdʒəs]　　　**adj.** 燦爛的　　　4th ★★★★★
The garden is gorgeous with various beautiful plants.
花園裡有各種美麗的植物，很絢麗燦爛。

1245 gossip ['gɑsəp]　　　　**v.** 閒聊　　　4th ★★★★★
I gossip with an old friend of mine for the whole night.
我和老友閒聊一整晚。

1246 government ['gʌvənmənt]　　**n.** 政府　　　4th ★★★★★
The government spent money on a firework display during the New Year's festival.
政府在新年節慶期間花錢施放煙火秀。

1247 gown [gaun]　　　　　**n.** 禮服　　　4th ★★★★★
With some embellishments, the ragged dress was magically turned into a dazzling ball gown.
有了飾品做搭配，原本破破爛爛的洋裝神奇地變成了絢爛耀眼的禮服。

1248 graceful ['gresfəl]　　　**adj.** 得體的　　　4th ★★★★★

068

The driver made a graceful apology to the lady for his carelessness.
司機為他的粗心大意，禮貌的向這位女士道歉。

1249 grade [gred]　　　　　　　　**n.** 等級　　　4th ★★★★★
The factory is in urgent need of lots of high-grade raw materials.
這間工廠急切需要大量的高級原物料。

1250 gradually ['grædʒuəlɪ]　　　**adv.** 逐漸地　　4th ★★★★★
The stray dog is getting used to the new environment gradually.
這隻流浪狗正逐漸適應新環境。

1251 graduation [ˌgrædʒu'eʃən]　　**n.** 畢業　　　4th ★★★★★
In order to promote the importance of English, several universities have decided to set a minimum English proficiency for graduation.
為了提升英語的重要性，已有幾間大學決定設立最低英文能力的畢業門檻。

1252 grain [gren]　　　　　　　　**n.** 穀物　　　5th ★★★★★
Some Asian countries export a large amount of grain to Europe every year.
有些亞洲國家每年會出口大量穀物到歐洲。

1253 grant [grænt]　　　　　　　**n.** 補助金　　4th ★★★★★
The Review Board could be considering discontinuing the grants given to several non-governmental organizations.
審查委員會可能考慮停止撥款給一些非政府組織。

1254 grasp [græsp]　　　　　　　**v.** 理解　　　4th ★★★★★
As a musical, Cats is visually stunning, but it is not always easy to grasp the meanings of the lyrics.
做為一齣音樂劇，「貓」在視覺上令人震撼，但要理解歌詞意義不是那麼容易。

1255 grass [græs]　　　　　　　　**n.** 草地　　　5th ★★★★★
Please don't play sports on the grass here.
不要在這裡的草地玩球。

1256 gratify ['grætə,faɪ]　　　　　**v.** 使喜悅　　3rd ★★★★★
It gratified me to learn that my favorite team won the final this morning.
今天早上我聽到最愛的球隊贏得總決賽，這讓我很開心。

1257 gratitude ['grætə,tjud]　　　**n.** 感謝　　　4th ★★★★★
The temple stages performances of Taiwanese opera every year as an expression of gratitude to the Goddess of Mercy.
每年歌仔戲團為了感謝觀世音菩薩的庇佑，會在廟宇搭台演出。

G

1258 gravity ['grævətɪ]　　n.　重要性　　4th ★★★★★
The lead was not aware of the gravity of the situation and didn't make an immediate decision.
領頭的人沒有察覺到事情的嚴重性，而沒有立即做出決策。

1259 graze [grez]　　v.　吃草　　4th ★★★★★
A herd of cattle are grazing in the field.
一群牛在牧場裡吃草。

1260 greedy ['gridɪ]　　adj.　貪婪的　　4th ★★★★★
Many politicians are greedy for power.
很多政界人士都貪圖權力。

1261 greenhouse ['grin,haus]　　n.　溫室　　4th ★★★★★
The industrialized nations that ratified the Kyoto Protocol pledged to limit the emissions of carbon dioxide and other greenhouse gases to alleviate global warming.
這些工業國家共同簽署京都協議書，承諾限制排放二氧化碳及其他溫室氣體以減緩全球暖化。

1262 greet [grit]　　v.　迎接　　5th ★★★★★
People find more and more often that when people call a business, they are greeted not by a human voice but by a "voice-mail center".
打電話到一家公司時，有越來越多人發現，回應的並非真人的聲音，而是「語音信箱中心」。

1263 gregarious [grɪ'gɛrɪəs]　　adj.　群居的　　3rd ★★★★★
Bees and grasshoppers are gregarious insects.
蜜蜂和蚱蜢是群居昆蟲。

1264 grill [grɪl]　　v.　烤　　5th ★★★★★
Mom is good at grilling or frying beef.
媽媽擅長烤、炸牛肉。

1265 grin [grɪn]　　v.　露齒笑　　3rd ★★★★★
The lovely girl grinned at me the moment I opened the door.
我開門時看見這可愛的女孩對我笑了笑。

1266 grocery ['grosərɪ]　　n.　雜貨　　4th ★★★★★
There is only one grocery store in the neighborhood of my house.
我家附近只有一間雜貨店。

069

1267 ground [graund]　　　　n.　場地　　5th ★★★★★

It is a long journey for many birds that live near the Bering Sea to fly from their feeding grounds to the Kenting National Park.
對棲息在白令海峽附近的鳥群，從原本的覓食區飛往墾丁國家公園是一段漫長的旅途。

1268 group [grup]　　　　n.　一群　　5th ★★★★★

Gypsies are a group of people who do not live in one place.
吉普塞人是一群沒有固定居所的人們。

1269 grow [gro]　　　　v.　生長　　5th ★★★★★

Charlie didn't recognize himself in the mirror after he grew a beard.
查理蓄鬍子後，他幾乎認不出鏡子裡的自己。

1270 grudging ['grʌdʒɪŋ]　　　　adj.　勉強的　　3rd ★★★★★

The chairperson gave a grudging consent on the proposal.
主席勉強答應這項提案。

1271 guarantee [ˌgærən'ti]　　　　n.　保證　　4th ★★★★★

Judicial justice is the foundation of social justice and the guarantee of social equality.
司法正義是社會正義的根本且為社會平等的保障。

1272 guess [ges]　　　　v.　猜　　5th ★★★★★

Does anybody here know the lady's age? I guess she is twenty-one.
在場有誰知道這位女士的年紀？我猜她二十一歲。

1273 guest [gest]　　　　n.　來賓　　5th ★★★★★

The party got louder as more guests arrived.
更多賓客的蒞臨使得派對更加喧嘩。

1274 guilty ['gɪltɪ]　　　　adj.　內疚的　　4th ★★★★★

Steve felt guilty after harming his parents with some harsh words.
史帝夫講了一些苛刻的話傷害父母，之後感到很內疚。

1275 habit ['hæbɪt]　　　　n.　習慣　　5th ★★★★★

Drinking is a habit Peter can't help indulging in.
彼得無法控制自己酗酒的習慣。

1276 habitat ['hæbə,tæt]　　　　n.　棲息地　　4th ★★★★★

Indonesia is a bird paradise, but hundreds of its 366 protected species are

threatened by habitat destruction and illegal activity.
印尼是鳥類天堂，但是三百六十六種保育鳥類受到棲息地遭破壞與非法活動的威脅。

1277 habitual [hə'bɪtʃuəl]　　　adj.　習慣的　　4th ★★★★★

Learning style means a person's natural, habitual, and preferred way of learning.
學習風格是指一個人天生習慣和偏好的學習方法。

1278 hail [hel]　　　v.　招呼　　3rd ★★★★★

After a long day working in the office, Alexander hailed a taxi to take him home.
亞歷山大在辦公室工作一整天後，招了一台計程車回家。

1279 half [hæf]　　　n.　一半　　5th ★★★★★

Half of the members didn't pass the English proficiency test.
一半的成員沒有通過英文能力測驗。

1280 hall [hɔl]　　　n.　大廳　　5th ★★★★★

To celebrate the 50th anniversary, teachers joined forces with parents to prepare the hall for the school play.
為了歡慶五十週年紀念日，老師們結集家長的力量準備學校活動的禮堂。

1281 hallucinate [hə'lusn‚et]　　　v.　出現幻覺　　3rd ★★★★★

After being lost in the sea for six days, John began to hallucinate. He saw things that weren't really there.
在海中迷失六天後，約翰開始出現幻覺。他看見許多並不存在的東西。

1282 halt [hɔlt]　　　v.　停止　　3rd ★★★★★

In April, the government took steps to halt water supplies to swimming pools and car-wash shops due to water shortages.
因應缺水問題，政府在四月採取措施，停止對游泳池和洗車店的供水。

1283 hammer ['hæmə]　　　n.　鐵鎚　　5th ★★★★★

Dad bought a hammer in the hardware store on the way home.
爸爸在回家的路上，到五金行買了支鐵鎚。

1284 handicapped ['hændɪ‚kæpt]　adj.　殘障的　　4th ★★★★★

Although koalas seem quiet, they should not be considered handicapped in racing because they can run as fast as rabbits.
雖然無尾熊看起來很文靜，但可別以為牠們不善於賽跑，牠們可以跑的和兔子一樣快。

1285 handle ['hændḷ]　　　v.　處理　　5th ★★★★★

You handled the situation really well. It's not easy.
你狀況處理的能力很好，這並不容易。

070

1286 handmade [ˈhændˌmed]　　　**adj.** 手工的　　　5th ★★★★★
The bakery is famous for its exotic handmade cookies.
這家店因異國風味的手工餅乾而出名。

1287 hanger [ˈhæŋɚ]　　　**n.** 掛鉤　　　5th ★★★★★
Overhang the coat on the hanger soon after you take it off.
外套脫掉後你要趕快用衣架吊起來。

1288 happen [ˈhæpən]　　　**v.** 發生　　　5th ★★★★★
Do you know anything about the accident which happened on the street yesterday?
關於昨天在街上發生的事故，你知道些什麼嗎？

1289 hard [hɑrd]　　　**adj.** 困難的　　　5th ★★★★★
We all demand silence from time to time, but silence is so hard to find.
有時候我們都需要寧靜，但卻很難有真正的寧靜。

1290 harassment [ˈhærəsmənt]　　　**n.** 騷擾　　　3rd ★★★★★
Sexual harassment is regarded as a serious violation of women's rights.
性騷擾被視為對女性人權的嚴重侵犯。

1291 hardly [ˈhɑrdlɪ]　　　**adv.** 幾乎不　　　5th ★★★★★
Many students could hardly recognize their homeroom teacher in junior high ten years after graduation.
許多學生畢業十年以後，都很難再認出當年國中的班導。

1292 harmful [ˈhɑrmfəl]　　　**adj.** 有害的　　　5th ★★★★★
Processing the plastic can lead to the release of harmful chemical substances into the water contained in the bottles.
塑料加工會使有害的化學物質釋放到瓶裝水裡。

1293 harmony [ˈhɑrmənɪ]　　　**n.** 和諧　　　4th ★★★★★
We hope that there will be no war in the world and that all people live in peace and harmony with each other.
願世界沒有戰爭，所有的人都可以和平共處。

1294 harvest [ˈhɑrvɪst]　　　**n.** 收成　　　4th ★★★★★
Since the orange trees suffered severe damage from a storm in the summer, the farmers are expecting a sharp decline in harvests this winter.
由於夏季的一場暴風雨讓橘子樹遭受嚴重損害，農民預計今年冬天的收成會大幅減少。

一考就上！考公職一定要會的3000單字

1295 hasten ['hesn]　　　**v.**　趕快　　　**4th** ★★★★★

We have to hasten to the station because there's not enough time.
時間不夠了，我們要趕緊趕到車站。

1296 hasty ['hestɪ]　　　**adj.**　匆促的　　　**4th** ★★★★★

Please don't come to a hasly conclusion.
請不要匆忙下定論。

1297 hate [het]　　　**v.**　討厭　　　**5th** ★★★★★

You are not listening. I hate to be interrupted when I'm speaking!
你都沒在聽，我討厭說話的時候被打斷。

1298 haunted ['hɔntɪd]　　　**adj.**　鬧鬼的　　　**4th** ★★★★★

The haunted house seems to be the landmark of the town.
這棟鬼屋似乎是該鎮的地標。

1299 hazardous ['hæzədəs]　　　**adj.**　危險的　　　**4th** ★★★★★

These jobs are less hazardous now because laws have been passed to ensure the reasonable safety of employees.
現在這些工作沒那麼危險了，因為已經通過多項法律，以確保僱員的妥善安全。

1300 head [hɛd]　　　**v.**　進前　　　**5th** ★★★★★

Before heading for the mountains, we need to come up with a thorough plan in case anything happens during the trip.
上山前，我們必須想出一個周密的計畫，以免旅途中有任何事情發生。

1301 headline ['hɛd‚laɪn]　　　**n.**　頭條新聞　　　**4th** ★★★★★

Did you see the headline in today's newspaper?
你有看到今天報紙的頭條新聞嗎？

1302 heal [hɪl]　　　**v.**　治療　　　**4th** ★★★★★

Becky hoped that the doctor could do something to heal her brother.
貝基希望醫生可以想辦法治癒她弟弟。

1303 health [hɛlθ]　　　**n.**　健康　　　**5th** ★★★★★

Lack of sleep is detrimental to your health.
睡眠不足對健康有害。

1304 hearing ['hɪrɪŋ]　　　**n.**　聽力　　　**5th** ★★★★★

People's hearing may be lost if they work for a long time in noisy factories.
如果人們長期在吵雜的工廠工作，他們有可能會喪失聽力。

1305 hearty [ˈhɑrtɪ]　　adj. 熱忱的　　4th ★★★★★
As soon as the manager noticed my presence, she immediately offered me warm coffee and a hearty welcome.
經理一看見我來了，馬上給我一杯熱咖啡和熱忱的歡迎。

1306 heat [hit]　　n. 炎熱　　5th ★★★★★
Since our classroom is not air-conditioned, we have to tolerate the heat during the hot summer days.
我們教室沒有冷氣，只得忍受夏季的炎熱。

1307 heaven [ˈhɛvən]　　n. 天堂　　5th ★★★★★
Muslims believe that the Prophet Muhammad rose to heaven from a rock in Jerusalem.
穆斯林相信先知穆罕默德從耶路撒冷的磐石上升到天堂。

1308 heavy [ˈhɛvɪ]　　adj. 重的　　5th ★★★★★
When typhoons attack Taiwan in summer, they often bring along heavy rains and strong winds.
颱風在夏季侵襲台灣時，常常挾帶豪雨強風。

1309 height [haɪt]　　n. 高度　　5th ★★★★★
In recent years, a craze for height has hit hard in industrializing Asian countries like Taiwan, Hong Kong and China.
近幾年來，對身高的狂熱已經襲捲亞洲的工業化國家，像是台灣、香港、中國。

1310 heir [ɛr]　　n. 繼承人　　3rd ★★★★★
The old man made his stepson his heir.
這位老先生立他的養子為繼承人。

1311 helmet [ˈhɛlmɪt]　　n. 安全帽　　4th ★★★★★
The traffic law requires all motorcyclists to wear helmets.
交通法令規定機車騎士都要戴安全帽。

1312 heredity [həˈrɛdɪtɪ]　　n. 繼承　　3rd ★★★★★
Culture is a social heredity.
文化是一種社會的傳承。

1313 heritage [ˈhɛrətɪdʒ]　　n. 遺產　　3rd ★★★★★
Students should be encouraged to read more classical works of literature; after all, they are the cultural heritage we have inherited from our wise ancestors.
我們應該鼓勵學生多讀一些古典文學作品，畢竟這些作品是傳承祖先智慧的文化遺產。

1314 hero [ˈhɪro]   **n.** 英雄   4th ★★★★★

At 26, Chien-Ming Wang was a national hero in his home country.
王建民在二十六歲那年，成了他家鄉的國家英雄。

1315 heroin [ˈhɛro‚ɪn]   **n.** 海洛英   4th ★★★★★

Nicotine is as addictive as heroin or cocaine
尼古丁和海洛英或古柯鹼一樣容易上癮。

1316 hesitate [ˈhɛzə‚tet]   **v.** 猶豫   4th ★★★★★

When Jack asked Helen to go to the movies with him, she hesitated, but a few minutes later she finally agreed.
傑克一開始約海倫去看電影時，海倫猶豫了一下，但幾分鐘後還是答應了。

1317 hesitation [‚hɛzəˈteʃən]   **n.** 猶豫   4th ★★★★★

The manager resigned without hesitation after he had been offered a better job in another company.
這位經理毫不猶豫的辭職了，因為另一家公司提供他一份更好的工作。

1318 heterodox [ˈhɛtərə‚dɑks]   **adj.** 異端的   3rd ★★★★★

The heterodox sermon is never acceptable in Christianity.
基督教絕對不會接受異端邪說。

1319 hibernate [ˈhaɪbə‚net]   **v.** 避寒   4th ★★★★★

During the winter, some animals hibernate or go into a very deep sleep.
有些動物在冬天會避寒或冬眠。

1320 hide [haɪd]   **v.** 躲   3rd ★★★★★

Hibernating animals usually hide away in a den or a hollow log, for protection and shelter during the cold winter months.
冬眠的動物通常會躲在洞穴或空心的木頭裡，藉此在寒冷的冬天裡得到保護和掩蔽。

1321 hierarchy [ˈhaɪə‚rɑrkɪ]   **n.** 階層   4th ★★★★★

Chinese families are arranged according to a hierarchy of seniority.
中國家庭強調長幼有序。

1322 highlight [ˈhaɪ‚laɪt]   **v.** 強調   4th ★★★★★

In his speech, Dr. Huang presented all the reports about the energy crisis to highlight the need for developing new energy resources.
黃博士在演講時，提出所有和能源危機有關的報告，強調發展新能源的必要性。

1323 hike [haɪk]   v.   健行   5th ★★★★★
The traditional image of summer camp is associated with hiking and campfires.
夏令營一般給人的傳統印象就是健行和營火。

1324 hinder ['hɪndə]   v.   妨礙   4th ★★★★★
Please don't hinder me in my work.
請不要妨礙我工作。

1325 hip [hɪp]   n.   臀部   5th ★★★★★
The policewoman is carrying a gun on her hip.
這位女警把槍放在屁股後面。

1326 hire [haɪr]   v.   雇用   5th ★★★★★
The injured included a security guard hired by the hotel, a Thai flight attendant, and three unidentified Korean guests.
傷者包含一名旅館聘雇的保安、一名泰國空姐，以及三位身份不明的韓國旅客。

1327 historian [hɪs'torɪən]   n.   歷史學家   5th ★★★★★
For many years, sociologists and historians have referred to the United States as social "melting pot."
許多年來，社會學家和歷史學家都稱美國是一個社會大熔爐。

1328 historical [hɪs'tɔrɪk]]   adj.   歷史的   5th ★★★★★
When in Rome, be sure to visit historical relics such as the Colosseum.
到羅馬的時候，別忘了去參觀像是古羅馬圓形劇場等歷史文物。

1329 history ['hɪstərɪ]   n.   歷史   5th ★★★★★
I am reading a history of the Internet. Did you know it began in the 1960's?
我在閱讀有關網路的歷史，你知道網路起源於六零年代嗎？

1330 hit [hɪt]   v.   打擊   3rd ★★★★★
The new medicine is still in experimental stages and will not hit the market until next year.
這項新藥還在實驗階段，明年才會正式上市。

1331 hobby ['hɑbɪ]   n.   嗜好   5th ★★★★★
Reading detective stories is one of Steve's favorite hobbies.
看偵探小說是史帝夫最喜愛的嗜好之一。

1332 hold [hold]   v.   握   5th ★★★★★

H

Among the Beatles' most popular songs was "I Want to Hold Your Hands" and "Hey, Jude".
披頭四最受歡迎的歌曲是「嘿！裘！」和「我想要牽著你的手」。

1333 hole [hol]　　　　　　　**n.** 洞　　　　　5th ★★★★★
Martha needs some thread to fix the hole in her pants.
瑪莎需要一些線來修補她褲子上的破洞。

1334 hollow ['hɑlo]　　　　**adj.** 空洞的　　　4th ★★★★★
I can't believe what Steven says because he has made hollow promises before.
我不相信史帝夫的話，因為他曾做過不實的承諾。

1335 homesick ['hom,sɪk]　　**adj.** 想家的　　　4th ★★★★★
When people go abroad, they usually feel homesick.
人們出國的時候，通常都會想家。

1336 honesty ['ɑnɪstɪ]　　　　**n.** 誠實　　　　5th ★★★★★
The health of society depends on simple virtues like honesty, decency, courage, and public spirits, not on the amount of per capita income.
社會的健康有賴誠實、莊重、勇氣和公德心等簡單的美德，不在於國民平均所得。

1337 honor ['ɑnɚ]　　　　　　**v.** 致敬　　　　4th ★★★★★
There's a shrine on the beach honoring the god of the sea.
海邊有一座向海神致敬的神殿。

1338 honorable ['ɑnərəbl]　　**adj.** 光榮的　　　4th ★★★★★
It is honorable to make a living with my own hands.
靠自己的雙手賺錢是很光榮的。

1339 horrible ['hɔrəbl]　　　　**adj.** 可怕的　　　5th ★★★★★
There was a horrible accident on the road this morning.
今早路上發生一起可怕的意外事故。

1340 hospitable ['hɑspɪtəbl]　　**adj.** 好客的　　　3rd ★★★★★
Dr. Chen is always hospitable to visitors from abroad. He gives them a good impression.
陳博士對外來的訪客總是十分慇勤好客，他給他們很好的印象。

1341 hospital ['hɑspɪtl]　　　**n.** 醫院　　　　5th ★★★★★
Only lying on the sick bed in a hospital do we realize how important health is.
只有當我們躺在醫院的病床上的時候，才了解健康有多重要。

1342 hospitality [ˌhɑspɪ'tælətɪ]　　**n.** 款待　　4th ★★★★★
Afford me the hospitality of your columns.
貴專欄若能刊登拙文，實是萬分榮幸。

1343 host [host]　　**n.** 主辦　　5th ★★★★★
The host city for the Games of the 2012 Olympiad will be the city of London.
2012年的奧運主辦城市將會是倫敦。

1344 hostile ['hɑstɪl]　　**adj.** 敵對的　　4th ★★★★★
China used to have a hostile relationship with that country.
中國跟那個國家曾經是敵對關係。

1345 hostility [hɑs'tɪlətɪ]　　**n.** 敵意　　4th ★★★★★
There is open hostility during the two politicians.
兩位政客之間存著公開的敵意。

1346 hour [aur]　　**n.** 小時　　5th ★★★★★
My manager commutes an hour each way to the factory.
我的經理每天來回各花一小時通勤到工廠。

1347 household ['haus,hold]　　**adj.** 家庭的　　4th ★★★★★
When children are old enough to help with household chores, the assignments tend to depend on gender.
當孩子大到可以幫忙做家事時，分派的工作通常因性別而有所不同。

1348 housework ['haus,wɜk]　　**n.** 家事　　5th ★★★★★
It was such a big house that all the children had to help with the housework.
這間房子實在太大了，所有的孩子都必須幫忙做家事。

1349 huge [hjudʒ]　　**adj.** 巨大的　　5th ★★★★★
The World Wide Web has made a huge impact on modern business and communication.
網際網路對現代商業和通訊有巨大的影響。

1350 human ['hjumən]　　**n.** 人類　　4th ★★★★★
All human beings and animals need air to survive.
人類萬物都必須依賴空氣而活。

1351 humanity [hju'mænətɪ]　　**n.** 全人類　　3rd ★★★★★
Paul thinks that one day all of humanity will be ruled by a single leader.
保羅認為有一天全人類都將被單一領導者所統治。

1352 humble [ˈhʌmbl̩]   **adj.** 謙卑的   4th ★★★★★
Be it ever so humble, there's no place like home.
雖然家裡如此簡陋，卻沒有其他地方能像家一樣。

1353 humid [ˈhjumɪd]   **adj.** 潮濕的   5th ★★★★★
This humid climate is only fit for coffee beans.
這種潮濕的天氣只適合種植咖啡豆。

1354 humiliation [hjuˌmɪlɪˈeʃən]   **n.** 羞辱   3rd ★★★★★
He seems to diminish in size and to be overwhelmed with humiliation.
他的聲望降低，並且被羞辱的不知所措。

1355 hungry [ˈhʌŋgrɪ]   **adj.** 飢餓的   5th ★★★★★
My dog tugs at my pants when he is hungry.
我的狗肚子餓時會猛拉我的褲子。

1356 hunt [hʌnt]   **v.** 打獵   4th ★★★★★
Robots have even taken up hunting in some places.
有些地方甚至利用機器人來打獵。

1357 hurricane [ˈhɝɪˌken]   **n.** 颶風   4th ★★★★★
A huge hurricane struck the island and caused great damage.
強大颶風侵襲島嶼並造成重大損傷。

1358 hurry [ˈhɝɪ]   **v.** 趕快   5th ★★★★★
He had better hurry if he is to make the deadline for submitting his paper.
如果他想在截止日以前把論文交出去的話，他最好趕快。

1359 hurt [hɝt]   **v.** 受傷   5th ★★★★★
The cat stepped on a nail and hurt its paw.
貓咪踩到了一根釘子，傷到牠的腳爪。

1360 hypersensitive   **adj.** 過份敏感的   3rd ★★★★★
[ˈhaɪpɚˈsɛnsətɪv]
Most children can be inattentive, hypersensitive, or impulsive at times.
大部分的孩子有時會漫不經心，過份敏感或太過衝動。

1361 hypothesis [haɪˈpɑθəsɪs]   **n.** 假設   3rd ★★★★★
Scientists usually make several hypotheses before they start to do experiments to test them.
科學家通常在實驗開始之前，會先做出許多假設。

074

1362 iceberg [ˈaɪsˌbɝg]　　　　　**n.** 冰山　　　4th ★★★★★
The iceberg will blockade the sea water from flowing freely.
冰山會阻擋海水自由流動。

1363 ice-breaking　　　　　**adj.** 破冰的　　5th ★★★★★
The minister paid an ice-breaking visit to the country.
部長破冰到該國訪問。

1364 idea [aɪˈdɪə]　　　　　**n.** 主意　　　5th ★★★★★
Nobody thinks the idea will work.
大家都認為這個想法不可行。

1365 ideal [aɪˈdɪəl]　　　　　**adj.** 理想的　5th ★★★★★
One and a half hours is the ideal time to keep museum visitors' eyes and minds sharp, and their feet happy!
參觀博物館的時間以一個半小時最為理想，人們才能保持觀察力和注意力的敏銳度以及雙腿的愉悅舒適。

1366 identical [aɪˈdɛntɪkl]　　　　　**adj.** 一致的　4th ★★★★★
Oliver has an identical twin brother.
奧利佛有個和他一模一樣的雙胞胎兄弟。

1367 identification [aɪˌdɛntəfəˈkeʃən] **n.** 身分證明　4th ★★★★★
From now on, all visitors to the building must show their identification in the lobby.
從現在開始，所有進入這棟建築物的訪客都必須在大廳出示他們的身分證件。

1368 identification card　　　**n.** 身分證　4th ★★★★★
Every citizen in our country should have a citizen identification card.
我們國家的每位公民都有一張身分證。

1369 identify [aɪˈdɛntəˌfaɪ]　　　**v.** 辨認　　4th ★★★★★
We have found some suspects. Can you help us identify the right one?
我們有一些嫌疑犯，你能幫我們辨認出真正的兇手嗎？

1370 identity [aɪˈdɛntətɪ]　　　**n.** 認同　　4th ★★★★★
After moving from China to America, he not only experienced culture shock but also suffered identity crisis.
他從中國搬到美國之後，不僅經歷文化衝擊，也受認同之苦。

1371 idle [ˈaɪdl]　　　　　　**v.** 空轉　　4th ★★★★★

You should turn your car off if it's going to idle for very long.
如果你的汽車要空轉很久，你應該要先熄火。

1372 idol [ˈaɪdl̩]　　　　　　　　n. 偶像　　　4th ★★★★★
The excellent baseball player is a superb idol of his fans.
這位傑出的棒球選手是他球迷心目中的超級偶像。

1373 ignorant [ˈɪgnərənt]　　　adj. 無知的　　4th ★★★★★
The foreigner is ignorant in most of the local traditions in Taiwan.
這個外國人對台灣當地傳統一無所知。

1374 ignore [ɪgˈnor]　　　　　　v. 忽視　　　4th ★★★★★
Mr. Chang always tries to answer all questions from his students. He will not ignore any of them even if they may sound stupid.
張老師總是盡力回答學生所有的問題，即使有些問題聽起來很蠢他也不會忽視。

1375 illegal [ɪˈligl̩]　　　　　　adj. 非法的　　5th ★★★★★
Murder is illegal in all countries.
謀殺在所有國家都是非法的。

1376 illegitimate [ˌɪlɪˈdʒɪtəmɪt]　adj. 非婚生的　3rd ★★★★★
The businessman accepted his illegitimate child and gave him most part of his heritage.
這位商人接受了自己的私生子，並讓他繼承大部分的財產。

1377 illicit [ɪˈlɪsɪt]　　　　　adj. 違法的　　3rd ★★★★★
The illicit distiller was given a suspended sentence.
這位非法的蒸餾酒製造商被處以緩刑。

1378 illiterate [ɪˈlɪtərɪt]　　　adj. 文盲的　　4th ★★★★★
Thanks to the educational refinement, very few people remain illiterate in Taiwan.
多虧教育改良，台灣幾乎沒有人是文盲。

1379 illness [ˈɪlnɪs]　　　　　n. 疾病　　　5th ★★★★★
The receptionist was absent on account of illness.
接待員因為生病所以缺席。

1380 illogical [ɪˈlɑdʒɪkl̩]　　　adj. 不合邏輯的　4th ★★★★★
The conclusion of the essay is not only ambiguous but illogical.
這篇文章的結尾不僅模糊不清，同時也不合邏輯。

075

1381 **ill-tempered** [ˈɪlˈtɛmpəd]　　**adj.** 脾氣不好的　　4th ★★★★★
Sean and his father are both ill-tempered.
尚恩和他父親脾氣都很暴躁。

1382 **illuminate** [ɪˈlumə,net]　　**v.** 照明　　3rd ★★★★★
The Christmas tree was illuminated with a number of small lamps.
聖誕樹上有很多小燈泡做裝飾。

1383 **illusion** [ɪˈljuʒən]　　**n.** 幻覺　　3rd ★★★★★
When a thirsty traveler sees a non-existing pool of water in the desert, he is having an optical illusion.
當一個乾渴的旅者在沙漠裡看到根本不存在的池水時，他看到的是幻覺。

1384 **illustration** [ɪ,lʌsˈtreʃən]　　**n.** 實例　　3rd ★★★★★
Rap's rise and sustained global popularity is a good illustration of how influential youth culture is on youth attitudes and behavior.
青年文化如何對年輕人的態度和行為造成影響，饒舌音樂的崛起和持續的全球普及是一個很好的例子。

1385 **image** [ˈɪmɪdʒ]　　**n.** 影像　　4th ★★★★★
Scott looked at his image in the mirror.
史考特看著他鏡子裡的影像。

1386 **imagination** [ɪ,mædʒəˈneʃən]　　**v.** 想像力　　4th ★★★★★
Harry Potter series is really about the power of imagination.
哈利波特系列書就是關於想像力的最佳見證。

1387 **imagine** [ɪˈmædʒɪn]　　**v.** 想像　　4th ★★★★★
I can't imagine what it would be like to be punched by a boxer.
我無法想像被一名拳擊手猛擊會是怎樣。

1388 **immediate** [ɪˈmidɪɪt]　　**adj.** 立即的　　4th ★★★★★
The company has taken immediate action to deal with the problem.
公司要立即行動來解決問題。

1389 **immediately** [ɪˈmidɪɪtlɪ]　　**adv.** 立刻　　4th ★★★★★
After four attempts, Mike finally passed his driving test and started to drive happily to work immediately.
麥克試了四次之後，終於通過駕照考試，然後立刻開始快樂開車上班。

I

1390 immensely [ɪˈmɛnslɪ]   **adv.** 極大地   3rd ★★★★★
Superstitions vary immensely throughout the world.
迷信在世界各地都不一樣。

1391 immigrate [ˈɪməˌgret]   **v.** 遷移   4th ★★★★★
Yoko's family immigrated to America when she was a baby.
在洋子還是小嬰兒時，全家人移民到美國。

1392 immune [ɪˈmjun]   **adj.** 免疫的   3rd ★★★★★
We must exercise regularly in order to strengthen our immune system, which helps us fight the diseases.
我們要經常運動增強免疫系統，這有助於我們對抗疾病。

1393 immunity [ɪˈmjunətɪ]   **n.** 免除   3rd ★★★★★
The goods from the duty free store is immunity from taxation.
免稅商店的商品無須課稅。

1394 impact [ˈɪmpækt]   **n.** 影響   4th ★★★★★
Computers have made a great impact on our lives. Nowadays almost everyone is using a computer to communicate with other people.
電腦對我們的生活造成了巨大的影響。如今，幾乎每個人都用電腦與他人交流。

1395 impair [ɪmˈpɛr]   **v.** 損傷   3rd ★★★★★
It's obvious that serious pollution will impair our health and environment.
嚴重的汙染明顯地損害我們的健康和環境。

1396 impartial [ɪmˈpɑrʃəl]   **adj.** 無私的   4th ★★★★★
My homeroom teacher is always impartial to all the students.
我的班導對所有學生都很公平。

1397 impatient [ɪmˈpeʃənt]   **adj.** 沒耐心的   5th ★★★★★
The impatient guy feels a little aggressive.
那個不耐煩的傢伙讓人感覺有些咄咄逼人。

1398 impeccable [ɪmˈpɛkəbl̩]   **adj.** 無瑕疵的   3rd ★★★★★
His writing skill is impeccable.
他的寫作技巧無可挑剔。

1399 impecunious [ˌɪmpɪˈkjunɪəs]   **adj.** 貧窮的   3rd ★★★★★
The impecunious candidate dramatically won the election.
這位一文不值的候選人戲劇性地當選。

076

1400 impede [ɪmˈpid]   **v.** 阻礙   3rd ★★★★★
The lack of subsidy will impede the progress of the project.
補助津貼短缺會阻礙計畫的進展。

1401 implement [ˈɪmpləmənt]   **n.** 提供   3rd ★★★★★
The association will implement a variety of sports facilities for members.
該協會將提供會員各種運動設施。

1402 implicit [ɪmˈplɪsɪt]   **adj.** 含蓄的   3rd ★★★★★
The buyer indicated an implicit threat during the negotiation.
談判過程中，買方含蓄的做出威脅。

1403 imply [ɪmˈplaɪ]   **v.** 暗示   4th ★★★★★
It's believed that silence usually implies resistance.
一般認為，沉默通常意味著反抗。

1404 impolite [ˌɪmpəˈlaɪt]   **adj.** 不禮貌的   5th ★★★★★
It's impolite to talk on the cell phone loudly at the restaurant.
在餐廳裡大聲講手機很不禮貌。

1405 import [ɪmˈport]   **v.** 進口   5th ★★★★★
Some countries in Southeast Asia import plenty of used cars from Taiwan.
東南亞的一些國家大量進口台灣的二手車。

1406 important [ɪmˈportnt]   **adj.** 重要的   5th ★★★★★
This is very important. Please pay attention to what I am going to announce.
這非常重要！請注意我將要宣布的事。

1407 impose [ɪmˈpoz]   **v.** 強加於   4th ★★★★★
In the United States, tobacco advertisements are not allowed on TV; likewise, our government imposes a ban on tobacco ads.
在美國，電視禁止播放菸草廣告，我國政府也同樣強行禁止。

1408 impossible [ɪmˈpɑsəbl̩]   **adj.** 不可能的   4th ★★★★★
It is impossible to imagine Paris without its cafés.
沒有咖啡館的巴黎是難以想像的。

1409 impress [ɪmˈprɛs]   **v.** 留下印象   4th ★★★★★
The high school athletes really impressed me with their skill.
那些中學生運動員的技能讓我印象深刻。

1410 impression [ɪmˈprɛʃən]   **n.**   印象   **4th** ★★★★★
The candidate left a favorable impression on the interviewers.
這位應徵者在面試官面前留下良好的印象。

1411 imprison [ɪmˈprɪzn]   **v.**   監禁   **3rd** ★★★★★
The fisherman was imprisoned for smuggling.
漁民因走私入獄。

1412 improve [ɪmˈpruv]   **v.**   改善   **4th** ★★★★★
The city mayor decided to launch a cell-phone etiquette campaign to improve people's cell-phone manners.
市長決定舉辦一個手機禮儀活動以改善人們的手機禮貌。

1413 improvement [ɪmˈpruvmənt]   **n.**   改善   **4th** ★★★★★
We may hope for an improvement in the weather tomorrow.
但願明天天氣會變好。

1414 improvise [ˈɪmprəvaɪz]   **v.**   臨時做   **3rd** ★★★★★
The mountain climber improvised a bandage out of his towel.
登山者臨時用毛巾做成繃帶。

1415 impulse [ˈɪmpʌls]   **n.**   衝動   **3rd** ★★★★★
Jane bought the camera on an impulse.
珍一時衝動買了那台相機。

1416 inaccessible [ˌɪnækˈsɛsəbḷ]   **adj.**   難進入的   **3rd** ★★★★★
So inaccessible is the panda's life in the forest that still very little is known about the reproduction of this animal.
貓熊在樹林裡的生活很難接近，所以這種動物的繁衍仍然少有人知。

1417 inactive [ɪnˈæktɪv]   **adj.**   不活動的   **4th** ★★★★★
There is an inactive volcano near the lake.
湖泊附近有一個休火山。

1418 inappropriate [ˌɪnəˈproprɪɪt]   **adj.**   不適宜的   **4th** ★★★★★
Such behavior is supposed to be inappropriate to the occasion.
在這種場合作出這種行為很不恰當。

1419 inarticulate [ˌɪnɑrˈtɪkjəlɪt]   **adj.**   口齒不清的   **3rd** ★★★★★
Some people will become inarticulate when they are nervous.
有些人緊張的時候會變得口齒不清。

1420 inauguration [ɪnˌɔgjəˈreʃən]　**n.**　就職典禮　3rd　★★★★★
The inauguration of a President of the United States takes place on January 20th.
美國總統就職典禮於一月二十日舉行。

1421 incapacitate [ˌɪnkəˈpæsəˈtet]　**v.**　使無法　3rd　★★★★★
Deter's wound incapacitates him from work.
迪特的傷勢讓他無法上班。

1422 incentive [ɪnˈsɛntɪv]　**n.**　動力　3rd　★★★★★
It was felt that the bonus for increased production would provide an incentive to work overtime.
有人認為產量增加而發給的額外津貼，會給人們想加班的動力。

1423 inch [ɪntʃ]　**n.**　英寸　4th　★★★★★
Some researchers and politicians still hold strong opposition against the liberalization plan of 8-inch wafer fabs to the mainland.
一些研究員和政界人士仍強烈反對將八吋晶圓廠移至中國的解放計劃。

1424 incident [ˈɪnsədnt]　**n.**　事件　3rd　★★★★★
Many important legal documents concerning the tragic incident have now been preserved in the museum.
有關那個悲劇事件的許多重要法律文件，現在都被保存在博物館裡。

1425 incinerate [ɪnˈsɪnəˌret]　**v.**　火化　3rd　★★★★★
Some farmers are used to incinerating branches or grass in the open air.
一些農民習慣露天焚燒樹枝或雜草。

1426 incline [ɪnˈklaɪn]　**v.**　有意　4th　★★★★★
The short message inclined the girl to set off immediately.
這封短訊讓女孩有意即刻動身。

1427 include [ɪnˈklud]　**v.**　包含　4th　★★★★★
Writers often make an outline of the things that they want to include in their story.
作家經常會先寫出他們想要包含在故事裡面的主題大綱。

1428 inclusive [ɪnˈklusɪv]　**adj.**　包含的　5th　★★★★★
The book costs NT$1,200, inclusive of packing and delivery.
這本書加上包裝和運費總共是一千兩百元。

1429 income [ˈɪnˌkʌm]　**n.**　收入　5th　★★★★★

After Mike pays all his bills, he doesn't have much spendable income left.
麥克付完所有帳單之後，他可花用的收入所剩不多。

1430 incompetent [ɪn'kɑmpətənt] **adj.** 不勝任的　4th ★★★★★
The young man is incompetent for managing a trading company.
這個年輕人沒有能力管理一家貿易公司。

1431 incomplete [ˌɪnkəm'plit] **adj.** 不完全的　4th ★★★★★
The Budda statue still remains incomplete.
佛祖雕像尚未完成。

1432 inconsistent [ˌɪnkən'sɪstənt] **adj.** 不一致的　3rd ★★★★★
The guy's actions are inconsistent with his words.
這傢伙言行不一。

1433 incorporate [ɪn'kɔrpə,ret] **v.** 合併　3rd ★★★★★
The engineer incorporated his assumption into the experiment.
工程師將他的假設加入實驗中。

1434 increase [ɪn'kris] **n.** 增加　4th ★★★★★
Sales rose even faster, so the company raised its dividend 10%, the first increase since 2009.
銷售額增長快速，公司因此調高了百分之十的股利，這是自2009年以來的首次成長。

1435 incredible [ɪn'krɛdəbl] **adj.** 不可思議的　4th ★★★★★
Jane never gave up, no matter how bad the situation was. Her tenacity was incredible.
無論情況有多糟糕，珍絕不放棄。她的堅持令人感到不可思議。

1436 independent [ˌɪndɪ'pɛndənt] **adj.** 獨立的　4th ★★★★★
Learning to budget your money is the first lesson you must learn to be independent.
學習獨立的第一堂課就是學習如何控制預算。

1437 index ['ɪndɛks] **n.** 指數　4th ★★★★★
I check the newest index of the stock market every day to see if my portfolio grows larger or smaller.
我每天都會核對最新的股市指數，看看我的投資組合是漲是跌。

1438 indicate ['ɪndə,ket] **v.** 顯示　4th ★★★★★
Many studies indicate that elderly people who have pets live longer than those who do not.
許多研究顯示家中有寵物的老年人比較長壽。

1439 indication [ˌɪndəˈkeʃən]　　n.　跡象　　4th　★★★★★
The gray clouds were an indication that rain was coming.
灰色雲層是快要下雨的徵兆。

1440 indict [ɪnˈdaɪt]　　v.　對⋯起訴　　3rd　★★★★★
The indicted suicide bomber harbored a vehement anti-social inclination and bore a deep-seated grudge against the government.
遭起訴的自殺炸彈客心懷一股強烈的反社會傾向和對政府的深層怨恨。

1441 indifference [ɪnˈdɪfərəns]　　n.　漠不關心　　4th　★★★★★
Some surveys show that increasing proportions of people are dissatisfied with the political system, or indifferent towards it.
許多調查顯示，越來越多的民眾對政治體制感到不滿，甚至漠不關心。

1442 indignant [ɪnˈdɪgnənt]　　adj.　憤慨的　　3rd　★★★★★
I am fiercely indignant at his remarks.
我對他的言論感到極度的憤慨。

1443 indispensable [ˌɪndɪsˈpɛnsəbl̩]　　adj. 不可或缺的　　3rd　★★★★★
The movie cannot run without the lead actress. She is indispensable.
這部電影沒有女主角無法開拍，她是不可或缺的人。

1444 individually [ˌɪndəˈvɪdʒuəlɪ]　　adv.　個別地　　4th　★★★★★
Our English teacher always emphasizes the importance of learning new words in context rather than learning each of them individually.
我們英文老師強調利用文章脈絡來學習新單字的重要性，會比一個個單獨學習來得好。

1445 induce [ɪnˈdjus]　　v.　促使　　3rd　★★★★★
Be sure to ask your doctor whether these pills will induce drowsiness; otherwise you might fall asleep while driving.
記得要問醫生這些藥丸是否會讓你昏昏欲睡，不然你開車時可能會睡著。

1446 indulgence [ɪnˈdʌldʒəns]　　n.　享受　　3rd　★★★★★
Women feel that lipstick is an indulgence, a quick pick-me-up when they can't afford a new outfit or jewelry.
當女人買不起新衣服或首飾時，她們認為口紅是一種能快速振奮心情的享受。

1447 industrial [ɪnˈdʌstrɪəl]　　adj.　工業的　　3rd　★★★★★
Diabetes alone claims on an average around 9% of total health budgets in industrial countries.
在工業化國家中，光是糖尿病平均就需要將近百分之九的醫療總預算。

1448 industrialization [ɪnˌdʌstrɪələ'zeʃən] **n.** 工業化 4th ★★★★★
The author of the novel The Lord of the Rings, Tolkien, witnessed the devastating effects of industrialization and the way in which it changed.
魔戒的作者托爾金目睹了工業化所帶來的毀滅性影響，以及其所帶來的改變。

1449 industry ['ɪndəstrɪ] **n.** 產業 4th ★★★★★
Steve Jobs' unrivaled mastery of technological innovations and aesthetics successfully transformed the landscape of consumer electronics industry.
史提夫賈伯斯對創新技術和美學方面無比的精熟，成功改變了消費性電子業的面貌。

1450 inevitable [ɪn'ɛvətəbḷ] **adj.** 不可避免的 4th ★★★★★
The tides of globalization become ever more inevitable and bring intense competitive pressure to the business leaders.
全球化的浪潮越來越無可避免，也為商界領袖帶來激烈的競爭壓力。

1451 inexhaustible [ˌɪnɪg'zɔstəbḷ] **adj.** 無窮盡的 4th ★★★★★
Light from the sun is practically inexhaustible; in other words, sunlight cannot be used up.
太陽光幾乎是無窮無盡的，也就是說，太陽光不可能會用盡。

1452 infancy ['ɪnfənsɪ] **n.** 初期 4th ★★★★★
Space exploration is still in its infancy.
太空探索還處於初級階段。

1453 infect [ɪn'fɛkt] **v.** 感染 4th ★★★★★
Officials at the Council of Agriculture confirmed that cattle on a southern Taiwan ranch have been infected by foot-and-mouth disease.
農委會官員證實台灣南部農場的牛群已感染口蹄疫。

1454 infection [ɪn'fɛkʃən] **n.** 感染 4th ★★★★★
The disease spreads very fast. Therefore, doctors suggest that everyone should wash hands to prevent infection.
這個疾病傳播的很快，所以醫生建議每個人都要洗手來預防感染。

1455 infectious [ɪn'fɛkʃəs] **adj.** 傳染性的 4th ★★★★★
We are entering a season when a lot of infectious diseases could break out.
我們進入了傳染病流行的季節。

1456 infer [ɪn'fɝ] **v.** 推論 4th ★★★★★
The police inferred the conclusion from the evidence they had found.
警方從已發現的證據推論出結果。

079

1457 inferiority [ɪnfɪrɪˈɑrɪtɪ]　　**n.** 劣等　　4th ★★★★★
His sense of inferiority made him isolated from the public.
他的自卑感使他與大眾脫離。

1458 infinite [ˈɪnfənɪt]　　**adj.** 無限的　　3rd ★★★★★
Body language covers the infinite range of movements, including the palatable ways to smile, to walk, to manipulate your eyes, or to move your hands and arms.
身體語言涵蓋的動作範圍很廣，包括愉快的微笑、走路方式、眼神的操作，或是手和胳膊的動作。

1459 infirm [ɪnˈfɜm]　　**adj.** 不堅定的　　4th ★★★★★
Cheer up! Don't be infirm of purpose.
振作起來！不要優柔寡斷！

1460 inflame [ɪnˈflem]　　**v.** 使憤怒　　4th ★★★★★
The lecturer's rude expressions inflamed the audience.
講師無禮的言詞激怒了觀眾。

1461 inflate [ɪnˈflet]　　**v.** 使膨脹　　4th ★★★★★
Children are inflating balloons to decorate their classroom.
孩子把氣球充氣來裝飾教室。

1462 inflation [ɪnˈfleʃən]　　**n.** 通貨膨脹　　4th ★★★★★
Due to inflation, prices for daily necessities have gone up and we have to pay more for the same items now.
因為通貨膨脹的關係，日常必需品的價錢上漲，同樣的商品我們現在得付更多錢了。

1463 influence [ˈɪnfluəns]　　**n.** 影響　　4th ★★★★★
Tides are caused by the influence of the moon and the sun.
潮汐的發生是受月亮和太陽的影響。

1464 influential [ˌɪnfluˈɛnʃəl]　　**adj.** 有影響力的　　4th ★★★★★
Those clues are influential in investigating the case.
這些線索對此案的調查有很大的影響。

1465 inform [ɪnˈfɔrm]　　**v.** 通知　　4th ★★★★★
Bella informed her fiancé of her safe arrival at the airport.
貝拉告知未婚夫說她已安全抵達機場。

1466 information [ˌɪnfɚˈmeʃən]　　**n.** 資訊　　5th ★★★★★

Computers can store large amounts of information.
電腦可以儲存大量的資訊。

1467 informative [ɪnˈfɔrmətɪv]   **adj.** 教育性的   4th ★★★★★
The report is informative. It can help you to have a better understanding of the current issues.
這篇報導具有教育意義，能幫助民眾對當前議題有更深入的了解。

1468 ingratiat [ɪnˈgreʃ͟ɪ͟ͅet]   **v.** 討好   3rd ★★★★★
The clerk intends to take an ingratiating attitude to her customers.
店員打算討好她的顧客。

1469 ingredient [ɪnˈgridɪənt]   **n.** 成分   4th ★★★★★
We're going to need a large basin to mix the ingredients for the cake.
我們需要一個大盆子來攪拌原料做蛋糕。

1470 inhabit [ɪnˈhæbɪt]   **v.** 棲息   4th ★★★★★
A variety of fresh water fish inhabit in the river.
這條河有很多種淡水魚棲息。

1471 inhabitant [ɪnˈhæbətənt]   **n.** 居民   4th ★★★★★
Some people say that the best way to learn another language is to go to the country where that language is spoken by its native inhabitants.
有些人說學習其他語言最好的方法，就是到該語言為母語的國家。

1472 inherit [ɪnˈhɛrɪt]   **v.** 遺傳   4th ★★★★★
There are studies to indicate that the tendency toward shyness may be inherited.
有研究指出，害羞的傾向可能是遺傳而來的。

1473 initially [ɪˈnɪʃəlɪ]   **adv.** 一開始   4th ★★★★★
The conference was initially scheduled to take place on August 8th, but due to the typhoon, it was canceled at the last minute.
會議原本計畫在八月八號舉行，但因為颱風的關係臨時取消了。

1474 initiative [ɪˈnɪʃətɪv]   **n.** 主動權   4th ★★★★★
Do not just sit and wait passively for a good chance to come to you. You have to take the initiative and create chances for yourself.
不要只是坐在那裡被動地等待好運找上門，你要主動為自己創造機會。

1475 injure [ˈɪndʒɚ]   **v.** 受傷   4th ★★★★★
The injured in the car accident were taken to the hospital by ambulances.
車禍的傷患被救護車送去醫院了。

080

1476 injury [ˈɪndʒərɪ]　　　　**n.** 受傷　　　**4th** ★★★★★
Rocky fell off his bike but he only received a minor injury.
洛基從他的自行車跌下來，但只受到輕傷。

1477 innocent [ˈɪnəsnt]　　　　**adj.** 清白的　　**3rd** ★★★★★
Every citizen has the right to be held innocent in all criminal cases, unless proved otherwise.
所有刑事案件中，每位公民都有權維持自己的清白，除非有其他證明並非如此。

1478 innovation [ˌɪnəˈveʃən]　　　**n.** 發明　　　**4th** ★★★★★
The top innovation, the Web, was created by British software consultant Tim Berners-Lee.
網路這頂尖的發明，是由一位英國軟體顧問Tim Berners-Lee所創造的。

1479 innovative [ˈɪnoˌvetɪv]　　　**adj.** 創新的　　**4th** ★★★★★
The new computer game Wii provides us with an innovative way of exercising. People now may play sports in their living rooms, which was unimaginable before.
Wii這款新電玩提供我們新穎的玩法。人們現在可以在客廳做運動，這在以前真是想像不到的。

1480 input [ˈɪnˌput]　　　　**v.** 輸入　　　**5th** ★★★★★
Listening is a skill to input sounds.
聽是一種聲音輸入的能力。

1481 inquisitive [ɪnˈkwɪzɪtɪv]　　　**adj.** 好問的　　**3rd** ★★★★★
The little boy is very inquisitive. He is interested in a lot of different things and always wants to find out more about them.
這個小男孩很愛發問。他對很不同的事情都很感興趣，而且總是想更深入了解。

1482 inscription [ɪnˈskrɪpʃən]　　　**n.** 碑文　　　**3rd** ★★★★★
Read the inscription on this stone. This building is now over 500 years old.
讀一讀石頭上的碑文，這座建築物已經有五百年的歷史了。

1483 insemination [ɪnˌsɛməˈneʃən]　**n.** 受孕　　　**3rd** ★★★★★
Aided by artificial insemination, Adriana Iliescu gave birth when she was 66 years old and became the oldest woman on record to give birth.
借助人工受精，Adriana Iliescu在六十六歲產子，創下最高齡生子的紀錄。

1484 insert [ɪnˈsɝt]　　　　**v.** 植入　　　**3rd** ★★★★★
Genetically modified foods are crops which are inserted with a gene from another species so that they will have certain features of that species.
基因改造食品是在作物中植入其他品種的基因，因此會含有該品種的某些特徵。

1485 inside ['ɪn'saɪd]   **adj.** 內部的   **5th** ★★★★★
The strong wind blew my umbrella inside out.
這道強風吹得我雨傘開花。

1486 insist [ɪn'sɪst]   **v.** 堅持   **4th** ★★★★★
The government insisted that seven cable TV channels shutting down for their programs were not good enough.
政府堅持將這七家有線電視頻道勒令停工，因為他們的節目都不夠優良。

1487 insomnia [ɪn'sɑmnɪə]   **n.** 失眠   **4th** ★★★★★
Jeffery refused to join his friends in a midnight cup of coffee because he was afraid it would give him insomnia.
傑佛瑞拒絕參加他朋友的深夜咖啡聚會，因為他怕會失眠。

1488 insomniac [ɪn'sɑmnɪæk]   **n.** 失眠患者   **3rd** ★★★★★
Insomniacs are those people who need to lie in the morning to catch up on lost sleep.
失眠的人早上需要躺在床上以補足喪失的睡眠。

1489 inspect [ɪn'spɛkt]   **v.** 檢查   **4th** ★★★★★
The water company inspects the pipelines and monitors the water supply regularly to ensure the safety of our drinking water.
自來水公司定期檢查管線和監測供水，以確保我們的飲用水的安全。

1490 inspection [ɪn'spɛkʃən]   **n.** 檢查   **4th** ★★★★★
An inspection of the balcony indicated no leaks.
檢查陽台發現沒裂縫。

1491 inspiration [ˌɪnspə'reʃən]   **n.** 靈感   **4th** ★★★★★
I just learned that Tivoli Gardens in Copenhagen, Denmark was the inspiration for the original Disneyland in L. A., California.
我剛剛才知道丹麥哥本哈根的蒂沃利花園，其靈感是來自加州迪士尼樂園的原型。

1492 inspire [ɪn'spaɪr]   **v.** 鼓舞   **4th** ★★★★★
The principal's example inspired a lot of young students to study hard.
校長的典範激勵很多年輕學子努力用功。

1493 instead [ɪn'stɛd]   **adv.** 卻   **4th** ★★★★★
I asked for a cheese cake but was given an apple pie instead.
我要的是起司蛋糕，但卻拿到蘋果派。

1494 instant ['ɪnstənt]　　　**adj.**　速食的　　4th ★★★★★
It's not good for our health to eat instant noodles every day.
天天吃泡麵對我們的健康不好。

1495 instinct ['ɪnstɪŋkt]　　　**n.**　本能　　4th ★★★★★
Each of the animals has the instinct of self-preservation.
每個動物都有自我保護的本能。

1496 institute ['ɪnstətjut]　　　**v.**　著手　　4th ★★★★★
The policeman instituted a search of the apartment building.
警察著手搜查一棟公寓大樓。

1497 institution [ˌɪnstə'tjuʃən]　　　**n.**　機構　　4th ★★★★★
Greenpeace, which aims to protect the environment, is an international institution.
綠色和平組織是一個國際性的機構，機構主旨是要保護環境。

1498 instructor [ɪn'strʌktə]　　　**n.**　講師　　4th ★★★★★
You should visit the instructor during the office hours to ask more questions.
你應該在講師的辦公時間去找他，問他更多問題。

1499 instruction [ɪn'strʌkʃən]　　　**n.**　教育　　4th ★★★★★
Most children receive instruction in English from the third grade at school.
大部分的英國小孩從小學三年級開始學習英語。

1500 instrument ['ɪnstrəmənt]　　　**n.**　儀器　　4th ★★★★★
When sailors want to find their position on the map, they use special instrument.
當水手想從地圖上找到自己的位置時，他們會用特別的儀器。

1501 insult ['ɪnsʌlt]　　　**n.**　侮辱　　3rd ★★★★★
To many people, verbal insults can be more hurtful and damaging than non-verbal or physical ones.
對很多人來說，言語上的侮辱比非言語或身體上的侮辱更傷人。

1502 insurance [ɪn'ʃurəns]　　　**n.**　保險　　4th ★★★★★
This firm specializes in selling insurance.
這間公司專門販賣保險。

1503 integrity [ɪn'tɛgrətɪ]　　　**n.**　正直　　3rd ★★★★★
People believed in the integrity of the judge, so they were shocked to hear that he was involved in the bribery scandal.
人們相信法官的正直，所以當他們得知他捲入賄選醜聞時非常震驚。

1504 intellectual [ˌɪntl̩ˈɛktʃuəl]　　**adj.** 智慧的　　4th ★★★★★
Although the intellectual property right is to be protected by law, the fans may think otherwise.
雖然法律保障智慧財產權，但歌迷們可不這麼想。

1505 intelligence [ɪnˈtɛlədʒəns]　　**n.** 智力　　4th ★★★★★
Many researchers have been interested in whether or not an individual's birth order has an effect on intelligence.
個體的出生順序是否會對其智力造成影響，研究人員對此一直很感興趣。

1506 intelligent [ɪnˈtɛlədʒənt]　　**adj.** 聰明的　　4th ★★★★★
Linda is the most intelligent among the students in her class.
琳達是班上所有學生中最聰明的。

1507 intense [ɪnˈtɛns]　　**adj.** 緊張的　　4th ★★★★★
Alice invariably experiences intense anxiety right before taking an important exam.
大考開始之前，愛麗絲總會感到極度焦慮。

1508 intend [ɪnˈtɛnd]　　**v.** 打算　　4th ★★★★★
Steven intends to buy a new house, so he needs to get a mortgage loan.
史帝夫想要買一棟新房子，因此他需要申請貸款。

1509 intensify [ɪnˈtɛnsəˌfaɪ]　　**v.** 加劇　　4th ★★★★★
The landslide in some mountainous areas has intensified in the last few years.
過去幾年中，一些山區的土石流已經加劇。

1510 intention [ɪnˈtɛnʃən]　　**n.** 意圖　　4th ★★★★★
Despite his intention to be on time, he is always late.
雖然他想要準時，但他總是遲到。

1511 intensive [ɪnˈtɛnsɪv]　　**adj.** 密集的　　4th ★★★★★
Avoid eating red meat and dairy products, which are the most emission-intensive foods.
我們要避吃紅肉和乳製品，這些都是碳排量最大的食物。

1512 intensively [ɪnˈtɛnsɪvlɪ]　　**adv.** 徹底地　　4th ★★★★★
The baby polar bear is being intensively studied by the scientists. Every move he makes is carefully observed and documented.
科學家正深入研究北極熊寶寶。它的每個動作都受到仔細的觀察和記錄。

082

1513 interact [ˌɪntəˈrækt]　　v.　互動　　**4th** ★★★★★
John is an experienced salesperson. Just observe closely how he interacts with customers and do likewise.
約翰是位經驗豐富的銷售員，只要仔細觀察他和客戶的互動並照做就可以了。

1514 interest [ˈɪntərɪst]　　n.　興趣　　**4th** ★★★★★
The key players in the energy market, requiring heavy capital investment, have little interest in innovation.
能源市場的主要投資者對創新開發興趣缺缺，因為所需投入的資金太龐大。

1515 interfere [ˌɪntəˈfɪr]　　v.　干擾　　**4th** ★★★★★
In Taiwan, using electronic devices is prohibited on domestic flights because it interferes with the communication between the pilots and the control tower.
台灣的國內航班禁止使用電子裝置，因為會干擾機師和塔臺間的通訊。

1516 international [ˌɪntəˈnæʃənl]　**adj.**　國際的　　**5th** ★★★★★
By visiting international websites, we can have direct contact with the whole world.
我們可以藉著上國外網站，直接和整個世界接觸。

1517 Internet [ˈɪntəˌnɛt]　　n.　網際網路　　**5th** ★★★★★
Unlike his classmates who stop by Internet cafes very often, John always goes home directly after school.
約翰和其他經常流連網咖的同學不一樣，他放學後總是直接回家。

1518 internship [ˈɪntɜnˌʃɪp]　　n.　實習　　**3rd** ★★★★★
In North America, the first year of resident hospital training has been known as an internship.
在北美，第一年的住院醫生培訓就叫做實習。

1519 interpret [ɪnˈtɜprɪt]　　v.　理解　　**4th** ★★★★★
It's difficult to interpret what people are saying when their mouths are full.
嘴巴塞滿東西時，很難理解人們在說些甚麼。

1520 interrogation [ɪnˌtɛrəˈgeʃən]　n.　訊問　　**3rd** ★★★★★
May I have my lawyer with me during the interrogation?
問訊時我可以帶律師嗎？

1521 intervention [ˌɪntəˈvɛnʃən]　　n.　干擾　　**3rd** ★★★★★
The professors undertook a collaborative project to establish a master's degree program in Early Childhood Intervention.
教授著手一項合作計畫，其內容是要開設一門有關幼兒干預的碩士課程。

1522 interview [ˈɪntəˌvju]　　　n.　面談　　5th ★★★★★
Charlie had to field some difficult questions in his interview.
查理必須在面試時巧妙答覆一些困難問題。

1523 intimate [ˈɪntəmɪt]　　　adj.　親密的　　3rd ★★★★★
The young couple sharing an intimate moment thought that no one was looking.
這對分享親密時刻的年輕夫婦以為沒有人在看。

1524 intolerant [ɪnˈtɑlərənt]　　　adj.　偏執的　　3rd ★★★★★
Some people can't stand intolerant people.
有些人受不了偏激的人。

1525 intonation [ˌɪntoˈneʃən]　　　n.　聲調　　4th ★★★★★
I can't make the intonation of my voice match a musical instrument.
我無法使我聲音的音調配合樂器。

1526 intrigue [ɪnˈtrig]　　　v.　激起好奇　　4th ★★★★★
The ancient Greek word for curls and locks is related to intriguing and tempting someone.
古希臘文字中，「捲」和「鎖」分別與激起某人好奇心和誘惑某人有關。

1527 introduce [ˌɪntrəˈdjus]　　　v.　引進　　5th ★★★★★
The Flight Safety Foundation has introduced from abroad the bird-dispersing equipment.
飛行安全基金會從國外引進可以驅散鳥群的設備。

1528 introduction [ˌɪntrəˈdʌkʃən]　　　n.　引入　　5th ★★★★★
The introduction of maize, or corn, from America has changed the cuisines of Europe very quickly.
美國引入的玉蜀黍或玉米，快速的改變了歐洲的飲食。

1529 intuitive [ɪnˈtjuɪtɪv]　　　adj.　直覺的　　3rd ★★★★★
The boy cried out from his intuitive response.
小男孩出於直覺反應放聲大哭。

1530 invaluable [ɪnˈvæljəb!]　　　adj.　無價的　　4th ★★★★★
Football is more than a sport; it is also an invaluable teacher.
足球不只是一項運動，更是一位無價的老師。

1531 invalid [ɪnˈvælɪd]　　　adj.　無效的　　3rd ★★★★★

083

Your permit to stay in Taiwan will be invalid by the end of this month.
你在台灣的居留證，有效期限是這個月的月底。

1532 invasion [ɪn've ʒən]　　　　　　**n.**　入侵　　　　3rd ★★★★★
The barbarians made an invasion upon the castle on the hilltop.
野蠻人入侵山頂上的城堡。

1533 invention [ɪn'vɛnʃən]　　　　　　**n.**　發明　　　　5th ★★★★★
Since the invention of the Internet, many people have predicted a paperless society.
自從網路發明了以後，許多人已經開始預測將來是無紙化的社會。

1534 inventory ['ɪnvən‚torɪ]　　　　　　**n.**　庫存　　　　5th ★★★★★
All branch stores are required to fill out the inventory report to check if there is enough merchandise on shelf and in stock.
所有分店都要填寫庫存報表，以檢查架上和倉庫的商品是否足夠。

1535 invest [ɪn'vɛst]　　　　　　**v.**　投資　　　　4th ★★★★★
It was unwise of him to invest all his money in stocks. He should have saved some in the bank.
他把所有錢投資在股票實在很不明智，應該在銀行存些錢。

1536 investment [ɪn'vɛstmənt]　　　　　　**n.**　投資　　　　4th ★★★★★
A country's financial infrastructure is an essential factor in investment evaluation.
一國的金融基礎建設是投資評估的重要因素。

1537 investigate [ɪn'vɛstə‚get]　　　　　　**v.**　調查　　　　4th ★★★★★
The authorities have chosen a group of smart detectives to set up a commission to investigate the murders that have caused social insecurity.
有關當局已經選定一批幹練的偵探組成委員會，調查造成社會不安的謀殺案。

1538 investigation [ɪn‚vɛstə'geʃən]　**n.**　調查　　　　4th ★★★★★
The motorcyclist was stopped by a policeman for a regular investigation.
警察將機車騎士攔下來做例行檢查。

1539 invisible [ɪn'vɪzəb]]　　　　　　**adj.**　看不見的　　　　4th ★★★★★
In the winter time, it is very common to see people killed by invisible gases due to the mishandling of their heater.
冬天的時候，普遍可見人們不當使用熱水器，而死於無形瓦斯外洩的事件。

1540 invitation [‚ɪnvə'teʃən]　　　　　　**n.**　邀請卡　　　　4th ★★★★★

Did everyone receive the wedding invitation?
每個人都收到喜帖了嗎？

1541 involve [ɪn'vɑlv]　　　　v.　涉及　　4th ★★★★★
The plot of most books involves a love story.
大多數書籍的情節都和愛情故事有關。

1542 Irish ['aɪrɪʃ]　　　　n.　愛爾蘭人　　3rd ★★★★★
The Irish have many different ways to describe a green landscape.
愛爾蘭人有許多不同的方法來描述一個綠色景觀。

1543 irrational [ɪ'ræʃənl]　　　adj.　無理性的　　4th ★★★★★
The supervisor became irrational with rage.
主管憤怒到失去理智。

1544 irresponsible [ˌɪrɪ'spɑnsəbl]　adj.　不負責的　　4th ★★★★★
It's irresponsible of you not to turn off the air-conditioner.
你沒有關掉空調真的很不負責。

1545 irreversible [ˌɪrɪ'vɜsəbl]　　adj.　不可逆的　　3rd ★★★★★
Finally, the chairperson made an irreversible decision.
主席最後做了一個無法更改的決定。

1546 irrevocable [ɪ'rɛvəkəbl]　　adj.　不可改變的　　3rd ★★★★★
The irrevocable promise reminds Tom to struggle constantly.
不能改變的承諾提醒湯姆要不斷努力。

1547 irritation [ˌɪrə'teʃən]　　　n.　生氣　　4th ★★★★★
The customer stared at the clerk in irritation.
顧客憤怒的盯著員工。

1548 island ['aɪlənd]　　　　n.　島嶼　　5th ★★★★★
Tom taught himself to spear fish while he was alone on the island.
湯姆獨自在島上期間，學會用矛刺捕水中的魚。

1549 isolation [ˌaɪs'leʃən]　　　n.　隔離　　3rd ★★★★★
Schizophrenia is a kind of syndrome caused partially by utter isolation from the outside world.
精神分裂症一部分是由於與外界完全隔離而造成的症候群。

084

J

1550 itchy ['ɪtʃɪ]   adj.   癢的   4th   ★★★★★
The girl felt itchy after she walked through the woods.
女孩走出樹林後覺得身體發癢。

1551 itinerary [aɪ'tɪnəˌrɛrɪ]   n.   行程   4th   ★★★★★
Our itinerary for tomorrow says we are to meet at 8:00 a.m. for breakfast.
我們明天的行程是早上八點碰面一起吃早餐。

1552 jealous ['dʒɛləs]   adj.   嫉妒的   5th   ★★★★★
Don't be jealous of my marks. You can do well, too.
不要羨慕我的成績，你也可以做得很好。

1553 jeopardize ['dʒɛpədˌaɪs]   v.   危害   3rd   ★★★★★
The government officials say that pollution could jeopardize our economic resources.
政府官員說污染會危害我們的經濟資源。

1554 jewelry ['dʒuəlrɪ]   n.   珠寶   4th   ★★★★★
They lost all their money and jewelry. The thief was believed to have entered through an unlocked window.
他們遺失了所有的錢和珠寶，小偷據信是從沒上鎖的窗戶進來的。

1555 jockey ['dʒɑkɪ]   n.   操作者   3rd   ★★★★★
A study indicates that most disc jockeys in dance clubs have lost part of their hearing.
一項研究指出，大部分在舞廳當DJ的人，都已喪失部份的聽力。

1556 join [dʒɔɪn]   v.   加入   5th   ★★★★★
Most young men in Taiwan join the army after they finish college.
台灣大部分的男生在大學畢業後就要去當兵。

1557 joke [dʒok]   v.   開玩笑   3rd   ★★★★★
Don't take what he said seriously. He was only joking.
不要把他說的話看得太嚴重，他只是在開玩笑。

1558 journal ['dʒɝnl]   n.   期刊   4th   ★★★★★
Michelle often reviews research papers for one of the top journals in comparative genetics.
米雪兒經常在一個頂尖的比較遺傳學期刊上，對他人的論文做出評論。

1559 journalist ['dʒɝnəlɪst]　　n.　記者　4th ★★★★★
Many journalists do not ascertain whether or not it is appropriate to interview that little girl during a tragic event for she is too young to understand the trauma.
那個小女孩因為年紀太小，無法了解自己所遭受的內心創傷，很多記者不確定在這期間採訪經歷悲劇事件的小孩是否妥當。

1560 journey ['dʒɝnɪ]　　n.　旅行　5th ★★★★★
Some animals have the ability to find their way home after making distant journeys.
有些動物到很遠的地方旅行後，還有能力找到回家的路。

1561 judge [dʒʌdʒ]　　v.　判斷　3rd ★★★★★
We can judge the success of your scheme only by taking into account the financial benefits over the next few years.
只考慮未來幾年的經濟獲利，我們就可以判斷你的計畫會成功。

1562 judgment ['dʒʌdʒmənt]　　n.　判斷　3rd ★★★★★
The course is for the students to learn to make sound judgments so that they can differentiate between fact and opinion without difficulty.
本課程是為了讓學生學習做出正確判斷，如此一來他們才能毫無困難地分辨事實和見解的不同。

1563 jury ['dʒurɪ]　　n.　陪審團　4th ★★★★★
The jury reached a verdict of "Not guilty."
陪審團判決無罪。

1564 justice ['dʒʌstɪs]　　n.　正義　4th ★★★★★
The smuggler was brought to justice.
走私者被繩之以法。

1565 justify ['dʒʌstə,faɪ]　　v.　辯護　4th ★★★★★
No argument can justify a war.
沒有任何言論可以替戰爭辯護。

1566 karate [kə'rɑtɪ]　　n.　空手道　4th ★★★★★
Karate is a good sport. It builds strength and confidence.
空手道是個好運動，可以鍛鍊力量和自信。

1567 keen [kin]　　adj.　渴望的　4th ★★★★★
My sister is very keen on keeping up with the current fashions.
我妹妹很渴望能趕上最新的時尚潮流。

085

1568 keyboard [ˈkiˌbord]　　　　**n.** 鍵盤　　3rd ★★★★★

In the future, the way we communicate with computers is very likely to change. We won't be mindlessly typing on keyboards but speaking to them.
未來我們和電腦互動的方式很可能會改變，不必費心在鍵盤上打字，而是直接說話。

1569 kidnap [ˈkɪdnæp]　　　　**v.** 綁架　　3rd ★★★★★

They demanded a huge ransom for the return of the little girl whom they had kidnapped.
他們綁架小女孩，並要求巨額贖金做為交換條件。

1570 kinship [ˈkɪnʃɪp]　　　　**n.** 親屬關係　　3rd ★★★★★

Loyalty, or an unspoken agreement to remain faithful and supportive, is more often expected in friendship than in kinship.
比起親情，我們更期待友情的忠誠，或那種對彼此心照不宣的忠貞和扶持。

1571 knife [naɪf]　　　　**n.** 刀子　　5th ★★★★★

Kevin asked his wife if she had any bandages, for he had just sliced his finger with a knife.
凱文問他太太有沒有繃帶，因為他剛剛被刀子劃傷手指。

1572 knit [nɪt]　　　　**v.** 編織　　4th ★★★★★

My grandmother knits me a new sweater every year for my birthday.
我祖母每年編織一件新毛衣祝賀我生日。

1573 knock [nɑk]　　　　**v.** 敲擊　　4th ★★★★★

Someone is knocking on the door. Would you please check it out for me?
有人在敲門，你可以幫我看看是誰嗎？

1574 knowledge [ˈnɑlɪdʒ]　　　　**n.** 知識　　5th ★★★★★

More and more students realize that with a good knowledge of English, they will have more opportunities to find a good job.
越來越多的學生了解到如果有紮實的英文知識，他們找到好工作的機會就越多。

1575 known [non]　　　　**adj.** 有名的　　3rd ★★★★★

She was one of the best known singers of her day.
她是她那個年代最知名的歌手之一。

1576 knuckle [ˈnkl]　　　　**n.** 關節　　5th ★★★★★

He cracked his knuckles as he tried to control his anger.
他把指關節弄的喀喀作響，試圖控制自己的憤怒。

1577 koala [koˈɑlə]   **n.** 無尾熊   5th ★★★★★
That little girl carries her toy koala everywhere she goes.
那個小女孩無論去任何地方都帶著她的玩具無尾熊。

1578 Korean [koˈriən]   **n.** 韓語   4th ★★★★★
More and more people in Taiwan are learning Korean now.
越來越多的台灣人現在正在學習韓語。

1579 label [ˈlebl̩]   **n.** 標籤   4th ★★★★★
The labels on your clothing are worth reading. They tell you what your clothing is made of.
衣服上的標籤值得一讀，上面會告訴你這件衣服的成份為何。

1580 labor [ˈlebɚ]   **v.** 勞動   5th ★★★★★
He labored five years on his essay.
他足足花了五年寫那篇論文。

1581 laboratory [ˈlæbrəˌtorɪ]   **n.** 實驗室   5th ★★★★★
The students learned chemistry in the laboratory.
學生們在實驗室學習化學。

1582 land [lænd]   **v.** 著地   5th ★★★★★
The plane developed engine trouble shortly after take-off and had to make an emergency landing.
這架飛機在起飛不久之後引擎發生故障，必須採取緊急迫降。

1583 landfill [ˈlændfɪl]   **n.** 垃圾掩埋場   3rd ★★★★★
According to one research, 90% of the bottles used are not recycled and lie for ages in landfills.
根據一項調查顯示，百分之九十用過的瓶瓶罐罐都沒回收，而是長年堆積在垃圾掩埋場。

1584 landlocked [ˈlændˌlɑkt]   **adj.** 內陸的   3rd ★★★★★
The oil of the landlocked country does not flow easily as it is left isolated from global markets.
內陸國家的石油在全球市場上的流動率不高，因為被孤立住了。

1585 landlord [ˈlændˌlɔrd]   **n.** 房東   3rd ★★★★★
I was upset about the condition of my apartment, so I made a complaint to my landlord.
我對公寓的屋況不是很高興，所以我向房東抱怨了一番。

A B C D E F G H I J K L M N O P Q R S T U V W X Y Z

086

1586 landmark ['lænd,mɑrk]　　　　**n.** 地標　　**5th** ★★★★★
As one of the tallest building in the world, Taipei 101 has become a new landmark of Taipei City.
台北101是全世界最高建築物之一，也成為台北市的新地標。

1587 landscape ['lænd,skep]　　　　**n.** 風景　　**4th** ★★★★★
The mountains of Taiwan create beautiful landscapes.
台灣的山脈創造美麗的風景。

1588 landslide ['lænd,slaɪd]　　　　**n.** 土石流　　**4th** ★★★★★
The week-long rainfall has brought about landslides and flooding in the mountain areas.
為期一週的降雨造成山區的土石流和水災。

1589 language ['læŋgwɪdʒ]　　　　**n.** 語言　　**5th** ★★★★★
As an international language, English allows people of different countries to converse.
英語是國際語言，讓不同國家的人得以溝通。

1590 large [lardʒ]　　　　**adj.** 大的　　**5th** ★★★★★
Jane was very happy that her speech last night attracted a large audience.
珍非常快樂，因為她昨晚的演講吸引一大群聽眾。

1591 latest ['letɪst]　　　　**adj.** 最新的　　**5th** ★★★★★
That car is the latest model. How it sells depends on the dealer.
那輛車是最新款，銷售量如何就要看業者怎麼做了。

1592 laugh [læf]　　　　**v.** 笑　　**5th** ★★★★★
Although laughing and smiling are genetic responses, the infant soon learns when to smile, laugh, and even how to laugh.
雖然大笑和微笑是基因反應，嬰兒很快就學會何時要微笑或大笑，甚至是要如何笑。

1593 launch [lɔntʃ]　　　　**v.** 進行　　**4th** ★★★★★
The Cambodia Daily is launching a world-wide campaign to wipe out malaria in Cambodia.
柬埔寨日報為了消滅柬埔寨國內的瘧疾，發動了一項全球性的活動。

1594 laundromat ['lɔndrəmæt]　　　　**n.** 洗衣店　　**5th** ★★★★★
Dad uses a basket to carry his clothes to the Laundromat.
爸爸用籃子把他的衣服帶到洗衣店去。

L

1595 laundry [ˈlɔndrɪ]　　　　n.　洗衣　　5th ★★★★★
Laundry detergent is a major source of pollution to the river.
洗衣粉是河川污染的一個主要污染源。

1596 lavatory [ˈlævəˌtorɪ]　　　　n.　盥洗室　　4th ★★★★★
On the plane the sign "Restroom" is usually replaced by the sign "Lavatory."
飛機上的廁所標誌通常用「Lavatory」代替「Restroom」。

1597 law [lɔ]　　　　n.　法律　　5th ★★★★★
About 3,000 police will be deployed to help maintain law and order in the election.
選舉時大約有三千名警力幫忙維持治安。

1598 lawsuit [ˈlɔˌsut]　　　　n.　訴訟　　3rd ★★★★★
Kelly went to his county's court and filed a lawsuit against the person who he felt was responsible for his loss.
凱利到地方法院向某人提出訴訟，他覺得那個人要為他的損失負責。

1599 lay [le]　　　　v.　使平靜　　4th ★★★★★
You don't need to be in such a hurry. Lay your breath and count to ten.
你不必那麼著急，平穩呼吸然後數到十。

1600 layer [ˈleɚ]　　　　n.　層　　4th ★★★★★
After the trip to the desert, the car was covered with a layer of dust. It needed washing.
這台車去過一趟沙漠旅程之後，蓋了一層灰，車該洗一洗了。

1601 layman [ˈlemən]　　　　n.　門外漢　　4th ★★★★★
The layman always finds it hard to realize how natural it is for the composer to compose.
對作曲家而言，作曲是一件相當自然的事，門外漢總是難以理解。

1602 layoff [ˈleˌɔf]　　　　n.　解雇　　4th ★★★★★
Citigroup Inc. plans to shed about 10 percent of its global workforce, and additional reductions would come from layoffs.
花旗集團計劃除去全球百分之十的勞動力，這額外的縮減就來自裁員。

1603 leader [ˈlidɚ]　　　　n.　領導人　　5th ★★★★★
Great leaders in every walk of life love to learn.
每一個偉大的領袖都熱愛學習。

1604 leadership [ˈlidɚʃɪp]　　　**n.**　領導　　**5th** ★★★★★
Under the leadership of newly elected president Barack Obama, the US is expected to turn a new page in politics and economy.
在新任總統歐巴馬的領導下，美國在政治和經濟上期望展開歷史的新頁。

1605 learning [ˈlɜnɪŋ]　　　**n.**　學習　　**4th** ★★★★★
Experience is generally considered much less important than book learning by educators.
對教育工作者來說，他們普遍認為唸書比經驗來得重要多了。

1606 lease [lis]　　　**n.**　租約　　**4th** ★★★★★
The lease states that you must vacate the apartment in good condition.
租約規定，你搬出公寓時，公寓狀況必須是完好的。

1607 leave [liv]　　　**v.**　離開　　**5th** ★★★★★
Anita leaves here for the United States to give a speech at a conference.
安妮塔將出發前往美國，她要在一場會議中發表演說。

1608 legal [ˈligl̩]　　　**adj.**　合法的　　**4th** ★★★★★
It is the accuser's right to appeal.
上訴是原告的權利。

1609 legend [ˈlɛdʒənd]　　　**n.**　傳說　　**3rd** ★★★★★
According to legend, each year was named after one of the 12 animals who came to see the dying Lord Buddha before he left the earth.
根據傳說，佛祖臨終前有十二隻動物前來探望，因此每一年就分別用這十二隻動物來命名。

1610 legislation [ˌlɛdʒɪsˈleʃən]　　　**n.**　立法　　**3rd** ★★★★★
It's very difficult to access the effects of the new legislation as it has only been implemented for two months.
這個新法才剛實行二個月，因此很難有所成效。

1611 legislative [ˈlɛdʒɪsˌletɪv]　　　**adj.**　立法的　　**4th** ★★★★★
The legislative branch of government is responsible for enacting and making new laws.
立法部門負責替政府頒布和制定新的法律。

1612 legislator [ˈlɛdʒɪsˌletɚ]　　　**n.**　立法委員　　**3rd** ★★★★★
To gain more reputation, some legislators would get into violent physical fights so that they may appear in TV news reports.
有些立委為了增加知名度，會大打出手好讓自己上電視。

1613 leisure [ˈliʒɚ]　　　　　　n.　休閒　　　4th ★★★★★
The leisure activities that children are encouraged to engage in vary by gender.
人們會依小孩的性別去鼓勵他們從事不同的休閒活動。

1614 lend [lɛnd]　　　　　　v.　借給　　　4th ★★★★★
I need some money. Could you lend me $10 until next week?
我需要錢，你可以借我十元嗎？我下禮拜還你。

1615 length [lɛŋθ]　　　　　　n.　長度　　　4th ★★★★★
This essay is clearly not satisfactory. It is only 100 words but the required length is 300 words.
這篇短文明顯令人不甚滿意，要求的篇幅長度為三百個字，但它只有一百個字。

1616 lengthy [ˈlɛŋθɪ]　　　　　adj.　冗長的　　4th ★★★★★
The speaker spent twenty minutes on one simple question. The explanation was so lengthy that we could not see the point clearly.
這位講者花了二十分鐘講解一個簡單的問題。他的解釋太冗長，我們無法清楚知道他所要傳達的重點。

1617 lessen [ˈlɛsn]　　　　　　v.　減少　　　5th ★★★★★
To lessen the risk of heart disease, you should start reducing your daily intake of oil and salt.
為了降低心臟病的風險，你應該開始減少每日油脂和鹽份的攝取。

1618 level [ˈlɛvl]　　　　　　n.　水準　　　5th ★★★★★
Water seeks its own level.
水往低處流。

1619 liberal [ˈlɪbərəl]　　　　adj.　自由的　　4th ★★★★★
John is not wealthy, but he is liberal with his money.
約翰並不富裕，但他花錢大方。

1620 library [ˈlaɪˌbrɛrɪ]　　　　n.　圖書館　　5th ★★★★★
Although the town is small, it has a library as complete as that of a large city.
雖然只是個小鎮，但鎮裡的圖書館和大城市的一樣完善。

1621 license [ˈlaɪsns]　　　　　v.　許可　　　4th ★★★★★
The exchange student has been licensed to practice medicine.
交換學生已經獲得執照可以開業行醫。

1622 lifetime ['laɪf,taɪm]　　　　　**n.**　一生　　5th ★★★★★
Some people call Sam a "Jack of all trades". He has had a great variety of jobs in his lifetime.
有些人稱山姆為「萬事通」，他的一生中做過很多不同的工作。

1623 lifestyle ['læɪf,staɪl]　　　　　**n.**　生活型態　　5th ★★★★★
Mrs. Lee's lifestyle is quite different from her husband's.
李太太的生活方式和她丈夫完全不同。

1624 lift [lɪft]　　　　　**v.**　抬起　　5th ★★★★★
The mother lifted her baby out of his pen.
媽媽從遊戲床裡抱起嬰兒。

1625 light [laɪt]　　　　　**adj.**　輕鬆的　　5th ★★★★★
My nephew likes to listen to light music as he reads.
我姪子看書的時候喜歡聽點輕音樂。

1626 lightweight ['laɪt'wet]　　　　　**adj.**　輕的　　4th ★★★★★
The new LCD television features a thin and lightweight body that you can easily carry anywhere you go.
新款液晶電視的特色是體型超薄超輕，可以讓你隨時隨地輕鬆帶著走。

1627 likely ['laɪklɪ]　　　　　**adj.**　可能的　　4th ★★★★★
As heavy fog is likely to affect air transportation for the next few days, passengers should contact airlines to confirm flight times.
濃霧很可能會影響未來幾天的航空交通，旅客應和航空公司確認航班時間。

1628 limit ['lɪmɪt]　　　　　**v.**　限制　　5th ★★★★★
Since there is only limited amount of oil and gas, we had better develop solar energy as soon as possible.
既然汽油和天然氣數量有限，我們最好儘快發展太陽能。

1629 line [laɪn]　　　　　**n.**　行　　5th ★★★★★
There are six lines in each stanza of the poem.
每一段有六行詩。

1630 link [lɪŋk]　　　　　**n.**　關聯　　5th ★★★★★
The link between conditions in the womb and breast cancer is very surprising.
子宮頸癌和乳癌之間的密切關聯令人吃驚。

1631 liquid ['lɪkwɪd] **n.** 液體 **3rd** ★★★★★
Be careful not to add too much liquid to the mixture.
小心不要在合劑裡加入過多液體。

1632 liquidate ['lɪkwɪˌdet] **v.** 清算 **3rd** ★★★★★
The board decided to liquidate the corporation by the end of the year.
董事會決定在年底進行公司清算。

1633 literate ['lɪtərɪt] **adj.** 文學的 **4th** ★★★★★
Almost all the children in the class are literate.
課堂上幾乎所有小孩都會讀書寫字。

1634 literature ['lɪtərətʃə] **n.** 文學 **4th** ★★★★★
My roommate fell asleep while reading her literature textbook.
我的室友在看文學課本時睡著了。

1635 litter ['lɪtə] **n.** 雜亂 **4th** ★★★★★
Dad was appalled at the litter of the yard.
爸爸被院子裡的髒亂嚇到。

1636 livelihood ['laɪvlɪˌhud] **n.** 生計 **4th** ★★★★★
Half a million poor Filipino farmers risked losing their livelihood.
五十萬菲律賓的貧困農民處於失去生計的風險中。

1637 lively ['laɪvlɪ] **adv.** 活潑地 **5th** ★★★★★
To make his room lively, he decorated it with pictures of his favorite sports figures.
為了使他的房間充滿朝氣，他用他最喜歡的運動人物照片做裝飾。

1638 load [lod] **v.** 裝載 **5th** ★★★★★
Please load new paper into the fax machine; I am sure someone sent us a fax.
請替傳真機補充紙張，我確定有人傳真給我們。

1639 loaf [lof] **n.** 一條 **5th** ★★★★★
Mom bought two loaves of bread at the supermarket.
媽媽在超市買了兩條麵包。

1640 loan [lon] **v.** 出借 **4th** ★★★★★
The National Palace Museum will continue to cooperate with Beijing's Palace Museum but will not loan artifacts to China.
故宮博物院會繼續與北京故宮合作，但不會把文物出借給中國。

1641 local ['lokl]   **adj.** 地方的   4th ★★★★★
Maya doesn't shop at national chain stores; she only buys from local companies.
馬雅不在全國連鎖店購物，她只從當地的公司購買。

1642 location [lo'keʃən]   **n.** 位置   4th ★★★★★
The new stadium was built at a convenient location, close to an MRT station and within walking distance to a popular shopping center.
新體育場蓋在交通便利的地段，靠近捷運站還有一座步行可及的著名購物中心。

1643 lodge [lɑdʒ]   **v.** 住宿   4th ★★★★★
The hikers lodged at a hostel in the mountains that night.
健行者晚上投宿於山間旅社。

1644 lofty ['lɔftɪ]   **adj.** 崇高的   3rd ★★★★★
All the people took pride in the soldier's lofty sentiment.
所有人對士兵的高尚情操引以為傲。

1645 log [lɔg]   **n.** 原木   4th ★★★★★
The cabin beside the path is made of logs.
小徑旁的小屋是用原木建的。

1646 logical ['lɑdʒɪkl]   **adj.** 邏輯的   4th ★★★★★
The scientist specializes in logical analysis.
科學家專攻邏輯分析。

1647 lonely ['lonlɪ]   **adj.** 孤獨的   5th ★★★★★
The old man has been living a lonely life for years.
這位老先生過了很多年的孤獨生活。

1648 long-running ['lɔŋrʌnɪŋ]   **adj.** 永續經營的   5th ★★★★★
The company is trying to reach their long-running goal.
公司正努力達到長期營運的目標。

1649 loom [lum]   **v.** 逼進   3rd ★★★★★
The hill loomed up out of the thick fog.
小山隱約出現在濃霧中。

1650 loose [lus]   **adj.** 鬆的   4th ★★★★★
The robber shook the security guard's loose arm and fled away.
劫匪朝保安的胳膊揮拳，然後逃之夭夭。

1651 loosen [ˈlusn]   **v.** 鬆開   3rd ★★★★★

Mr. Chen loosened his collar and tie as soon as he arrived home.
陳先生一回到家就鬆開自己的衣領和領帶。

1652 lose [luz]   **v.** 失去   5th ★★★★★

In order to lose weight and keep in good shape, people should exercise regularly, and avoid diet pills or crash diets.
為了減肥和維持良好身形，人們應該經常運動，避免吃藥或節食。

1653 loss [lɔs]   **n.** 遺失   5th ★★★★★

The family had to cope with the loss of their dog.
這家人必須處理痛失愛犬的問題。

1654 lottery [ˈlɑtərɪ]   **n.** 彩券   4th ★★★★★

When John, a bar owner, won the lottery, he was so happy that he said that all the drinks were on the house.
酒吧老闆約翰中了樂透，開心的告訴大家飲料不用錢。

1655 loud [laud]   **adj.** 喧鬧的   4th ★★★★★

About twenty-eight million Americans suffer serious hearing loss, and the likely cause in more than a third of the cases is too much exposure to loud noise.
約有二千八百萬人患有嚴重的聽力喪失，超過三分之一的案例顯示，有可能是因為過度暴露於吵雜的噪音所導致。

1656 lucrative [ˈlukrətɪv]   **adj.** 獲利的   3rd ★★★★★

The restaurant is a lucrative business because people love its food.
這家餐廳的生意很好，因為人們喜歡這裡的食物。

1657 luggage [ˈlʌgɪdʒ]   **n.** 行李   5th ★★★★★

The hotel porter assisted the guest with his luggage.
飯店的服務人員幫房客提行李。

1658 lunar [ˈlunɚ]   **adj.** 月亮的   4th ★★★★★

As the Chinese Lunar New Year comes near, a still-seen tradition is a year-end feast called "Wei-Ya."
每當農曆新年即將到來時，一個依然可見的傳統就是叫做「尾牙」的年終盛宴。

1659 lure [lur]   **n.** 誘惑力   3rd ★★★★★

The countryside has a lure for retired people from cities.
農村對於從城市退休的人們來說，很具吸引力。

090

1660 luxurious [lʌg'ʒurɪəs]   **adj.** 奢侈的   4th ★★★★★
The president flies in a luxurious jet.
總統乘坐豪華噴射機旅行。

1661 luxury ['lʌkʃərɪ]   **n.** 享受   4th ★★★★★
I am studying so hard for the forthcoming entrance exam that I do not have the luxury of a free weekend to rest.
我為了即將來臨的入學考用功讀書，根本沒有辦法享受周末的休憩。

1662 magazine [ˌmæɡə'zin]   **n.** 雜誌   5th ★★★★★
If you want to borrow magazines, tapes, or CDs, you can visit the library.
如果你想借雜誌、錄音帶或是CD，你可以去圖書館。

1663 magic ['mædʒɪk]   **n.** 魔術   5th ★★★★★
Magic is believed to have begun with the Egyptians, in 1700 BC.
據說魔術起源於西元前一千七百年的埃及。

1664 magician [mə'dʒɪʃən]   **n.** 魔術師   5th ★★★★★
Magicians were thought of as freaks and were only allowed to perform in a circus before.
以前魔術師被視作怪胎，而且只能在馬戲團裡表演。

1665 magnetic [mæɡ'nɛtɪk]   **adj.** 有磁性的   3rd ★★★★★
Salmon use special magnetic navigation to figure out which way to travel.
鮭魚利用一種特別的磁性導航來分辨旅行的方向。

1666 magnificent [mæɡ'nɪfəsənt]   **adj.** 宏偉的   3rd ★★★★★
These magnificent buildings date back to the period of Japanese occupation.
這些宏偉建築物可追溯到日據時代。

1667 main [men]   **adj.** 主要的   5th ★★★★★
According to recent studies, there are three main reasons why students procrastinate.
根據最近的研究，學生喜歡拖延主要有三個原因。

1668 mainframe ['men͵frem]   **n.** 主機   5th ★★★★★
We have worked to repair the damage of our mainframe computer, but you may experience some Internet connection problems for a few days.
我們已經修好受損的中央處理機，不過在未來幾天，你可能會遇到網路連線問題。

M

1669 mainland ['menlənd]   **n.** 大陸   4th ★★★★★
St. Valentine's Day has been slowly adopted in both Taiwan and Mainland China as Lover's Day.
西洋情人節慢慢為台灣和中國大陸所接受，將那天視為情人間的日子。

1670 maintain [men'ten]   **v.** 保持   4th ★★★★★
Despite living in different countries, the two families have maintained a close friendship.
這兩家人雖然住在不同的國家，但他們還是維持相當親密的友誼。

1671 majority [mə'dʒɔrətɪ]   **n.** 大多數   4th ★★★★★
A majority of the population of Taiwan is bilingual, with many trilingual and even quadrilingual speakers.
台灣大多數人口會說雙語，也有許多人會三種語言，甚至四種語言。

1672 male [mel]   **adj.** 男性的   4th ★★★★★
The idea of long hair as a symbol of male strength is even mentioned in the Bible, in the story of Samson and Delilah.
事實上在聖經參孫和大利拉的故事裡，就提及了長頭髮象徵男性力量的概念。

1673 mall [mɔl]   **n.** 購物中心   5th ★★★★★
My friends and I had nothing to do on Sunday so we just walked around the mall.
我朋友和我週日無所事事，所以就在購物中心到處逛逛。

1674 malnourished [mæl'nɜrɪʃt]   **adj.** 營養不良的   3rd ★★★★★
The majority of population in this African country is malnourished.
非洲國家大多數的人口都是營養不良。

1675 malnutrition [ˌmælnju'trɪʃən]   **n.** 營養不良   3rd ★★★★★
Most of the children in this area suffer from malnutrition.
這個地區大多數的小孩都受營養不良之苦。

1676 malodorous [mæl'odərəs]   **adj.** 惡臭的   3rd ★★★★★
There is a malodorous swamp where no living things exist.
充滿惡臭的沼澤沒有任何生物存在。

1677 manage ['mænɪdʒ]   **v.** 設法做到   4th ★★★★★
The mountain climbers managed to cross the river before the sunset.
登山者設法要在日落之前渡河。

091

1678 management ['mænɪdʒmənt]　**n.** 管理　4th ★★★★★
Many people have poor time management skills and often try to do too much in too little time.
許多人的時間管理很差，常常想用很少的時間做很多事。

1679 manager ['mænɪdʒɚ]　**n.** 經理　4th ★★★★★
John's boss is going to promote him from his position as assistant manager to a new position as manager.
約翰的老闆要把約翰從副理拉拔到經理的職位。

1680 mandatory ['mændə,torɪ]　**adj.** 義務的　3rd ★★★★★
It's mandatory to pay taxes for citizens.
公民有義務納稅。

1681 manner ['mænɚ]　**n.** 態度　4th ★★★★★
As a result of his obtrusive manner, Jim's work as a waiter lasted only for one day.
由於吉姆的態度莽撞，他服務生的工作只維持了一天。

1682 manual ['mænjuəl]　**adj.** 手工的　4th ★★★★★
The old man has been a manual worker, a carpenter, for more than forty years.
這位老先生是木匠，他已經做工超過四十年了。

1683 manuscript ['mænjə,skrɪpt]　**n.** 原稿　4th ★★★★★
The dictionary is still in manuscript.
這本字典仍在手稿階段。

1684 map [mæp]　**n.** 地圖　5th ★★★★★
Leo usually reads the map carefully before he starts for somewhere new to him.
里昂在動身前往陌生的地方時，通常會先仔細看過地圖。

1685 margin ['mɑrdʒɪn]　**n.** 邊緣　4th ★★★★★
Don't forget to leave a narrower margin on the left-hand side of your sheet of paper.
不要忘了在你的表單左手邊留下一點頁面空白。

1686 marginal ['mɑrdʒɪnl]　**adj.** 邊際的　3rd ★★★★★
With all the extra manpower put in the project, we can only see marginal effects.
儘管所有額外的勞動力都來執行這項計劃，我們也只能看到邊際效應。

1687 marine [mə'rin]　**n.** 海軍陸戰隊　4th ★★★★★

My father hasn't been a marine for many years, but he still acts like one.
我父親已有好幾年不當海軍陸戰隊隊員，但他還是表現得煞有其事。

1688 mark [mɑrk] **n.** 目標 5th ★★★★★
The factory director wishes the new product would hit the mark.
廠長希望能成功推出新產品。

1689 marker [mɑrkɚ] **n.** 標記 5th ★★★★★
The fence served as a boundary marker of the farm.
柵欄農場作為界線的標記。

1690 market ['mɑrkɪt] **n.** 市場 5th ★★★★★
Maybe someone will buy your old junk at a flea market.
也許有人會在跳蚤市場買你的舊物。

1691 marketing ['mɑrkɪtɪŋ] **n.** 行銷 4th ★★★★★
Understanding the language and culture in target markets in foreign countries is one of the keys to successful international marketing.
了解國外目標市場的語言和文化，是成功國際行銷的關鍵之一。

1692 marriage ['mærɪdʒ] **n.** 婚姻 5th ★★★★★
Some people prefer to follow a predictable pattern in their life: school, then marriage and children.
有些人喜歡遵照生活中可預料的模式：學校、結婚，然後生子。

1693 married ['mærɪd] **adj.** 已婚的 5th ★★★★★
Last month, fifty couples, who were married for fifty years and more, celebrated their golden anniversary in the city hall.
上個月，有五十對結婚超過五十年的夫妻，在市政府慶祝他們的金婚紀念。

1694 martyr ['mɑrtɚ] **n.** 犧牲者 3rd ★★★★★
Most Americans like to think of themselves as martyrs to work.
大部份美國人喜歡把自己想成工作的犧牲者。

1695 marvelous ['mɑrvələs] **adj.** 妙極的 4th ★★★★★
We loved Jim Anderson's latest book. It was marvelous.
我們愛死了Jim Anderson的新書，那本書真是妙極了。

1696 mass [mæs] **n.** 團 4th ★★★★★
Sometimes a huge mass of snow slides down a mountain side, which is an avalanche.
有時，會有非常巨大的一團雪滑落山腰，這就是雪崩。

1697 massive [ˈmæsɪv]　　　　**adj.** 大規模的　　5th ★★★★★
Nuclear power stations are massive and complex structures.
核電廠是規模又大又複雜的結構。

1698 massage [məˈsɑʒ]　　　　**n.** 按摩　　4th ★★★★★
The office lady usually has a massage after work.
女性上班族通常下班後會去按摩。

1699 master [ˈmæstɚ]　　　　**v.** 精通　　5th ★★★★★
It's never easy to master a foreign language in a short time.
很難在短時間內能精通外語。

1700 masterpiece [ˈmæstɚˌpis]　　**n.** 傑作　　4th ★★★★★
It's one of the great masterpieces of Chinese art.
這是中國藝術的偉大傑作之一。

1701 match [mætʃ]　　　　**v.** 使相配　　4th ★★★★★
The forecasted weather did not match the sunshine at the game.
比賽時的大太陽和天氣預報不符合。

1702 material [məˈtɪrɪəl]　　　　**n.** 材料　　4th ★★★★★
To protect our environment, we should recycle materials like paper and metals.
為了保護我們的環境，我們應該回收像紙張及金屬的材料。

1703 matter [ˈmætɚ]　　　　**n.** 事件　　5th ★★★★★
We haven't seen John for a long time. As a matter of fact, we have lost track of him.
我們好長一段時間沒看到約翰了，事實上，我們已經跟他失聯了。

1704 mature [məˈtjur]　　　　**v.** 長成　　4th ★★★★★
The small fish which are now being released into the lake will mature in about eighteen months' time.
放生到湖裡的小魚大約十八個月後會長成大魚。

1705 maxim [ˈmæksɪm]　　　　**n.** 座右銘　　3rd ★★★★★
You had better lay the maxim to your heart.
你最好把你的座右銘放在心上。

1706 maximum [ˈmæksəməm]　　**n.** 最大值　　4th ★★★★★
The CEO is trying to achieve the maximum of efficiency with the minimum of labor.
這位執行長試著用最少的勞動力來達到最大效益。

M

1707 meal [mil]　　　　　**n.** 餐　　　　5th ★★★★★
Drew's pants felt tight after the large meal.
茱兒大吃一頓後覺得褲頭很緊。

1708 mean [min]　　　　　**v.** 意指　　　　5th ★★★★★
It's all Greek to me. Maybe Sam knows what it means. Let's go ask him about it.
我完全不懂，也許山姆知道是什麼意思，我們來去問他。

1709 meaningful ['minɪŋfəl]　　**adj.** 有意義的　　5th ★★★★★
It is quite meaningful to read and write for real purposes through blogging.
藉由博客，人們會因實際目的來閱讀和抒寫，這相當有意義。

1710 means [minz]　　　　　**n.** 方法　　　　4th ★★★★★
In the past, bicycles were used mainly as a means of transportation.
以前腳踏車主要是做交通工具使用。

1711 meanwhile ['min,hwaɪl]　　**adv.** 同時地　　4th ★★★★★
I am hard at work; meanwhile, my wife is at home taking a nap.
我努力工作，而與此同時我妻子在家睡午覺。

1712 measurement ['mɛdʒəmənt]　**n.** 測量　　　4th ★★★★★
Measurements are needed in many everyday activities.
很多日常活動都需要用到測量。

1713 mechanic [mə'kænɪk]　　**n.** 技工　　　4th ★★★★★
My brother is a mechanic and he fixes my car for free.
我哥哥是機械工，他免費修理我的車。

1714 mechanical [mə'kænɪkḷ]　　**adj.** 機械的　　4th ★★★★★
My flight to Hong Kong was delayed because of a mechanical problem.
因為機器故障的緣故，我到香港的班機延誤了。

1715 mediator ['midɪ,etə]　　**n.** 調停者　　3rd ★★★★★
The respectable archbishop has agreed to play the mediator between the government and the protesting people.
可敬的大主教已同意擔任政府與抗議群眾之間的調停者。

1716 medical ['mɛdɪkḷ]　　**adj.** 醫藥的　　5th ★★★★★
Adults and children over twelve years of age take two spoonfuls of this medical liquid every six hours.
十二歲以上的兒童和成年人每隔六小時就服用這瓶藥液，每次兩匙。

The 3000 vocabularies you must know in public service exam

093

1717 medicine [ˈmɛdəsn]　　　**n.** 藥　　　5th ★★★★★
This medicine is good for heart disease. But its possible side effect is low blood pressure.
這種藥對心臟病很好，但是可能帶來低血壓的副作用。

1718 medium [ˈmidɪəm]　　　**n.** 媒體　　　4th ★★★★★
Despite the media attention, many teenagers still find it hard to talk about school bully.
儘管受到媒體關注，許多青少年還是很難開口談論校園霸凌的問題。

1719 meeting [ˈmitɪŋ]　　　**n.** 會議　　　5th ★★★★★
The time for the meeting is still up in the air.
會議的確切時間尚未決定。

1720 melt [mɛlt]　　　**v.** 融化　　　5th ★★★★★
Sugar melts in water, and so does salt.
糖溶於水，鹽也是。

1721 memento [mɪˈmɛnto]　　　**n.** 紀念品　　　3rd ★★★★★
I bought a boomerang and a toy koala as mementos of my trip to Australia.
我去澳洲旅行時，買了回力鏢和無尾熊玩偶當做紀念品。

1722 memo [ˈmɛmo]　　　**n.** 備忘錄　　　5th ★★★★★
It's a memo to the accounting department asking for more subsidies.
這個備忘錄是用來提醒會計部提供更多補貼。

1723 memory [ˈmɛmərɪ]　　　**n.** 記憶力　　　5th ★★★★★
He has an excellent memory; he can easily learn every name in this book by heart.
他有絕佳的記憶力，他可以輕易記住這本書裡的每個名字。

1724 mend [mɛnd]　　　**v.** 修補　　　4th ★★★★★
Mother is mending the hole in my pants now.
母親現在正在修補我褲子上的破洞。

1725 mention [ˈmɛnʃən]　　　**n.** 提及　　　4th ★★★★★
The celebrity took all the credit for writing the book without mentioning his co-author.
這位名人沒有提到他的共同作者，他把撰寫這本書的一切功勞搶走。

1726 menu [ˈmɛnju]　　　**n.** 菜單　　　5th ★★★★★
Can I get you something to drink while you are looking at the menu?
你在看菜單的同時要喝點什麼嗎？

M

1727 merchant ['mɜtʃənt] n. 商人 4th ★★★★★
Bonnie doesn't know how to make cell phones, but as a merchant, she is good at selling them.
邦妮不知道如何製造手機，但她身為一個零售商，善於推銷它們。

1728 merge [mɜdʒ] v. 合併 3rd ★★★★★
The board decided to merge the subsidiary with its parent company.
董事會決定要合併母公司和子公司。

1729 merit ['mɛrɪt] n. 優點 4th ★★★★★
Patience is one of his merits.
耐心是他的優點之一。

1730 message ['mɛsɪdʒ] n. 訊息 5th ★★★★★
After Patty firmly said no, Mark finally got the message and left her alone.
佩蒂堅決拒絕了馬克，馬克這才恍然大悟並不再打擾她。

1731 messy ['mɛsɪ] adj. 凌亂的 5th ★★★★★
He only cleans up his room when it gets really messy.
房間真的亂到不行的時候他才會去整理。

1732 metal ['mɛtl] n. 金屬 4th ★★★★★
The brown metal you see is copper.
你看到的棕色金屬是銅。

1733 metaphor ['mɛtəfə] n. 隱喻 4th ★★★★★
Sunlight is the metaphor for freedom and the joy of living.
陽光是自由和快樂生活的隱喻。

1734 method ['mɛθəd] n. 方法 5th ★★★★★
By using active method to observe and search the neighborhood, police can be more effective in fighting crime.
警察藉由積極觀察和搜尋鄰近地區的方法，能更有效的打擊犯罪。

1735 metropolitan [,mɛtrə'pɑlətn] adj. 都市的 4th ★★★★★
After 20 years of living in a small village, the old man wanted a more metropolitan way of life.
老先生住在小村莊二十年之後，開始想要一個比較都市化的生活。

1736 microscopic ['maɪkrə'skɑpɪk] adj. 微觀的 4th ★★★★★

094

The researcher is doing a microscopic examination under a microscope in the laboratory.
研究人員在實驗室用顯微鏡作微觀檢查。

1737 middle [ˈmɪdḷ]　　　　　**adj.** 中間的　　　5th ★★★★★

The Middle East has been a very tense region for many years.
中東多年來一直是個非常緊張的地區。

1738 migrate [ˈmaɪˌgret]　　　　**v.** 遷移　　　4th ★★★★★

Some birds migrate to warmer areas in the wintertime.
有些鳥類在冬季時會遷移到較溫暖的地區。

1739 migration [maɪˈgreʃən]　　　　**n.** 遷移　　　4th ★★★★★

It's a documentary of the spring migration of the wild ducks.
這是一部關於野鴨在春季遷徙時的紀錄片。

1740 migratory [ˈmaɪgrəˌtorɪ]　　　**adj.** 移棲的　　　4th ★★★★★

Formosan landlocked salmons are a migratory fish.
櫻花鉤吻鮭是迴游魚類。

1741 mild [maɪld]　　　　　**adj.** 輕微的　　　5th ★★★★★

According to the health official, the rate of increasing number of cases is not beyond what is expected and the symptoms of all the patients are mild.
根據衛生局的說法，病例數量增加的比例並沒有超過預期，患者的症狀也都很輕微。

1742 million [ˈmɪljən]　　　　**n.** 百萬　　　5th ★★★★★

The writer's novels continue to give pleasure to millions all over the world.
這位作家的小說繼續為世界上無數的人帶來樂趣。

1743 military [ˈmɪləˌtɛrɪ]　　　　**adj.** 軍隊的　　　4th ★★★★★

As military officers, women must work hard enough to get the job done.
女生當軍官必須要夠努力才能完成工作。

1744 mind [maɪnd]　　　　　**n.** 理智　　　5th ★★★★★

She must have lost her mind to do such a crazy thing.
她一定是瘋了才會做出這種事。

1745 miner [ˈmaɪnɚ]　　　　　**n.** 礦工　　　4th ★★★★★

The miner was very dirty from his day at work.
礦工在工作天裡都是髒兮兮的。

1746 mineral [ˈmɪnərəl]　　　n.　礦物質　　4th ★★★★★
Mineral water is strongly recommended if you are going to have a trip to the desert.
如果你要到沙漠旅行，強烈推薦帶礦泉水。

1747 minimal [ˈmɪnəməl]　　adj.　極小的　　3rd ★★★★★
In a capitalistic economy, the role of government in business is minimal.
在資本主義經濟中，政府在商業上扮演的作用很小。

1748 minimize [ˈmɪnəˌmaɪz]　　v.　減到最小　　3rd ★★★★★
A variety of preventive measures are now on call in order to minimize the potential damage caused by the deadly disease.
各種預防措施都在隨時待命中，就是為了減少致命疾病可能造成的危害。

1749 minimum [ˈmɪnəməm]　　n.　最小量　　4th ★★★★★
The class needs a minimum of six students to continue.
這門課需要至少六個人才能繼續開課。

1750 minister [ˈmɪnɪstə]　　n.　部長　　4th ★★★★★
After the President's inauguration ceremony, new minister assumed office on May 20, 2008.
總統就職典禮過後，新部長將於二千零八年五月二十日上任。

1751 minority [maɪˈnɔrətɪ]　　n.　少數　　4th ★★★★★
Farmers are in a minority in this country.
這個國家的農民是少數。

1752 miracle [ˈmɪrəkl̩]　　n.　奇蹟　　4th ★★★★★
It's believed that the patient's recovery is a miracle.
據說這位病人能康復是奇蹟。

1753 miraculous [mɪˈrækjələs]　　adj.　不可思議的　　4th ★★★★★
The explorer experienced several miraculous things during his journey.
探險家在旅程中有一些不可思議的經歷。

1754 mirror [ˈmɪrə]　　n.　鏡子　　5th ★★★★★
Breaking a mirror is said to be a sign of bad luck.
打破鏡子據說是不幸的徵兆。

1755 miss [mɪs]　　v.　錯過　　5th ★★★★★

The tour group was so lucky—they almost missed the tram!
那個旅遊團很幸運，他們差一點就要錯過電車了。

1756 miserable ['mɪzərəbl]　　**adj.** 悲慘的　3rd ★★★★★
The workers' lives were miserable: they worked in all kinds of weather, earning only enough money to buy simple food and cheap clothes.
工人的生活悲慘，他們無論晴雨都要工作，賺的錢也只夠買簡單的食物和廉價的衣服。

1757 mistake [mɪ'stek]　　**n.** 錯誤　5th ★★★★★
If James had taken my advice, he would not have made such a stupid mistake.
如果詹姆士接受我的勸告，他就不會犯這種愚蠢的錯誤。

1758 mitigate ['mɪtə,get]　　**v.** 緩和　3rd ★★★★★
It's unclear how to mitigate the effects of industrialization on the costal area.
現在還不清楚該如何減輕工業化對濱海地區造成的影響。

1759 mix [mɪks]　　**v.** 混合　5th ★★★★★
Many different tribes are mixed together in the mountain area.
在山區，許多不同的部落會融合在一起。

1760 mixture ['mɪkstʃə]　　**n.** 混合　5th ★★★★★
The roots of Western civilization can be traced to the mixture of Greek and Roman cultures, known as classical culture.
西方文明的根源可以追溯到希臘和羅馬的混合文化，又稱古典文化。

1761 model ['madl]　　**n.** 模範　4th ★★★★★
American heroes and heroines have generally provided solid role models for young people to follow.
美式英雄普遍提供了可靠的角色榜樣讓年輕人仿效。

1762 moderate ['madərɪt]　　**adj.** 適中的　4th ★★★★★
Regular, moderate exercise will relieve muscle tension, keep the muscles firm, and make the heart and blood vessels healthy.
定期和適度的運動會紓緩肌肉緊張，維持肌肉結實，並有益於心臟和血管健康。

1763 modern ['madən]　　**adj.** 現代化的　4th ★★★★★
Thousands of flood-damaged books are saved, thanks to modern technology.
多虧了現代科技，上千本被洪水毀壞的書本都救回來了。

1764 modest ['madɪst]　　**adj.** 謙遜的　5th ★★★★★
The model student is always modest in his behavior.
模範生的行為表現總是很得體。

1765 modify ['mɑdə,faɪ] **v.** 修正 4th ★★★★★

The scientist modified his speech to make it easier for children to understand the threat of global warming.
科學家改變自己的說話方式，讓孩子能更容易了解全球暖化造成的威脅。

1766 modulate ['mɑdʒə,let] **v.** 調整 3rd ★★★★★

The lecturer can modulate his voices according to the size of the room where he speaks.
演講者可以根據演說場地的大小，來調整自己的聲音。

1767 moist [mɔɪst] **adj.** 潮濕的 5th ★★★★★

Grant's clothes are moist from the light rainfall.
格蘭的衣服被小雨淋濕了。

1768 moisturize ['mɔɪstʃə,raɪz] **v.** 滋潤 4th ★★★★★

Sandy moisturizes her skin with lotion every night.
山迪每天晚上擦乳液滋潤肌膚。

1769 molest [mə'lɛst] **v.** 侵犯 3rd ★★★★★

Kindly do not molest the patients here.
請不要騷擾這裡的病人。

1770 momentarily ['momən,tɛrəlɪ] **adv.** 暫時 3rd ★★★★★

The spokesman hesitated momentarily and then said "no comments".
發言人猶豫了一下，然後說：「無可奉告！」。

1771 momentous [mo'mɛntəs] **adj.** 重要的 4th ★★★★★

The birth of a baby is a momentous occasion in a family.
一個嬰兒的誕生是家族的重要時刻。

1772 momentum [mo'mɛntən] **n.** 動力 3rd ★★★★★

Let's not lose the momentum; keep up the good work.
我們不要失去動力，再接再厲吧！

1773 monarchy ['mɑnəkɪ] **n.** 君主政治 3rd ★★★★★

The revolutionaries overthrew the monarchy at last.
革命黨人終於推翻帝制。

1774 monetary ['mʌnə,tɛrɪ] **adj.** 金融的 3rd ★★★★★

Some countries tighten monetary policy to avoid inflation.
一些國家緊收貨幣政策，以避免通貨膨脹。

1775 monitor ['manətə]　　　　v.　監控　　　★★★★★
The slow student's progress is being monitored by his instructors.
老師密切注意這個理解力較差的學生其學習進展。

1776 monopoly [mə'napli]　　　　n.　壟斷　　　★★★★★
No country has a monopoly on morality or truth, whose principles should be established with general agreements.
沒有一個國家能控制道德或真理的原則，這些事應該是由普羅大眾的認同所建立的。

1777 monotonous [mə'natənəs]　　adj.　單調的　　★★★★★
The preacher's monotonous voice was so boring that it put me to sleep.
牧師單調的聲音如此無趣，所以我睡著了。

1778 monstrously ['manstrəsli]　　adv.　非常　　★★★★★
I was monstrously touched by his selfless assistance.
我對他無私的幫助大受感動。

1779 monthly ['mʌnθli]　　　　adj.　每月的　　★★★★★
I find it more economical to buy a monthly train ticket than to pay for each ride each day.
我發現買火車月票比每天支付單程費用划算。

1780 monument ['manjəmənt]　　n.　紀念碑　　★★★★★
The government erected a monument to the memory of the brave firefighters.
政府立碑紀念勇敢的消防隊員。

1781 mood [mud]　　　　　n.　心情　　　★★★★★
I'm not in the mood to go out to the tea house tonight.
我今晚沒有心情去茶館。

1782 moody ['mudɪ]　　　　adj.　喜怒無常的　★★★★★
One day Charlotte is happy and smiling, and the next day she's angry or depressed. She's a very moody person.
夏綠蒂這天還開心的笑著，隔天就變得生氣或沮喪，她是個喜怒無常的人。

1783 moonlight ['mun,laɪt]　　n.　月光　　　★★★★★
I think everything looks more beautiful in moonlight.
我認為在月光下一切看起來更美。

1784 morality [mə'rælətɪ]　　n.　道德　　　★★★★★
The rich man has a high standard of morality. He never takes advantage of other

people.
這位富人的道德標準很高，從不會佔他人便宜。

1785 mortal ['mɔrtl]　　adj.　致命的　4th ★★★★★
Jean's injury was minor, and fortunately not mortal.
珍的傷勢輕微，且幸運的是無生命危險。

1786 mortgage ['mɔrgɪdʒ]　　n.　貸款　3rd ★★★★★
As most people do not have enough money to pay for a house, they try to secure a mortgage from a bank.
大部分的人沒有足夠的錢買房子，所以他們會向銀行貸款。

1787 mortuary ['mɔrtʃu,ɛrɪ]　　n.　停屍間　3rd ★★★★★
The bodies had been placed in the mortuary until the funeral took place two weeks later.
屍體安置在太平間兩個星期，直到葬禮舉行。

1788 mostly ['mostlɪ]　　adv.　大部分地　5th ★★★★★
John spends his free time on computer games mostly.
約翰把空閒時間都花在電玩上。

1789 motion ['moʃən]　　n.　動作　5th ★★★★★
Linda is interested in observing the motion of the planets.
琳達對於觀察行星的運行很感興趣。

1790 motivate ['motə,vet]　　v.　刺激　4th ★★★★★
The teacher's speech motivated the students to work harder on their studies.
老師的演講鼓勵學生更用心學習。

1791 motivation [,motə'veʃən]　　n.　動機　4th ★★★★★
In our company I am afraid there is very little motivation to work hard.
我害怕上班時沒有努力工作的動力。

1792 motorcycle ['motə,saɪkl]　　n.　機車　5th ★★★★★
You had better put on your helmet before you start your motorcycle.
你發動機車以前，最好先戴上安全帽。

1793 motto ['moto]　　n.　座右銘　4th ★★★★★
John is an aggressive businessman who would do anything necessary to achieve success. His motto is that "The end justifies the means".
約翰是個積極的商人，為了成功他會不惜做任何事。他的座右銘是「以正當手段達到目的」。

1794 mourn [morn]　　　　　**v.**　哀悼　　4th ★★★★★
The mother mourned over the death of her young child.
這位母親哀悼她早逝的孩子。

1795 mouthful ['mauθfəl]　　　**n.**　一口　　5th ★★★★★
Mr. Huang had just a mouthful of dinner before taking the train.
黃先生搭火車前只吃了一點點晚餐。

1796 move [muv]　　　　　**v.**　移動；搬運　4th ★★★★★
She just moved to the city two weeks ago, so she is far behind the other students in the class.
她兩個禮拜前剛搬進城裡，所以在學校還跟不上其他學生。

1797 movie ['muvɪ]　　　　　**n.**　電影　　5th ★★★★★
Demi Moore is Helen's favorite actress. She's seen all of her movies.
黛咪摩爾是海倫最喜歡的女演員，她看過黛咪所有的電影。

1798 muchness ['mʌtʃnɪs]　　　**n.**　大量　　3rd ★★★★★
They are all much of a muchness.
他們都大同小異。

1799 multimedia [mʌltɪ'midɪə]　　**n.**　多媒體　4th ★★★★★
It is obvious that we are in the multimedia age.
很明顯的，我們現在處於多媒體的世代。

1800 multiply ['mʌltəplaɪ]　　　**v.**　增加　　4th ★★★★★
Bacteria can multiply if the water is kept on the shelves for too long or if it is exposed to heat or direct sunlight.
如果水放在架上太久或直接接觸高溫或陽光，會使細菌繁殖。

1801 murder ['mɝdɚ]　　　　　**n.**　謀殺案　4th ★★★★★
In the recent months, the siren of public safety was set off by several astonishing murders in Taiwan.
近幾個月來，台灣發生幾件令人震驚的謀殺案，使公共安全拉起警報。

1802 muscle ['mʌsl̩]　　　　　**n.**　肌肉　　4th ★★★★★
You can firm your muscles by going to the gym and following a strict exercise regime.
你可以上健身房或遵守嚴格的運動計畫來增強你的肌肉。

一考就上！
考公職一定要會的3000單字

1803 museum [mju'zɪəm]　　　**n.**　博物館　　5th ★★★★★
This museum is proud of its many ancient paintings collected through generations.
這些世代相傳的古畫是博物館引以為傲的收藏。

1804 mustache ['mʌstæʃ]　　　**n.**　小鬍子　　4th ★★★★★
Neal is too young to grow a mustache.
尼爾太年輕不能蓄小鬍子。

1805 mutual ['mjutʃuəl]　　　**adj.**　互相的　　4th ★★★★★
A happy marriage must be based on mutual respect and understanding between husband and wife.
幸福的婚姻必須建立在丈夫和妻子之間的相互尊重和體諒。

1806 myriad ['mɪrɪəd]　　　**n.**　無數　　3rd ★★★★★
In brief, the transforming global economy creates a myriad of new opportunities for the emerging markets.
簡而言之，轉變中的世界經濟為新興市場帶來無數的新機會。

1807 mystery ['mɪstərɪ]　　　**n.**　不可思議　　4th ★★★★★
Tipping can be a mystery for people living in countries where this practice is uncommon.
有些國家不習慣給小費，那裡的人們會覺得這個做法很不可思議。

1808 narrow ['næro]　　　**adj.**　狹窄的　　4th ★★★★★
Living overseas has changed Johnson's worldview entirely. His narrow perspective has been broadened.
海外生活徹底改變了強生的世界觀，擴大了他原本狹隘的眼界。

1809 nation ['neʃən]　　　**n.**　國家　　4th ★★★★★
The Kingdom of Bhutan is a landlocked nation situated between India and China.
不丹王國是位於印度和中國間的內陸國家。

1810 national ['næʃən]]　　　**adj.**　國家的　　4th ★★★★★
The Director General of National Police Agency is the highest ranking police officer in Taiwan.
警政署長是台灣位階最高的警務人員。

1811 native ['netɪv]　　　**adj.**　本地的　　4th ★★★★★
Many of the native Taiwanese above the age of fifty or so speak Japanese as a second language.
許多五十歲以上或五十歲左右的台灣本省人，第二外語是日文。

098

1812 natural [ˈnætʃərəl]　　　　**adj.** 自然的　　5th ★★★★★
Typhoons are natural phenomena well-known to Taiwan residents.
颱風對台灣居民而言是眾所皆知的自然現象。

1813 nearby [ˈnɪrˌbaɪ]　　　　**adv.** 附近　　4th ★★★★★
This city is located ideally, providing easy access to beaches, rivers, wineries, and nearby ski fields.
這座城市的地點很理想，方便人們前往海灘、河流、釀酒廠和附近的滑雪場。

1814 nearly [ˈnɪrlɪ]　　　　**adv.** 將近　　3rd ★★★★★
According to scientists, adults spend nearly a third of their lives asleep while infants sleep twice that much or even more.
根據科學家研究，成人一生花了近三分之一的時間睡覺，而嬰兒則是成人的兩倍甚至更多。

1815 necessary [ˈnɛsəˌsɛrɪ]　　　　**adj.** 必要的　　5th ★★★★★
Most people do not think that language classes are necessary.
大部分的人認為上語言課是沒有必要的。

1816 need [nid]　　　　**n.** 需要　　5th ★★★★★
The company cannot but answer every need of its customers.
公司必須回應每一位顧客的需求。

1817 needle [ˈnidl]　　　　**n.** 針　　4th ★★★★★
I need a needle to sew my pants.
我需要一根針來縫我的褲子。

1818 negative [ˈnɛɡətɪv]　　　　**adj.** 負面的　　4th ★★★★★
The doctor point out that stress, loneness, and lack of friends can have a negative influence on sick people.
醫生指出壓力、寂寞和缺少朋友對病人來說有負面的影響。

1819 neglect [nɪɡˈlɛkt]　　　　**v.** 忽視　　4th ★★★★★
Ben neglected his work too much and he soon lost his job.
班過於忽視他的工作，所以很快就失業了。

1820 negotiate [nɪˈɡoʃɪˌet]　　　　**v.** 談判　　4th ★★★★★
The government has sent delegates to negotiate with Japan for a free-trade agreement.
政府派代表到日本談判自由貿易協定。

1821 negotiation [nɪˌgoʃɪˈeʃən]　　**n.** 談判　　4th ★★★★★
Nowadays, negotiation is a much better and wiser means than military force to solve differences or problems between nations.
如今，相較於使用軍事武力，談判是更好、更明智的手段來解決國與國之間的紛爭。

1822 neighbor [ˈnebɚ]　　**n.** 鄰居　　5th ★★★★★
My neighbor Paul called an ambulance to send his dad to the hospital this morning.
我的鄰居保羅今早打電話給救護車送他的父親去醫院。

1823 neighborhood [ˈnebɚˌhud]　　**n.** 社區　　5th ★★★★★
We'd love to have you drop by since you just moved to the neighborhood and don't have many friends here.
既然你剛搬到附近，沒有很多朋友，歡迎有空來我們家坐坐。

1824 nephew [ˈnɛfju]　　**n.** 姪子　　4th ★★★★★
My brother's son is my nephew.
我兄弟的兒子就是我的姪子。

1825 nervous [ˈnɝvəs]　　**adj.** 緊張的　　5th ★★★★★
The examinee was very nervous while he waited for the doctor.
這位受檢者等待醫生時很緊張。

1826 network [ˈnɛtˌwɝk]　　**n.** 電視網　　3rd ★★★★★
The largest television network in America is not ABC, CBS, or Fox.
美國最大的電視公司不是ABC、CBS，也不是Fox。

1827 nevertheless [ˌnɛvɚðəˈlɛs]　　**conj.** 然而　　4th ★★★★★
I don't think I can win a tennis match against Joyce. Nevertheless, I will try to play as well as I can.
我不認為我能在網球賽中贏過喬思，然而我會盡力打好球。

1828 news [njuz]　　**n.** 消息　　5th ★★★★★
The doctor floored Marriott with the bad news.
醫生的壞消息給了馬裏奧特很大的打擊。

1829 newspaper [ˈnjuzˌpepɚ]　　**n.** 報紙　　5th ★★★★★
Wendell replied to a job advertisement for bus drivers in the newspaper.
溫德爾應徵報紙上求職廣告中的公車司機。

099

1830 nibble [ˈnɪbl̩]　　　　　**v.**　一點點的咬　🏃 ★★★★★
Silkworms nibbled away the mulberry leaves.
蠶寶寶一點一點的吃著桑葉。

1831 nickname [ˈnɪkˌnem]　　　**n.**　綽號　🏃 ★★★★★
Chad has the nickname "Fatty" as he always looks chubby.
因為查德看起來總是胖嘟嘟的，所以他的綽號是「小胖」。

1832 nightmare [ˈnaɪtˌmɛr]　　　**n.**　噩夢　🏃 ★★★★★
American kids love Halloween treats, but a bucket of Halloween candy can be a dentist's nightmare.
美國小孩都喜歡萬聖節糖果，但這一桶桶的糖果卻是牙醫的惡夢。

1833 nocturnal [nɑkˈtɝnl̩]　　　**adj.**　夜行的　🏃 ★★★★★
Owls are nocturnal birds, and bats are nocturnal animals.
貓頭鷹是夜行鳥類，而蝙蝠是夜行動物。

1834 nod [nɑd]　　　　　　**v.**　點頭　🏃 ★★★★★
When asked if he really wanted to marry Lucy, Peter nodded his head without hesitation.
當彼得被問到是否真的要娶露西，他毫不猶豫地點頭。

1835 noise [nɔɪz]　　　　　　**n.**　噪音　🏃 ★★★★★
Avalanches happen when the snow on the mountain is disturbed by wind, earth movements, loud noises, or even by people skiing.
當山上的雪受到風、地層移動、巨大噪音或人類滑雪的干擾影響，就會發生雪崩。

1836 noisy [ˈnɔɪzɪ]　　　　　**adj.**　吵鬧的　🏃 ★★★★★
If you feel anxious, you had better stay away from noisy areas.
如果你覺得心煩氣躁，最好離吵鬧的區域遠一點。

1837 nominate [ˈnɑməˌnet]　　　**v.**　提名　🏃 ★★★★★
The rich man was nominated for Mayor twice, but he was never elected.
那位有錢人二度被提名參選市長，但他從未當選。

1838 nominee [ˌnɑməˈni]　　　　**n.**　候選人　🏃 ★★★★★
The senator has become the Democratic nominee for the presidency.
這位參議員成為民主黨提名的總統候選人。

1839 normally [ˈnɔrml̩ɪ]　　　　**adv.**　正常地　🏃 ★★★★★

Children normally have a distrust of new foods.
小孩子通常對新食物感到戒慎恐懼。

1840 notable ['notəbl]　　　**adj.** 顯著的　　4th ★★★★★
The house is notable as the famous enterpriser's birthplace.
這房子因為是知名企業家的出生地而受到關注。

1841 notice ['notɪs]　　　**v.** 注意　　5th ★★★★★
I've noticed that many boys have messy hairstyles nowadays.
我注意到時下許多男孩有著凌亂的髮型。

1842 notify ['notə,faɪ]　　　**v.** 通知　　4th ★★★★★
Should you encounter any problems regarding the new system, please notify the tech support ASAP.
萬一遇到任何有關新系統的問題，請盡速告知技術支持。

1843 notion ['noʃən]　　　**n.** 想法　　4th ★★★★★
You need to have a clear notion of what to do in the future.
你對於未來的路應該要有清楚的想法。

1844 notorious [no'torɪəs]　　　**adj.** 惡名昭彰的　　4th ★★★★★
This district is notorious for its bad security.
這個地區因治安敗壞而聲名狼藉。

1845 notoriously [no'torɪəslɪ]　　　**adv.** 聲名狼藉地　　4th ★★★★★
The city is notoriously dangerous with many gang members causing trouble all the time. Everybody knows it is unwise to wander on the streets alone.
這座城市有許多惹事生非的幫派份子，因此聲名狼藉非常危險，每個人都知道獨自在街上漫步是不智的。

1846 nourish ['nɜɪʃ]　　　**v.** 養育　　4th ★★★★★
The poor mother nourished her baby with rice milk, but not fresh milk.
這位可憐的母親用米漿餵養她的寶寶，而不是新鮮的牛奶。

1847 novel ['nɑvl]　　　**n.** 小說　　5th ★★★★★
My father enjoys not only reading poems but also reading novels.
我父親喜歡讀詩也喜歡讀小說。

1848 nuisance ['njusns]　　　**n.** 討厭的事　　3rd ★★★★★
The drunken man was charged with causing a public nuisance. People in the neighborhood were annoyed by his rude behaviors.
酒醉男子被控妨害風化，附近的人們都被他粗野的行為惹惱。

100

O

1849 number ['nʌmbə]   **n.** 數字   5th ★★★★★
After a series of games lost, he knew his days were numbered.
輸了一連串的比賽後，他知道自己來日不多了。

1850 numerous ['njumərəs]   **adj.** 很多的   4th ★★★★★
The stars in the sky are more numerous when you go outside the city.
當你走出城市，天空中有更多的星星。

1851 nutrient ['njutrɪənt]   **n.** 營養物   4th ★★★★★
Young children need a lot of nutrients to help them grow.
幼童需要大量的營養幫助他們成長。

1852 oath [oθ]   **n.** 誓言   3rd ★★★★★
All the new senators have to take an oath in the inauguration.
所有新上任的參議員都要在就職典禮中宣示。

1853 obedience [ə'bidjəns]   **n.** 服從   4th ★★★★★
The commanding officer expected unquestioning obedience from his soldiers.
指揮官要求士兵對他絕對服從。

1854 obese [o'bis]   **adj.** 肥胖的   3rd ★★★★★
Obese children are supposed to change their diet.
肥胖兒童應該改變自己的飲食。

1855 obesity [o'bisətɪ]   **n.** 肥胖   3rd ★★★★★
Obesity can result from a diet high in fat.
肥胖起因於高脂肪的飲食。

1856 object ['ɑbdʒɪkt]   **n.** 物體   4th ★★★★★
When you take photos, you can move around to shoot the target object from different angles.
照相的時候，你可以四處移動，從不同的角度拍目標物。

1857 objection [əb'dʒɛkʃən]   **n.** 反對   4th ★★★★★
Despite the objections of the White House, the Senate voted today to cut off aid to Somalia.
儘管白宮反對，參議院今天投票中斷對索馬利亞的援助。

1858 objective [əb'dʒɛktɪv]   **n.** 目標   4th ★★★★★
My son's objective in life is being an excellent judge.
我兒子的人生目標是成為一位優秀的法官。

1859 obligation [ˌɑbləˈgeʃən] **n.** 債務 4th ★★★★★

Most companies, faced with the economic downturn, need to have strong solvency, with assets valuable enough to meet obligations and operations in the long term.
面對經濟不景氣，大部分公司需要強大的償債能力，其資產價值需足以應付長期的債務款項和營運。

1860 oblige [əˈblaɪdʒ] **v.** 迫使 3rd ★★★★★

According to the agreement, employers are legally obliged to pay the minimum wage to their employees.
根據協議，雇主有義務依法支付員工最低工資。

1861 obscure [əbˈskjur] **adj.** 模糊的 3rd ★★★★★

It is not easy to define "art" and "crafts" clearly because the line between them is an obscure one.
很難清楚界定「藝術」和「工藝」，因為其中的界線模糊。

1862 observation [ˌɑbzɝˈveʃən] **n.** 觀察 4th ★★★★★

Children gain knowledge about the world around them in part from observation and experience.
小孩部分是靠著觀察和經驗得到這世界上的知識。

1863 observe [əbˈzɝv] **v.** 觀察 4th ★★★★★

In order to write a report on stars, we decided to observe the stars in the sky every night.
我們為了要寫有關星星的報導，決定每晚觀察天上的星星。

1864 obsess [əbˈsɛs] **v.** 迷住 3rd ★★★★★

The student was obsessed with fear of failure.
這個學生為失敗的恐懼搞到心神不寧。

1865 obsolete [ˈɑbsəˌlit] **adj.** 陳舊的 3rd ★★★★★

The original model has been rendered obsolete and replaced by the new one.
原始的模式已經過時了，用新的取而代之。

1866 obstacle [ˈɑbstək!] **n.** 障礙 3rd ★★★★★

For many college students, financial burden can be the single biggest obstacle in the way of finishing their degrees.
對許多大學生來說，財務負擔是完成學位唯一最大的障礙。

1867 obstruction [əbˈstrʌkʃən] **n.** 阻礙 3rd ★★★★★

101

There is an obstruction in the pipe. I need to remove it now.
這個管子堵住了，我現在要把它清一清。

1868 obtrusive [əb'trusɪv]　　　**adj.** 冒失的　　4th ★★★★★
As a result of his obtrusive manner, Jim's work as a waiter lasted only for one day.
吉姆的態度冒失，他服務生的工作只做了一天。

1869 obtain [əb'ten]　　　**v.** 獲得　　4th ★★★★★
I have not obtained a raise in the past three years, so it's hard for me to make both ends meet.
我已經三年沒有加薪了，所以收支平衡對我來說有點困難。

1870 obviously ['ɑbvɪəslɪ]　　　**adv.** 明顯地　　4th ★★★★★
This new computer is obviously superior to the old one because it has many new functions.
這台新電腦明顯優於舊式的，因為新式有很多新功能。

1871 occasion [ə'keʒən]　　　**n.** 場合　　4th ★★★★★
Angela only drinks champagne on special occasions.
安琪拉只在特殊場合喝香檳。

1872 occupation [ˌɑkjə'peʃən]　　　**n.** 職業　　4th ★★★★★
The woman is a composer by occupation.
這個女人的職業是作曲家。

1873 occupied ['ɑkjupaɪd]　　　**adj.** 忙碌的　　4th ★★★★★
The secretary was occupied in dealing with e-mails this afternoon.
祕書今天下午忙著處理電子郵件。

1874 occur [ə'kɝ]　　　**v.** 發生　　4th ★★★★★
When heat from the Sun is trapped near the Earth's surface, the greenhouse effect occurs.
當太陽的熱能停滯在地球表面時，溫室效應就發生了。

1875 ocean ['oʃən]　　　**n.** 海洋　　4th ★★★★★
The foreign model's beautiful eyes were blue like the ocean.
那個外國模特兒有著像海一樣藍的美麗雙眼。

1876 offend [ə'fɛnd]　　　**v.** 冒犯　　4th ★★★★★
The customer's vulgar language offended the waitress.
顧客的粗言穢語冒犯了女服務生。

1877 offensive [ə'fɛnsɪv]   **adj.** 冒犯的   4th ★★★★★
The sharp noise is offensive to my ears.
尖銳的噪音讓我的耳朵很不舒服。

1878 offer ['ɔfə]   **v.** 提供   4th ★★★★★
As they cannot see eye to eye on the buyout offer, the negotiators are at loggerheads without any possibility of a breakthrough.
由於雙方談判人無法在收購價中取得共識，在不可能有所進展的情形下陷入僵局。

1879 officer ['ɔfəsə]   **n.** 警官   5th ★★★★★
An officer always works persistently and diligently on the cases he deals with.
警官總是努力不懈地辦理他負責的案件。

1880 official [ə'fɪʃəl]   **adj.** 正式的   4th ★★★★★
My two friends are getting married but they haven't picked the date to make it official.
我的兩個朋友要結婚了，但他們還沒有挑日子正式公佈。

1881 offset ['ɔf,sɛt]   **v.** 抵消   3rd ★★★★★
Domestic losses will be offset by developing overseas markets.
拓展海外市場將會抵消國內虧損。

1882 oil [ɔɪl]   **n.** 石油   5th ★★★★★
When most people think of Latin American oil, their thoughts turn to Venezuela and Mexico.
人們一想到拉丁美洲的石油，他們的思緒會轉向委內瑞拉和墨西哥的石油。

1883 ointment ['ɔɪntmənt]   **n.** 軟膏   4th ★★★★★
You have to put some ointment with antibiotics on your cuts to prevent them from infection.
你得在傷口上擦一點抗生素軟膏，以防止感染。

1884 omnivorous [ɑm'nɪvərəs]   **adj.** 雜食的   3rd ★★★★★
Turtles and monkeys are both omnivorous.
烏龜和猴子都是雜食性。

1885 ongoing ['ɑn,goɪŋ]   **adj.** 進行的   4th ★★★★★
The negotiations are still ongoing because no agreement has been reached.
因為還未達成任何協議，談判仍在進行中。

1886 onslaught ['ɑn‚slɔt]　　n.　突擊　　3rd ★★★★★
The city counselor made a violent onslaught on the government.
城市的法律顧問猛烈攻擊政府。

1887 online ['ɔn‚laɪn]　　adv.　網路上　　4th ★★★★★
A website for electronic books has opened online, but it is not going to anger the publishing industry.
線上電子書的網站已經開通，但並不會惹惱出版業。

1888 opera ['ɑpərə]　　n.　歌劇　　4th ★★★★★
It's not a good idea to bring children to an opera.
帶兒童到歌劇院不是一個好主意。

1889 operate ['ɑpə‚ret]　　v.　運作　　4th ★★★★★
Employees are required to follow the standard operating procedures and to act accordingly.
員工必須依循標準作業程序，然後照著做。

1890 operation [‚ɑpə'reʃən]　　n.　活動　　4th ★★★★★
That group was excellent at handling clandestine operations.
那個團隊擅長祕密行動。

1891 opinion [ə'pɪnjən]　　n.　意見　　4th ★★★★★
People have different opinions about the dangers of children using the Internet.
有關小孩使用網路的危險性，大家各執己見。

1892 opponent [ə'ponənt]　　n.　對手　　3rd ★★★★★
The tall boy is a tough opponent; he plays tennis very well.
那個高個子男孩是一個強硬的對手，他網球打得非常好。

1893 opportunity [‚ɑpə'tjunətɪ]　　n.　機會　　4th ★★★★★
He is too stubborn a person to take advantage of the opportunity.
他太頑固了，害得自己沒有好好把握機會。

1894 opposition [‚ɑpə'zɪʃən]　　n.　反對　　4th ★★★★★
The new tax policy proposed for the next fiscal year has been severely criticized by the opposition party leaders.
在野黨的領導人嚴厲批評了下一個會計年度所發布的新稅收政策。

1895 oppression [ə'prɛʃən]　　n.　壓迫　　3rd ★★★★★

A number of Taiwanese elites used to suffer from political oppression ten years Ago.
十年前許多台灣精英份子受到政治迫害。

1896 optimistic [ˌɑptə'mɪstɪk]　　**adj.** 樂觀的　　3rd ★★★★★
In boom years, optimistic books sell well, while pessimism rules the bookstore in recession.
景氣好的時候，勵志書籍賣得很好，而悲觀主義的書籍在景氣蕭條時卻主掌書局銷量。

1897 option ['ɑpʃən]　　**n.** 選擇　　4th ★★★★★
With online shopping, one can get hundreds of options when looking for a cell phone.
由於網路購物的興起，一個人在選購手機時可以有好幾百個選擇。

1898 oration [o'reʃən]　　**n.** 演說　　3rd ★★★★★
The priest delivered a funeral oration in the honor of the deceased.
神父發表一篇弔詞來紀念死者。

1899 orchestra ['ɔrkɪstrə]　　**n.** 交響樂團　　4th ★★★★★
The orchestra played a Beethoven symphony.
樂隊演奏一首貝多芬的交響樂。

1900 order ['ɔrdə]　　**n.** 點餐　　5th ★★★★★
May I take your order?
可以幫您點菜嗎？

1901 ordinary ['ɔrdn,ɛrɪ]　　**adj.** 平常的　　4th ★★★★★
In the ordinary way, I should pick up my girl friend at the station.
按慣例我應該到車站接我女友。

1902 organ ['ɔrgən]　　**n.** 器官　　4th ★★★★★
Some animals have organs in their bodies that produce light.
有些動物體內的器官會產生光。

1903 organization [ˌɔrgənə'zeʃən]　　**n.** 組織　　4th ★★★★★
This is the first time for a local organization to host an international conference and to provide all the facilities and services for this special event.
這是當地組織第一次主辦國際會議，並為這場特別盛會提供所有的設施與服務。

1904 organize ['ɔrgə,naɪz]　　**v.** 籌劃　　4th ★★★★★
I am writing to you to explore the possibility of organizing this event with your

company. Our cooperation last year was a great success.
我寫信給你是為了探討這次活動是否有可能和貴公司一同舉辦。去年我們的合作非常成功。

1905 orientation [ˌorɪɛnˈteʃən]　　**n.** 新生訓練　　3rd ★★★★★

All the students are required to attend the two-day orientation program so that they can have a complete understanding of the university they are admitted to.
所有學生都必須參加為期兩天的迎新活動，讓他們對自己考上的大學有完整的了解。

1906 origin [ˈɔrədʒɪn]　　**n.** 起源　　4th ★★★★★

The origin is the starting point.
起源就是出發點。

1907 original [əˈrɪdʒənl]　　**adj.** 最初的　　4th ★★★★★

Mr. Lee bought the suit at half of the original price.
李先生用半價買了這套西裝。

1908 ornament [ˈɔrnəmənt]　　**n.** 裝飾　　4th ★★★★★

The Christmas tree is decorated with a lot of ornaments.
聖誕樹上裝飾著很多小飾品。

1909 other [ˈʌðɚ]　　**adj.** 其他的　　5th ★★★★★

This CD-RW is designed for use in the United States of America. Sale or use of this product in some other countries may break local laws.
這片CD僅用於美國本地。在其他國家銷售或使用會違反當地法律。

1910 outbreak [ˈautˌbrek]　　**n.** 爆發　　4th ★★★★★

Health officials warned that the recent outbreak of dengue fever could spread to northern Taiwan.
衛生官員警告說，最近爆發的登革熱可能蔓延到台灣北部。

1911 outlet [ˈautˌlɛt]　　**n.** 商店　　3rd ★★★★★

Kentucky Fried Chicken has 1,100 outlets in China, about twice as many as those of McDonald's.
肯德基在中國有一千一百家分店，大約是麥當勞的兩倍多。

1912 outline [ˈautˌlaɪn]　　**n.** 輪廓　　3rd ★★★★★

It was so dark that we could only see the outline of the mountains against the sky.
天這麼黑，我們只看得到天空襯托下山的輪廓。

1913 outstanding [ˈautˈstændɪŋ]　　**adj.** 傑出的　　4th ★★★★★

The player's outstanding performance won him a gold medal in the Olympic Games.
這名球員出色的表現為他贏得奧運金牌。

1914 outward ['autwəd]　　　　adj. 外部的　　　4th ★★★★★
One's inner beauty cannot always be seen from their outward appearances.
人的內在美並不一定可以從外在面貌看出來。

1915 outweigh [aut'we]　　　　v. 勝過　　　4th ★★★★★
The two pails outweigh those three people.
這兩桶東西比那三個人還重。

1916 oven ['ʌvən]　　　　n. 烤箱　　　5th ★★★★★
The pie is hot from the oven.
派剛從烤箱拿出來，很燙。

1917 overall ['ovɚ,ɔl]　　　　adj. 總的　　　5th ★★★★★
The overall length of the bridge is ten meters.
這座橋的總長度是十公尺。

1918 overcoat ['ovɚ,kot]　　　　n. 大衣　　　5th ★★★★★
The guest took off his overcoat soon after he entered the hall.
客人進入大廳後就把大衣脫掉。

1919 overcome [,ovɚ'kʌm]　　　　v. 克服　　　4th ★★★★★
To overcome budget shortages, some small schools in rural areas have set up cooperative programs to share their teaching and library resources.
為了克服預算短缺，農村地區的一些學校建立合作方案，分享彼此的教學和圖書資源。

1920 overdraft ['ovɚ,dræft]　　　　n. 透支　　　3rd ★★★★★
She has an enormous overdraft to pay off.
她有一大筆透支要償還。

1921 overhead ['ovɚ'hɛd]　　　　adj. 頭上的　　　5th ★★★★★
We are advised to put our carry-on baggage either under the seat in front of us or in the overhead compartment.
我們應該把隨身行李放在座位前方的地板或座位上方的行李架。

1922 overhear [,ovɚ'hɪr]　　　　v. 偷聽　　　4th ★★★★★
The maid accidently overheard what the host was singing.
女僕偶然聽到主人在唱歌。

104

1923 overjoy [ˌovɚˈdʒɔɪ]　　　**v.**　使狂喜　　4th ★★★★★
It overjoys me to hear of your promotion.
聽到你升職我非常開心。

1924 overload [ˌovɚˈlod]　　　**v.**　負擔過重　　5th ★★★★★
These companies are overloaded with debt and often operate with low returns on capital.
這些公司負債累累，而且通常運作時，資本的報酬率都很低。

1925 overlook [ˌovɚˈluk]　　　**v.**　眺望　　4th ★★★★★
The Drake Hotel in downtown Chicago sits overlooking Lake Michigan.
德雷克飯店坐落在芝加哥市中心，俯瞰密西根湖。

1926 overnight [ˈovɚˈnaɪt]　　　**adv.**　整夜　　5th ★★★★★
I stayed overnight at my friend's the night before.
前天晚上我在朋友家過夜。

1927 overpass [ˌovɚˈpæs]　　　**n.**　天橋　　5th ★★★★★
There is an overpass connecting the teaching building and the laboratory.
這座天橋連接教學大樓和實驗室。

1928 overprice [ˌovɚˈpraɪs]　　　**v.**　定價過高　　5th ★★★★★
I think they overprice the blouse.
我覺得這件襯衫的定價過高。

1929 oversee [ˈovɚˈsi]　　　**v.**　監督　　4th ★★★★★
The new manager oversees all office matters and makes sure that everything is no sooner said than done.
新任經理負責所有公事，並確保每件事都能說到做到。

1930 overstay [ˈovɚˈste]　　　**v.**　逗留過久　　5th ★★★★★
No one is allowed to overstay at the exhibition hall.
超過規定時間任何人都不能在展示廳逗留。

1931 overtake [ˌovɚˈtek]　　　**v.**　超過　　4th ★★★★★
A heavy motorcycle overtook the car few minutes ago.
一輛重機在幾分鐘前超越一台轎車。

1932 overturn [ˌovɚˈtɝn]　　　**v.**　推翻　　4th ★★★★★
The government will be overturned by the rebels sooner or later.
政府遲早會被反叛份子推翻。

一考就上！考公職一定要會的3000單字

1933 overwhelm [ˌovɚˈhwɛlm]　　**v.**　壓倒　　3rd ★★★★★
Feeling overwhelmed by the heavy work in the office, I need a vacation.
我被辦公室繁重的工作給壓垮了，我需要度假。

1934 overwork [ˈovɚˈwɜk]　　**v.**　工作過度　　3rd ★★★★★
People who overwork tend to have a higher risk of heart diseases.
工作過度的人通常有更高的風險得到心臟病。

1935 owl [aul]　　**n.**　貓頭鷹　　5th ★★★★★
The mouse moving under tree leaves was caught by an owl.
貓頭鷹抓住在樹葉下方移動的老鼠。

1936 owner [ˈonɚ]　　**n.**　擁有者　　5th ★★★★★
When an invention is patented, no one may make, use, or sell it without the permission of the patent's owner.
當某項發明取得專利權時，若未經專利所有人的允許，任何人不得製造、使用或出售該項發明。

1937 pace [pes]　　**n.**　速度　　5th ★★★★★
Cultural learning moves at a very fast and intense pace during the first year of life.
人在出生的第一年，對於文化學習有相當快速和大幅度的進展。

1938 package [ˈpækɪdʒ]　　**n.**　包裹　　5th ★★★★★
You can pay more money for shipping to ensure that your package arrives in time.
你可以付多一點運費以確保你的包裹及時送達。

1939 packed [pækt]　　**adj.**　擁擠　　5th ★★★★★
The place was packed. There was no room to move around.
那地方很擁擠，沒有走動的空間。

1940 page [pedʒ]　　**n.**　頁　　5th ★★★★★
An editor will format the layout of magazine pages.
編輯將會設計雜誌封面的編排。

1941 pain [pen]　　**n.**　痛苦　　5th ★★★★★
The patient moaned all night. I could clearly hear the long low sounds he made. He must have been under great pain.
病人整夜呻吟。我能清楚聽見他發出的又長又低的聲音。他當時一定是非常痛苦。

1942 pale [pel]　　**adj.**　蒼白的　　5th ★★★★★

The girl turned pale at the sight of blood.
女孩一看到血就臉色發白。

1943 pamphlet ['pæmflɪt]　　　**n.**　小冊子　　🌗 ★★★★★ 3rd

Does the pamphlet you picked up at the information desk tell you if there is a gift store somewhere in this museum?
你從服務台拿的小冊子上，有沒有指示博物館的禮品店在哪裡？

1944 panel ['pænl]　　　**n.**　面板　　4th ★★★★★

Many satellites in space are equipped with large panels whose solar cells transform sunlight directly into electric power.
很多外太空的衛星都備有太陽能蓄電板，能將陽光直接轉化為電能。

1945 panoramic [ˌpænə'ræmɪk]　　**adj.**　全景的　　3rd ★★★★★

No visit to Taipei would be complete without a panoramic view of the city from the top of Taipei 101. In other words, Taipei 101 is a must-go place.
沒有從台北101的頂樓俯看全景，台北之旅就不算完整。也就是說，台北101大樓是必遊景點。

1946 paper ['pepɚ]　　　**n.**　論文　　5th ★★★★★

When preparing to write a research paper, I always go to the library to gather as much information as possible.
當我準備要寫一篇研究報告時，總會到圖書館盡可能多蒐集些資料。

1947 paperwork ['pepɚˌwɜk]　　**n.**　書面作業　　4th ★★★★★

Please fill out the paperwork before getting in line.
排隊之前請先填寫這份文件。

1948 parachute ['pærəˌʃut]　　**n.**　降落傘　　4th ★★★★★

It should be extremely exciting to do a parachute jump in the high sky.
高空跳傘應該非常令人興奮。

1949 parade [pə'red]　　　**n.**　遊行　　4th ★★★★★

After the baseball team won the national championship, the town quickly put together a parade to greet the returning heroes.
棒球隊贏得全國冠軍後，該鎮馬上組成一支遊行隊伍迎接英雄的歸來。

1950 paradise ['pærəˌdaɪs]　　**n.**　天堂　　4th ★★★★★

The amusement park is supposed to be a paradise for children.
遊樂園是孩子們的天堂。

P

1951 paralyze ['pærə,laɪz]　　**v.**　使癱瘓　　3rd ★★★★★
Thousands of people flooded into the city to join the demonstration; as a result, the city's transportation system was almost paralyzed.
數以千計的人們湧進城裡參加示威遊行，結果造成全市的交通系統大癱瘓。

1952 part [pɑrt]　　**n.**　部分　　5th ★★★★★
Timing is often the important part of any decision.
做決定時，時機通常佔了很重要的部分。

1953 partial ['pɑrʃəl]　　**adj.**　偏袒的　　5th ★★★★★
It's not proper for a teacher to be partial to anyone in the class.
對老師來說，偏袒班上任何一個學生是不妥當的。

1954 participate [pɑr'tɪsə,pet]　　**v.**　參與　　4th ★★★★★
In recent years, Taiwan has made great strides in enhancing its international image and gaining greater exposure, participating actively in a number of major international events.
最近幾年，台灣已經有很大的進展，不僅提高了國際形象及得到較多曝光，也積極參與許多國際活動。

1955 participation [pɑr,tɪsə'peʃən]　　**n.**　參與　　4th ★★★★★
Tom practiced hard for the qualification for the participation in the national contest.
湯姆為了取得參加全國大賽的資格，非常努力練習。

1956 participant [pɑr'tɪsəpənt]　　**n.**　參與者　　4th ★★★★★
The seminar was held in such a warm room that many of the participants dozed off.
研討會在一個相當溫暖的房間裡舉行，許多與會者因而打起瞌睡。

1957 particularly [pə'tɪkjələlɪ]　　**adv.**　特別地　　4th ★★★★★
The snow in past winter was particularly harsh.
去年冬天的雪下得特別惡劣。

1958 partnership ['pɑrtnə,ʃɪp]　　**n.**　夥伴關係　　3rd ★★★★★
To combat crime and restore social order, it is urged to establish a partnership between police and citizens.
為了打擊犯罪和維護社會秩序，社會呼籲警民之間建立夥伴關係。

1959 passer-by ['pæsə'baɪ]　　**n.**　路人　　4th ★★★★★
In yesterday's protest, the demonstrator distributed leaflets of their claims against air pollution to passers-by.
在昨天的抗議中，示威者分發傳單聲明他們反對困擾空氣污染。

1960 passage ['pæsɪdʒ]　　　　**n.** 走廊　　4th ★★★★★
There was a screen at the end of the passage.
走廊的盡頭有一個屏幕。

1961 passenger ['pæsndʒə]　　**n.** 乘客　　4th ★★★★★
The cable car can carry six passengers once.
纜車一次可乘載六名乘客。

1962 passion ['pæʃən]　　　　**n.** 熱愛　　4th ★★★★★
The girl has a passion for classical music.
這個女孩熱愛古典音樂。

1963 passive ['pæsɪv]　　　　**adj.** 被動的　　4th ★★★★★
Mr. Johnson was disappointed at his students for having a passive learning attitude.
強生老師對於學生被動的學習態度感到失望。

1964 passport ['pæs,port]　　**n.** 護照　　5th ★★★★★
Now that our passports have been stolen, Officer, what do you recommend us to do?
警察先生，現在我們的護照被偷了，你建議我們該怎麼做呢？

1965 pastime ['pæs,taɪm]　　**n.** 消遣　　4th ★★★★★
Flying kites is a traditional New Year pastime in Japan.
放風箏在日本新年是一項傳統消遣活動。

1966 patent ['pætnt]　　　　**n.** 專利　　3rd ★★★★★
Microsoft Company got a patent for its invention. Anyone who manufactures the same product will be fined.
微軟公司為其發明申請了專利，任何製造同樣產品的人將被罰款。

1967 patient ['peʃənt]　　　　**adj.** 有耐心的　　5th ★★★★★
My little sister has become more patient as she has aged.
我的妹妹隨著年齡增長，變得越來越有耐心。

1968 patiently ['peʃəntlɪ]　　**adv.** 有耐心地　　5th ★★★★★
When I arrived at our meeting place, I saw my father waiting patiently.
當我到和爸爸相約的地方時，看見他正耐心的等著。

1969 patrol [pə'trol]　　　　**n.** 巡邏　　3rd ★★★★★

A patrol officer is ticketing John for driving on the shoulder.
巡邏員警開了約翰一張罰單，因為他開上路肩。

1970 **patron** [ˈpetrən]　　　　n.　顧客　　　3rd ★★★★★

I had been the store's most loyal patron until the new management raised the prices.
在新的經營者提高價位之前，我一直都是這家店的忠實顧客。

1971 **pattern** [ˈpætən]　　　　n.　模式　　　4th ★★★★★

Bees dance their signals, flying in certain patterns that tell other bees where to find nectar for honey.
蜜蜂藉由飛舞傳遞訊號，他們特定的飛行模式是為了告訴其他蜜蜂，哪裡有可以採集成蜂蜜的花蜜。

1972 **pave** [pev]　　　　v.　鋪設　　　4th ★★★★★

Jackie Robinson paved the way for black and white people to play baseball together.
傑奇羅賓森為了讓黑人和白人能一起打棒球鋪路。

1973 **pay** [pe]　　　　v.　支付　　　5th ★★★★★

Sandy had to pay a lot of interest on her house loan.
珊蒂必須支付很多房貸利息。

1974 **payment** [ˈpemənt]　　　　n.　款項　　　5th ★★★★★

Jack made his final car payment, and now he has no debt.
傑克付了最後一筆車款，現在他沒有負債。

1975 **peak** [pik]　　　　n.　山頂　　　5th ★★★★★

Some people believe that Colorado's peaks are the home to only bears and mountain man who look like bears.
有些人認為只有熊和看起來像熊的山人，才會以科羅拉多州的山峰為棲所。

1976 **peculiar** [pɪˈkjuljə]　　　　adj.　獨特的　　　4th ★★★★★

Madison has a peculiar interest in writing stories about talking rabbits.
曼德森對撰寫有關會說話的兔子的故事書有特殊興趣。

1977 **peculiarity** [pɪˌkjulɪˈærətɪ]　　　　n.　怪癖　　　3rd ★★★★★

My sister's peculiarity is that she sometimes laughs for no reason.
我妹的怪癖是她有時候會沒來由的大笑。

1978 **pedal** [ˈpɛdl̩]　　　　v.　騎　　　4th ★★★★★

The child will pedal his tricycle to the playground.
小孩子會騎著他的兒童三輪車到操場。

1979 **pedestal** ['pɛdɪstḷ]　　　　**n.**　底座　　🚫 ★★★★★
The statue will be put on the pedestal made of marble.
這座雕像會裝上大理石的底座。

1980 **pedestrian** [pə'dɛstrɪən]　　**n.**　行人　　🚫 ★★★★★
Pedestrians should walk through the zebra crossing when crossing the road.
行人穿越馬路時應該走斑馬線。

1981 **peel** [pil]　　　　　　**v.**　剝　　🚫 ★★★★★
You have to peel the banana before you eat it.
吃香蕉之前你要先剝香蕉皮。

1982 **penalty** ['pɛnḷtɪ]　　　　**n.**　處罰　　🚫 ★★★★★
Some people believe that the death penalty is an extreme form of punishment.
有些人認為死刑是一種極端的懲罰。

1983 **penetrate** ['pɛnə,tret]　　　**v.**　穿透　　🚫 ★★★★★
The bullet is able to penetrate a wall one hundred meters away.
這顆子彈能夠穿透百米寬的牆。

1984 **penetration** [,pɛnə'treʃən]　**n.**　洞察力　🚫 ★★★★★
The CEO is a man of penetration and he can grasp the key point very soon.
這位執行長富有洞察力，他可以很快領略要點。

1985 **penguin** ['pɛngwɪn]　　　　**n.**　企鵝　　🚫 ★★★★★
The young penguin was killed by a fierce seal near the coast.
這隻年幼的企鵝在岸邊被凶猛的海豹吃掉。

1986 **pension** ['pɛʃən]　　　　　**n.**　退休金　🚫 ★★★★★
A Federal Bankruptcy judge in Chicago approved the United Airline's decision to terminate its employees' pension plans yesterday.
芝加哥一位聯邦破產判決法官，在昨日批准了美國聯合航空終止僱員退休金的決定。

1987 **people** ['pipḷ]　　　　　　**n.**　人們　　🚫 ★★★★★
No matter how inconvenient country life may be, many people have escaped from big cities to rural areas.
無論鄉村生活是多麼的不方便，還是有許多人從大城市逃往農村。

1988 pepper [ˈpɛpɚ]　　　　**n.** 辣椒　　　5th ★★★★★
Some people are allergic to the smell of pepper powder.
有些人對辣椒粉的氣味過敏。

1989 perceive [pəˈsiv]　　　　**v.** 察覺　　　4th ★★★★★
With his excellent social skills, Steven has been perceived as a great communicator by all his colleagues.
因為史帝夫出色的社交能力，一直以來同事們都認為他是個厲害的溝通者。

1990 percent [pɚˈsɛnt]　　　　**n.** 百分比　　　5th ★★★★★
Eleven percent of Taiwanese aircraft hit by birds have suffered damage, according to statistics released by the Flight Safety Foundation.
根據飛行安全基金會的統計顯示，台灣的飛機有百分之十一是遭鳥類撞擊而受損。

1991 percentage [pɚˈsɛntɪdʒ]　　　　**n.** 百分比　　　4th ★★★★★
By 2020, the country with the highest percentage of aging population will be Japan.
到了2020年，日本將會是人口高齡化比例最高的國家。

1992 perception [pɚˈsɛpʃən]　　　　**n.** 看法；知覺　　　5th ★★★★★
Helen Keller altered our perception of the disabled, and achieved many deeds no one has ever done before.
海倫凱勒改變我們對殘障者的看法，也完成許多沒人做過的事跡。

1993 perfect [ˈpɝfɪkt]　　　　**adj.** 完美的　　　5th ★★★★★
Practice makes perfect.
熟能生巧。

1994 perfection [pɚˈfɛkʃən]　　　　**n.** 完美　　　5th ★★★★★
The ancient tradition still remains in perfection.
古老的傳統還是保存得很完善。

1995 perforate [ˈpɝfəˌret]　　　　**v.** 穿孔　　　4th ★★★★★
The bullet perforated the gangster's chest and he died at once.
子彈穿過歹徒的胸膛，他當場死亡。

1996 perform [pɚˈfɔrm]　　　　**v.** 表現　　　5th ★★★★★
My cousin's poor health has affected how he performs in school.
我的表弟身體不好，這也影響到他在學校的表現。

1997 performance [pɚˈfɔrməns]　　　　**n.** 表演　　　5th ★★★★★

The frequencies of these good performances are declining.
這些精采表演演出次數正在下降。

1998 perfume ['pɜfjum]　　　**n.** 香水　　5th ★★★★★
She is used to wearing this brand of perfume.
她習慣擦這個牌子的香水。

1999 period ['pɪrɪəd]　　　**n.** 期間　　5th ★★★★★
Before An Lee's films started to attract worldwide attention, he stayed home for a period of time while his wife worked to support the family.
李安的電影還沒受世界矚目以前，有好一段時間都待在家，由他太太工作支撐家計。

2000 perish ['pɛrɪʃ]　　　**v.** 滅亡　　4th ★★★★★
The village perished in floods and most of the villagers died.
這個村莊遭洪水滅村，大部分的村民也難逃一劫。

2001 permanent ['pɜmənənt]　　　**adj.** 固定的　　4th ★★★★★
Lucy is trying hard to get a permanent job in Taipei.
露西正努力試著要在台北找到一個長期工作。

2002 permeate ['pɜmɪ,et]　　　**v.** 瀰漫　　4th ★★★★★
The smoke permeated the restaurant and all the customers rushed out.
濃煙瀰漫了整間餐廳，顧客爭先恐後跑了出去。

2003 permission [pəˈmɪʃən]　　　**n.** 允許　　4th ★★★★★
Your car will be towed away if you park it here without permission.
如果你未經允許就把車停在這裡，你的車子會被吊走。

2004 permit [pəˈmɪt]　　　**v.** 允許　　4th ★★★★★
For safety reasons, no one is permitted to use a cellular phone on the plane.
為了安全著想，飛機上禁止使用手機。

2005 pernicious [pəˈnɪʃəs]　　　**adj.** 惡性的　　3rd ★★★★★
The thin woman has been suffering from pernicious anemia for several years.
這個瘦弱的女人已經有好幾年都受惡性貧血之苦。

2006 perpetuate [pəˈpɛtʃu,et]　　　**v.** 使永恆　　3rd ★★★★★
The monument was erected to perpetuate the memory of the great general.
為了永遠紀念這位偉大的將軍而建了這座紀念碑。

2007 **perplex** [pəˈplɛks]　　　　**v.**　使困惑　　~~3rd~~ ★★★★★

My brother tried to perplex me with difficult math question.
我弟試圖用困難的數學問題難倒我。

2008 **persist** [pəˈsɪst]　　　　**v.**　持續存在　　~~4th~~ ★★★★★

Superstitions persist everywhere in the world.
迷信在世界上到處都有。

2009 **persistent** [pəˈsɪstənt]　　　**adj.**　堅持的　　~~4th~~ ★★★★★

Mary had to work full-time to support her family, but she still earned her college degree by being persistent in her studies.
瑪莉為了養活家人必須上全職班，但她還是靠著堅定的毅力完成大學學業。

2010 **person** [ˈpɝsn]　　　　**n.**　人　　~~4th~~ ★★★★★

He is a conservative person. He doesn't like changes but enjoys old ways of thinking.
他是個保守的人，不喜歡改變，只喜愛舊有的思考方式。

2011 **personal** [ˈpɝsn̩]　　　　**adj.**　個人的　　~~4th~~ ★★★★★

For your safety, when you make a friend on the Internet, don't reveal too much personal information in the e-mail at the beginning stage.
為了你的安全著想，結交網友時，不要一開始就在電子郵件裡透露太多個人訊息。

2012 **personality** [ˌpɝsn̩ˈælətɪ]　　**n.**　個性　　~~4th~~ ★★★★★

Quiet people don't usually have the personality to host TV shows.
文靜的人沒有電視節目主持人的特徵。

2013 **personnel** [ˌpɝsn̩ˈɛl]　　　**n.**　人事　　~~4th~~ ★★★★★

I planned to apply for the position of the personnel manager.
我打算應徵人事經理的職位。

2014 **perspective** [pəˈspɛktɪv]　　**n.**　觀點　　~~4th~~ ★★★★★

Immigrants bring different perspectives to the country, teaching local people about other countries and cultures.
移民帶給一個國家不同的觀點，教導當地民眾其他的國家和文化。

2015 **perspiration** [ˌpɝspəˈreʃən]　　**n.**　辛苦　　~~3rd~~ ★★★★★

Genius is one percent inspiration and ninety-nine percent perspiration.
天才是靠百分之一的靈感和百分之九十九的努力。

2016 persuade [pə'swed]   **v.**   說服   4th ★★★★★
Chelsea said she was going to stay home, but I persuaded her to come out.
切爾西說要待在家裡，但我勸她出來走走。

2017 persuasive [pə'swesɪv]   **adj.** 有說服力的   4th ★★★★★
In writing, you take a persuasive position on an issue and try to make the reader believe that your position is correct.
在寫作時，針對一項議題你要舉出具說服力的論點，並讓讀者相信你的論點是正確的。

2018 peruse [pə'ruz]   **v.**   閱讀   3rd ★★★★★
I only had a moment to peruse the newspaper quickly this morning.
今天早上，我只有一點時間匆匆讀了報紙。

2019 perseverance [ˌpɜsə'vɪrəns]   **n.**   毅力   3rd ★★★★★
Perseverance can overcome any difficulty.
毅力可以克服任何困難。

2020 pessimist ['pɛsəmɪst]   **n.**   悲觀者   3rd ★★★★★
A poor person has no right to be pessimist.
可憐的人沒有悲觀的權利。

2021 pessimistic [ˌpɛsə'mɪstɪk]   **adj.** 悲觀的   3rd ★★★★★
Don't take a pessimistic view of life.
不要悲觀看待人生。

2022 pesticide ['pɛstɪˌsaɪd]   **n.**   殺蟲劑   3rd ★★★★★
Using too much pesticide is never good to the environment.
使用太多農藥對環境沒有任何益處。

2023 petition [pə'tɪʃən]   **n.**   請願   3rd ★★★★★
All the representatives petitioned the CEO to take immediate measures.
全體代表請求執行長採舉立即措施。

2024 petty ['pɛtɪ]   **adj.** 瑣碎的   4th ★★★★★
The accountant purchased some bottles of water from petty expenses.
會計人員用零星費用買了些瓶裝水。

2025 petulant ['pɛtʃələnt]   **adj.** 任性的   4th ★★★★★
As the only child in her family, Amy is both selfish and petulant. Even her grandparents find it hard to reason with her when she is having a fit.
艾咪是獨生女，她又自私脾氣又差，連祖父母都發現很難在她情緒爆發時跟她講理。

P

2026 pharmacy [ˈfɑrməsɪ]　n.　藥品　3rd ★★★★★
Stacy works for a major drug company and sells pharmacies to doctors and hospitals.
史黛西在一家大型製藥公司工作，負責銷售藥品給醫生和醫院。

2027 phenomenon [fəˈnɑmə,nɑn]　n.　現象　3rd ★★★★★
Haley's Comet is a phenomenon that a person usually only sees once in his lifetime.
哈雷彗星是稀有現象，人們通常一生只會看到一次。

2028 philosophical [,fɪləˈsɑfɪk̩]　adj.　泰然自若的　4th ★★★★★
Many people are not philosophical about their losses.
許多人無法泰然自若面對自己的損失。

2029 phlegmatic [flɛgˈmætɪk]　adj.　遲鈍的　3rd ★★★★★
The phlegmatic student is making a gradual progress now.
這個遲鈍的學生正逐漸進步。

2030 phonograph [ˈfonə,græf]　n.　留聲機　3rd ★★★★★
This classic phonograph can still work well.
這台傳統留聲機仍可以正常運作。

2031 photocopier [ˈfotə,kɑpɪə]　n.　影印機　5th ★★★★★
I want to make some A4 copies but I've never used a photocopier before.
我想用A4大小的紙印東西，但是我從來沒有用過影印機。

2032 phrase [frez]　n.　片語　4th ★★★★★
Look up what the adjective phrase means.
查查看這個形容詞片語什麼意思。

2033 physical [ˈfɪzɪk̩]　adj.　生理的　4th ★★★★★
The effect of physical and mental demands and pressures on the human body may be thought of as stress.
身心的需求和壓力對人體所造成的影響，可以被視為壓力。

2034 pickpocket [ˈpɪk,pɑkɪt]　n.　扒手　4th ★★★★★
We should be aware of pickpockets on the crowded bus.
我們在擁擠的公車上要注意扒手。

2035 picturesque [,pɪktʃəˈrɛsk]　adj.　如畫的　4th ★★★★★

My family spent a joyful weekend in a picturesque village.
我們全家在風景如畫的村莊度過一個愉快的週末。

2036 piece [pis]　　　　　　**n.** 一片　　5th ★★★★★
I'm very hungry. Can I have a piece of cake?
我非常餓，可以吃一片蛋糕嗎？

2037 pilgrim ['pɪlgrɪm]　　　　**n.** 朝聖者　　4th ★★★★★
People who travel from one place to another for religious reasons are pilgrims.
為了宗教因素從一處旅行至另一處的人，我們稱之為朝聖者。

2038 pilot ['paɪlət]　　　　　　**n.** 飛行員　　5th ★★★★★
To fly a balloon, the pilot burns wood or gas to make hot air, which makes the balloon rise.
為了讓熱氣球飛起來，飛行員燃燒木材或氣體來製造熱空氣，使熱氣球上升。

2039 pioneer [ˌpaɪə'nɪr]　　　　**n.** 先鋒　　4th ★★★★★
Jean Piaget, a psychologist and pioneer in the study of child intelligence, was born in Switzerland in 1896.
皮亞捷出生於一八九六年的瑞士，是一位心理學家，也是研究兒童智力的先驅。

2040 piracy ['paɪrəsɪ]　　　　**n.** 盜版　　3rd ★★★★★
Many entertainment celebrities, on April 5, 2002, attended an anti-piracy demonstration in Taipei.
二千〇二年四月五日，許多演藝名人出席了在台北的一場反盜版示威活動。

2041 pirate ['paɪrət]　　　　　**n.** 海盜　　4th ★★★★★
Pirates off the coast of Africa are a big problem today.
非洲海岸邊的海盜是當今一大問題。

2042 pitch [pɪtʃ]　　　　　　**v.** 投擲　　4th ★★★★★
Wang Chien-Ming does not give up many home runs when he pitches.
王建民投球時不常被打出全壘打。

2043 pitiable ['pɪtɪəbl]　　　　**adj.** 可憐的　　4th ★★★★★
The beggar was so pitiable that I could not but give him a few dollars.
那個乞丐看起來好可憐，我不由得給他幾塊錢。

2044 pity ['pɪtɪ]　　　　　　**n.** 可惜　　4th ★★★★★
It's a pity that you have to leave so soon. I sincerely hope that you will come back very soon.
真可惜你必須這麼早離開，我衷心希望你很快就回來。

P

2045 pitiful ['pɪtɪfəl]　　　**adj.** 慈悲的　　4th ★★★★★
The woman is pitiful to poor children from single parent families.
這個女人很同情來自單親家庭的貧窮小孩。

2046 plagiarism ['pledʒə,rɪzəm]　　**n.** 抄襲　　3rd ★★★★★
The graduate student was accused of plagiarism in his latest report.
這位研究生最近的一篇報告被控抄襲。

2047 plain [plen]　　　**adj.** 簡單的　　4th ★★★★★
The math question is quite plain for most of the students in the gifted class.
這個數學問題對資優班的學生來說，相當簡單。

2048 plan [plæn]　　　**v.** 計畫　　5th ★★★★★
Susan is planning to have a party during her husband is on his business trip abroad.
蘇珊計畫在她老公到國外出差的時候，辦一場派對。

2049 plane [plen]　　　**n.** 飛機　　5th ★★★★★
If you want to travel from Taipei to Hualien faster, you should take a plane.
如果你要快一點從台北到花蓮，你應該搭飛機。

2050 plant [plænt]　　　**n.** 植物　　5th ★★★★★
The young plants receive the sunlight and water that they need in the nursery.
幼小的植物在苗圃得到其所需的陽光和水。

2051 planet ['plænɪt]　　　**n.** 星球　　4th ★★★★★
We can slow down the climate change by making personal commitment to protect our planet.
我們可以靠著個人努力來保護我們的星球，減緩氣候的變遷。

2052 plastic ['plæstɪk]　　　**adj.** 塑膠的　　5th ★★★★★
Susan's plastic bag broke because she put too much candy in it.
蘇珊的塑膠袋破了，因為她在裡頭裝了太多糖果。

2053 plate [plet]　　　**n.** 本壘　　5th ★★★★★
We are looking forward to the pitcher's return to the plate.
我們期待投手重返本壘板。

2054 platform ['plæt,fɔrm]　　　**n.** 政綱　　5th ★★★★★
It is never easy to see the ruling party and the opposition party sharing the same

platform.
要看到執政黨與反對黨用相同的政綱是絕不可能的。

2055 playful ['plefəl]　　　　　**adj.** 打趣的　　5th ★★★★★
It is a world that avoids heavy scientific-sounding language in favor of words that are simple, fresh and playful.
這個世界的用語傾向簡單、新鮮、開玩笑的口吻，避免沉重和聽起來極為嚴謹的話語。

2056 pleasant ['plɛzənt]　　　　**adj.** 愉快的　　5th ★★★★★
Thanks a lot for such a pleasant evening.
非常感謝讓我擁有這麼一個愉快的夜晚。

2057 pleasure ['plɛʒɚ]　　　　　**n.** 樂意　　5th ★★★★★
My dad takes pleasure in mowing the lawn every Sunday.
我爸爸樂於在每星期日修剪草坪。

2058 pledge [plɛdʒ]　　　　　　**v.** 保證　　3rd ★★★★★
Many citizens have pledged their participation in an act to make our cities clean.
許多市民已經承諾要以身作則，維持我們的城市的整潔。

2059 plentiful ['plɛntɪfəl]　　　　**adj.** 多的　　4th ★★★★★
Of all living creatures on earth, insects are the most plentiful.
地球上的所有生物中，以昆蟲最為繁多。

2060 plenty ['plɛntɪ]　　　　　　**n.** 豐富　　4th ★★★★★
There are plenty of band-aids in the first aid kit.
急救箱裡有許多急救繃帶。

2061 plight [plaɪt]　　　　　　　**n.** 保證　　4th ★★★★★
People who don't think ahead and plan for their future often find themselves in sorry plight.
不願意長遠思考和計畫未來的人，往往發現自己處於困境中。

2062 plug [plʌg]　　　　　　　　**v.** 插入插頭　　4th ★★★★★
Don't forget to plug in your phone so that it works tomorrow.
不要忘了把你的手機接上電源以便明天使用。

2063 plumber ['plʌmɚ]　　　　　**n.** 水管工　　4th ★★★★★
The faucet in the kitchen had been leaking for days. We should call the plumber to fix the problem.
廚房水龍頭漏水好幾天了，我們應該打電話叫水管工來修理。

P

2064 **poem** ['poɪm]　　　　　**n.** 詩　　　5th ★★★★★
This student is particularly good at memory. He is successful in learning the long poem by heart.
這個學生的記憶力特別好，他成功背下一首長詩。

2065 **poison** ['pɔɪzn]　　　　　**v.** 中毒　　　4th ★★★★★
In case of food poisoning, young children are especially vulnerable.
如果發生食物中毒，幼小孩童尤其首當其衝。

2066 **poisonous** ['pɔɪznəs]　　　**adj.** 有毒的　　　4th ★★★★★
Mattel recalled some of its toys made in China after they were found poisonous and harmful to the children.
美泰兒公司發現在中國製造的玩具有毒且對兒童有害後，召回了一些玩具。

2067 **police** [pə'lis]　　　　　**n.** 警方　　　4th ★★★★★
The police asked the girl's parents not to give away to the kidnappers' request.
警方請求女孩的雙親，不要對綁匪的要求讓步。

2068 **policy** ['pɑləsɪ]　　　　　**n.** 政策　　　4th ★★★★★
Aiden has some liberal beliefs about changing government policy.
艾登有一些關於改變政府政策的宏觀理念。

2069 **polite** [pə'laɪt]　　　　　**adj.** 有禮貌的　　　5th ★★★★★
I like to go shopping in that department store because the clerks there are very polite and nice.
我喜歡去那家百貨公司逛，因為那裡的店員都非常禮貌且友善。

2070 **politics** ['pɑlətɪks]　　　**n.** 政治學　　　4th ★★★★★
They always argue about politics and never can agree on anything.
他們總是爭論有關政治的事，但從未達成任何共識。

2071 **pollute** [pə'lut]　　　　　**v.** 汙染　　　4th ★★★★★
Burning paper money on festival days can pollute the air.
在節慶日焚燒紙錢會污染空氣。

2072 **pollution** [pə'luʃən]　　　**n.** 汙染　　　4th ★★★★★
The air pollution was caused by the farmers who burned the waste in the field after the harvest.
農夫採收完後燃燒廢物，導致空氣汙染。

2073 polyglot ['pɑlɪ‚glɑt]　　　**n.**　語言天才　　4th ★★★★★
A polyglot is a person who has a good command of many different languages.
一個通曉多國語言的人，就是能夠靈活使用多國語言。

2074 pool [pul]　　　　　　**n.**　水池　　5th ★★★★★
When it gets hot outside, dad fills up the pool with the hose.
外面的天氣開始熱了起來，爸爸用軟管把水池注滿水。

2075 poor [pur]　　　　　　**adj.**　不健康的　　5th ★★★★★
The young man was well qualified for the position, but the committee finally turned
down his application on account of his poor health.
這位年輕人很適合那個職位，但委員會最後因為他的健康問題拒絕錄用他。

2076 popular ['pɑpjələ]　　　　**adj.**　受歡迎的　　5th ★★★★★
Ximending is popular with almost all the young people in Taipei.
西門町受到全台北市年輕人的歡迎。

2077 popularity [‚pɑpjə'lærətɪ]　　**n.**　名氣　　5th ★★★★★
The singer's popularity increases even though she gave birth to a new baby.
那位歌星縱使產下新生兒，她的名氣還是攀升。

2078 population [‚pɑpjə'leʃən]　　**n.**　人口　　4th ★★★★★
The world's population is now estimated to be over six billion.
世界人口目前估計超過六十億。

2079 portion ['porʃən]　　　　**n.**　部分　　4th ★★★★★
To the great annoyance of many readers, a considerable portion of the space in
any newspaper is occupied by advertisements.
每份報紙有相當大的版面都被廣告所占據，這對讀者來說，很令人惱怒。

2080 portable ['portəbl]　　　　**adj.**　可攜帶的　　5th ★★★★★
Julie wants to buy a portable computer so that she can carry it around when she
travels.
茱莉想買台筆電，這樣她在旅行時就可以隨身攜帶。

2081 portfolio [port'folɪ‚o]　　　**n.**　有價證券　　4th ★★★★★
A cautious investor knows how to diversify his portfolio. He won't put all the eggs
in one basket.
謹慎的投資者知道如何使有價證券多樣化。他不會將所有雞蛋放在同一個籃子裡。

P

2082 pose [poz]　　　　　　　**v.**　造成　　**5th** ★★★★★
A research shows it is familiar people, not strangers, who pose the most risk.
一項研究指出，構成最大危險的是熟人，而非陌生人。

2083 positive [ˈpɑzətɪv]　　　**adj.**　正面的　　**4th** ★★★★★
When played properly, some music can have positive effects on learning and attitude.
有些音樂彈奏得宜的時候，可以在學習上和態度上有正面的影響。

2084 possess [pəˈzɛs]　　　　**v.**　擁有　　**4th** ★★★★★
Andrew is now working at a factory, but his dream is to possess a business run by him.
安德魯現在在一家工廠上班，但他的夢想是擁有一間自己掌管的企業。

2085 possibility [ˌpɑsəˈbɪlətɪ]　　**n.**　可能性　　**4th** ★★★★★
I don't know if I'll pass my test today, but it's a possibility.
我不知道今天我是否會通過測驗，但我覺得有可能。

2086 possible [ˈpɑsəbḷ]　　　**adj.**　可能的　　**5th** ★★★★★
Hitchhiking from city to city sounds interesting, but it's not possible to hitchhike from planet to planet.
搭便車旅行於不同城市間聽起來很有趣，但在行星間是不可能的。

2087 postage [ˈpostɪdʒ]　　　**n.**　郵資　　**4th** ★★★★★
The postage stamp has been around for only a relatively short period of time.
郵票的出現其實是最近才發生的事。

2088 postpone [postˈpon]　　　**v.**　拖延　　**4th** ★★★★★
If this customer still has not agreed to the agenda, we should consider postponing the meeting.
如果這位客人還是不同意會議議程的話，我們應該考慮將會議延期。

2089 potato [pəˈteto]　　　　**n.**　馬鈴薯　　**5th** ★★★★★
She bought some carrots, potatoes and lettuce to make salad.
她買一些紅蘿蔔、馬鈴薯和萵苣來做沙拉。

2090 potential [pəˈtɛnʃəl]　　　**n.**　可能性　　**4th** ★★★★★
A gun in the wrong hands has the potential to hurt somebody.
槍如果落入壞人之手，有可能會傷害到他人。

2091 **poultry** ['poltrɪ]　　　　　**n.** 家禽　　　**3rd** ★★★★★
Chickens, ducks and geese are all poultry.
雞、鴨、鵝都屬於家禽類。

2092 **pour** [por]　　　　　**v.** 傾倒　　　**4th** ★★★★★
After you pour my glass of milk, check to see if my toast is ready.
你把牛奶倒在我的杯子後，去看看我的麵包是不是可以吃了。

2093 **poverty** ['pɑvətɪ]　　　　　**n.** 貧窮　　　**5th** ★★★★★
The businessman fell into poverty after he got bankrupt.
這名商人破產後陷入貧困。

2094 **powder** ['paudɚ]　　　　　**n.** 粉末　　　**5th** ★★★★★
The naughty boy crushed the crayon to powder under his feet.
這個頑皮的男孩用腳把粉筆踩得粉粹。

2095 **power** ['paur]　　　　　**n.** 力量　　　**5th** ★★★★★
Many people believed that the water had the power to make one young.
許多人都相信水有讓人變年輕的力量。

2096 **powerful** ['paurfəl]　　　　　**n.** 強力的　　　**5th** ★★★★★
The fire in the fireworks factory in Changhua set off a series of powerful explosions and killed four people.
位於彰化的一家煙火工廠發生火災，引起一連串大爆炸，有四人因此死亡。

2097 **practice** ['præktɪs]　　　　　**v.** 練習　　　**3rd** ★★★★★
You need to practice your swimming skills, if you don't want to be drowned.
如果你不想溺水的話，就得練習你的游泳技巧。

2098 **pragmatically** [præg'mætɪkəlɪ]　**adv.** 實際上　　　**3rd** ★★★★★
Pragmatically speaking, the tolerate length of a film is defined by the length of time an audience is willing to sit.
客觀來說，觀眾能夠容忍的片長取決於他們願意坐多久的時間。

2099 **praise** [prez]　　　　　**n.** 讚美　　　**4th** ★★★★★
Hsu Fang-yi, a young Taiwanese dancer, recently performed at Lincoln Center in New York and won a great deal of praise.
年輕的台灣舞者許芳宜，最近在紐約的林肯中心演出，大獲好評。

2100 **precaution** [prɪ'kɔʃən]　　　　　**n.** 預防措施　　　**4th** ★★★★★

It is imperative that people should take precautions before they go on a skiing trip.
重要的是，人們在滑雪前，應該先做好預防措施。

2101 precious ['prɛʃəs]　　　　**adj.** 珍貴的　　*4th* ★★★★★
Water has been considered to be a precious commodity. People are not supposed to take it for granted.
水一直都是珍貴的日常用品，人們不應該視為理所當然。

2102 precinct ['prisɪŋkt]　　　　**n.** 分局　　*3rd* ★★★★★
Officer Chang is from the Ta-An Police Precinct of the Taipei Municipal Police Department.
張警官服務於台北市警察局的大安派出所。

2103 precise [prɪ'saɪs]　　　　**adj.** 準確的　　*4th* ★★★★★
The mechanic is always very precise in following instructions.
機械師總是非常精確地遵照操作指示。

2104 predecessor ['prɛdɪ'sɛsə]　　**n.** 原先的產品　　*4th* ★★★★★
The American car of the 1980s is quite different from its predecessors.
1980年代的美國車和原先的產品有很大的不同。

2105 predict [prɪ'dɪkt]　　　　**v.** 預測　　*4th* ★★★★★
Though it is too early to say whether the storm will make shift in Taiwan, it is predicted heavy rain for northern and eastern parts of the island over the coming days.
雖說颱風是否轉向台灣還言之過早，不過未來幾天台灣北部和東部預計會下大雨。

2106 predominantly [prɪ'dɑmɪnəntlɪ] **adv.** 佔優勢地　　*3rd* ★★★★★
A widening gap between rich and poor is threatening to shatter Japan's view of itself as a predominantly middle-class country.
日漸擴大的貧富差距正逐步粉碎日本自以為是中產階級國家中的主流的想法。

2107 prefer [prɪ'fɜ]　　　　**v.** 寧可　　*5th* ★★★★★
We are used to this room now and prefer not to change to another one.
我們已經習慣這個房間了，最好不要再換另一間。

2108 preference ['prɛfərəns]　　**n.** 偏好　　*4th* ★★★★★
George has a strong preference for marble floors.
喬治對大理石地板有強烈的偏好。

2109 pregnancy ['prɛgnənsɪ]　　**n.** 懷孕　　*4th* ★★★★★

Smoking or drinking during pregnancy can cause a child to be born deformed.
懷孕時抽菸或喝酒會導致畸形兒。

2110 prejudice ['prɛdʒədɪs]　　n.　偏見　　4th ★★★★★
She is likely to have a prejudice against the boy from a single-parent family.
她很可能會對這個單親家庭的男孩有偏見。

2111 premature [ˌprimə'tjur]　　adj.　過早的　　4th ★★★★★
Try not to make a premature conclusion without second thinking.
不要未經深思熟慮就過早下定論。

2112 premiere [prɪ'mjɛr]　　n.　首映　　3rd ★★★★★
The world premier of the action movie will be at Hoover Theater on November 10.
這部動作片將會在十一月十日於胡佛戲院舉行全球首映。

2113 premise ['prɛmɪs]　　n.　房屋　　3rd ★★★★★
In order to promote inward investment, the government is planning to provide free premises of offices and factories for three years.
為了促進外來投資，政府計畫提供三年免費的辦公室和工廠用地。

2114 prepare [prɪ'pɛr]　　v.　預備　　5th ★★★★★
We did not have time to read the whole novel, so the teacher prepared an epitome for us.
我們沒有時間讀完整本小說，所以老師替我們準備了摘要。

2115 prescribe [prɪ'skraɪb]　　v.　開處方　　4th ★★★★★
The doctor prescribed some painkillers for my complaint.
我身體不適，醫生開了些止痛藥給我。

2116 prescription [prɪ'skrɪpʃən]　　n.　處方藥　　4th ★★★★★
After Allen got out of the clinic, he went to the pharmacy to have the prescription filled.
艾倫離開診所去藥局拿藥。

2117 prescriptive [prɪ'skrɪptɪv]　　adj.　規定的　　3rd ★★★★★
Most students think their teacher's guidelines on homework are too prescriptive.
大多數學生認為，老師對於家庭作業的標準過於約定俗成。

2118 presence ['prɛzns]　　n.　面前　　5th ★★★★★
John played the romantic song on the guitar in the presence of his classmates.
約翰在全班同學面前用吉他彈奏浪漫的曲子。

P

2119 present [prɪˈzɛnt]   **v.** 展現   4th ★★★★★
I'll present a demonstration of the new computer system. Then you'll know how powerful it is.
我將示範新的電腦系統，然後你就知道這套系統有多強。

2120 preserve [prɪˈzɝv]   **v.** 保存   4th ★★★★★
While adapting to western ways of living, many Asian immigrants in the US still try hard to preserve their own cultures and traditions.
許多住在美國的亞洲移民在適應西方生活的同時，仍努力保存自己的文化和傳統。

2121 president [ˈprɛzədənt]   **n.** 總統   4th ★★★★★
The last name of the late U.S. President John F. Kennedy is Kennedy.
美國前總統約翰甘迺迪的姓氏為甘迺迪。

2122 pressure [ˈprɛʃɚ]   **n.** 壓力   4th ★★★★★
His parents' high expectation puts him under tremendous pressure to win the first prize.
父母對他的期望很高，令他在爭取冠軍的過程中承受很大的壓力。

2123 prestigious [prɛsˈtɪdʒɪəs]   **n.** 著名的   5th ★★★★★
Founded in 1952, the MIT Sloan School of Management is one of the world's most prestigious colleges of commerce.
麻省理工學院於一九五二年創立，是世界上最著名的商學院之一。

2124 presumptuous [prɪˈzʌmptʃuəs]   **adj.** 放肆的   3rd ★★★★★
It seems to be presumptuous of the assistant to talk on the cell phone in the meeting.
助理在會議中講手機似乎是很放肆的行為。

2125 pretend [prɪˈtɛnd]   **v.** 假裝   4th ★★★★★
Most politicians try to impress people by showing how smart they are, but President Bush does the opposite; that is, he likes to pretend you're telling him something he didn't know.
許多政治家藉著表現自己的聰明才智，留給民眾好印象。但布希總統反其道而行，他喜歡假裝沒聽過你所說的事。

2126 pretty [ˈprɪtɪ]   **adv.** 相當地   5th ★★★★★
This is a pretty mess.
場面相當混亂。

2127 prevail [prɪˈvel]   **v.** 勝過   4th ★★★★★

The girl was prevailed upon to stay overnight because it happened to rain heavily.
因為下起大雨，女孩被說服留下來過夜。

2128 prevent [prɪ'vɛnt]　　　　**v.** 預防　　　4th ★★★★★

To prevent students from parking in the parking area assigned for faculty members, the school administration imposed a new regulation.
為了避免學生把車停在教職員停車區，學校行政部門實行了一項新規定。

2129 preventive [prɪ'vɛntɪv]　　　**adj.** 預防　　　4th ★★★★★

Failure to take preventive measures against pollution may eventually make a threat to human survival.
如果不針對污染採取預防措施，最終可能會威脅到人類生存。

2130 preview ['pri‚vju]　　　　**v.** 預習　　　4th ★★★★★

Previewing the lesson before class gives me a better idea about what the teacher is going to teach.
課前預習讓我對老師要教的東西有更清楚的想法。

2131 previous ['priviəs]　　　　**adj.** 先前的　　　4th ★★★★★

What distinguishes this approach from previous attempts to deal with breast cancer?
這種治療乳癌的方法，和之前的有什麼不同？

2132 price [praɪs]　　　　**n.** 價錢　　　5th ★★★★★

I should have bought that TV set when it had a discount price last week.
早知道上禮拜那台電視機在打折的時候，我就應該把它買下來。

2133 primary ['praɪ‚mɛrɪ]　　　　**adj.** 主要的　　　5th ★★★★★

The primary goal of many businesses is to make money.
許多企業的主要目標是為了賺錢。

2134 primitive ['prɪmətɪv]　　　　**adj.** 原始的　　　4th ★★★★★

It is a primitive instinct to flee a place of danger.
遇到危險就逃跑是人類的原始本能。

2135 principal ['prɪnsəpl]　　　　**n.** 校長　　　3rd ★★★★★

The principal tells the press that many safety measures have been taken, so having another campus accident in the same place again is very inconceivable.
校長告訴媒體，學校已經採取許多安全措施，所以在同樣的地方發生另一件校園意外是微乎其微。

P

2136 principle ['prɪnsəpl]　　　n.　原理　　4th ★★★★★
Learning the basic pronunciation principles helps students spell English words more easily.
學習基本的發音原理可以幫助學生更輕鬆背英文單字。

2137 printer ['prɪntɚ]　　　n.　印表機　　5th ★★★★★
Before printing any document, you need to connect the printer to the computer.
要列印任何文件之前，你必須先將印表機連上電腦。

2138 prior ['praɪɚ]　　　adj.　在先的　　5th ★★★★★
Given the increasingly high rate of divorce, many couples, prior to marriage, are advised to consider getting a prenuptial agreement.
有鑑於離婚率的增加，會建議夫妻在結婚前考慮簽署一份婚前協議。

2139 priority [praɪˈɔrətɪ]　　　n.　優先權　　4th ★★★★★
Healthcare workers, pregnant women and children aged between six months and six years are set to be priority recipients of immunization vaccine against the H1N1 virus.
醫護人員、孕婦和出生六個月到六歲間的兒童能優先施打免疫疫苗。

2140 prison ['prɪzn]　　　n.　監獄　　4th ★★★★★
Frank was caught trying to smuggle drugs into jail, which made him face a six-year sentence in prison.
法蘭克因為企圖走私毒品入獄，他將面臨六年刑期。

2141 privacy ['praɪvəsɪ]　　　n.　隱私　　4th ★★★★★
Newlyweds really value their privacy.
新婚夫婦都會十分珍惜他們的私生活。

2142 private ['praɪvɪt]　　　adj.　私人的　　4th ★★★★★
Most of the rooms in the White House are private, but there are five rooms that anyone can visit.
白宮大部分的房間都是私人的，但有五間房可供任何人進去參觀。

2143 privation [praɪˈveʃən]　　　n.　窮困　　5th ★★★★★
A lot of people died of privation in the country score years ago.
好幾年前，這個國家有很多人死於貧困。

2144 privilege ['prɪvlɪdʒ]　　　n.　特權　　4th ★★★★★
Jack was given the rare privilege of using the president's office, which made others quite jealous.
傑克獲准使用董事長的辦公室，這項罕見的特權讓很多人忌妒。

116

2145 probability [ˌprɑbəˈbɪlətɪ]　　**n.**　可能性　　5th ★★★★★
The probability of me playing basketball with Kobe Bryant is essentially zero.
我和柯比布萊恩打籃球的可能性基本上是零。

2146 probation [proˈbeʃən]　　**n.**　緩刑　　3rd ★★★★★
The jury put the thief under two years' probation.
陪審團給小偷兩年的緩刑。

2147 problem [ˈprɑbləm]　　**n.**　問題　　5th ★★★★★
Buffy is hoping one of her peers knows the answer to the problem.
巴菲希望她的其中一位同事知道問題的答案。

2148 procedure [prəˈsidʒə]　　**n.**　程序　　4th ★★★★★
If Kato follows the procedure, he shouldn't have any trouble.
如果加藤遵照程序，他應該不會有任何麻煩。

2149 process [ˈprɑsɛs]　　**n.**　過程　　4th ★★★★★
The writing and editing process is done on a computer, and therefore people don't need to use paper.
寫作和編輯的過程都在電腦上完成，所以不需要紙張。

2150 procession [prəˈsɛʃən]　　**n.**　遊行　　4th ★★★★★
We managed to catch a glance of Queen Elizabeth as the procession passed.
當遊行隊伍通過時，我們極力想要看到伊莉莎白女王一眼。

2151 produce [prəˈdjus]　　**v.**　生產　　4th ★★★★★
The fertile soil produced excellent crops.
肥沃的土壤生產優良的農作物。

2152 product [ˈprɑdəkt]　　**n.**　產品　　4th ★★★★★
Foreign products are always much more expensive than local ones.
國外的產品總是比國內的產品貴。

2153 production [prəˈdʌkʃən]　　**n.**　作品　　4th ★★★★★
The movie trilogy of The Lord of the Rings is a New Zealand production.
魔戒的電影三部曲是在紐西蘭製作的。

2154 productive [prəˈdʌktɪv]　　**adj.**　多產的　　4th ★★★★★
Mr. Lin is a very productive writer; he publishes at least five novels every year.
林先生是位多產的作家，他每年至少會出版五本小說。

2155 profession [prəˈfɛʃən]　　**n.** 職業　　4th ★★★★★
Accounting is a profession which has always interested me.
我一直都對會計這個職業很有興趣。

2156 professional [prəˈfɛʃənl]　　**adj.** 專業的　　4th ★★★★★
Fans of professional baseball and football argue continually over which is America's favorite sport.
職業棒球和職業足球的球迷們不停爭辯何者為美國人最愛的運動。

2157 professor [prəˈfɛsə]　　**n.** 教授　　4th ★★★★★
The professor can give nice advice for any that wants to learn Japanese well.
教授給了那些想要學好日文的人一些很棒的建議。

2158 proficiency [prəˈfɪʃənsɪ]　　**n.** 精通　　4th ★★★★★
Miss Chang attains proficiency at teaching English.
張小姐對英語教學很熟練。

2159 profile [ˈprofaɪl]　　**n.** 人物簡介　　4th ★★★★★
The popular show is known for its high profile guests like politicians, actors, and singers.
這個當紅的節目以其高知名度的來賓著稱，如政治人物，演員和歌手。

2160 profit [ˈprɑfɪt]　　**n.** 利潤　　4th ★★★★★
Since the business is slow this year, we have not made any profit.
由於今年的生意清淡，我們還沒賺到什麼錢。

2161 profitable [ˈprɑfɪtəbl]　　**adj.** 有利潤的　　4th ★★★★★
Selling fried chicken at the night market doesn't seem to be a decent business, but it is actually quite profitable.
在夜市賣鹽酥雞看起來不是個體面的工作，但其實很賺錢。

2162 progress [ˈprɑgrɛs]　　**n.** 進度　　4th ★★★★★
If you are learning another language, you can't allow your inhibition to control your progress.
如果你在學習新的語言，你不能壓抑自己的進度。

2163 progressive [prəˈgrɛsɪv]　　**adj.** 前進的　　4th ★★★★★
The troops made a progressive advance before dawn.
軍隊在破曉前逐步向前邁進。

117

2164 prohibit [prəˈhɪbɪt]　　　v. 禁止　　　4th ★★★★★
Eating and drinking in the language lab are strictly prohibited.
語言實驗室嚴禁飲食。

2165 project [ˈprɑdʒɛkt]　　　n. 計畫　　　4th ★★★★★
The dean says that the project is just a waste of money.
校長說這項計畫不過是浪費錢罷了。

2166 promote [prəˈmot]　　　v. 推廣　　　4th ★★★★★
The Indian government can legally block sites promoting hate speech, terrorism or pornography, but in reality sites are rarely banned.
印度政府可以合法阻止推廣仇恨言論、恐怖主義或色情的網站，但實際上這些網站卻很少被禁止。

2167 promotion [prəˈmoʃən]　　　n. 晉級　　　4th ★★★★★
Miss Liu finally got promotion after she worked at the company for ten years.
劉小姐在公司待了十年後終於升職了。

2168 prompt [prɑmpt]　　　adj. 迅速的　　　4th ★★★★★
The shopkeeper is always prompt in her payment.
店主總是準時繳款。

2169 pronounce [prəˈnauns]　　　v. 發音　　　4th ★★★★★
Reading lessons are opportunities to teach pronunciation for many teachers.
對許多老師來說，閱讀課是教導發音的好機會。

2170 proof [pruf]　　　n. 證據　　　4th ★★★★★
Without further proof, the police had to release the man under arrest.
警察沒有進一步的證據，只好將已逮捕的男子釋放。

2171 propel [prəˈpɛl]　　　v. 推進　　　4th ★★★★★
The ferry is propelled by steam.
渡輪靠蒸氣推進。

2172 properly [ˈprɑpəlɪ]　　　adv. 完全地　　　4th ★★★★★
We all do not understand why properly.
我們都不是完全了解為什麼。

2173 proportion [prəˈporʃən]　　　n. 比率　　　4th ★★★★★
A large proportion of the earth's surface is covered with water.
水覆蓋地表佔了很大的比例。

P

2174 proposal [prə'pozl]　　　**n.**　提案　　　4th ★★★★★
The mayor has made a proposal for a special budget of fifty million dollars to help reconstruct the disaster area.
市長提出了一項五千萬特別預算的提案幫助重建災區。

2175 propose [prə'poz]　　　**v.**　提議　　　4th ★★★★★
The young man proposed marriage to his girlfriend at the theater.
這位年輕人在戲院向他女朋友求婚。

2176 pros and cons　　　**n.**　利弊得失　　　3rd ★★★★★
Have you considered the pros and cons of buying a house instead of renting an apartment?
你有考慮過不租房子而改買房子的利弊得失嗎？

2177 prosecute ['prɑsɪ,kjut]　　　**v.**　控告　　　3rd ★★★★★
It surprised us all that the shoplifter was neither prosecuted nor even arrested.
令我們驚訝的是，扒手既沒有被告，甚至也沒有被逮捕。

2178 prosecution [,prɑsɪ'kjuʃən]　　　**n.**　起訴　　　3rd ★★★★★
The prosecution will be abandoned if the stolen money is returned.
如果歸還偷來的錢，將會撤銷告訴。

2179 prosecutor ['prɑsɪ,kjutə]　　　**n.**　檢察官　　　3rd ★★★★★
The prosecutor sued the shopkeeper for sexual harassment.
檢察官以性騷擾起訴店主。

2180 prospect ['prɑspɛkt]　　　**n.**　前景　　　4th ★★★★★
Andy's company makes investment plans according to the prospects of the market. His job is to extrapolate future developments based on current trends.
安迪的公司依據市場前景擬訂投資計畫，而他的工作是照現在趨勢推斷未來發展。

2181 prospective [prə'spɛktɪv]　　　**adj.**　未來的　　　4th ★★★★★
Mrs.Lee admires her prospective son-in-law a lot.
李太太很欣賞她的準女婿。

2182 prosperity [prɑs'pɛrətɪ]　　　**n.**　繁榮　　　3rd ★★★★★
Language never develops independently. It is closely related to the prosperity or the decline of the people who speak it.
語言從未獨立發展過，它和使用族群的興衰有著密切關聯。

A B C D E F G H I J K L M N O P Q R S T U V W X Y Z

The 3000 vocabularies you must know in public service exam

118

2183 prosperous [ˈprɑspərəs]　　　　adj.　繁榮的　　　4th ★★★★★
Korea has shown exceptional growth in the economy over the past three years. Now it is more prosperous than many other Asian countries.
過去三年來韓國已在經濟方面展現卓越成長，現在它比其他許多亞洲國家還繁榮。

2184 protect [prəˈtɛkt]　　　　v.　保護　　　4th ★★★★★
Joe loved going to concerts but always wore earplugs to protect him.
喬愛聽音樂會，卻總是戴耳塞保護自己。

2185 protection [prəˈtɛkʃən]　　　　n.　保護　　　4th ★★★★★
If I were you, I would purchase more insurance, just for your own protection.
如果我是你，我會買更多保險來保障自己。

2186 protein [ˈprotiɪn]　　　　n.　蛋白質　　　3rd ★★★★★
One gram of protein contains four calories, and one gram of fat contains nine calories.
一克的蛋白質含四卡路里，而一克的脂肪含九卡路里。

2187 protest [prəˈtɛst]　　　　v.　抗議　　　4th ★★★★★
Both men and women are protesting for equal rights of the sexes.
男人和女人都正在為爭取性別的平等權進行抗議。

2188 protocol [ˈprotəˌkɑl]　　　　n.　草案　　　4th ★★★★★
Not only have the lobbying groups been backing up the new protocol, but several industry labor unions are now voicing their stern support for it.
不僅是遊說團體支持這項新協議，還有一些工會也對此表示堅定的支持。

2189 proud [praud]　　　　adj.　自豪的　　　5th ★★★★★
The coach was proud because his basketball team won the championship.
教練很自豪，因為他帶領的籃球隊得到冠軍。

2190 prove [pruv]　　　　v.　證明　　　4th ★★★★★
With an exhaustive list of references, Dr. Lee's research project proves to be a most thorough and complete study of the subject.
李教授有一份詳盡的參考資料，他的研究專題證實是這門學科最全面徹底的研究。

2191 proverb [ˈprɑvɝb]　　　　n.　諺語　　　4th ★★★★★
According to an ancient Roman proverb, a sound body is the sign of a sound mind.
根據一個古羅馬的諺語所言，健全的精神寓于健康的身體。

2192 provide [prə'vaɪd]　　v.　提供　　4th ★★★★★
We provide an interest-free, twelve-month installment plan.
我們提供十二期零利率的分期方案。

2193 province ['prɑvɪns]　　n.　省份　　4th ★★★★★
The devastating earthquake has buried over 18,000 lives in southwestern China's Sichuan province.
慘絕人寰的地震導致中國西南方的四川省有超過一萬八千個人遭活埋。

2194 provoke [prə'vok]　　v.　激怒　　3rd ★★★★★
Disastrous "urban renewal" in the 1950s provoked such a furious backlash that Boston now has some of the best-preserved historic buildings and neighborhoods in the country.
災難性的都市重建於五〇年代在波士頓引起激烈反彈，所以波士頓擁有許多目前美國境內保留最完善的歷史建築和街景。

2195 psychological [ˌsaɪkə'lɑdʒɪk]]　　adj.　心理的　　3rd ★★★★★
A trip to the supermarket has now become an exercise in psychological warfare.
現在到超市購物已經成為一場心理戰。

2196 psychologist [saɪ'kɑlədʒɪst]　　n.　心理學家　　3rd ★★★★★
Many psychologists today say that dreams are the bridge between our conscious and unconscious mind.
現今許多心理學家都說，夢是我們意識和潛意識之間的橋樑。

2197 psychology [saɪ'kɑlədʒɪ]　　n.　心理學　　3rd ★★★★★
The psychology that works in physical stores is just as powerful on the Internet.
在實體商店購物的心理運作和在網路上一樣激烈。

2198 psychosomatic　　adj.　身心失調的　　3rd ★★★★★
[ˌsaɪkoso'mætɪk]
The doctor said that her problems were more than merely psychosomatic.
醫生說她的問題不只是身心失調而已。

2199 publicity [pʌb'lɪsətɪ]　　n.　名聲　　4th ★★★★★
That company got bad publicity after people found out that they were harming the environment.
人們發現那家公司一直在破壞生態環境，名聲掃地。

2200 public ['pʌblɪk]　　n.　公眾　　4th ★★★★★

Kissing in public has been and still is frowned on by many people in China.
在中國，許多人還是覺得在公共場合親吻很不妥當。

2201 publish ['pʌblɪʃ]　　　　　　**v.**　出版　　　4th ★★★★★
When J. K. Rowling's Harry Potter was first published, readers rushed to the bookstores to buy her book.
J. K.羅琳的哈利波特甫出版，讀者便衝到書店去買她的新書。

2202 pump [pʌmp]　　　　　　　**v.**　抽水　　　5th ★★★★★
The fire fighter pumped water out of a cellar soon after the typhoon.
颱風過後不久，消防員從地下室抽水出來。

2203 punch [pʌntʃ]　　　　　　**v.**　用拳頭打　4th ★★★★★
The kid broke a bone in his arm when he punched the wall.
這個孩子用拳頭搥了一下牆壁，把自己手臂的骨頭弄斷了。

2204 punish ['pʌnɪʃ]　　　　　　**v.**　處罰　　　4th ★★★★★
Jack's parents are too tolerant of their son's bad behavior. They did not even punish him when he cheated in the exam.
傑克的父母太過於容忍兒子的壞行徑。他們甚至連他考試作弊時也沒有懲處他。

2205 purchase ['pɜtʃəs]　　　　　**v.**　購買　　　4th ★★★★★
David spent all his money on his new apartment; he had no more for the purchase of a new car.
大衛把所有的錢花在他的新公寓上，他沒有多餘的錢買新車。

2206 purity ['pjurətɪ]　　　　　　**n.**　純淨　　　5th ★★★★★
Diamonds are evaluated on the basis of their weight, purity, and color.
鑽石依據重量、純度和色澤來決定其價值。

2207 purpose ['pɜpəs]　　　　　　**n.**　目的　　　4th ★★★★★
The main purpose for building the Dubai Tower is for the Arab world to honor its industrialization.
建造杜拜塔的主要目的是讓阿拉伯世界景仰自身的工業化成果。

2208 purse [pɜs]　　　　　　　　**n.**　皮包　　　5th ★★★★★
My girlfriend always has tissues in her purse.
我女朋友的手提包裡總備有面紙。

2209 pursuit [pə'sut]　　　　　　**n.**　追捕　　　4th ★★★★★
The police officer is in pursuit of the criminal.
警方人員正在追捕罪犯。

2210 qualification [ˌkwɑləfəˈkeʃən] **n.** 資格 4th ★★★★★
In fact, the old man has no qualification to practice medicine.
事實上，這位老人沒有資格開業行醫。

2211 qualify [ˈkwɑləˌfaɪ] **v.** 具…資格 4th ★★★★★
Barney disliked that book so much that he said it shouldn't qualify as literature.
巴尼不喜歡那本書，他說這本書根本不夠格稱作文學。

2212 quality [ˈkwɑlətɪ] **n.** 品質 4th ★★★★★
We have heard that your company manufactures and exports high quality sporting goods.
我們聽說你公司專門製造以及出口高級的運動用品。

2213 quantity [ˈkwantətɪ] **n.** 數量 4th ★★★★★
The summer in Taiwan is humid; the large quantity of water in the air makes it feel even hotter and more uncomfortable.
台灣的夏天很潮濕，空氣中大量的水分使得夏天更熱且更難受。

2214 quantum [ˈkwantəm] **adj.** 飛躍的 3rd ★★★★★
The appointment of a female minister is a quantum leap for gender equality.
這位女性部長的任命，對於性別平等來說，是一個飛躍性的進展。

2215 quarantine [ˈkwɔrənˌtin] **n.** 隔離 3rd ★★★★★
Animals entering Britain from abroad are put in quarantine for three months.
從國外進口到英國的動物必須隔離三個月。

2216 quarrel [ˈkwɔrəl] **n.** 爭吵 4th ★★★★★
Quarrels arise because our desires conflict with those of others.
爭吵發生的原因是因為利益和他人相左。

2217 quarter [ˈkwɔrtə] **n.** 季度 4th ★★★★★
What is projected for the sales in the first quarter may not necessarily be the final sales volume at the end of the quarter.
第一季所預測的銷售情況，不一定是本季結束時的最終銷售額。

2218 query [ˈkwɪrɪ] **n.** 疑問 4th ★★★★★
If you have any queries regarding this offer, simply call our helpline.
如果您對此優惠有任何疑問，請撥打我們的客服專線。

2219 quest [kwɛst] **v.** 追求 4th ★★★★★

The team will continue its quest for Olympic gold this afternoon.
這支團隊今天下午將繼續追求奧運金牌。

2220 question [ˈkwɛstʃən]   **n.** 問題   5th ★★★★★
Our literature teacher likes us to generate as many questions as we can before his class so we can hold a discussion during class time.
我們的文學老師喜歡我們在上課前設想各種問題，這樣在課堂上就可以討論。

2221 quickly [ˈkwɪklɪ]   **adv.** 快速地   4th ★★★★★
Sugars are a form of carbohydrates, but the body uses them quickly and without much benefit.
糖是碳水化合物的一種形式，但我們的身體吸收很快，也沒有多少好處。

2222 quiet [ˈkwaɪət]   **adj.** 安靜的   4th ★★★★★
Parents often have to tell their children to keep quiet during church.
在教堂做禮拜時，父母常告誡他們的子女要安靜。

2223 quiz [kwɪz]   **v.** 盤問   3rd ★★★★★
Four men are being quizzed by police about the murder.
警方正在詢問四名男子有關謀殺案的事。

2224 quotation [kwoˈteʃən]   **n.** 報價   3rd ★★★★★
The representative gave me a quotation for a new apartment.
這位代表給我一間新公寓的報價。

2225 quote [kwot]   **v.** 報價   3rd ★★★★★
Please quote me your lowest price.
請報最低價給我。

2226 race [res]   **n.** 種族   5th ★★★★★
The improved race of horse is much more stronger.
品種改善的馬更強壯。

2227 radiantly [ˈredɪəntlɪ]   **adv.** 燦爛地   3rd ★★★★★
Jennifer smiled radiantly at her wedding; she was so happy.
珍妮佛在她的婚禮上笑得燦爛，非常開心。

2228 radical [ˈrædɪkl]   **adj.** 基本的   4th ★★★★★
You need to understand radical principles well when studying physics.
學習物理時你需要好好瞭解其基本原理。

R

2229 rage [redʒ]   **n.** 憤怒   4th ★★★★★
Utada worries about filling her parents with rage if she fails a test.
宇多田擔心若考試不及格她的父母會很憤怒。

2230 raise [rez]   **v.** 舉起   5th ★★★★★
A basketball player could raise his arm and reach the ceiling.
一位籃球選手舉高他的手臂就可以摸到天花板。

2231 range [rendʒ]   **v.** 涵蓋   4th ★★★★★
Prices at the new restaurant range from $5.00 to $20.00.
這間餐廳的價格從五美元到二十美元不等。

2232 rank [ræŋk]   **n.** 位階   4th ★★★★★
Sam's job isn't great, but he plans on moving up in the ranks of the company over the years.
山姆的工作不是很重要，但他計劃在幾年後能提升在公司的位階。

2233 ransack ['rænsæk]   **v.** 仔細搜索   3rd ★★★★★
The police ransacked the warehouse to look for illegal drug.
警察徹底搜索倉庫，想找出非法毒品。

2234 rapid ['ræpɪd]   **adj.** 快速的   5th ★★★★★
Many people find it hard to keep up with the rapid development of modern technology.
許多人發現要趕上現代科技的快速發展很困難。

2235 rapidly ['ræpɪdlɪ]   **adv.** 快速地   5th ★★★★★
The telephone is widely considered as the most rapidly evolving technological device today.
大家普遍認為電話是現今技術設備中發展最迅速的。

2236 rare [rɛr]   **adj.** 稀有的   5th ★★★★★
Teddy has been to libraries across the country seeking the rare book.
泰迪為了尋找罕見的書去過全國各地的圖書館。

2237 rarely ['rɛrlɪ]   **adv.** 很少   5th ★★★★★
Although he is a chef, Roberto rarely cooks his own meals.
雖然羅伯托是位廚師，卻鮮少為自己下廚。

2238 rate [ret]   **n.** 速率   5th ★★★★★

This company is going downhill at a great rate.
這間公司正大幅走下坡。

2239 rather ['ræðɚ]　　　　　adv. 寧願　　　4th ★★★★★
An officer would rather do the right things than do things right during his patrol duty.
官員在執勤時寧願開始就做正確的選擇，而不要事後補救。

2240 reach [ritʃ]　　　　　n. 可及範圍　　　4th ★★★★★
Keep the medicine away from the reach of children under six years old.
藥物要放在六歲以下小孩拿不到的地方。

2241 readily ['rɛdɪlɪ]　　　　　adv. 容易地　　　4th ★★★★★
Feeding birds has become so popular that prepared feed mixtures are readily available.
飼養鳥類已經變得非常流行，到處都能買到調製好的混合飼料。

2242 realistic [rɪə'lɪstɪk]　　　　　adj. 現實的　　　4th ★★★★★
Although your plans look good, you have to be realistic and consider what you can actually do.
雖然你的計畫看起來很棒，但你必須現實點，想想你實際上可以做什麼。

2243 realize ['rɪə‚laɪz]　　　　　v. 了解　　　4th ★★★★★
When I saw that my classroom was empty, I realized that it must be Sunday.
我看到教室空無一人時，才想到那天一定是星期日。

2244 realm [rɛlm]　　　　　n. 領域　　　3rd ★★★★★
In particular, the impact of the Internet on e-commerce has created a new realm of enforcement challenges for customs.
特別是，網路對電子商務的衝擊，對海關執法創造了一個新的挑戰領域。

2245 reason ['rizn]　　　　　n. 理由　　　5th ★★★★★
Insufficient preparation and injuries are often the reasons for an athlete's poor performance in a contest.
運動員在比賽時表現欠佳通常有兩個原因，缺乏足夠的練習或是受傷。

2246 reasonable ['riznəbl]　　　　　adj. 合理的　　　5th ★★★★★
Fast food is available almost 24 hours a day and it is usually served at a reasonable price.
速食幾乎二十四小時都買的到，而且價格通常很合理。

2247 rebel [rɪ'bɛl]   **v.** 反叛   4th ★★★★★
The masses rebelled the local government for the sake of unfair taxation.
群眾反抗當地政府不公平的稅收。

2248 rebellious [rɪ'bɛljəs]   **adj.** 造反的   4th ★★★★★
The coach used to regard Leo as a rebellious and trouble-making member before.
教練曾經認為李歐是個叛逆又愛惹麻煩的隊員。

2249 recall [rɪ'kɔl]   **v.** 回想   4th ★★★★★
If the dreamer is wakened immediately after his dream, he can usually recall the entire dream.
如果做夢的人在做完夢後立刻被叫醒,他通常可以回想起整場夢境。

2250 receive [rɪ'siv]   **v.** 接收   4th ★★★★★
We received some small gifts in our stockings on Christmas.
聖誕節時我們會在長統襪裡收到一些小禮物。

2251 recent ['risnt]   **adj.** 最近的   4th ★★★★★
Cody's skin is still tan from his recent trip to the beach.
科迪前陣子去海灘旅行後,皮膚到現在還是棕褐色。

2252 recession [rɪ'sɛʃən]   **n.** 不景氣   3rd ★★★★★
Stock prices of fast-food restaurants have bulked up during the recession.
速食餐廳的股價在景氣衰退期間暴漲。

2253 recharge [ri'tʃɑrdʒ]   **v.** 充電   4th ★★★★★
My cell phone, which keeps beeping to remind me of recharging it, is low on battery.
我的手機快要沒電了,一直發出嗶嗶聲提醒我要充電。

2254 receipt [rɪ'sit]   **n.** 收據   4th ★★★★★
You'll need the store receipt to show proof of purchase if you want to return any items you bought.
如果你想要退回你所買的商品,需要收據作為購買憑證。

2255 receptionist [rɪ'sɛpʃənɪst]   **n.** 接待員   4th ★★★★★
The attitude of receptionists from a governmental office is frequently unfriendly.
政府部門裡的接待員,態度經常不友善。

2256 recipe ['rɛsəpɪ]   **n.** 食譜   4th ★★★★★

Grandmother promised to teach me some of her recipes this year.
祖母答應今年要教我一些她的烹飪秘訣。

2257 reciprocal [rɪ'sɪprək!]   **adj.** 相互的   4th ★★★★★
When we talk about "each other" or "one another," we refer to reciprocal relationships, meaning that the relationships are bi-directional.
當我們談論到「對方」或「彼此」時，指的是相互間的關係，意味這些關係是雙向的。

2258 reckless ['rɛklɪs]   **adj.** 魯莽的   4th ★★★★★
A report shows that the reckless drivers are to blame in nine out of ten accidents.
據報導顯示，十起車禍中有九起都得怪罪於粗心的駕駛。

2259 recognize ['rɛkəg,naɪz]   **v.** 認出   4th ★★★★★
Jerry didn't recognize his primary school classmate Mary until he listened to her self-introduction.
傑瑞聽到瑪莉的自我介紹後，才認出原來她是他的小學同學。

2260 recommend [,rɛkə'mɛnd]   **v.** 推薦   4th ★★★★★
If you ever come to my hometown, I can recommend a few good restaurants.
如果你要來我的家鄉，我可以推薦一些好餐廳。

2261 reconcile ['rɛkənsaɪl]   **v.** 和解   3rd ★★★★★
After years of legal battle for custody, the divorced couple finally reconciled. They were aware that maintaining a good relationship was the best choice for themselves and for the children.
經過多年的監護權法律爭戰，這對離婚夫妻終於和解了。他們明白維持良好關係對他們本身及孩子都是最好選擇。

2262 record ['rɛkəd]   **n.** 記錄   5th ★★★★★
Could I check on your driving record?
我可以查查你的駕駛記錄嗎？

2263 recover [rɪ'kʌvə]   **v.** 恢復   4th ★★★★★
My mom is recovering from a severe illness.
我母親從重病中逐漸康復。

2264 recovery [rɪ'kʌvərɪ]   **n.** 恢復   4th ★★★★★
Tom was very ill a week ago, but now he looks healthy. We are amazed by his quick recovery.
湯姆一個禮拜前病得很重，但他現在看起來很健康，我們都很驚訝他的恢復如此迅速。

R

2265 **recreational** [ˌrɛkrɪ'eʃən]]　**adj.** 娛樂的　~~4th~~ ★★★★★
Peter is now living on a budget of NT$100 per day. He cannot afford any recreational activities.
彼得每天的生活預算只有一百塊，他負擔不起任何娛樂活動。

2266 **recruit** [rɪ'krut]　**v.** 招募　~~3rd~~ ★★★★★
The new party was largely recruited from the middle classes.
新政黨的主要招募對象是中產階級。

2267 **recruitment** [rɪ'krutmənt]　**n.** 招募　~~4th~~ ★★★★★
A lot of companies are forced to cut down graduate recruitment.
很多公司被迫減少招聘大學畢業生。

2268 **recycle** [ri'saɪk]]　**v.** 回收　~~5th~~ ★★★★★
Irene does not throw away used envelopes. She recycles them by using them for taking telephone messages.
艾琳沒有把用過的信封丟掉，她將信封回收，做為留言的便條紙。

2269 **reduce** [rɪ'djus]　**v.** 減少　~~4th~~ ★★★★★
Because air is so basic to life, it is very important to keep that air clean by reducing or preventing air pollution.
空氣是賴以生存的基礎，減輕或預防空氣污染以保持空氣清淨是很重要的。

2270 **reduction** [rɪ'dʌkʃən]　**n.** 降低　~~4th~~ ★★★★★
What reduction will you make on this article?
你會對這篇文章做哪些刪減？

2271 **reef** [rif]　**n.** 礁　~~3rd~~ ★★★★★
Artificial reefs provide a haven where fish can find the shelter they need and rest from strong currents.
人工魚礁為魚群提供了一個避難所，牠們可以找到所需的庇護，也可以從強勁的水流中暫緩旅途。

2272 **refer** [rɪ'fɝ]　**v.** 指涉　~~4th~~ ★★★★★
New Zealand and Australia are often referred to as the "land down under".
紐西蘭和澳大利亞通常被指涉為「南方大陸」。

2273 **reference** ['rɛfərəns]　**n.** 參考　~~4th~~ ★★★★★
It's important to include a bibliography, citing all referenced works, as part of your research project.
你在做專題報告時，索引和參考資料要納入報告的一部分，這很重要。

2274 reflect [rɪˈflɛkt] 　　　 v.　反射　　 4th ★★★★★
How we react to an event reflects our values and beliefs
我們對一個事件做出的回應，反映了我們的價值觀和信仰。

2275 reflective [rɪˈflɛktɪv] 　　 adj.　沉思的　 4th ★★★★★
After hearing the news, they sat in a reflective silence without saying a word.
在聽完這個消息後，他們坐著沉思，不發一語。

2276 reform [ˌrɪˈfɔrm] 　　　　 n.　改革　　 4th ★★★★★
The President must account for his governmental reforms.
總統必須為他的政府改革負責。

2277 refreshing [rɪˈfrɛʃɪŋ] 　　 adj.　暢快的　 4th ★★★★★
Tea is enjoyed worldwide as a refreshing and stimulating drink.
世界各地的人都喜歡喝茶，大家都認為茶是一種暢快又刺激的飲料。

2278 refrigerator [rɪˈfrɪdʒəˌretə] 　 n.　冰箱　　 5th ★★★★★
Please keep the ice cream in the refrigerator soon, or it will melt.
請把冰淇淋放進冰箱，不然會融化。

2279 refuge [ˈrɛfjudʒ] 　　　　 n.　避難所　 4th ★★★★★
The climbers took a rest in a mountain refuge near a lake.
登山客在山上靠近湖泊的避難所休息。

2280 refugee [ˌrɛfjuˈdʒi] 　　　 n.　難民　　 4th ★★★★★
Hundreds of refugees fled across the border to another country.
數百位難民越過邊境逃往他國。

2281 refund [rɪˈfʌnd] 　　　　 n　退款　　 4th ★★★★★
If the camera you bought is defective, you can bring it back and ask for a refund.
如果你買的相機有瑕疵，可以拿回來要求退款。

2282 refuse [rɪˈfjuz] 　　　　 v.　拒絕　　 4th ★★★★★
Although there were many setbacks in his career as a writer, Henry refused to give up, and eventually he gained national recognitions.
雖然亨利的作家生涯有許多挫折，但他不放棄，最終獲得國人的認同。

2283 regard [rɪˈgɑrd] 　　　　 n.　敬重　　 4th ★★★★★
The tasty dishes at this restaurant have earned the chef high regard.
這家餐廳的美味佳餚贏得主廚很高的評價。

2284 regarding [rɪˈgɑrdɪŋ]　　**prep.** 關於　　~~4th~~ ★★★★★
The Office of Media Relations issued a press release to clarify some recent doubts regarding the company's quarterly earnings report.
媒體公關部發出新聞稿，對最近公司的季度盈利報告澄清一些疑慮。

2285 regardless [rɪˈgɑrdlɪs]　　**prep.** 不論　　~~4th~~ ★★★★★
The company treated all the job applications with equal consideration, regardless of age, race, or gender.
該公司不論年齡、種族或性別，對所有應試者抱以同等的考量。

2286 region [ˈridʒən]　　**n.** 地區　　~~4th~~ ★★★★★
Apart from the polar region, it is difficult to imagine a more inhospitable environment on Earth than a desert.
除了極地以外，很難想像在地球上還有比沙漠更不適合居住的環境。

2287 regional [ˈridʒənl]　　**adj.** 地區的　　~~4th~~ ★★★★★
Chinese is a language with many regional differences. People living in different areas often speak different dialects.
中文有許多地區性差異，生活在不同地區的人們往往講不同的方言。

2288 register [ˈrɛdʒɪstɚ]　　**v.** 註冊　　~~4th~~ ★★★★★
Jeff tried to register for art class but it had already filled up.
傑夫想要註冊藝術課程班，但已經額滿了。

2289 registration [ˌrɛdʒɪˈstreʃən]　　**n.** 行照　　~~4th~~ ★★★★★
A driver should always have his/her driver's license and registration when he/she is driving.
開車時駕照和行照要隨時帶在身邊。

2290 regret [rɪˈgrɛt]　　**v.** 後悔　　~~4th~~ ★★★★★
She felt a great regret at having spent her money in that way.
她非常後悔那樣花錢。

2291 regularly [ˈrɛgjələlɪ]　　**adv.** 一般地　　~~4th~~ ★★★★★
Their group is regularly made up of old people. George and Mary are the only two members that are under forty.
他們這個團體是由老人家組成的。喬治和瑪麗是唯二年齡低於四十歲的成員。

2292 regulation [ˌrɛgjəˈleʃən]　　**n.** 規則　　~~4th~~ ★★★★★
There is a regulation that bicycle riders should wear a helmet.
明文規定腳踏車騎士應該戴安全帽。

2293 reincarnation [ˌriɪnkɑr'neʃən] **n.** 轉世 3rd ★★★★★
Whenever a Dalai Lama died, a search began for his reincarnation.
達賴去世後，轉世靈童的尋找便會展開。

2294 reinforce [ˌriɪn'fɔrs] **v.** 補強 4th ★★★★★
The tailor reinforced the pockets on my jacket with double stitching.
裁縫師縫上雙縫線來補強我夾克的口袋。

2295 reject [rɪ'dʒɛkt] **v.** 駁回 4th ★★★★★
I am sorry that the appeal has been rejected by the High Court.
我很遺憾上訴已被高等法院駁回。

2296 rejection [rɪ'dʒɛkʃən] **n.** 拒絕 4th ★★★★★
Sandy has applied for tens of jobs, but all she got is rejection letters.
珊迪已經應徵十幾份工作，但都拿到拒絕信。

2297 rejuvenate [rɪ'dʒuvənet] **v.** 回復青春 3rd ★★★★★
Many people believed that the water of the Fountain of Youth had the power to rejuvenate young.
許多人相信，青春之泉的水有回復年輕的力量。

2298 relate [rɪ'let] **v.** 相關 3rd ★★★★★
An estimated 1.2 billion people do not have access to clean drinking water. More than five million people die each year from water-related diseases.
估計約十二億人喝不到乾淨飲水，每年更有超過五百萬人死於與水有關的疾病。

2299 relationship [rɪ'leʃən'ʃɪp] **n.** 關係 4th ★★★★★
In the past few years, I have developed an important relationship with my mentor.
過去這幾年下來，我和我的指導老師已有很密切的關係。

2300 relax [rɪ'læks] **v.** 放鬆 4th ★★★★★
The best strategy for avoiding stress is to learn how to relax.
預防壓力的最好辦法就是學習如何放鬆。

2301 release [rɪ'lis] **v.** 釋放 4th ★★★★★
Laughter provides physical release from stress.
大笑可以讓人在生理上釋放壓力。

2302 relevant ['rɛləvənt] **adj.** 有關的 4th ★★★★★
Before an operation, a surgeon must check every relevant detail of the patient's

medical history.
手術前，外科醫師一定要檢查病人病史裡的每個相關細節。

2303 reliable [rɪˈlaɪəbl̩]　　adj. 可靠的　　~~4th~~ ★★★★★
An unnamed but reliable source told CNN News that several high-ranking officers were involved in the scandal.
一個不具名的可靠消息來源告訴CNN，許多高階長官都有涉入那宗醜聞。

2304 relief [rɪˈlif]　　n. 寬心　　~~4th~~ ★★★★★
What a relief! You have just taken a load off my mind.
真是鬆了一口氣!你剛卸下我心中一顆大石頭。

2305 relieve [rɪˈliv]　　v. 緩和　　~~4th~~ ★★★★★
Using a heating pad or taking warm baths can sometimes help to relieve pain in the lower back.
使用電毯或洗熱水澡有時可以幫助緩和下背部的疼痛。

2306 religious [rɪˈlɪdʒəs]　　adj. 宗教的　　~~4th~~ ★★★★★
The religious fanatic believed that all people were evil sinners.
那位宗教狂熱分子認為所有人都是邪惡的罪人。

2307 reluctant [rɪˈlʌktənt]　　adj. 不情願的　　~~4th~~ ★★★★★
They were reluctant to accept the offer without knowing all the details.
他們在不知道所有細節以前，是不會接受這份工作的。

2308 remain [rɪˈmen]　　v. 留下　　~~4th~~ ★★★★★
His speedy recovery from a fatal car accident still remains an enigma for a lot of people.
他從致命車禍中快速復原，在許多人心中始終是一個難解的謎。

2309 remark [rɪˈmark]　　v. 談論　　~~4th~~ ★★★★☆
Some of Judy's relatives remarked on the change in her since her marriage.
茱蒂的一些親戚談論到她婚後的改變。

2310 remarkably [rɪˈmarkəblɪ]　　adv. 顯著地　　~~4th~~ ★★★★★
The young Taiwanese pianist performed remarkably well and won the first prize in the music contest.
這位年輕的台灣鋼琴家表現出眾，並在音樂比賽中得到第一名。

2311 remedy [ˈrɛmədɪ]　　v. 補救　　~~4th~~ ★★★★★
Although the manager apologized many times for his poor decision, there was

nothing he could do to remedy his mistake.
儘管經理為他的失策道歉了很多次，還是無法補救他的錯誤。

2312 remember [rɪ'mɛmbɚ]   **v.**   記得   5th ★★★★★
I spoke to him on the phone yesterday. I remember telling him about the meeting today.
我昨天和他通電話，我記得我有告訴他關於今天的會議。

2313 remind [rɪ'maɪnd]   **v.**   提醒   5th ★★★★★
The old cottage reminded the Swedish man of his grandparent's home.
老舊的農舍使這位瑞典人想起他祖父母的家。

2314 reminder [rɪ'maɪndɚ]   **n.**   催單   4th ★★★★★
The landlady will send her tenant a reminder if he doesn't pay the rent on schedule.
這位女房東的房客若沒按時繳房租，她就會寄催單給他。

2315 remonstrate [rɛmən‚stret]   **v.**   告誡   3rd ★★★★★
Steven remonstrate her son about his studies when the exam is approaching.
考試即將來臨，史蒂芬告誡她的兒子要加緊唸書。

2316 remote [rɪ'mot]   **adj.**   遙遠的   4th ★★★★★
The young doctor decided to work in a remote hospital to help the poor.
這位年輕醫生決定到偏遠的醫院工作幫助窮困的人。

2317 remove [rɪ'muv]   **v.**   消除   4th ★★★★★
Growing forests produce oxygen and remove carbon dioxide, which is the major cause of global warming.
種植森林可以增加氧氣並消除全球暖化的元兇——二氧化碳。

2318 renewable [rɪ'njuəbl]   **adj.**   可更新的   4th ★★★★★
Beijing plans to spend $185th billion by 2020 to develop renewable energy.
北京計劃到二零二零年以前，要投資一千八百五十點零零億美元發展再生能源。

2319 renovate ['rɛnə‚vet]   **v.**   革新   3rd ★★★★★
The school has decided to renovate the old gym instead of building a new one from scratch.
學校決定不要重蓋新的體育館，而是把舊的體育館翻新。

2320 renowned [rɪ'naund]   **adj.**   著名的   4th ★★★★★
Having a great voice and charisma, A-Mei has become a renowned figure in the

entertainment business in Asia.
阿妹因為擁有絕佳的嗓音和個人魅力，在亞洲演藝圈成為一位家喻戶曉的名人。

2321 rent [rɛnt]   **v.** 租   **4th** ★★★★★
My friends and I rented a cabin in the woods during the winter.
冬天的時候我和朋友在樹林租了一間小木屋。

2322 repair [rɪ'pɛr]   **v.** 維修   **4th** ★★★★★
The gym is closed on Monday for routine maintained work. The facilities are kept in good condition by the regular checking and repairing.
健身房每週一休息做例行維護工作、定期檢查和維修好使這些設施保持良好狀態。

2323 replacement [rɪ'plesmənt]   **n.** 更換   **4th** ★★★★★
If dissatisfied with something they have bought, customers can return it to the store and receive a replacement product or refund cash.
客戶如果對他們購買的東西不滿意，他們可以回到商店兌換同值商品或是退錢。

2324 represent [ˌrɛprɪ'zɛnt]   **v.** 象徵   **4th** ★★★★★
In the classical Greek period, curly hair was not only the fashion, but it also represented an attitude towards lIfe.
在古希臘時期，捲髮不僅是時尚，也代表了對生活的態度。

2325 reputation [ˌrɛpjə'teʃən]   **n.** 名聲   **4th** ★★★★★
If you attack a person's reputation, he or she will take revenge sooner or later.
如果你攻擊一個人的名譽，他或她遲早會報復的。

2326 require [rɪ'kwaɪr]   **v.** 要求   **4th** ★★★★★
Employees of this company are required to switch off all the lights before leaving in order to save the energy.
這家公司的員工在離開前必須關閉所有的燈以節省能源。

2327 research [rɪ's3tʃ]   **n.** 研究   **4th** ★★★★★
Research has also found that men and women suffer from compulsive shopping at about the same rate.
研究發現男人和女人有購物衝動的比率是一樣的。

2328 rescue ['rɛskju]   **n.** 救援   **4th** ★★★★★
The crew abandoned the burning ship and was saved by the rescue team.
船員放棄著火的船並被搜救隊救起。

2329 reserve [rɪ'z3v]   **v.** 預定   **4th** ★★★★★

During the peak season, you must reserve hotel rooms at least three months in advance.
旅遊旺季期間，你必須至少提前三個月訂房。

2330 resident ['rɛzədənt]　　　　n.　居民　　4th ★★★★★
Most of the city residents come to realize that the mass rapid transit system is a far better substitute for their cars. They feel a strong dependence on it now.
許多市民體認到捷運是汽車的絕佳代替品，他們現在感受到強烈的依賴感。

2331 resolve [rɪ'zɑlv]　　　　n.　決心　　4th ★★★★★
There is no scarcity of opportunity to make a living at what you love; there's only a scarcity of resolve to make it happen.
做自己熱愛的事情維生永遠不缺機會，缺的只有實現它的決心。

2332 resort [rɪ'zɔrt]　　　　n.　勝地　　4th ★★★★★
Kenting National Park is my favorite summer resort.
墾丁國家公園是我最愛的夏日勝地。

2333 resource [rɪ'sors]　　　　n.　資源　　4th ★★★★★
We should emphasize the importance of recycling because of the limited resources on Earth.
我們要強調回收的重要，因為地球上的資源有限。

2334 restless ['rɛstlɪs]　　　　adj.　不安定的　　4th ★★★★★
Somerset Maugham wrote about a restless man's quest for inner understanding.
毛姆寫的是有關焦躁不安的男人追尋內在同感的故事。

2335 resume [ˌrɛzju'me]　　　　n.　履歷表　　4th ★★★★★
When preparing to find a new job, there is no more valuable document you can prepare than your résumé.
準備找新工作時，你的履歷是最重要的文件。

2336 repetitive [rɪ'pɛtɪtɪv]　　　　adj.　重複的　　4th ★★★★★
The highly repetitive structure of music helps children learn to trust themselves and enhance their self-confidence and sense of accomplishment.
高度重複的音樂模式可以幫助孩子學會信任自己，加強自信和成就感。

2337 replace [rɪ'ples]　　　　v.　取代　　4th ★★★★★
The rise of oil prices made scientists search for new energy resources to replace oil.
由於油價上漲，科學家開始尋找新能源來取代石油。

2338 reply [rɪ'plaɪ]　　　　　n.　回應　　4th ★★★★★

We've enclosed a stamped and addressed envelope for your reply, and would be pleased to reciprocate at any time.
我們已附上供你回覆的回郵信封，並且樂於隨時回報。

2339 report [rɪ'port]　　　　　v.　報告　　5th ★★★★★

The woman wanted to report a burglary because her house was broken.
這位女人想要通報一起竊盜案，因為她家遭人闖空門了。

2340 representative [rɛprɪ'zɛntətɪv]　n.　代表　　4th ★★★★★

Not knowing what the sales representative was trying to do, the lady looked perplexed.
這位女士看起來不知所措，因為她不知道業務代表想做什麼。

2341 reputation [ˌrɛpjə'teʃən]　　　n.　名譽　　4th ★★★★★

If you attack a person's reputation or good name, he or she will take revenge sooner or later.
如果你攻擊一個人的名譽或好名聲，對方遲早會報仇。

2342 request [rɪ'kwɛst]　　　　　v.　請求　　4th ★★★★★

Thank you for your letter of March 10, requesting our catalog and a price list of our products.
感謝您三月十日索取我們型錄及產品價目表的信件。

2343 researcher [ri'sɝtʃɚ]　　　　n.　研究人員　　4th ★★★★★

Some researchers warn that at least half of the languages now spoken throughout the world are facing extinction within this century.
有些研究人員警告，現在全世界有至少一半的語言將在本世紀面臨滅亡。

2344 resemble [rɪ'zɛmbl̩]　　　　v.　相似　　4th ★★★★★

The couple resemble each other in taste.
這對夫妻的品味相似。

2345 reservation [ˌrɛzɚ'veʃən]　　n.　預定　　4th ★★★★★

I want to check in, and I've already made a reservation.
我想要辦入房手續，而且已經訂房了。

2346 reserve [rɪ'zɝv]　　　　　v.　保留　　4th ★★★★★

This piece of land is reserved for wild animals and plants; it is not open for the general public.
這塊地是預留給野生動植物的，不對外開放。

2347 residential [ˌrɛzəˈdɛnʃəl]　　　**adj.** 住宅的　　　**4th** ★★★★★

The foreigner didn't satisfy the residential qualifications to get a work permit.
這位外國人不符合居住資格，無法拿到工作許可。

2348 resign [rɪˈzaɪn]　　　**v.** 辭職　　　**4th** ★★★★★

The old manager decided to resign from his post for his poor health.
老邁的經理因為健康欠佳而決定辭職。

2349 resist [rɪˈzɪst]　　　**v.** 抵抗　　　**4th** ★★★★★

How can anyone resist the attempt of my grandmother's home-style fried potatoes?
怎麼可能有人抗拒得了我奶奶親手做的炸薯條？

2350 resistant [rɪˈzɪstənt]　　　**adj.** 抵抗的　　　**4th** ★★★★★

It goes without saying that a healthy diet will create a body resistant.
健康的飲食可以產生抵抗力，這是人盡皆知的事。

2351 resolution [ˌrɛzəˈluʃən]　　　**n.** 解決　　　**4th** ★★★★★

Hopes of a peaceful resolution to the conflict between the two parties have faded. The likelihood of reaching a satisfactory settlement of the dispute is very bleak.
和平解決兩造衝突的希望破滅，要圓滿解決爭端的可能性非常渺茫。

2352 resolve [rɪˈzɑlv]　　　**v.** 決議　　　**4th** ★★★★★

The Central Bank resolved on a stringent foreign exchange policy to deter market participants from speculative currency activity.
中央銀行決定實行嚴格的外匯政策，以防止貨幣市場參與者從事投機活動。

2353 respect [rɪˈspɛkt]　　　**n.** 尊敬　　　**4th** ★★★★★

The Maori and all New Zealanders have a strong respect for the land and various specific requirements are set up to protect their environment.
毛利人和所有的紐西蘭人都十分尊敬他們的土地，因而設立許多規定來保護環境。

2354 respond [rɪˈspɑnd]　　　**v.** 回應　　　**4th** ★★★★★

Your printer is not responding. You haven't hooked it up to the computer.
你的印表機沒有反應，你沒有把它連上電腦。

2355 response [rɪˈspɑns]　　　**n.** 回應　　　**4th** ★★★★★

Her response seemed spontaneous, but was in fact planned carefully and rehearsed beforehand.
她的回應看起來很隨性，但其實早就已經小心計畫並且練習過的。

A B C D E F G H I J K L M N O P Q R S T U V W X Y Z

2356 responsibility [rɪ͵spɑnsəˈbɪlətɪ] **n.** 責任 **4th** ★★★★★
As the pilot of the aircraft, you have the responsibility to use everything in your way to ensure safe flight.
身為機長,你有責任盡一切努力來確保飛行安全。

2357 responsible [rɪˈspɑnsəbḷ] **adj.** 負責的 **4th** ★★★★★
The legislative branch of government is responsible for enacting and making new laws.
政府的立法部門負責頒布法令以及制定新法。

2358 restaurant [ˈrɛstərənt] **n.** 餐廳 **5th** ★★★★★
Fire consumed the entire restaurant in less than an hour. Fortunately, all the diners and staff escaped unhurt.
大火不到一小時就吞噬了整間餐廳,幸好所有的顧客和員工都平安逃了出來。

2359 restrict [rɪˈstrɪkt] **v.** 限制 **4th** ★★★★★
This is a restricted area. Ordinary people are not allowed to enter.
這是一個管制區域,一般人不准進入。

2360 result [rɪˈzʌlt] **n.** 結果 **4th** ★★★★★
There is a lot of pressure on high school students to obtain very good exam results in order to enter national universities.
獲得好成績以進入國立大學,對高中生來說壓力很大。

2361 retailer [ˈritelɚ] **n.** 零售商 **3rd** ★★★★★
The success of Wal-Mart, the world's largest retailer, can be chiefly attributed to the low-price strategy.
全球零售業龍頭沃爾瑪的成功主要歸功於它的低價策略。

2362 retain [rɪˈten] **v.** 維持 **3rd** ★★★★★
An attractive investment environment is a key for this country to retain the support and interest of the international business community.
一個國家要維持國際商業社會對它的支持和興趣,誘人的投資環境是關鍵。

2363 retaliate [rɪˈtælɪ͵et] **v.** 報復 **3rd** ★★★★★
If we impose import duties, other countries may retaliate against us.
如果我們徵收進口關稅,其他國家可能會抵制我們。

2364 retirement [rɪˈtaɪrmənt] **n.** 退休 **4th** ★★★★★
The new retirement policy would cause the company to lose the support of the employees who benefit from the current system.
這家公司員工受益於目前的制度,新制會使公司失去員工的支持。

128

2365 retreat [rɪ'trit]　　　v.　退縮　　4th ★★★★★
Children must be allowed to retreat into their own worlds without parental intrusion.
必須要讓孩子不受父母干擾，回到屬於他們自己的世界。

2366 retribution [ˌrɛtrɪ'bjuʃən]　n.　報應　　3rd ★★★★★
Some people believe the day of retribution is approaching.
很多人相信審判日即將到來。

2367 retrieve [rɪ'triv]　　　v.　收回　　3rd ★★★★★
I would like to retrieve my laptop which I left in the department office.
我想要拿回我放在辦公室的筆電。

2368 retrospect ['rɛtrəˌspɛkt]　v.　追憶　　3rd ★★★★★
My grandmother is really nostalgic. She usually retrospects in her childhood.
我祖母很懷舊，她常常回想起她的童年。

2369 retrospective [ˌrɛtrə'spɛktɪv]　adj.　回顧的　3rd ★★★★★
The painter's retrospective exhibition will be held in the city library.
這位畫家的回顧展將在市立圖書館舉行。

2370 return [rɪ'tɜn]　　　v.　回　　5th ★★★★★
As soon as I graduate from this university, I am going to return to my mother country.
我大學畢業之後，就要馬上回到祖國。

2371 reuse [ˌri'juz]　　　v.　再利用　　5th ★★★★★
We can protect our environment by following the 3Rs: recycling, reusing and reducing waste.
我們可以遵循3R來保護我們的環境：回收、再利用和減少廢物。

2372 reveal [rɪ'vil]　　　v.　揭示　　3rd ★★★★★
Nothing more thoroughly reveals your personality than the table you set.
你擺餐具的樣子最能顯示出你的個性。

2373 revenge [rɪ'vɛndʒ]　　v.　報復　　3rd ★★★★★
She decided to revenge herself on those who insulted her.
她決定報復那些羞辱她的人。

2374 revenue ['rɛvəˌnju]　　n.　收益　　3rd ★★★★★

The term that describes governmental income from which public expenses are met is revenue.
用來償付公共支出，描述政府收入的詞就是「收益」。

2375 review [rɪˈvju]　　　　v.　再檢查　　5th ★★★★★
The court decided to review the scene of the crime.
法院決定再檢查一次犯罪現場。

2376 revision [rɪˈvɪʒən]　　　n.　修正　　4th ★★★★★
The revision of the book is quite different from the original one.
這本書的修訂版和原版有很大的差異。

2377 revive [rɪˈvaɪv]　　　　v.　甦醒　　4th ★★★★★
We tried to revive him for two hours but he was gone.
我們花了兩個小時試圖喚醒他，但他還是離開人世了。

2378 revolution [ˌrɛvəˈluʃən]　　n.　革命　　3rd ★★★★★
More than one hundred million people worldwide have joined the cyber-socializing revolution.
全球超過一億以上的人口都參與了網路社交的革命。

2379 revolutionize [rɛvəˈluʃənˌaɪz]　v.　徹底改革　4th ★★★★★
Changes to global trade environment have revolutionized the way the world does business.
全球貿易環境的轉變已經徹底改變了這個世界做生意的方法。

2380 reward [rɪˈwɔrd]　　　　v.　獎賞　　4th ★★★★★
Those sales representatives were rewarded for their dedication to the company.
這些業務代表因為他們對公司的貢獻而得到獎賞。

2381 rhythm [ˈrɪðəm]　　　　n.　節奏　　3rd ★★★★★
The roots of rock and roll are actually very diverse; it is a style of music that developed from rhythm and blues, gospel, jazz, and American country music.
搖滾樂的根源其實非常多元，他的音樂風格是從藍調節奏、福音音樂、爵士樂和美國鄉村音樂發展而來的。

2382 ridicule [ˈrɪdɪkjul]　　　n.　嘲笑　　3rd ★★★★★
Don't cast ridicule upon your younger brother.
不要嘲笑你弟弟。

2383 rim [rɪm]　　　　　　n.　邊緣　　3rd ★★★★★

129

Don't place your cell phone at the rim of the table.
不要把你的手機放在桌子邊緣。

2384 ring [rɪŋ]   **v.** 打電話   5th ★★★★★
I'll ring you back later.
我待會回電給你。

2385 rise [raɪz]   **v.** 上升   5th ★★★★★
The safety of food sold on the market has been a rising issue in the society these years.
市面上所販售的食物，其安全性在近年來逐漸成為一項熱門議題。

2386 risk [rɪsk]   **n.** 風險   4th ★★★★★
When you gamble, you take a risk.
你賭博就是在冒險。

2387 ritual ['rɪtʃʊrl]   **n.** 習慣   4th ★★★★★
Japanese gift-giving rituals show how tremendously important these acts are in that culture.
日本的送禮習俗說明了這件事在其文化中有多麼重要。

2388 rival ['raɪvl̩]   **adj.** 敵對的   4th ★★★★★
Mr. Lee debated with his rival candidate on some public issues.
李先生和他的參選對手辯論一些公開議題。

2389 robber ['rɑbɚ]   **n.** 搶匪   4th ★★★★★
A convenience store's surveillance tape enabled the police to catch the robber in an hour.
便利商店的監視器幫助警察在一個小時內抓到搶匪。

2390 robot ['robət]   **n.** 機器人   4th ★★★★★
Robots are entering into all kinds of activities.
各式各樣的活動都有機器人的參與。

2391 romantic [rə'mæntɪk]   **adj.** 浪漫的   5th ★★★★★
Anthropologist used to believe that romantic love was invented by Europeans in the Middles Ages.
人類學家曾認為，浪漫愛情是歐洲中世紀的產物。

2392 rotate ['rotet]   **v.** 使輪流   3rd ★★★★★
Farmers often rotate crops to help preserve the quality of the soil.
農夫經常輪種作物有助於維護土壤的品質。

2393 roughly [ˈrʌflɪ]   **adv.** 粗略地   **5th** ★★★★★

There has been an increase of roughly two thousand order forms for the company.
這間公司粗估大約增加了二千筆訂單。

2394 route [rut]   **n.** 路線   **4th** ★★★★★

This is the shortest route from the museum to the station.
從博物館到車站，這條路程最短。

2395 routine [ruˈtin]   **n.** 例行公事   **4th** ★★★★★

Every night, they go through the same routine. For example, he throws open the bedroom window, she closes it.
他們每晚都做相同的事，舉例來說，他會突然打開臥室窗戶，然後她就會把它關起來。

2396 row [ro]   **n.** 一排   **5th** ★★★★★

There is a row of huge horsetail trees along the sidewalk.
人行道上有一排巨型杉樹。

2397 royal [ˈrɔɪəl]   **adj.** 皇家的   **4th** ★★★★★

Our next door neighbors moved in last year and have kept a very low profile since then. Not many people know that they are the relatives of the royal family in Japan.
我們隔壁鄰居去年搬進來，從那時候起他們就一直保持低調。很少人知道他們是日本皇室的親戚。

2398 rude [rud]   **adj.** 無禮   **4th** ★★★★★

In many cultures, it is considered rude if we interrupt other people's conversation.
在許多文化中，打斷別人的談話很不禮貌。

2399 ruin [ˈruɪn]   **v.** 摧毀   **4th** ★★★★★

We have spent an entire semester planning this trip. But a newly developing typhoon might ruin the whole thing.
我們花了一整個學期規劃這次的旅行，但一個新形成的颱風可能會毀了一切。

2400 rule [rul]   **n.** 規則   **4th** ★★★★★

On construction sites, workers should observe the rules and wear helmets at all times for their own safety.
工地的工人應該要遵守規則，時時刻刻戴上安全帽以策安全。

2401 rural [ˈrurəl]   **adj.** 農村的   **4th** ★★★★★

In many countries, there is a drift of population from rural areas to the cities.
許多國家都有人口從鄉村地區流動到城市的趨勢。

130

2402 rush [rʌʃ]　　　　　　　　　　**n.** 匆促　　　4th ★★★★★
If you're not in a rush to leave, could you stay and help me?
如果你不急於離開，你能留下來幫我嗎？

2403 rust [rʌst]　　　　　　　　　　**n.** 鏽　　　4th ★★★★★
The pipes have browned from years of rust.
鐵做的管子由於多年來的生鏽已變成褐色。

2404 sack [sæk]　　　　　　　　　　**n.** 袋子　　　4th ★★★★★
Santa had a toy for me in his sack.
聖誕老人的布袋裡有一個玩具要給我。

2405 sacrifice ['sækrə͵faɪs]　　　　**n.** 犧牲　　　4th ★★★★★
Generally speaking, parents in Asia make more sacrifices for their children than those in the west.
一般說來，比起西方父母，亞洲父母為子女作更多犧牲。

2406 safety ['seftɪ]　　　　　　　　**n.** 安全　　　5th ★★★★★
Airplane pilots are responsible for the safety of hundreds of people on board.
機長要對機上數百名乘客的安全負責。

2407 salary ['sæʲlərɪ]　　　　　　　**n.** 薪資　　　5th ★★★★★
The hard work that Blair does merits a raise in salary.
布萊爾努力工作值得加薪。

2408 sample ['sæmpl̩]　　　　　　　**n.** 樣品　　　5th ★★★★★
Enclosed please find their sample and catalogue.
請參考附寄的樣品和型錄。

2409 sanitary ['sænə͵tɛrɪ]　　　　　**adj.** 衛生的　　　3rd ★★★★★
Sanitary conditions in this neighborhood are extremely terrible. Therefore some contagious diseases are very widespread.
這個社區的衛生條件非常糟糕，因而到處都散播著一些傳染病。

2410 satellite ['sætl̩͵aɪt]　　　　　　**n.** 人造衛星　　　3rd ★★★★★
Free of the time and space, satellite distance learning is one of the most popular media for gaining new information nowadays.
衛星遠程教育因為無時空限制，是現今獲取新訊息最熱門的媒體之一。

2411 satisfaction [͵sætɪs'fækʃən]　　**n.** 滿足　　　4th ★★★★★

S

Betty likes nothing more than to read. For her, reading is a spiritual experience that gives her great personal satisfaction.
貝蒂最喜歡閱讀，對她而言，閱讀是一種心靈經驗，為她帶來極大的自我滿足。

2412 satisfy ['sætɪsˌfaɪ]   v.   滿足   4th ★★★★★
Tom always works hard to make his own money to satisfy his material needs.
湯姆認真工作賺錢，好滿足他的物質需求。

2413 sauce [sɔs]   n.   醬汁   5th ★★★★★
The main ingredients for this sauce are tomatoes, mushrooms, peppers, and garlic.
這份醬汁的主要成分是番茄、蘑菇、胡椒、蒜頭。

2414 save [sev]   v.   儲蓄   5th ★★★★★
Marian's salary is the same as mine, but she has saved lots of money because she manages her money better than I.
瑪利亞的薪水和我一樣，但她存了很多錢，因為她的財務管理做得比我好。

2415 saving ['sevɪŋ]   n.   節省   5th ★★★★★
The device can produce a ten percent saving on fuel.
這項裝置可以節省百分之十的燃料。

2416 savvy ['sævɪ]   n.   見識   3rd ★★★★★
He is well known for his political savvy and strong management skills.
他因其政治頭腦和強而有力的管理技能聞名。

2417 scale [skel]   n.   規模   th ★★★★★
A powerful earthquake registering 6.8 on the Richter scale rocked Taiwan on March 31, 2002.
二千零二年三月三十一日，一場芮氏規模六點八的強震撼動台灣。

2418 scam ['skæm]   n.   詐騙   3rd ★★★★★
Their scam is selling fake antiques to foreign tourists.
他們的花招是賣仿冒古董給外國遊客。

2419 scan [skæn]   v.   瀏覽   4th ★★★★★
Many passengers scanned the newspaper while waiting for the train.
很多乘客在等火車的時候會瀏覽一下報紙。

2420 scandal ['skændl̩]   n.   醜聞   3rd ★★★★★
The minister step down office for the sake of the political scandal.
部長為了政治醜聞下台。

2421 scapegoat ['skep,ɡot]   **n.** 代罪羔羊   **3rd** ★★★★★
Eliminating problems by transferring the blame to others is often called scapegoat.
藉著怪罪他人來解決問題，通常稱為尋找代罪羔羊。

2422 scarce [skɛrs]   **adj.** 缺乏的   **4th** ★★★★★
Water becomes scarce when it doesn't rain for a long while.
好一段時間不下雨時，就會缺水。

2423 scarcely ['skɛrslɪ]   **adv.** 幾乎不   **4th** ★★★★★
Badly injured in the car accident, Jason could scarcely move his legs and was sent to the hospital right away.
傑森在車禍中受了重傷，他的雙腳幾乎不能動，馬上被送去醫院。

2424 scared [skɛrd]   **adj.** 恐懼的   **5th** ★★★★★
I loved swimming, but I am too scared to jump off the high diving board.
我熱愛游泳，但從高聳的跳水板往下跳讓我很害怕。

2425 scary ['skɛrɪ]   **adj.** 可怕的   **5th** ★★★★★
A really scary movie will give me terrible nightmares.
一部真正的恐怖片會讓我做可怕的惡夢。

2426 scatter ['skætɚ]   **v.** 散落   **4th** ★★★★★
The mirror slipped out of the little girl's hand, and the broken pieces scattered all over the floor.
鏡子從小女孩的手上滑了出來，碎片散落一地。

2427 scene [sin]   **n.** 一場戲   **4th** ★★★★★
The director filmed the scene many times until it was done to his satisfaction.
導演一幕戲要拍很多次，直到他滿意為止。

2428 scenery ['sinərɪ]   **n.** 風景   **4th** ★★★★★
The tourists enjoyed wholeheartedly the breathtaking scenery along the coast highway between Hualien and Ilan.
遊客全神貫注欣賞著花蓮和宜蘭之間濱海公路的美景。

2429 schedule ['skɛdʒul]   **n.** 時間表   **4th** ★★★★★
Following a schedule and doing things on time is extremely important in today's busy world.
在今日繁忙的世界裡，照著時間表做事，並準時完成非常重要。

2430 scheme [skim]　　　　　　n.　方案　　　4th ★★★★★

It's important to keep your plans small and manageable, and work well within your budget, rather than undertake a grandiose scheme.
重要的是，不要著手於宏偉的方案，而是要使計畫維持在小規模且易於管理，並在預算之內順利進行。

2431 scholar ['skɑlɚ]　　　　　　n.　學者　　　4th ★★★★★

Having published many important papers, he enjoys a high reputation as a scholar.
他是一位聲望很高的學者，發表過許多重要的文件。

2432 scholarship ['skɑlɚˌʃɪp]　　n.　獎學金　　　4th ★★★★★

David is now the best student in high school. It's certain that he will get a scholarship to the state university.
大衛是高中最優秀的學生，他肯定可以拿到獎學金去唸州立大學。

2433 scientific [ˌsaɪən'tɪfɪk]　　adj.　科學的　　　4th ★★★★★

You had better take a scientific approach to the situation.
你最好用科學方法來處理這個狀況。

2434 scientist ['saɪəntɪst]　　　n.　科學家　　　4th ★★★★★

Based on their study results, scientists have found that there is a close connection between stressful jobs and increased illness.
根據科學家的研究結果，他們發現了工作壓力和病痛增加之間有密切的關連。

2435 scold [skold]　　　　　　v.　責備　　　4th ★★★★★

John has been scolded by his boss for over ten minutes now. Apparently, she is not happy about his being late.
約翰已經被老闆罵了十分鐘以上，看來她對約翰的遲到不是很高興。

2436 scoop [skup]　　　　　　n.　杓子　　　4th ★★★★★

Helen asked her brother to buy her two scoops of chocolate ice cream.
海倫叫哥哥買兩球巧克力冰淇淋給她。

2437 score [skor]　　　　　　n.　分數　　　5th ★★★★★

You need a minimum score of seventy to pass this test.
你最低要考七十分才能通過測驗。

2438 scout [skaut]　　　　　　v.　搜尋　　　3rd ★★★★★

The Chiou family scouted the neighborhood for their lost dog.
邱家人為了他們走失的小狗找遍了這附近地區。

2439 scratch [skrætʃ]　　　　v.　搔癢　　　3rd ★★★★★

It is not easy for old people to scratch their backs, so they need help when their backs itch.
老人家很難幫自己抓背，所以背癢的時候，就需要他人幫忙。

2440 scream [skrim]　　　　v.　尖叫　　　4th ★★★★★

The woman lost her temper and screamed at the vendor.
這個女人大發雷霆，對著小販尖叫。

2441 screen [skrin]　　　　n.　螢幕　　　4th ★★★★★

One of the ways by which website companies make money is from the advertisements that flash on the screens.
網路公司賺錢的方法之一，就是從電腦視窗彈跳出來的廣告。

2442 sculpture ['skʌlptʃɚ]　　　　n.　雕刻　　　3rd ★★★★★

The world's largest collection of Khmer sculpture resides at Angkor, the former royal capital of Cambodia.
吳哥是柬埔寨的前皇家首都，該地集結了最多的高棉雕刻。

2443 search [sɝtʃ]　　　　v.　搜查　　　4th ★★★★★

Officer Lee searched the suspect's pockets and found a Beretta model 92FS 9mm pistol.
李警官搜查嫌犯的口袋，找到了一把九毫米口徑的貝瑞塔手槍。

2444 season ['sizn]　　　　n.　季節　　　3rd ★★★★★

During the World Cup football season, the wives whose husbands have their eyes fixed on the scoreboard indeed become the so-called "World Cup widows."
每逢世界盃足球季，許多太太因她們的丈夫只關心足球賽事，而成了所謂的「世界盃寡婦」。

2445 seat [sit]　　　　n.　座位　　　5th ★★★★★

The play will begin in ten minutes, so we should go to our seats now.
表演再十分鐘就要開始了，我們應該要趕快就座。

2446 second ['sɛkənd]　　　　adj.　第二的　　　5th ★★★★★

The latest evidence shows that second-hand smoke can not only lower children's IQ but also cause lung cancer.
最新的證據顯示，吸二手煙不但會導致嬰兒的智力降低，還會造成肺癌。

2447 secondary ['sɛkən͵dɛrɪ]　　　　adj.　次要的　　　5th ★★★★★

Simon loves his work. To him, work always comes first, and family and friends are

secondary.
西蒙熱愛他的工作。對他來說，工作永遠是首要，家庭和朋友是次要的。

2448 secretary [ˈsɛkrəˌtɛrɪ]　　　n.　秘書　　5th ★★★★★
A different secretary seems to answer the phone every time I call that company.
每次我打電話給那家公司似乎都是不同的秘書接的。

2449 section [ˈsɛkʃən]　　　n.　區域　　4th ★★★★★
That section of the city is for commercial buildings only so there are many businessmen working there.
城市的那個地段只做商業建築用，所以有很多商人在那裡做買賣。

2450 secure [sɪˈkjur]　　　v.　確保　　4th ★★★★★
Remember to secure yourself against accidents before starting off.
記得在出發前要確保自己安全，預防意外的發生。

2451 security [sɪˈkjurətɪ]　　　n.　安全　　4th ★★★★★
Most people work in order to have financial security.
大部分的人工作是為了確保財務上安全。

2452 seed [sid]　　　n.　種子　　4th ★★★★★
Many popular drinks, like coffee, cola, and cocoa, are all made from the seeds of trees.
許多流行飲品是由樹的種子製成的，像是咖啡、可樂、可可亞。

2453 seek [sik]　　　v.　尋找　　4th ★★★★★
Seeking peace and clean air, many people have moved from cities to rural areas.
許多人為了尋找平靜以及乾淨的空氣，會從城市搬到鄉間。

2454 seem [sim]　　　v.　似乎　　5th ★★★★★
The spiritual woman seemed to be talking to the air.
那位通靈的女人似乎在對空氣說話。

2455 seldom [ˈsɛldəm]　　　adv.　很少　　5th ★★★★★
Seldom did I make any mistake during my past five years of service in the company.
我在這間公司工作的五年當中鮮少犯錯。

2456 select [səˈlɛkt]　　　adj.　精選的　　4th ★★★★★
Gold card members will be offered special discounts on select merchandise each month.
金卡會員每個月都享有精選商品的特價優惠。

2457 **selfish** [ˈsɛlfɪʃ]　　　　　**adj.** 自私的　　5th ★★★★★
Because he is very selfish, he has few friends.
他很自私，所以他沒什麼朋友。

2458 **self-sufficient** [ˈsɛlfsəˌfɪʃənt] **adj.** 自足的　　4th ★★★★★
Some countries in Africa are not self-sufficient in crops.
非洲某些國家在糧食上無法自給自足。

2459 **send** [sɛnd]　　　　　**v.** 寄送　　5th ★★★★★
With e-mails, people don't need to use paper to send and receive letters and messages.
有了電子郵件，人們不再需要用紙張收發信件和訊息。

2460 **sensory** [ˈsɛnsərɪ]　　　　**adj.** 感覺的　　5th ★★★★★
Our brains interpret our sensory impressions for us. For instance, the images of things we look at must go to the brain so we can actually "see" them.
大腦會詮釋我們的感官印象。舉個例子來說，我們所見到的圖像會傳至大腦，經過詮釋讓我們能真正「看到」它們。

2461 **semester** [səˈmɛstə]　　　　**n.** 學期　　5th ★★★★★
I am taking some evening classes this semester, and I have a lot of homework.
這學期我修了許多夜間課程，而且有很多回家作業。

2462 **seminar** [ˈsɛməˌnɑr]　　　　**n.** 研討會　　4th ★★★★★
The biologists held a number of seminars to discuss important topics last week.
上個禮拜生物學家舉辦了多次研討會，討論許多重要主題。

2463 **senior** [ˈsinjə]　　　　**adj.** 高級的　　5th ★★★★★
The senior managers, with whom we are meeting next week, are promising a big money deal.
下星期我們要和高階主管開會，他們承諾會有一筆巨額交易。

2464 **sensation** [sɛnˈseʃən]　　　　**n.** 知覺　　4th ★★★★★
The boy had a sensation of dizziness after standing in the sun for a long while.
男孩站在陽光下一段時間後，感到頭暈目眩。

2465 **sense** [sɛns]　　　　**n.** 感覺　　4th ★★★★★
Using only its sense or smell, a single dog can search an area eight times faster than a search team of twenty people.
一隻狗在搜查一個地區時，單靠感覺或嗅覺就比一支二十人的搜查隊伍快上八倍。

2466 sensible ['sɛnsəbl]　　　**adj.** 明智的　　4th ★★★★★
It should be sensible of you to refuse the invitation.
你拒絕邀請應是明智的作法。

2467 sensitive ['sɛnsətɪv]　　　**adj.** 敏感的　　4th ★★★★★
Many sounds are not sensed by human ears because, unlike other animals, our ears are not as sensitive.
有很多的聲音人耳聽不見，因為我們和其他動物不同，我們的耳朵沒有那麼靈敏。

2468 sentence ['sɛntəns]　　　**v.** 判決　　4th ★★★★★
Billy was sentenced by the judge to three days in jail because of drunk driving.
比利因為酒後駕車，遭法官判處入獄三天。

2469 sentimental [ˌsɛntə'mɛntl]　　**adj.** 情緒的　　4th ★★★★★
This is a typical television soap opera, and millions of people watch these stormy, sentimental stories every day.
這是一部典型的肥皂劇，數百萬的觀眾每天收看這些灑狗血又傷感的故事。

2470 separate ['sɛpəˌret]　　　**adj.** 個別的　　4th ★★★★★
A college student, blind in both eyes by two separate accidents, is seeing now through the eyes of a dead marine.
因兩場車禍而雙眼全盲的大學生，現在透過一位已逝海軍的眼睛重見光明。

2471 separately ['sɛpərɪtlɪ]　　　**adv.** 分開地　　4th ★★★★★
This T-shirt's composition is 100% cotton. Wash separately, and do not tumble dry.
這件T恤是百分之百純棉，要分開洗且不能烘乾。

2472 sergeant ['sɑrdʒənt]　　　**n.** 警官　　4th ★★★★★
I'm very proud of my job because I'm a police sergeant.
我是一位警官，我對自己的工作十分自豪。

2473 series ['siriz]　　　**n.** 系列　　4th ★★★★★
In most cases, we go through a series of four to six sleep cycles each night.
在大多數情況下，我們每晚會經過一系列四至六個睡眠週期。

2474 serious ['sɪrɪəs]　　　**adj.** 嚴重的　　5th ★★★★★
The large number of students quitting schools reflects how serious the drop-out problem has been.
大量的學生輟學反映出退學問題的嚴重性。

134

2475 service ['sɝvɪs]　　　　　n.　服務　　5th ★★★★★
A car depreciates after a couple of years of service.
汽車在使用兩、三年後折舊。

2476 serving ['sɝvɪŋ]　　　　　n.　一份　　4th ★★★★★
Doctors recommend us to eat five to eight servings of fruits and vegetables daily to keep healthy.
醫生建議我們每天吃五到八份蔬果來維持健康。

2477 settle ['sɛtl]　　　　　v.　使安定　　4th ★★★★★
After traveling in Europe for ten years, he wants to settle down in Taiwan.
他在歐洲旅行十年之後，想要在台灣安定下來。

2478 settler ['sɛtlə]　　　　　n.　定居者　　4th ★★★★★
Polynesian people from other Pacific islands were probably the first settlers in Honolulu.
太平洋島上的玻里尼西亞人很可能是檀香山的第一批定居者。

2479 severe [sə'vɪr]　　　　　adj.　嚴重的　　4th ★★★★★
I've had severe pains in my stomach since dinner.
晚餐之後我的肚子就一直劇烈疼痛。

2480 sewage ['sjuɪdʒ]　　　　　n.　下水道　　4th ★★★★★
To prevent sewage from entering the waterways and protect public health, the city councilman strongly demanded that the sewage system be improved in three months.
為了防止污水進入河道以保障公眾健康，市議員強烈要求在三個月內改進污水處理系統。

2481 sex [sɛks]　　　　　n.　性　　4th ★★★★★
One of our great challenges is how we need to talk more freely and openly about sex.
我們最大的挑戰之一是如何更自在和開放地談論性。

2482 sexually ['sɛkʃuəlɪ]　　　　　adv.　性慾地　　4th ★★★★★
A woman reporter complained one of them sexually harassed her in a locker room.
一名女記者抱怨他們其中一人在更衣室裡對她性騷擾。

2483 shallow ['ʃælo]　　　　　adj.　淺的　　4th ★★★★★
The pool is shallow, so don't jump in head-first.
水池很淺，所以不要頭先入水。

2484 shame [ʃem]　　　v.　羞辱　　5th ★★★★★
Vincent shamed his family's name when he was put in jail.
文生入獄使他的家族名聲蒙羞。

2485 shape [ʃep]　　　v.　形成　　5th ★★★★★
Both a person's heredity and his environment help to shape his character.
個人的遺傳和生長的環境都會幫助形成他的性格。

2486 share [ʃɛr]　　　v.　共享　　5th ★★★★★
Why not share our money?
我們何不共享我們的錢呢？

2487 shareholder [ˈʃɛrˌholdə]　　n.　股東　　5th ★★★★★
A notice calling for an emergency meeting to be held on May 1st is issued to all
the shareholders.
五月一號將召開一場緊急會議，已經發送公告給所有股東了。

2488 sharp [ʃɑrp]　　　adj.　尖銳的　　5th ★★★★★
Spades are made with sharp metal tips and are useful in gardening.
鏟子是用鋒利的金屬尖頭製成，對園藝很有幫助。

2489 sheet [ʃit]　　　n.　表格　　3rd ★★★★★
The balance sheet, prepared by the accountants, has shown that the company
made a profit last month.
會計師所製作的資產負債表顯示出該公司上個月有賺錢。

2490 shelter [ˈʃɛltə]　　n.　避難所　　4th ★★★★★
This shelter gives homeless people a place to sleep when it's cold outside.
外面的天氣很冷時，避難所給無家可歸者一個睡覺的地方。

2491 shine [ʃaɪn]　　　v.　照耀　　4th ★★★★★
The longer the sun shines, the warmer the earth's surface is.
太陽照射的時間越長，地表就越溫暖。

2492 shoot [ʃut]　　　v.　射擊　　4th ★★★★★
The seal at the circus could shoot a basketball through a hoop.
馬戲團裡的海豹可以將籃球射進籃框。

2493 shortage [ˈʃɔrtɪdʒ]　　n.　缺乏　　5th ★★★★★
This year's East Asia Summit meetings will focus on critical issues such as energy

conservation, food shortages, and global warming.
今年東亞高峰會將集中討論一些重要議題，例如能源節約、食物短缺、全球暖化。

2494 shortly [ˈʃɔrtlɪ]　　　adv. 不久　　4th ★★★★★
The man was severely injured in last weekend's tragic car accident and died shortly afterwards.
那男子在上禮拜的一場車禍中受重傷，不久後就死亡了。

2495 shot [ʃɑt]　　　n. 射擊　　4th ★★★★★
David plays basketball well. He's quick and makes good shot.
大衛的籃球打的很好，他動作很快而且射籃很準。

2496 should [ʃud]　　　aux. 應該　　5th ★★★★★
All of us, young and old, should take part in recycling programs to help conserve natural resources.
不分老少，我們所有人都應該參與回收計劃，以幫助保護自然資源。

2497 shoulder [ˈʃoldɚ]　　　v. 肩負　　5th ★★★★★
Being the only child in the family, he shoulders the full responsibility of taking care of his parents.
他是家中的獨生子，所以肩負照顧雙親的全責。

2498 showcase [ˈʃoˌkes]　　　v. 使展現　　4th ★★★★★
The hour-long program will showcase the culture of Taiwan and is scheduled to be screened at the end of the year.
這部一小時的節目將會展現台灣文化，計畫將在年底時播出。

2499 shower [ˈʃauɚ]　　　n. 淋浴　　5th ★★★★★
Well, you'd better take a hot shower right now, or you'll catch a cold.
你現在最好去洗個熱水澡，不然你會感冒。

2500 shrink [ʃrɪŋk]　　　v. 縮小　　3rd ★★★★★
When people reach a certain age, they shrink. They might become a few inches shorter.
人們到達某一個年齡時，體型會縮小，可能會矮個幾公分。

2501 sibling [ˈsɪblɪŋ]　　　n. 兄弟姐妹　　3rd ★★★★★
In a dispute between siblings, parents usually take the side of the younger child because that child is weaker and smaller.
兄弟姐妹之間有糾紛時，父母通常偏袒較年輕的孩子，因為那個孩子較弱小。

2502 sight [saɪt]　　　　n.　視力　　4th ★★★★★
The salesman received a sight bill from the financial department.
推銷員接到從財務部門傳來的即期匯票。

2503 sign [saɪn]　　　　n.　告示牌　　4th ★★★★★
Signs asking visitors to keep their hands off the art are everywhere in the Louvre Museum, Paris.
巴黎的羅浮宮到處都有標示，要求旅客不得用手碰觸藝術品。

2504 signal ['sɪgn̩]　　　　v.　做信號　　4th ★★★★★
He signaled to the waiter that he was ready to order food by closing up the menu folder in his hands.
他將手中的菜單合起來向服務生示意他已經準備好要點餐了。

2505 signature ['sɪgnətʃɚ]　　　　n.　簽名　　4th ★★★★★
You can go on the class trip if you get your parent's signature.
如果你得到父母的簽名，就可以參加班級旅行。

2506 significance [sɪg'nɪfəkəns]　　　　n.　重要性　　3rd ★★★★★
The significance of most events takes time to recognize.
大多數事件的重要性需要時間來確認。

2507 significant [sɪg'nɪfəkənt]　　　　adj.　明顯的　　3rd ★★★★★
There is a significant change in weather after Moon Festival.
中秋節過後，天氣有明顯的變化。

2508 silence ['saɪləns]　　　　n.　沈默　　5th ★★★★★
The monk has spoken a word since his vow of silence.
修道士自從立誓沉默後到現在只講過一句話。

2509 silent ['saɪlənt]　　　　adj.　安靜的　　5th ★★★★★
Reading is primarily a silent activity.
閱讀本是一項安靜的活動。

2510 similar ['sɪmələ]　　　　adj.　相似的　　4th ★★★★★
People who have similar interests can discuss interactively on blogs.
興趣相仿的人可以在部落格上交流討論。

2511 simultaneously [saɪməl'tenɪəslɪ]　adv.　同時地　　3rd ★★★★★
The president's speech will be broadcast simultaneously on television and radio

so that more people can listen to it at the time when it is delivered.
總統的演講會同時在電視和廣播中播出，這樣就可以有更多的人可以聽的見。

2512 since [sɪns]　　　　conj. 自從　　5th ★★★★★
Jerusalem was divided between Israel and Jordan until 1967; since then Israel has held all city.
耶路撒冷以前由以色列和約旦共享，一九六七年以後，就由以色列掌管整座耶路撒冷。

2513 sincere [sɪn'sɪr]　　　adj. 誠懇的　　4th ★★★★★
Daphne likes her boss because he is friendly and sincere.
黛芬喜歡她的老闆，因為他既友善又誠懇。

2514 single ['sɪŋgl]　　　　adj. 單一的　　4th ★★★★★
The deadline is only three days away. We can't ignore the waste of a single minute in doing the work.
截止日期只剩三天了，我們在做事時不能浪費任何一分鐘。

2515 sink [sɪŋk]　　　　　v. 下沉　　5th ★★★★★
After the storm last night, many ships sank to the bottom of the ocean.
經過了昨晚的暴風雨後，許多輪船都沉到海洋的底部。

2516 site [saɪt]　　　　　n. 地點　　4th ★★★★★
The Globe, a famous theater in London, was rebuilt not far from its original site.
倫敦知名的全球劇院，在距離原址不遠處重建。

2517 situate ['sɪtʃu,et]　　　v. 使坐落　　4th ★★★★★
Like pearls scattered in the East Sea, the Penghu archipelago is situated in the southwest of the Taiwan Strait.
澎湖列島位於台灣海峽西南方，猶如一堆散落在東海之濱的珍珠。

2518 size [saɪz]　　　　　n. 尺寸　　4th ★★★★★
Your heart is a bundle of muscles about the size of your fist.
你的心臟是一捆肌肉，大小大約像你的拳頭一樣。

2519 skeptical ['skɛptɪkl]　　adj. 懷疑的　　3rd ★★★★★
They all believe it will work, but I am quite skeptical about it.
他們都相信這會成功，但是我有點懷疑。

2520 skill [skɪl]　　　　　n. 技巧　　5th ★★★★★
Using time effectively is a valuable skill that everyone must master.
善用時間是每個人都必須學會的寶貴技巧。

2521 skyscraper [ˈskaɪˌskrepɚ]　　n.　摩天大樓　4th ★★★★★
There are more and more skyscrapers built in the newly developed zone.
新興開發區蓋了越來越多的摩天大樓。

2522 slang [slæŋ]　　n.　俚語　4th ★★★★★
Textese is a term for the abbreviations and slang most commonly used among young people today.
簡訊語言是以縮寫和俚語的方式來表達的語言，為時下青年廣泛使用。

2523 slash [slæʃ]　　v.　縮減　4th ★★★★★
The newly elected mayor pledged to slash the red tape to help the disadvantaged families.
新當選的市長承諾要削減繁瑣規則，以幫助弱勢家庭。

2524 slice [slaɪs]　　n.　片　5th ★★★★★
My aunt took out two slices of bread to make a sandwich.
我的阿姨拿出兩片土司來做三明治。

2525 slick [slɪk]　　n.　浮油　5th ★★★★★
The head of Environmental Protection Administration made a public apology for the inappropriate handling of the oil slick at Kenting.
環保署的負責人為墾丁浮油事件的不當處理公開道歉。

2526 slide [slaɪd]　　v.　滑動　4th ★★★★★
The avalanche gets bigger as it slides down the mountain, carrying with rocks and fallen trees.
雪崩時從山上挾帶的岩石和倒下的樹木，讓崩塌更為嚴重。

2527 slippery [ˈslɪpərɪ]　　adj.　滑的　5th ★★★★★
The ground is slippery. Hold onto the rope and don't let go.
地面很滑，要抓好繩子別鬆手。

2528 slogan [ˈsloɡən]　　n.　標語　4th ★★★★★
The advertisers spent all day trying to think of a catchy slogan.
廣告商花了一整天的時間試著想出一句引人注意的廣告標語。

2529 slope [slop]　　v.　傾斜　4th ★★★★★
The road slopes down after this right turn.
這條道路右轉後是斜坡。

2530 smart [smɑrt]　　adj. 聰明的　　5th ★★★★★
The representative is smart in his dealings.
這位代表在商業往來上十分精明。

2531 smile [smaɪl]　　v. 微笑　　5th ★★★★★
The man's eyes seemed to twinkle as he smiled.
這男人微笑時眼睛似乎閃閃發光。

2532 smoke [smok]　　v. 抽菸　　5th ★★★★★
Lung cancer, one of the major killers in Taiwan, has long been associated with air pollution and smoking.
肺癌長期以來都和空氣污染以及吸煙有關，是台灣主要的致命死因之一。

2533 smooth [smuð]　　adj. 光滑的　　4th ★★★★★
The finish of the table is really smooth and shiny.
那張完工後的桌子真是又滑又亮。

2534 smother ['smʌðɚ]　　v. 厚厚覆蓋　　3rd ★★★★★
Men who eat a lot of tomatoes or pizza smothered with stuff may be giving themselves a hedge against prostate cancer.
吃很多番茄或比薩上放滿酌料的人，有助於預防前列腺癌。

2535 smuggle ['smʌgl̩]　　v. 私運　　4th ★★★★★
The customs officials are so incompetent that many illegal goods have been smuggled in.
海關人員很不稱職，讓許多非法物品走私進來。

2536 snack [snæk]　　n. 零食　　5th ★★★★★
Ted has eaten a lot of snacks while watching TV. He no longer has any appetite for dinner.
泰德一邊看電視一邊吃了很多零食，使他沒有胃口吃晚飯。

2537 sneeze [sniz]　　v. 打噴嚏　　4th ★★★★★
The SARS virus spreads through droplets by sneezing or coughing.
SARS病毒藉由打噴嚏或咳嗽等飛沫傳染。

2538 sniff [snɪf]　　v. 嗤之以鼻　　3rd ★★★★★
You shouldn't have sniffed at the officer.
你不應該對長官嗤之以鼻。

S

2539 soak [sok]　　　　　　　　**v.**　吸收　　　**3rd** ★★★★★
The manager required his staff to soak the latest information from the market constantly.
經理要求員工要持續不斷吸收市場的最新資訊。

2540 soapbox ['sop,bɑks]　　　**n.**　臨時演說台　**5th** ★★★★★
The politician became a soapbox orator after resignation.
這位政治家辭職後成為街頭演說者。

2541 soar [sor]　　　　　　　　**v.**　飛漲　　　**3rd** ★★★★★
Prices soared as a result of the inflation.
物價上漲是通貨膨漲的結果。

2542 soccer ['sɑkɚ]　　　　　　**n.**　足球　　　**5th** ★★★★★
The boy became a player on the school soccer team from this semester.
這個男孩這學期開始成為足球校隊的球員。

2543 social ['soʃəl]　　　　　　**adj.**　社交的　**4th** ★★★★★
Unlike her social sister, Nancy is shy and does not like to go to parties or make new friends.
南西和她外向的姊姊不一樣,她很害羞,不喜歡參加派對或交新朋友。

2544 society [sə'saɪətɪ]　　　　**n.**　社會　　　**4th** ★★★★★
In a democratic society, everyone can fight for his own human rights.
在民主社會裡,每個人都可以爭取自身人權。

2545 software ['sɔft,wɛr]　　　**n.**　軟體　　　**5th** ★★★★★
The two companies made an agreement to develop software together.
這兩家公司達成協議,要共同開發軟體。

2546 soil [sɔɪl]　　　　　　　　**n.**　土壤　　　**4th** ★★★★★
Some chemicals like DDT can remain in soil for years, resulting in vegetables and fruits that are harmful to our health.
一些化學品如DDT會殘留在土裡,導致蔬果危害人體健康。

2547 solar ['solɚ]　　　　　　　**adj.**　太陽的　**4th** ★★★★★
The system of converting solar energy into electrical energy would do very little damage to the environment.
該系統利用太陽能轉換成電能,所以幾乎不會對環境構成破壞。

138

2548 soldier ['soldʒɚ]   n.   士兵   4th ★★★★★
Napoleon was a French soldier who became emperor of France.
拿破崙是一名法國士兵,後來成為法國皇帝。

2549 solid ['sɑlɪd]   n.   固體   3rd ★★★★★
It's hard to scoop this ice cream because it's frozen solid.
要挖出這球冰淇淋很難,因為已經結凍了。

2550 solution [sə'luʃən]   n.   解決   4th ★★★★★
You will feel much better if you work on solutions to your upsetting situations.
如果你試著解決現下的混亂,你會感覺好一點。

2551 solve [sɑlv]   v.   解決   3rd ★★★★★
The problem was so difficult that most students could not solve it.
這個問題很困難,大部分的學生都無法解決。

2552 somehow ['sʌm,haʊ]   adv.   以某種方式   4th ★★★★★
This may look difficult, but I know things will work out somehow.
這看起來很難,但我知道事情總是會有出路的。

2553 someone ['sʌm,wʌn]   pro.   某人   5th ★★★★★
When a police officer doesn't have search permission, he can't go into someone's house to look for something.
若警察沒有搜查許可,他就不能進入別人的家中找東西。

2554 sometimes ['sʌm,taɪmz]   adv.   有時候   5th ★★★★★
The wood from willow trees is sometimes used to make boxes.
柳樹的木材有時用來做成箱子。

2555 somewhat ['sʌm,hwɑt]   adv.   有點   5th ★★★★★
Arnold is somewhat sore from his workout yesterday.
阿諾因昨天的訓練而感到稍微疼痛。

2556 sore [sor]   adj.   疼痛   5th ★★★★★
Tyler's jaw gets sore when he chews gum.
泰勒嚼口香糖時下顎會疼痛。

2557 sorrow ['saro]   n.   悲傷   5th ★★★★★
It is a great sorrow for a parent to cope with the death of their child.
處理孩子的死亡對父母是個極大的悲痛。

2558 sound [saund]　　　n.　聲音　　4th ★★★★★

It's very difficult for people who sleep silently to put up with the sound of snoring.
睡覺安靜的人很難忍受打鼾的聲音。

2559 source [sors]　　　n.　來源　　4th ★★★★★

Laundry detergent is a major source of pollution to the river.
洗衣精是河川污染的主要來源。

2560 south [sauθ]　　　adv.　南方　　5th ★★★★★

Birds head south to warmer climate when cold weather comes.
當寒冷的天氣到來時，鳥兒會飛到天氣較溫暖的南方。

2561 souvenir ['suvəˌnɪr]　　　n.　紀念品　　4th ★★★★★

I bought some key chains as souvenirs of my trip to Rome.
我去羅馬旅行時買了一些鑰匙圈當作紀念品。

2562 spacious ['speʃəs]　　　adj.　寬敞的　　4th ★★★★★

What she wanted most was a spacious house to live in.
她最想要的就是住在一間寬敞的房子裡。

2563 span [spæn]　　　n.　一段時間　　3rd ★★★★★

The extended life span has led to a growing population in Taiwan.
平均壽命的延長使台灣人口日益增加。

2564 spare [spɛr]　　　v.　節省　　3rd ★★★★★

These books are very expensive, I know, but you should spare no expenses where the education of your children is concerned.
我知道這些書籍很貴，但是孩子的教育費可不能省。

2565 special ['spɛʃəl]　　　adj.　特別的　　5th ★★★★★

Many people enjoy scuba diving, which requires special training in the use of oxygen underwater.
許多人喜歡潛水，這需要在水下使用氧氣的特別訓練。

2566 specialty ['spɛʃəltɪ]　　　n.　特製品　　4th ★★★★★

The Michelin three-star chef took his protege into confidence to fully disclose the recipes of all his luscious specialties.
這位米其林三星級廚師將自己所有的特色佳餚食譜都傳授給門生。

2567 species ['spiʃɪz]　　　n.　物種　　4th ★★★★★

139

Many species of marine animals and fish are directly at risk due to the temperature rise because they simply cannot survive in warmer waters.
由於溫度上升，很多海洋物種和魚類面臨直接風險，因為它們根本無法生存在溫暖的水域。

2568 specific [spɪˈsɪfɪk]　　　**adj.** 特定的　　**4th** ★★★★★
There are two kinds of invitations in western cultures, which are general and specific.
西方文化有兩種類型的邀請：一般和特定。

2569 specifically [spɪˈsɪfɪk]ɪ]　**adv.** 特定地　**4th** ★★★★★
I specifically asked for a room facing the sea, but the manager told me that the only room left was facing the woods.
我特別要求一間面海的房間，但經理告訴我，只剩下一間面對森林的房間。

2570 specialize [ˈspɛʃəlˌaɪz]　　　**v.** 專攻　　**4th** ★★★★★
Mary wants to specialize in literature at college, so she tries to read as many literary works as possible.
瑪麗想在大學專攻文學，所以她盡量多看文學作品。

2571 spectacle [ˈspɛktəkl]　　　　**n.** 景象　　**3rd** ★★★★★
The northern lights, known as the aurora borealis, are one of nature's most dazzling spectacles.
北極的光線是大自然最耀眼的景觀之一，稱之為極光。

2572 spectacular [spɛkˈtækjələ]　**adj.** 壯觀的　**3rd** ★★★★★
Thousands of tourists visit Antarctic every year to see its spectacular ice, snow, and wildlife.
每年有成千上萬的遊客到南極欣賞壯觀的冰雪和野生動物。

2573 spectator [spɛkˌtetə]　　　　**n.** 觀眾　　**3rd** ★★★★★
Athletes and sports competitors compete in organized, officiated sports events to entertain spectators.
運動員和運動選手於有組織的正式賽事中競賽，以娛樂觀眾。

2574 speech [spitʃ]　　　　　　　**n.** 演說　　**4th** ★★★★★
My mind often drifted during the boring speech.
我的心思經常在無趣的演講陷入神遊。

2575 speed [spid]　　　　　　　　**n.** 速度　　**4th** ★★★★★
The maximum speed limit on this road is thirty kilometers per hour.
這條道路最高行車速限是每小時三十公里。

S

2576 spend [spɛnd]　　　　v. 度過　　5th ★★★★★
I am thinking about spending my vacation in South Asia.
我想要去南亞度假。

2577 spicy [ˈspaɪsɪ]　　　　adj. 辣的　　5th ★★★★★
They had a spicy conversation about the conclusion made in the meeting.
他們辛辣地談論會議結果。

2578 spin [spɪn]　　　　v. 旋轉　　4th ★★★★★
Movements in break dancing include spinning on the head, jumping from the knees to the toes, and doing pantomime.
霹靂舞的動作包括大地板動作、小地板動作、隨意舞步。

2579 spirit [ˈspɪrɪt]　　　　n. 精神　　4th ★★★★★
The football team played with a noble spirit.
那支足球隊以高尚的精神踢球。

2580 spiritually [ˈspɪrɪtʃuəlɪ]　　　adv. 精神上　　4th ★★★★★
Jessica is a very religious girl because she believes that she is always spiritually supported by her god.
潔西卡是個非常虔誠的女孩，她相信上帝會在精神上支持她。

2581 splash [splæʃ]　　　　v. 濺起　　4th ★★★★★
On a rainy day, fast-moving motorcycles or automobiles may splash mud and dirt all over you.
下雨天的時候，快速移動的汽機車可能會把泥濘濺起，弄得你滿身都是。

2582 spit [spɪt]　　　　v. 吐　　3rd ★★★★★
The old man spit out betel nut juice and some got on my shoe.
老人亂吐檳榔汁，有些還吐在我鞋子上。

2583 split [splɪt]　　　　v. 剝開　　3rd ★★★★★
Split the banana in half so that we can both eat some.
把香蕉切成兩半，這樣我們兩個都可以吃一些。

2584 spoil [spɔɪl]　　　　v. 損壞　　4th ★★★★★
When it come to oranges, those you recommended me to buy two days ago had so many spoiled.
說到橘子，兩天前你推薦我買的橘子很多都是壞的。

140

2585 sponsor ['spɑnsɚ]   v. 贊助   3rd ★★★★★
Our trip to the meeting in Taipei was sponsored by the city government. The funding was plenty.
我們到台北開會的出差費是由市政府所贊助，經費很足夠。

2586 sport [sport]   n. 運動   5th ★★★★★
The 2002 Winter Olympic Games, held in Salt Lake City, Utah, were the first major international sports event to take place in the U.S.A. after the September eleventh attacks.
二千零二年，美國猶他州鹽湖城所舉行的冬季奧運會，是美國自九一一攻擊後第一個大型國際體育賽事。

2587 sportsmanship ['sportsmən,ʃɪp] n. 運動家精神 5th ★★★★★
Andrew had good sportsmanship. He still wore a smile on his face though he lost the competition.
安德魯有運動家的精神，就算輸了比賽，他的臉上還是帶著笑容。

2588 spot [spɑt]   n. 現場   5th ★★★★★
The thief was caught on the spot yesterday.
昨天小偷當場被捕。

2589 sprain [spren]   v. 扭傷   3rd ★★★★★
Jolie sprained her ankle so that she couldn't play basketball for a month.
裘莉扭傷腳踝，導致她一個月都不能打籃球。

2590 spread [sprɛd]   v. 散佈   4th ★★★★★
The rumor is spread all over town that Jack is going to get married.
城裡到處流傳傑克要結婚的謠言。

2591 square [skwɛr]   adj. 公正的   5th ★★★★★
I don't think it's a square deal.
我不認為這是一項正當交易。

2592 squeeze [skwiz]   v. 擠壓   4th ★★★★★
My grandmother squeezes my cheek every time I visit her.
每次我去探視奶奶時，她都會擰我的臉頰。

2593 squelch [skwɛltʃ]   v. 鎮住   5th ★★★★★
I tried to squelch the laugh rising in my throat, but seeing the boss looking all over his desk for the glasses he had pushed up on his head was too funny.
我想要忍住喉頭裡的笑聲，但看著老闆在他的桌上到處找著架在頭上的眼鏡，實在太好笑。

2594 **stab** [stæb]   **v.** 刺   **4th** ★★★★★
Two policemen were stabbed by the suspect, when handling a domestic violence case.
兩位員警在處理家暴案件時,被嫌疑犯給刺傷了。

2595 **stabilize** ['stebl‚aɪz]   **v.** 使穩定   **3rd** ★★★★★
After an unpredictable fourth quarter, the economy is expected to stabilize toward the coming year.
經歷了令人意外的第四季,明年的經濟預估會穩定下來。

2596 **stadium** ['stedɪəm]   **n.** 體育場   **4th** ★★★★★
Next year our baseball team is getting a new stadium.
明年我們的棒球隊會有新的球場。

2597 **staff** [stæf]   **n.** 全體職員   **4th** ★★★★★
The entire staff chipped in money for their boss' birthday.
全體員工都出錢為他們老闆過生日。

2598 **stage** [stedʒ]   **n.** 舞台   **5th** ★★★★★
The audience quieted down when the conductor came on stage to begin directing the orchestra.
交響樂的指揮一上台開始指揮,觀眾便安靜下來。

2599 **stain** [sten]   **n.** 玷汙   **3rd** ★★★★★
Blood on clothing is a stubborn stain.
衣服上的血跡是個難洗的污漬。

2600 **standard** ['stændəd]   **n.** 格式   **4th** ★★★★★
Please structure your webpage's text and media using HTML standards.
請使用HTML格式來組織你的網頁文字和媒體。

2601 **standpoint** ['stænd‚pɔɪnt]   **n.** 立場   **4th** ★★★★★
Before telling a lie to protect someone, we should evaluate the circumstances from the standpoint of the deceived.
在我們要說謊去包庇一個人之前,應該要從蒙騙者的觀點去評估整的情況。

2602 **stare** [stɛr]   **v.** 注視   **4th** ★★★★★
The cat is staring at the flame from the candle.
貓咪盯著蠟燭上的火焰。

2603 start [stɑrt]　　　　　　　　**v.** 開始；出發　　**5th** ★★★★★
John suggested that the manager buy a gift for Lynn, who will be leaving the company and starting a business of her own.
約翰建議經理買份禮物給琳恩，因為她即將離開公司自己創業。

2604 starve [stɑrv]　　　　　　　**v.** 使挨餓　　**3rd** ★★★★★
Anorexia is an eating disorder where people starve themselves.
厭食症是一種飲食失調，人們會讓自己挨餓。

2605 state [stet]　　　　　　　　**n.** 州　　**4th** ★★★★★
California State University, Long Beach is located in the City of Long Beach, ten miles from the harbor and 25 miles from the Los Angeles International Airport.
加州大學長灘分校位於長灘市，與港口相距十英里，與洛杉磯國際機場相距二十五英里。

2606 station ['steʃən]　　　　　　**n.** 車站　　**5th** ★★★★★
Would you please tell me how to get to the nearest train station?
你可以告訴我最近的車站該怎麼去嗎？

2607 statue ['stætʃu]　　　　　　**n.** 雕像　　**4th** ★★★★★
The Statue of Liberty stands on a pedestal.
自由女神像由一個底座支撐著。

2608 stature ['stætʃɚ]　　　　　　**n.** 水準　　**3rd** ★★★★★
Georgia O'Keeffe was a woman artist of international stature.
格魯吉亞奧基夫是一位國際級的女藝術家。

2609 status ['stetəs]　　　　　　**n.** 身分　　**4th** ★★★★★
In ancient Egypt, as long ago as 1500 BC, the outward appearance expressed the person's status, role in society and political position.
早在公元前一千五百年的古埃及，外表即表示一個人在社會和政治上的身份地位。

2610 steady ['stɛdɪ]　　　　　　**adj.** 穩定的　　**4th** ★★★★★
The three major illnesses, circulatory system diseases, cancers, and diabetes will be on steady increase along with the rise of aging population.
隨著人口高齡化的興起，循環系統疾病、癌症和糖尿病這三大疾病，將逐步增加。

2611 steam [stim]　　　　　　　**v.** 蒸　　**4th** ★★★★★
My uncle had a steamed bun and soybean milk for breakfast this morning.
我的舅舅今天早上吃了饅頭和豆漿當早餐。

2612 stereo ['stɛrɪo]　　　　　n.　立體音響　　**4th** ★★★★★
In almost every home, a stereo or television will fill the rooms with sound.
幾乎每個家庭的房間裡都有立體音響或電視機的聲音。

2613 stereotype ['stɛrɪə,taɪp]　　n.　刻板印象　　**4th** ★★★★★
Stereotypes are a kind of gossip about the world, a gossip that makes us pre-judge people before we ever lay eyes on them.
刻板印象是一種對世界的流言蜚語。流言蜚語會讓我們在尚未看見某些人之前，就產生先入為主的判斷。

2614 stick [stɪk]　　　　　　v.　被⋯困住　　**4th** ★★★★★
We are stuck with the buck. However, if we think it is a right thing to do, we must do it right away.
我們被反彈聲浪困住了。但如果我們認為這麼做是對的，還是必須馬上實行。

2615 stiff [stɪf]　　　　　　adj.　硬梆梆的　　**4th** ★★★★★
My bed used to feel stiff but now it's broken in.
我的床以前覺得硬梆梆的，但現在還蠻舒適的。

2616 stimulus ['stɪmjələs]　　　n.　刺激　　**3rd** ★★★★★
The Republic of China Consumer Voucher is an economic stimulus package.
中華民國的消費券是一項刺激經濟的配套方案。

2617 stingy ['stɪndʒɪ]　　　　adj.　吝嗇的　　**4th** ★★★★★
Most Chinese businesspeople seem to be too stingy to get involved in charity.
大部分中國商人似乎都吝於參與慈善事業。

2618 stock [stɑk]　　　　　n.　存貨　　**4th** ★★★★★
The store has a large stock of canned food.
這家商店有一大堆罐頭食品的存貨。

2619 stomachache ['stʌmək,ek]　n.　胃痛　　**5th** ★★★★★
Mary is suffering from a stomachache and needs to eat food which is easy to digest.
瑪麗患有胃痛，需要吃容易消化的食物。

2620 storage ['storɪdʒ]　　　　n.　儲藏　　**4th** ★★★★★
Onions can be divided into two categories, which are fresh onions and storage onions.
洋蔥可分為兩大類：新鮮洋蔥和庫存洋蔥。

142

2621 store [stor]　　　　　　　**v.**　儲存　　**5th** ★★★★★

The human brain is like a super computer, storing millions of bits of information that can be recalled instantly.
人類的大腦就像一台超級電腦，裡頭儲存了幾百萬筆訊息，可以讓人立即回想。

2622 storm [stɔrm]　　　　　　　**n.**　暴風雨　　**5th** ★★★★★

The storm did a lot of harm to the southern part of the island.
暴風雨對本島南部造成很大的損傷。

2623 stow [sto]　　　　　　　**v.**　裝進　　**3rd** ★★★★★

The cargo has been stowed in the ship's hold.
已經把貨物裝載到船艙了。

2624 straight [stret]　　　　　　　**adj.**　直的　　**4th** ★★★★★

Draw a straight line to connect the two points.
畫一條直線連接這兩點。

2625 straighten ['stretn]　　　　　　　**v.**　整頓　　**4th** ★★★★★

Let's straighten out our accounts and check how much we owe each other.
我們來好好理清我們的帳目，再查對欠了彼此多少錢。

2626 strand [strænd]　　　　　　　**v.**　擱淺　　**3rd** ★★★★★

A school of dolphins stranded at the coast, some of which were dead.
一群海豚擱淺在岸邊，其中有幾隻死了。

2627 stranger ['strendʒɚ]　　　　　　　**n.**　陌生人　　**5th** ★★★★★

Sorry, I'm a stranger here myself, so I don't know that place.
抱歉，我不是本地人，我不知道那個地方。

2628 strangle ['stræŋgl]　　　　　　　**v.**　壓制　　**3rd** ★★★★★

The country's economic plight is strangling its scientific institutions.
該國的經濟困境扼殺了其科學機構。

2629 street [strit]　　　　　　　**n.**　街道　　**5th** ★★★★★

An officer is familiar with the neighborhood he patrols, such as streets, businesses, people, and problems.
警察要對他巡邏的社區很熟悉，像是街道、店家、居民、治安問題。

2630 strength [strɛŋθ]　　　　　　　**n.**　力量　　**4th** ★★★★★

Hercules had the strength of ten men.
希臘神話大力士赫克力士擁有十個人的力氣。

2631 **strengthen** [ˈstrɛŋθən]   v.   加強   **4th** ★★★★★
People who exercise regularly can strengthen their hearts.
運動規律的人可以增強心臟功能。

2632 **strenuous** [ˈstrɛnjuəs]   adj.   費力的   **3rd** ★★★★★
The clerks had a strenuous day taking stock.
店員辛苦的盤點存貨一整天。

2633 **stress** [strɛs]   n.   壓力   **4th** ★★★★★
Almost three-quarters of American high school juniors said they felt stress at least once a week, some almost daily.
有將近四分之三的美國高中生說他們一週至少感到壓力一次，有些則是幾乎每天。

2634 **stressful** [ˈstrɛsfəl]   adj.   有壓力的   **4th** ★★★★★
My life has been so stressful that my health is getting worse.
我的生活壓力很大，使我的健康越來越差了。

2635 **stretch** [strɛtʃ]   v.   伸展   **4th** ★★★★★
The cat woke up, stretched, and then walked over to its bowl of milk.
貓醒來伸伸懶腰，然後朝牠的牛奶碗走去。

2636 **strict** [strɪkt]   adj.   嚴格的   **5th** ★★★★★
The chocolate cake in the bakery next door is so tempting, but I probably need to stop thinking about it since I am on a very strict diet.
隔壁麵包店的巧克力蛋糕好吸引人，但我最好停止去想，因為我現在正屬行一項節食計畫。

2637 **strike** [straɪk]   v.   攻擊   **4th** ★★★★★
The computer virus, which was designed to strike on April 26, is reported to have affected over 60 million computers worldwide.
根據報導，此電腦病毒已於四月二十六日發動攻擊，全世界有超過六千萬台電腦受到影響。

2638 **structure** [ˈstrʌktʃə]   n.   結構   **4th** ★★★★★
Children in every culture learn their native language, kinship terms and family structure without thinking about them.
每個文化的小孩都是在毫無意識的情況下習得母語、親屬稱謂和家庭結構。

2639 **struggle** [ˈstrʌgl]   v.   奮鬥   **4th** ★★★★★
The young man struggled to succeed in business.
年輕人為了事業成功而努力奮鬥。

143

S

2640 stubborn ['stʌbən]   adj. 固執的   4th ★★★★★
John is a very stubborn person. It is difficult to get him to change his mind.
約翰很固執，很難讓他改變自己的想法。

2641 studio ['stjudɪ‚o]   n. 工作室   4th ★★★★★
The band recorded their music at a studio the night before.
樂團前天晚上在錄音室錄製他們的音樂。

2642 study ['stʌdɪ]   n. 研究   4th ★★★★★
Studies have shown that the closer the blood relationship between two people, the closer they are likely to be in intelligence.
研究顯示，兩個血緣關係越近的人，智力也會越相近。

2643 stuff [stʌf]   v. 填塞   4th ★★★★★
Betty stuffed all of her books into her schoolbag on the first day of school.
貝蒂第一天上學時把她所有的書都塞進書包裡。

2644 style [staɪl]   n. 風格   5th ★★★★★
Chad wants to open an Italian style restaurant in Tainan.
查德想要在台南開一家義大利風格的餐廳。

2645 stylish ['staɪlɪʃ]   adj. 流行的   5th ★★★★★
The girl is a stylish dresser and she spends a lot of money on new clothes.
這個女孩穿著時髦，她花了很多錢買衣服。

2646 subject ['sʌbdʒɪkt]   adj. 須經…的   4th ★★★★★
The program should be subject to the CEO's approval.
這個方案應該經過總裁批准。

2647 submit [səb'mɪt]   v. 提出   3rd ★★★★★
The motion has been submitted to the board.
這項提議已提交董事會。

2648 subscribe [səb'skraɪb]   v. 訂閱   3rd ★★★★★
In many rural areas, there are still many people who do not even subscribe to a newspaper.
在一些鄉村地區，還是有許多人連報紙都沒有訂閱。

2649 subsequently ['sʌbsɪ‚kwɛntlɪ]   adv. 隨後   4th ★★★★★
Subsequently, the company decided to cancel the contract.
公司隨後決定取消合同。

2650 **subsidiary** [səb'sɪdɪ,ɛrɪ]　　n.　子公司　　**3rd** ★★★★★
The subsidiary is in Hong Kong, but the parent company is in Taiwan.
子公司在香港，但母公司在台灣。

2651 **subsidy** ['sʌbsədɪ]　　n.　補助金　　**3rd** ★★★★★
We ought to take advantage of the subsidies from the government.
我們應該善用政府補助的津貼。

2652 **subsidize** ['sʌbsə'daɪz]　　v.　補助　　**3rd** ★★★★★
The organization has been subsidized by the government for years.
這個組織已靠政府補助多年。

2653 **subsist** [səb'sɪst]　　v.　維持生命　　**3rd** ★★★★★
The survivor subsisted for three days on seaweeds and water.
生還者三天來靠著海草和水維持生命。

2654 **substance** ['sʌbstəns]　　n.　物質　　**3rd** ★★★★★
Fossil fuels, such as oil or coal, release harmful substances into the air when they are burned.
石油或煤等化石燃料燃燒時，會釋放有害物質到空氣中。

2655 **substitute** ['sʌbstə,tjut]　　v.　替代　　**3rd** ★★★★★
Our chemistry teacher was on a one-month sick leave, so the principal had to find a teacher to substitute for her.
我們的化學老師請了一個月的病假，所以校長要幫她找一個代課老師。

2656 **suburb** ['sʌbɝb]　　n.　郊區　　**4th** ★★★★★
With the completion of several public transportation projects, such as the MRT, commuting to work has become easier for people living in the suburbs.
隨著捷運等多項大眾交通工具的完工，通勤上班對於住在郊區的人來說變得更容易了。

2657 **succeed** [sək'sid]　　v.　成功　　**5th** ★★★★★
A plan or project may falter, even if it finally succeeds.
一項計畫即使最後成功了，中途也難免會躑躅。

2658 **success** [sək'sɛs]　　n.　成功　　**5th** ★★★★★
The musician owed his success to his parents for giving him music lessons.
音樂家將他的成功歸功於父母栽培他上音樂課。

2659 **successful** [sək'sɛsfəl]　　adj.　成功的　　**4th** ★★★★★

A truly successful person displays both an inner and an outer quality of success.
一個真正成功的人，他的內在和外在都會表現出成功的特質。

2660 such [sʌtʃ]　　　　　　　　　adv. 如此地　　　4th ★★★★★
American fast food restaurants such as McDonald's and Kentucky Fried Chicken are quite popular in Taiwan.
美國的速食店如麥當勞和肯德基在台灣都很受歡迎。

2661 sue [su]　　　　　　　　　v. 控告　　　4th ★★★★★
The woman decided to sue for divorce because of her husband's violent treatment.
這位婦人因為丈夫的暴力相向而訴請離婚。

2662 suffer ['sʌfɚ]　　　　　　　　v. 受苦　　　4th ★★★★★
The population suffers more overweight-related problems than it did ten years ago.
和十年前比起來，現在有越來越多人深受因體重過重而併發的問題。

2663 sugar ['ʃugɚ]　　　　　　　　n. 糖　　　5th ★★★★★
Eating too much sugar is bad for your teeth as well as your health.
吃太多糖對你的牙齒和健康都不好。

2664 suggest [sə'dʒɛst]　　　　　　v. 建議　　　4th ★★★★★
The CFO suggested that the company should cut down on the unnecessary expenditure.
這位財務部長建議公司應該縮減不必要的預算。

2665 surgery ['sɝdʒərɪ]　　　　　　n. 外科手術　　　4th ★★★★★
The death of two conjoined twins following unprecedented surgery to separate them has prompted an outpouring of the grief around the world.
首例的分離手術造成這對連體嬰死亡，激起世界各地源源不絕的悲痛。

2666 suicide ['suə,saɪd]　　　　　　n. 自殺　　　4th ★★★★★
No one could understand why he committed suicide. He seemed to have everything to live for.
沒有人理解為什麼他要自殺，在外人看來他已經擁有了一切。

2667 suit [sut]　　　　　　　　　n. 控告　　　3rd ★★★★★
Failure to follow the terms of a contract is enough reason for a court suit.
沒有遵守合約上的條款足夠構成向法庭提起訴訟的理由。

2668 suitable ['sutəbl̩]   adj. 合適的   4th ★★★★★
The movie has some adult situations, so it is not suitable for children.
這部電影有些色情鏡頭，所以不適合孩童觀看。

2669 sum [sʌm]   n. 總額   4th ★★★★★
Coffee experts are willing to pay large sums of money for high-quality coffee beans.
咖啡行家願意為了高品質的咖啡豆付一大筆錢。

2670 summarize ['sʌmə,raɪz]   v. 做摘要   4th ★★★★★
After you finish reading the whole article, please summarize it into a few sentences.
請你在讀完整段文章後，將文章摘要成幾行句子。

2671 summit ['sʌmɪt]   n. 高峰會   4th ★★★★★
The World Congress of Accountants is a summit where 5,000 accountants meet to discuss the industry's important issues.
世界會計師高峰會有五千名會計師聚在一起討論該行業的重要議題。

2672 sunlight ['sʌn,laɪt]   n. 陽光   4th ★★★★★
Rainbows are formed when sunlight passes through small drops of water in the sky.
當陽光穿透天空的小水滴時，就會形成彩虹。

2673 superb [su'pɝb]   adj. 超級的   5th ★★★★★
The superb food at the hotel made up for the uncomfortable rooms
這間旅館的美食，彌補了房間不適的缺點。

2674 superficial ['supə'fɪʃəl]   adj. 膚淺的   4th ★★★★★
I try to judge people by their character, not by something as superficial as physical appearance.
我儘量以個性來評論一個人，而不是以像外貌這類膚淺的東西。

2675 superior [sə'pɪrɪə]   adj. 優越的   4th ★★★★★
This new computer is obviously superior to the old one because it has many new functions.
這台新電腦明顯比舊的那台優越，因為有很多新功能。

2676 superstition [,supə'stɪʃən]   adj. 迷信的   4th ★★★★★
Superstitions are sometimes esteemed as part of a cultural heritage.
有時候迷信也視為文化遺產的一部分。

S

2677 supervisor ['supɚˌvaɪzɚ] **n.** 主管 4th ★★★★★
The supervisor will be given a one-year leave of absence.
主管會有一年的休假。

2678 supplement ['sʌpləmənt] **v.** 補充 3rd ★★★★★
A salary in accordance with the skills and expertise will be supplemented by a car allowance.
薪水是依照能力和專業技能來發放，另外含有交通津貼作為補助。

2679 supply [sə'plaɪ] **n.** 供應 4th ★★★★★
On the sunny day, the store sold out of its supply of sunglasses.
商店在大晴天時將庫存的太陽眼鏡銷售一空。

2680 support [sə'port] **v.** 支持 4th ★★★★★
The president supports getting rid of nuclear weapons.
總統支持撤除核武。

2681 suppose [sə'poz] **v.** 認為 4th ★★★★★
I'd rather suppose the movie to be good.
我認為這部片應該會不錯。

2682 sure [ʃur] **adv.** 確定 5th ★★★★★
When traveling around the world, business people like to make sure that they have access to a computer at all times.
商務人員在世界各地旅行時，他們希望確保隨時都可使用電腦。

2683 surface ['sɝfɪs] **n.** 表面 3rd ★★★★★
I could feel the coarse surface on my feet when I wasn't wearing my shoes.
我沒有穿鞋時，我的腳可以感覺到地面的粗糙。

2684 surge [sɝdʒ] **v.** 湧現 3rd ★★★★★
The loneliness and isolation shared by urban dwellers contribute to a new type of crime to surge in modern society.
城市居民的寂寞和孤獨，導致現代社會湧現了一個新興的犯罪手法。

2685 surpass [sɚ'pæs] **v.** 超過 3rd ★★★★★
The Internet has surpassed newspapers as a medium of mass communication. It has become the main source for national and international news for people.
網路已經超越報紙成為主要的大眾傳播媒介，是人們獲悉國內外新聞的主要來源。

2686 **surplus** ['sɝpləs]　　　　**n.** 盈餘　　　**4th** ★★★★★
The cell phone company has a trade surplus of NT500 million.
這家電信公司有新台幣五百萬元的貿易盈餘。

2687 **surprise** [sə'praɪz]　　　　**v.** 驚訝　　　**5th** ★★★★★
My grandmother likes to surprise people. She never calls beforehand to inform us of her visits.
我的祖母喜歡給大家驚喜，她從來不會事先打電話告訴我們她要來。

2688 **surround** [sə'raund]　　　　**v.** 環繞　　　**4th** ★★★★★
We all breathe the air that surrounds the Earth.
我們呼吸著環繞地球的空氣。

2689 **surroundings** [sə'raundɪŋz]　　**n.** 環境　　　**4th** ★★★★★
It is true that the surroundings will affect one's work and studies.
環境的確會影響我們的工作和課業。

2690 **survey** [sə'veɪ]　　　　**v.** 調查　　　**3rd** ★★★★★
The police surveyed the scene of crime carefully for fear of missing any clue that was related to the murder.
警察仔細調查犯罪現場，深怕錯過任何和謀殺案相關的線索。

2691 **survive** [sə'vaɪv]　　　　**v.** 生還　　　**4th** ★★★★★
Many fish are unable to survive in open water because larger fish can catch them too easily.
許多小魚無法在海裡生存，因為大魚很容易就抓到它們了。

2692 **suspect** [sə'spɛkt]　　　　**n.** 嫌疑犯　　**4th** ★★★★★
The police searched the house of the suspect thoroughly. They almost turned the whole house upside down.
警察在嫌犯的家中作地毯式的搜查，他們幾乎要把整個房子翻過來了。

2693 **suspend** [sə'spɛnd]　　　　**v.** 吊銷　　　**4th** ★★★★★
He couldn't drive because his license was suspended for three months.
他不能開車，因為他的駕照被吊銷三個月。

2694 **suspense** [sə'spɛns]　　　　**n.** 擔心　　　**4th** ★★★★★
John proposed to May, but she kept him in suspense for several days before she said that she would marry him.
約翰向瑪莉求婚，她在說願意之前讓約翰擔心了好幾天。

2695 **suspicion** [sə'spɪʃən]　　　**n.**　嫌疑　　**4th** ★★★★★
A urine test cleared Mr. Wang of the suspicion of drug abuse.
驗尿結果洗刷了王先生藥物濫用的嫌疑。

2696 **suspicious** [sə'spɪʃəs]　　　**adj.**　可疑的　　**4th** ★★★★★
When we receive text messages of promotions from a company, we must be suspicious of possible false advertisement out of which the company wants to make profit.
收到某公司促銷活動的簡訊時，我們要懷疑這可能是該公司為了賺錢的不實廣告。

2697 **sustainable** [sə'stenəbl]　　　**adj.**　能維持的　　**3rd** ★★★★★
The organization aims to create a sustainable peace.
這個機構的目標是創造永續的和平

2698 **sweep** [swip]　　　**v.**　打掃　　**5th** ★★★★★
She is sweeping with a broom.
她用掃把掃地。

2699 **swift** [swɪft]　　　**adj.**　敏捷的　　**3rd** ★★★★★
The swift fox jumped over the black bear.
敏捷的狐狸從黑熊身上跳過去。

2700 **swing** [swɪŋ]　　　**v.**　使回轉　　**5th** ★★★★★
The driver swung his car around the street corner.
司機開車沿著街角轉彎。

2701 **switch** [swɪtʃ]　　　**v.**　轉變　　**5th** ★★★★★
Angelina drives fast and switches lanes often.
安潔莉娜開快車，而且經常變換車道。

2702 **symbol** ['sɪmbl]　　　**n.**　象徵　　**4th** ★★★★★
In Taiwan, some high school uniforms are symbols of excellence and honor.
在台灣，有些高中制服象徵卓越與榮譽。

2703 **symbolic** [sɪm'balɪk]　　　**adj.**　象徵的　　**4th** ★★★★★
What most distinguishes humans from other creatures is our ability to create and manipulate a wide variety of symbolic representations.
人類和其他動物最大的不同，就是我們能夠創造和使用各種各樣的符號標示。

2704 **sympathetic** [͵sɪmpə'θɛtɪk]　　　**adj.**　同情的　　**3rd** ★★★★★

Learning that the war had taken away his beloved wife and three children, we all felt sympathetic for him.
我們得知戰爭奪走他心愛的妻子和三名子女後，都對他感到很同情。

2705 sympathize ['sɪmpə,θaɪz]　　v.　表示同情　　3rd ★★★★★
A lot of people sympathizes with the divorced woman raising three children on her own.
一個離婚女子獨立扶養三個小孩，讓很多人深感同情。

2706 sympathy ['sɪmpəθɪ]　　n.　同情　　3rd ★★★★★
We really feel sympathy for the victim's misfortune.
我們真的很同情受害者的不幸遭遇。

2707 symptom ['sɪmptəm]　　n.　徵兆　　3rd ★★★★★
A mild fever is one of the first symptoms of SARS.
輕微的發燒是SARS的初期症狀之一。

2708 syndrome ['sɪn,drom]　　n.　症候群　　3rd ★★★★★
AIDS is the abbreviation for Acquired Immune Deficiency Syndrome.
愛滋病是後天免疫缺乏症候群的縮寫。

2709 system ['sɪstəm]　　n.　系統　　4th ★★★★★
Writers need to classify a mass of information by means of some orderly system.
作家需要條理分明的系統將資料分類。

2710 taboo [tə'bu]　　n.　禁忌　　3rd ★★★★★
There is a taboo in their culture that a pregnant woman must not look at a dead cat.
他們的文化有一個禁忌，那就是懷孕的婦女不可以看到死掉的貓。

2711 tacit ['tæsɪt]　　adj.　不明言的　　3rd ★★★★★
The clerk's quietness is likely to be a tacit permission to give me a special discount.
店員默不作聲可能是要給我特別折扣的默許。

2712 tag [tæg]　　n.　標籤　　5th ★★★★★
This designer suit carries a price tag of £2,000.
這套設計師西裝售價兩千英鎊。

2713 takeover ['tek,ovɚ]　　n.　接管　　5th ★★★★★
The annual meeting of the WHO this September will be a two-day program dealing solely with the takeover proposal.
世界衛生組織今年九月的年度會議將為期兩天，課程只涉及收購建議。

2714 talk [tɔk]　　　　v.　談話　　5th ★★★★★
Sam said that he would talk to the girl but he got timid when he saw her.
山姆說他會去和這女孩說話，但當他看到她時卻退縮了。

2715 talent ['tælənt]　　　n.　才藝　　5th ★★★★★
A producer for a popular television show is always looking for people with unusual talent to perform on the show.
當紅的綜藝節目製作人總是不停尋找有特殊才能的人上節目表演。

2716 tangle ['tæŋgl]　　　v.　使糾纏　　3rd ★★★★★
The buyer chose to go through a third person, an agent, rather than tangle the problem himself.
買家寧願透過第三方採購，也就是代理人，而不想惹上一堆問題。

2717 tanker ['tæŋkə]　　　n.　油輪　　5th ★★★★★
Ships such as oil tankers are extremely large, and can be built by only a small number of shipyards.
像油輪這種超大的船隻，只有少數的船廠有辦法建造。

2718 tap [tæp]　　　　n.　水龍頭　　5th ★★★★★
Many people like to drink bottled water because they feel that tap water may not be safe.
許多人喜歡喝瓶裝水，因為他們覺得自來水不安全。

2719 target ['tɑrgɪt]　　　n.　目標　　5th ★★★★★
The strong hunter aimed his gun at the target and fired.
獵人拿著他的槍對準目標然後開槍。

2720 taste [test]　　　　v.　品嚐　　5th ★★★★★
I don't like the soup tastes too much of onions.
我不喜歡湯裡有太多洋蔥的味道。

2721 tax [tæks]　　　　n.　稅金　　4th ★★★★★
How much income tax did you pay last year?
你去年繳多少所得稅？

2722 technically ['tɛknɪk!ɪ]　　adv.　技術上　　4th ★★★★★
Rapid advancement in motor engineering makes it technically possible to build a flying car in the near future.
電機工程發展很迅速，將來的技術也許可以建造出飛行汽車。

2723 technician [tɛk'nɪʃən]　　**n.**　技術員　　**4th** ★★★★★
We will be unable to make any copies until the technician has the machine functioning properly.
技術員把機器修理好之前，我們無法影印任何東西。

2724 technological [tɛknə'lʊdʒɪkl]　**adj.**　科技的　　**4th** ★★★★★
Without much contact with the outside world for many years, John found many technological inventions foreign to him.
約翰好幾年沒有和外在世界接觸，他發現許多科技發明對他而言很陌生。

2725 technology [tɛk'nɑlədʒɪ]　　**n.**　科技　　**4th** ★★★★★
The computer fair will feature several new products and technologies.
電腦展將以展示數件新產品與新科技。

2726 teenager ['tin,edʒɚ]　　**n.**　青少年　　**5th** ★★★★★
Recent studies have shown that alcohol is the leading gateway drug for teenagers.
近期研究顯示，酒精是促使青少年染上毒癮的主要途徑。

2727 teller ['tɛlɚ]　　　**n.**　出納員　　**5th** ★★★★★
The paying teller gave two more thousand dollars to the client carelessly.
出納員不小心多給了客戶兩千塊錢。

2728 temperament ['tɛmprəmənt]　**n.**　性格　　**4th** ★★★★★
I don't like to work with someone with a nervous temperament.
我不喜歡和神經質的人共事。

2729 temperature ['tɛmprətʃɚ]　　**n.**　溫度　　**4th** ★★★★★
The liquid water becomes solid ice in low temperatures.
液態水在低溫下結成冰。

2730 temple ['tɛmpl]　　　**n.**　神殿　　**4th** ★★★★★
Jerusalem is the ancient Hebrew capital, where King Solomon built the Temple.
耶路撒冷是古希伯來首都，所羅門王在此建造聖殿。

2731 temporarily ['tɛmpə,rɛrəlɪ]　**adv.**　暫時地　　**4th** ★★★★★
These pills can temporarily relieve cold symptoms. If pain or fever persists, or if redness or swelling is present, consult a doctor, these could be signs of a serious condition.
這些藥丸可以暫時減緩感冒症狀。如果持續感到疼痛或發燒，或產生發紅或腫脹，請諮詢醫生，這可能是一種罹患重疾的跡象。

2732 temptation [tɛmp'teʃən]　　　n.　誘惑　　　4th ★★★★★
A good government official has to resist the temptation of money and make the right decision.
一個好的政府官員必須能夠抗拒金錢的誘惑，做出正確的決定。

2733 tend [tɛnd]　　　v.　傾向　　　3rd ★★★★★
Office workers suffer from back problems because they tend to sit still for long period of time.
辦公室職員有背痛的毛病，因為他們總是長時間坐著不動。

2734 tendency ['tɛndənsɪ]　　　n.　趨勢　　　3rd ★★★★★
With rising oil prices, there is an increasing tendency for people to ride bicycles to work.
隨著油價的飆漲，人們騎腳踏車上班有逐漸增加的趨勢。

2735 tension ['tɛnʃən]　　　n.　壓力　　　4th ★★★★★
Too much tension gives me a headache. I can't take the stress anymore.
大多壓力讓我的頭很痛，我沒辦法再承受了。

2736 tentatively ['tɛntətɪvlɪ]　　　adv.　暫時地　　　3rd ★★★★★
I don't know for sure what I am going to do this weekend, but tentatively I plan to visit an old friend of mine in southern Taiwan.
我不確定這週末要做什麼，但我暫時計畫要到南台灣拜訪一位老朋友。

2737 term [tɝm]　　　n.　術語　　　4th ★★★★★
"Environmental autism" is a term that psychologists use to name the condition of some children.
「環境幽閉症」這個術語是心理學家用來說明一些兒童的狀況。

2738 terminal ['tɝmənḷ]　　　adj.　末期的　　　3rd ★★★★★
The old man is suffering from terminal cancer.
這位老人受癌症末期之苦。

2739 terminate ['tɝmə,net]　　　v.　終止　　　3rd ★★★★★
The suppliers will claim compensation if we partially terminate our contract with them.
如果我們和供應商終止部分合約，他們會要求賠償。

2740 terrify ['tɛrə,faɪ]　　　v.　使恐怖　　　4th ★★★★★
Terrified by the intensity of an earlier earthquake, most residents of this village are making efforts to strengthen the constructions of their houses.
大部分的村民被先前地震的強度嚇壞了，所以正努力加強他們房子的結構。

2741 territory [ˈtɛrəˌtorɪ]　　　n.　領土　　**4th** ★★★★★
Male howler monkeys use their loud voices to fight for food, mates, or territory.
雄性吼猴會用他們的大嗓門來爭奪食物、配偶或領土

2742 test [tɛst]　　　n.　測驗　　**5th** ★★★★★
With so many assignments and tests, high school students should learn to budget their time carefully in order to finish everything in time.
中學生有這麼多功課及考試，他們應該學習仔細安排時間並及時完成每件事。

2743 testimony [ˈtɛstəˌmonɪ]　　　n.　證據　　**4th** ★★★★★
The testimony given by the witness was a far cry from the truth.
目擊證人所提供的證詞和事實相距甚遠。

2744 text [tɛkst]　　　n.　原文　　**4th** ★★★★★
The children's book has many pictures surrounding the text.
小孩子書裡的課文周圍有很多圖片。

2745 theater [ˈθɪətə]　　　n.　戲院　　**5th** ★★★★★
The movie theater is between the disco pub and the pet store.
電影院在迪斯可酒吧和寵物店的中間。

2746 theme [θim]　　　n.　主題　　**4th** ★★★★★
The major theme in the coming issue of the best-selling monthly magazine will be "Love and Peace".
這本暢銷月刊下個月的主題是「愛與和平」。

2747 theory [ˈθiərɪ]　　　n.　理論　　**4th** ★★★★★
Scientists always hope that the theory we discover today can be confirmed by future research.
科學家總是希望我們現在發現的理論，可以藉由未來的研究得到證實。

2748 therapist [ˈθɛrəpɪst]　　　n.　治療學家　　**3rd** ★★★★★
Therapists find that treatment of those people who seek help because they are unable to stop smoking or overeating is rarely successful.
治療學家發現，戒菸失敗或暴飲暴食的人在尋求幫助時，所做的治療鮮少成功。

2749 therefore [ˈðɛrˌfor]　　　adv.　因此　　**4th** ★★★★★
Steve has several meetings to attend every day; therefore, he has to work on a very tight schedule.
史帝夫每天都要參加很多會議，所以他每天的工作行程都很緊繃。

2750 thief [θif]　　　　　　　　　**n.** 小偷　　　5th ★★★★★
The thief stole my wallet and hit me in the head.
小偷把我的錢包偷走又打我的頭。

2751 thrill [θrɪl]　　　　　　　　**n.** 興奮　　　4th ★★★★★
Surfers get a thrill from the big ocean waves they ride.
衝浪的人在海浪中馳乘得到快感。

2752 thrust [θrʌst]　　　　　　　**v.** 塞入　　　4th ★★★★★
He thrust the present into my hands and ran off.
他把禮物塞進我的手中然後就跑走了。

2753 thorough ['θɝo]　　　　　　**adj.** 徹底的　　4th ★★★★★
A thorough analysis of market anticipation can increase the success rate of a new product.
詳盡的市場預測分析可以提高新產品的成功率。

2754 though [ðo]　　　　　　　　**conj.** 雖然　　5th ★★★★★
John enjoys listening to pop music, though he is not good at singing at all.
約翰雖然不會唱歌，但他很喜歡聽流行音樂。

2755 thought [θɔt]　　　　　　　**n.** 想法　　　5th ★★★★★
Because people are different from each other, each one has unique thoughts and ideas.
每個人都是與眾不同的，各自擁有自己獨特的想法。

2756 thousand ['θauznd]　　　　　**n.** 千　　　5th ★★★★★
Man first walked on American soil approximately fifteen to twenty thousand years ago.
人類大約是在一萬五千年到兩萬年前首次踏進美洲大陸的土地。

2757 threat [θrɛt]　　　　　　　　**n.** 威脅　　　4th ★★★★★
In the past, many people died from pneumonia. But thanks to modern medicine, pneumonia is no longer such a threat.
過去有許多人死於肺炎，幸虧現代醫學的進步，肺炎已經不再是一種威脅。

2758 throughout [θru'aut]　　　　**prep.** 遍佈　　4th ★★★★★
There are more than two thousand chain stores throughout the country.
全國各地有超過兩千家連鎖店。

T

2759 thunderstorm [ˈθʌndəˌstɔrm]　　n.　雷雨　　5th ★★★★★
Do not take shelter under trees in a thunderstorm because lightning often strikes tall objects.
大雷雨時不要躲到樹下，因為閃電通常會擊中高的物體。

2760 ticket [ˈtɪkɪt]　　　　　　n.　門票　　5th ★★★★★
Tickets to the coming concert are available at many bookstores in town.
鎮上很多書店都能買到即將到來的演唱會門票。

2761 tight [taɪt]　　　　　　adj.　緊的　　4th ★★★★★
Darren ties his shoes into a very tight knot.
達文在他鞋子上綁一個非常緊的結。

2762 tip [tɪp]　　　　　　　　n.　小費　　5th ★★★★★
My boss gave the driver a nice tip for his special attention.
我老闆因為司機的特別照料而給他不少小費。

2763 tiredness [ˈtaɪrdnɪs]　　n.　疲倦　　5th ★★★★★
Half of sleep-deprived managers admitted to shouting at colleagues because of tiredness.
有半數睡眠被剝奪的經理承認，曾因疲倦而對同事吼叫。

2764 title [ˈtaɪtl]　　　　　　n.　標題　　5th ★★★★★
David didn't read the book. He only glanced at the title.
大衛沒有讀這本書，他只是瞄了一下標題。

2765 toast [tost]　　　　　　n.　敬酒　　4th ★★★★★
I'd like to propose a toast to our guest, Professor Chen.
我想要跟我們的貴賓陳教授敬一杯。

2766 tolerance [ˈtɑlərəns]　　n.　容忍　　4th ★★★★★
The boxer has a high tolerance for pain.
拳擊手非常會忍痛。

2767 token [ˈtokən]　　　　　n.　象徵　　4th ★★★★★
Susan and Don usually call each other "sweetheart," "dear," or some other tokens of affection.
蘇珊和唐通常互稱對方為「愛人」、「親愛的」或其他象徵愛情的用語。

2768 tolerate [ˈtɑləˌret]　　　v.　容受　　4th ★★★★★

We had to tolerate an unbearable five-hour delay at the airport because of the smog.
因為濃霧的關係，我們得在機場忍受班機延誤五個小時。

2769 toll [tol]   **n.** 過路費   4th ★★★★★
To drive through that bridge, you must pay a toll of two U.S. dollars.
為了開過那座橋，你必須支付過路費兩元美金。

2770 tongue [tʌŋ]   **n.** 舌頭   5th ★★★★★
Did I say "a lot of dime"? Oh, I'm really sorry. I meant to say "a lot of time." It was a slip of tongue.
我剛說「很多小錢」？喔，真是抱歉！我的意思是說「很多時間」，舌頭打結了。

2771 topic ['tɑpɪk]   **n.** 主題   4th ★★★★★
The books in the library cover a wide variety of topics that range from language to science.
圖書館內的書籍涵蓋了各式主題，從語言類到科學類都有。

2772 tornado [tɔr'nedo]   **n.** 龍捲風   4th ★★★★★
Florida suffered from several tornadoes this past summer.
今年夏天佛羅里達遭受到多個龍捲風的襲擊。

2773 toss [tɔs]   **v.** 扔擲   3rd ★★★★★
Toss me the keys! I'll drive.
把鑰匙扔給我! 我來開車。

2774 totally ['totl̩ɪ]   **adv.** 完全地   4th ★★★★★
The telephone has changed beyond recognition in recent years. In both form and function, it has become totally different from what it was before.
電話已經今非昔比，無論是在外型或是功能上，都和以前完全不一樣。

2775 tough [tʌf]   **adj.** 剛強的   4th ★★★★★
Search dogs must be able to learn quickly and be tough enough to withstand severe weather.
搜查犬必須夠堅強才能承受險峻的天氣。

2776 tourist ['turɪst]   **n.** 觀光客   5th ★★★★★
Formosan Green Island, though small, attracts tourists because of its natural beauty.
台灣的綠島雖小，卻因為其天然美景吸引了許多觀光客。

2777 tournament ['tɜnəmənt]　　　n.　錦標賽　　4th ★★★★★
Each participant received a tournament memento with its mascot printed.
每位參賽者獲得了印有吉祥物的比賽紀念品。

2778 tow [to]　　　v.　拖吊　　5th ★★★★★
The car parked beside the red line was towed away.
停在紅線旁的車子被拖吊。

2779 toxic ['tɑksɪk]　　　adj.　有毒的　　4th ★★★★★
Plastic has become extraordinarily important in our daily life, but the process of burning or recycling it often creates toxic chemicals.
塑膠在我們的日常生活中變得特別重要，但在燃燒或回收的過程中，常常會製造有毒化學物。

2780 track [træk]　　　v.　追蹤　　4th ★★★★★
I want to see how this machine tracks and manages data reporting.
我想看看這台機器如何追蹤和管理數據報告。

2781 trade [tred]　　　v.　交易　　4th ★★★★★
People first started using money in order to trade.
人們為了交易首次開始使用鈔票。

2782 traditional [trə'dɪʃənḷ]　　　adj.　傳統的　　4th ★★★★★
Online education is more economical and efficient than traditional schooling.
線上教學和傳統學校教育比較起來更經濟也更有效率。

2783 traffic ['træfɪk]　　　n.　交通　　5th ★★★★★
The foreigner has a basic idea about the traffic laws in Taipei.
這個外國人對台北的交通規則有基本的了解。

2784 tragedy ['trædʒədɪ]　　　n.　悲劇　　4th ★★★★★
The tragedy of life lies in having no goal to reach.
人生的悲劇在於沒有任何目標可以實現。

2785 train [tren]　　　v.　訓練　　5th ★★★★★
Search dogs are trained to find missing people.
搜查犬受過訓練，專門尋找失蹤人口。

2786 trail [trel]　　　n.　足跡　　4th ★★★★★
The aboriginal boy has been on all of the trails in the mountain area.
這個原住民男孩的足跡遍及了整個山區。

2787 trait [tret]   **n.** 特徵   4th ★★★★★
One of John's pleasant traits is generosity.
慷慨大方是約翰討人喜歡的特徵之一。

2788 tranquil ['træŋkwɪl]   **adj.** 平靜的   4th ★★★★★
Blue creates a tranquil and quiet feeling in many people.
藍色讓許多人產生平靜和安心的感覺。

2789 transact [træns'ækt]   **v.** 交易   3rd ★★★★★
The company transacts business with a large number of factories.
公司和很多工廠都有交易。

2790 transaction [træn'zækʃən]   **n.** 交易   3rd ★★★★★
Most banks will charge their customers a certain amount of money for each transaction.
大部分的銀行會對每一筆交易酌量向客戶收錢。

2791 transcript ['træn͵skrɪpt]   **n.** 成績單   3rd ★★★★★
Enclosed is a copy of my transcript from National Taiwan University, along with the letters of reference you requested.
附件是一份我在台灣大學的成績單，還有您要求的推薦信。

2792 transform [træns'fɔrm]   **v.** 轉型   3rd ★★★★★
The 60s was a period when the country transformed from agriculture-based to export-oriented economy.
六零年代是這個國家的轉型期，從農業經濟轉變為出口經濟。

2793 transit ['trænsɪt]   **n.** 運輸   3rd ★★★★★
The term MRT stands for Mass Rapid Transit.
MRT這個詞代表大眾捷運系統。

2794 translate [træns'let]   **v.** 翻譯   4th ★★★★★
The secretary is translating the document from Spanish to Chinese for her boss.
秘書幫老闆把文件從西班牙文翻成中文。

2795 transmit [træns'mɪt]   **v.** 傳送   4th ★★★★★
The parcel was transmitted by rail.
這份包裹是靠鐵路傳送。

2796 transplant [træns'plænt]   **v.** 移植   3rd ★★★★★

Men who receive transplanted kidneys from women are more likely to reject them.
男性患者接受女性的腎臟移植較容易會有器官排斥作用。

2797 transportation [ˌtrænspəˈteʃən]　**n.** 交通工具　3rd ★★★★★
We don't have enough transportation for tonight's show.
我們沒有足夠的交通工具去看今晚的表演。

2798 trap [træp]　**v.** 設陷阱捕捉　4th ★★★★★
The witch tried to trap the children in her house.
巫婆試圖在她的房子裡設陷阱誘捕小孩。

2799 travel [ˈtrævl̩]　**v.** 旅行　5th ★★★★★
Baseball scouts travel the world to find the best players.
棒球球探行遍全球各地尋找最好的球員。

2800 treasure [ˈtrɛʒɚ]　**n.** 寶藏　4th ★★★★★
The crew of the ship was very happy to find the treasure.
船上的船員非常高興能找到寶藏。

2801 treatment [ˈtritmənt]　**n.** 治療　4th ★★★★★
It's better for you to travel with medical insurance, so that you can get treatment when you get injured.
旅行時保個醫療平安險比較好，這樣當你受傷了就可以得到治療。

2802 trendy [ˈtrɛndɪ]　**adj.** 時髦的　3rd ★★★★★
Recently a lot of trendy restaurants have been opened in this area. It has become very hard to find any traditional and inexpensive places to go for a meal.
最近這個地區開了很多新潮的餐廳，要找到一個傳統又便宜的地方吃頓飯已經變得非常困難。

2803 trip [trɪp]　**n.** 旅行　5th ★★★★★
Lance's mouth was swollen from his trip to the dentist.
藍斯在看牙醫的途中嘴巴就腫了。

2804 triple [ˈtrɪpl̩]　**v.** 成為三倍　3rd ★★★★★
The number of people who call in sick due to work stress has tripled in the past five years.
最近五年來，因為工作壓力而請病假的人數是以前的三倍。

2805 trivial [ˈtrɪvɪəl]　**adj.** 瑣碎的　3rd ★★★★★
Jennifer doesn't get along with her roommate. She often gets into a fight with her

The 3000 vocabularies you must know in public service exam

about trivial things.
珍妮佛和室友處得不好，她們常為一些微不足道的小事爭吵。

2806 tropical [ˈtrɑpɪkl]　　adj. 熱帶的　　4th ★★★★★
Sugar cane grows better in tropical climates because it needs a lot of sunlight for growth.
甘蔗較適合生長在熱帶氣候，因為生長需要大量的陽光。

2807 troublesome [ˈtrʌblˌsəm]　　adj. 麻煩的　　5th ★★★★★
That girl is known to be one of the most troublesome students in the class.
那女孩是課堂上最麻煩的學生之一。

2808 truck [trʌk]　　n. 卡車　　5th ★★★★★
A motorcyclist ran through a red light and was struck by a passing truck.
摩托車騎士闖紅燈，被一台經過的卡車撞上。

2809 tsunami [tsuˈnɑmi]　　n. 海嘯　　3rd ★★★★★
During the tsunami in Asia, news organizations often ran pictures that ordinary people had posted on Web sites.
亞洲海嘯期間，新聞機構經常發表一些民眾張貼在網站上的照片。

2810 tuition [tjuˈɪʃən]　　n. 學費　　4th ★★★★★
Wendy hopes to be the recipient of that scholarship. If she gets it, her college tuition will be covered for two years.
溫蒂希望得到那筆獎學金。如果她得到了，她兩年的大學學費就有著落了。

2811 tumultuous [tjuˈmʌltʃuəs]　　adj. 喧囂的　　3rd ★★★★★
The football team celebrated its victory in a tumultuous fashion.
足球隊歡心鼓舞地慶祝他們的勝利。

2812 tune [tjun]　　n. 音調　　4th ★★★★★
The piano sounds like it's out of tune.
鋼琴聲聽起來好像走音了。

2813 turn [tɜn]　　v. 改變　　5th ★★★★★
Well-prepared food will turn bad if stored too long.
熟食如果放太久會壞掉。

2814 turtle [ˈtɜtl]　　n. 海龜　　5th ★★★★★
Although marine turtles spend most of their time at sea, they come to land to lay their eggs.
雖然海龜大部分的時間都待在海裡，但牠們會爬到陸地下蛋。

2815 twice [twaɪs]　　adj. 兩次　　4th ★★★★★
I love Mexican food. I have it at least twice a week.
我喜歡墨西哥菜，我一個禮拜至少會吃兩次。

2816 twig [twɪg]　　n. 樹枝　　4th ★★★★★
David looked up when he heard the twig snap.
大衛聽到樹枝劈啪地響時往上看了一下。

2817 twin [twɪn]　　n. 雙胞胎　　5th ★★★★★
Jim and Joe are twin brothers, but they don't look alike.
吉姆和喬是雙胞胎兄弟，但是他們長得一點也不像。

2818 type [taɪp]　　n. 類型　　5th ★★★★★
May I know what type of machine you have?
請問你用哪款機型？

2819 typhoon [taɪˈfun]　　n. 颱風　　5th ★★★★★
All flights were cancelled due to the typhoon.
因為颱風的因素，所有班機都取消了。

2820 typical [ˈtɪpɪk!]　　adj. 典型的　　4th ★★★★★
Typical behavior for the bear is to sleep for the entire winter.
冬眠是熊的典型行為。

2821 typically [ˈtɪpɪklɪ]　　adv. 典型地　　4th ★★★★★
People who were born on very high mountains typically have larger lungs to help breathing than those who live at sea level do.
在高地出生的人，肺通常比住在海平面的人還要大，這樣可以幫助他們呼吸。

2822 ultimatum [ˌʌltəˈmetəm]　　n. 最後通牒　　3rd ★★★★★
The professor finally issued an ultimatum to Tim; retake the examination or fail in the course.
教授終於發出最後通牒給提姆，看是要重考一次或者被當。

2823 umbrella [ʌmˈbrɛlə]　　n. 傘　　5th ★★★★★
It looks fine now. But I'm carrying my umbrella in case it rains later.
天氣現在看起來很好，但我還是帶著傘以防等會下雨。

2824 unacceptable [ˌʌnəkˈsɛptəb!] adj. 不能接受的　　4th ★★★★★
The outline of the project should be unacceptable.
這份企劃大綱不應該被接受。

153

2825 unanimously [juˈnænəməslɪ]　**adv.**　無異議地　**3rd** ★★★★★
The twenty seven European Union heads of state unanimously agreed to sign on to a package of energy measures at a summit in Brussels; none of them voted against it.
二十七位歐盟領袖在一次布魯塞爾的高峰會中，全體同意簽署一套能源措施方案。沒有人反對。

2826 unapproachable [ˌʌnəˈprotʃəbl̩]　**adj.**　孤傲的　**4th** ★★★★★
Peter doesn't get along with his colleagues because he is an unapproachable sort of person.
彼德和同事處得不好，因為他是那種難以親近的人。

2827 unattended [ˌʌnəˈtɛndɪd]　**adj.**　沒人管的　**4th** ★★★★★
It may be against the law to leave young children unattended.
留著年幼的小孩無人看管，可能會觸犯法律。

2828 uncertainty [ʌnˈsɝtntɪ]　**n.**　不確定　**4th** ★★★★★
Resilient people can stay unfazed even in the time of relentless uncertainty.
適應力強的人，即使在動盪無情的時代，也能處之泰然。

2829 unconscious [ʌnˈkɑnʃəs]　**adj.**　未察覺的　**4th** ★★★★★
The stock dealer was unconscious of having made a serious error.
這位股市交易員尚未驚覺自己犯了一個嚴重的錯誤。

2830 uncountable [ʌnˈkauntəbl̩]　**adj.**　不可數的　**4th** ★★★★★
Some nouns are countable and some are uncountable.
有些名詞可數，有些不可數。

2831 uncover [ʌnˈkʌvɚ]　**v.**　揭露　**4th** ★★★★★
The police uncovered a plot to assassinate the mayor last night.
警方昨晚破獲一起暗殺市長的陰謀。

2832 undercover [ˌʌndɚˈkʌvɚ]　**adj.**　暗中進行的　**3rd** ★★★★★
The undercover policeman should be ready for any risks.
臥底警察應該準備好面對任何風險。

2833 underground [ˈʌndɚˌgraund]　**adj.**　地下的　**3rd** ★★★★★
Spelunking is a sport where explorers go deep inside underground caves that are dark and wet.
深穴探勘是一項運動，探勘者必須要深入又濕又黑的地下洞穴。

2834 underprivileged [ˌʌndəˈprɪvəlɪdʒd] **adj.** 貧困的 *3rd* ★★★★★
The social welfare system ought to provide the underprivileged people with sufficient support.
社會福利系統應該要提供低下階層的人足夠的資助。

2835 understand [ˌʌndəˈstænd] **v.** 了解 *3rd* ★★★★★
To understand the world, a child needs firsthand experience with many opportunities to observe, to experiment, and to get hands dirty.
孩子為了了解這個世界，需要很多親身體驗的機會來觀察、實驗和動手做。

2836 undertake [ˌʌndəˈtek] **v.** 進行 *4th* ★★★★★
The city government has not undertaken the sewage pipe replacement project to date due to a labor shortage.
市政府因為勞工短缺，沒有實行下水道管線的替換方案。

2837 unemployment [ˌʌnɪmˈplɔɪmənt] **n.** 失業 *4th* ★★★★★
A period of reduced economic activity and rising unemployment is called a depression, or a recession.
在一段時間裡，經濟活動減少和失業率提升，稱作蕭條或不景氣。

2838 unexpected [ˌʌnɪkˈspɛktɪd] **adj.** 出乎意外的 *4th* ★★★★★
An emergency is an unexpected and dangerous situation that must be dealt with immediately.
意外是一種出乎意料的危險情況，必須馬上處理。

2839 unfortunately [ʌnˈfɔrtʃənɪtlɪ] **adv.** 不幸地 *4th* ★★★★★
Jackson has been trying to avoid Susan's friends after he married Helen, but unfortunately he ran into some of Susan's close friends yesterday.
傑克森和海倫結婚之後，一直試著避開蘇珊的朋友，但不幸地，他昨天碰到一些蘇珊的閨中密友。

2840 uniform [ˈjunəˌfɔrm] **n.** 制服 *5th* ★★★★★
Before I start my job, I put on my uniform and look at myself in the mirror to make sure that I look neat.
我在開始工作之前，會先穿上制服，然後看著鏡中的自己確保看起來整齊。

2841 union [ˈjunjən] **n.** 結合 *4th* ★★★★★
In a wedding banquet it is common to see a pair of ice-sculpted swans that represent the union of the new couple.
婚宴上常常會看見一對冰雕天鵝，象徵新婚夫妻的結合。

154

2842 **unique** [ju'nik]　　　**adj.** 獨特的　　**5th** ★★★★★
When you choose an Internet handle make sure that it is a unique name.
當你選擇一個網路帳號的時候，要確定是夠獨特的名字。

2843 **universe** ['junə,vɜs]　　**n.** 宇宙　　**4th** ★★★★★
The United States will continue the venture to the unknown universe even after the loss of two space shuttles, Challenger and Columbia.
美國雖然失去了挑戰者號和哥倫比亞號這兩艘太空梭，還是會繼續到未知的宇宙冒險。

2844 **university** [,junə'vɜsətɪ]　　**n.** 大學　　**4th** ★★★★★
The freshmen entered their first year of university with ripe minds.
新生第一年進入大學已具有成熟的心智。

2845 **unrealistic** [,ʌnrɪə'lɪstɪk]　　**adj.** 不切實際的　　**4th** ★★★★★
A common mistake found in parenthood is that parents often set unrealistic goals for their children.
父母親教育孩子時的一個常見錯誤就是，他們常常替子女設立不切實際的目標。

2846 **unnecessary** [ʌn'nɛsə,sɛrɪ]　**adj.** 不必要的　　**4th** ★★★★★
The rise in prices has caused many customers to reconsider unnecessary purchases.
價格提升導致許多顧客重新考慮一些不必要的消費。

2847 **unreasonable** [ʌn'riznəb!]　**adj.** 不合理的　　**4th** ★★★★★
It is unreasonable to regard any language as the property of a particular nation.
把任何一種語言視為一個特定國家的資產並不合理。

2848 **unreliable** [,ʌnrɪ'laɪəb!]　　**adj.** 不可靠的　　**4th** ★★★★★
Hearing the art critic's bitter and unreliable comments on her new painting, Molly started a heated argument with him.
茉莉聽到藝術評論家對她的新作品惡毒且不實的評論，她便與他起了激烈的爭吵。

2849 **unsatisfactory** [,ʌnsætɪs'fæktərɪ]　**adj.** 不理想的　**4th** ★★★★★
The disappointed teacher informed him that he was making unsatisfactory progress in his studies.
老師失望的告訴他，他的學業進展不太理想。

2850 **until** [ən'tɪl]　　　**conj.** 直到　　**5th** ★★★★★
The burglar alarm on my car had been turned on every night until last night.
我的車子每晚警鈴大作，一直到昨天晚上才停止。

2851 unusual [ʌnˈjuzuəl]　　adj.　奇特的　　5th ★★★★★
My colleague read an unusual detective story last night.
我的同事昨晚看了一本很特別的偵探小說。

2852 unveil [ʌnˈvel]　　v.　揭示　　4th ★★★★★
A statue of George Johnson was unveiled in recognition of his making a sizable bequest to the alma mater.
為了紀念喬治強森為母校付出為數可觀的遺贈，推出了他的雕像。

2853 upbringing [ˈʌpˌbrɪŋɪŋ]　　n.　教養　　4th ★★★★★
The misconduct of a student should not be ignored. As it has a lot to do with the child's upbringing, parents need to be involved in the counseling process.
家長不應該忽視學生的不當行為，因為這跟孩子的成長有很大的關聯，他們必須參與輔導過程。

2854 update [ʌpˈdet]　　v.　更新　　4th ★★★★★
If you want to keep your computer from being attacked by new viruses, you need to constantly renew and update your anti-virus software.
如果你不想讓新病毒入侵你的電腦，你必須持續更新防毒軟體。

2855 upgrade [ˈʌpˌgred]　　v.　升級　　4th ★★★★★
After many years of extensive research, Taiwanese computer companies have upgraded their quality.
台灣的電腦公司經過了多年的持續研究，品質儼然已經提升。

2856 uphold [ʌpˈhold]　　v.　維護　　4th ★★★★★
The duty of a police officer is to ensure public safety and uphold law and order.
警察的任務就是要確保公共安全以及維護法律秩序。

2857 upset [ʌpˈsɛt]　　adj.　不安的　　4th ★★★★★
I don't regret telling her what I thought even if it might have upset her.
我不後悔告訴她我的想法，即使她可能會因此感到不安。

2858 urban [ˈɝbən]　　adj.　都市的　　4th ★★★★★
Crime is growing at a rapid rate, especially in urban areas.
犯罪率快速增加，都市地區尤然。

2859 urge [ɝdʒ]　　v.　催促　　4th ★★★★★
The government urges people at cross-purposes to judge the second-generation health insurance policy on its own merits.
政府敦促立場不同的人，要根據兩代健康保險政策的優點，作為判斷基礎。

155

2860 urgent [ˈɝdʒənt]　　　　adj. 緊急的　　4th ★★★★★
The workers are urgent for payment of arrears of wages.
這些工人催促支付積欠的工資。

2861 use [juz]　　　　v. 使用　　5th ★★★★★
Advertisers will sometimes use half-truths.
廣告業者有時候只說出一半的真相。

2862 useful [ˈjusfəl]　　　　adj. 有用的　　5th ★★★★★
The most useful carbohydrates come from vegetables such as wheat and corn.
最有益的碳水化合物來自蔬菜，像是大麥或玉米。

2863 usurp [juˈzɝp]　　　　v. 篡奪　　3rd ★★★★★
Step-parents may exercise too little control over children for fear that they are usurping the rights of the child's natural parent.
繼父母較少管教孩子，因為他們害怕會篡奪親生父母的權利。

2864 usher [ˈʌʃə]　　　　v. 引領　　4th ★★★★★
The receptionist ushered me into the manager's office and offered me a tea.
接待員引領我到經理的辦公室，然後遞給我一杯茶。

2865 utensil [juˈtɛnsl]　　　　n. 家庭用品　　3rd ★★★★★
We decided to buy some utensils for our new apartment, including a refrigerator, a vacuum cleaner, and a dishwasher.
我們要替新公寓添購一些家庭用品，包括冰箱、吸塵器、洗碗機。

2866 utilize [ˈjutl͵aɪz]　　　　v. 利用　　3rd ★★★★★
When active patrol methods are utilized, law enforcement can be more effective in combating crime.
要是我們積極利用巡邏方法，執法就可以更有效打擊犯罪。

2867 vacant [ˈvekənt]　　　　adj. 空缺的　　4th ★★★★★
Due to the yearly bonus system, the one hundred vacant positions in this high-tech company have attracted many applicants from around the island.
這間科技公司的年度分紅體制，吸引各地的人來應徵這一百個職缺。

2868 vaccination [͵væksnˈeʃən]　　　　n. 接種　　3rd ★★★★★
Seasonal flu vaccinations began yesterday, leading to long lines at hospitals and health center across the island.
昨天季節性感冒疫苗開始施打，全島居民在醫院和健康中心前大排長龍。

2869 vaccine [væk'sin]   **n.** 疫苗   **3rd** ★★★★★
The discovery of the new vaccine is an important breakthrough in the fight against avian flu.
新疫苗的發現在對抗禽流感上是一件重大的突破。

2870 vain [ven]   **adj.** 徒然的   **4th** ★★★★★
I knocked loudly in the vain hope that someone might answer.
我大聲敲門，懷抱著徒然的希望，枉想有人會回應。

2871 vainglorious [‚ven'glorɪəs]   **adj.** 自負的   **3rd** ★★★★★
The vainglorious lawyer lost his case and disappointed his client.
這位自負的律師打輸了官司，也讓他的客戶失望。

2872 valid ['vælɪd]   **adj.** 正確的   **4th** ★★★★★
For the experiment to be valid, acceptable and effective, it is essential to record the data accurately.
為了讓實驗正確、可信且有效，精確記錄數據很重要。

2873 value ['vælju]   **n.** 價值   **5th** ★★★★★
If silver becomes more scarce than gold, it will no doubt have a greater value.
如果銀變得比金還要稀少，無疑會有更大的價值。

2874 vanish ['vænɪʃ]   **v.** 消失   **4th** ★★★★★
Telling me that he had to take a train home in ten minutes, he vanished into the street.
他告訴我他必須在十分鐘內搭火車回家，然後就消失在街上。

2875 variety [və'raɪətɪ]   **n.** 多樣化   **4th** ★★★★★
The mall has a variety of clothing stores.
大型購物中心有各式各樣的服裝店。

2876 various ['vɛrɪəs]   **adj.** 各式各樣的   **4th** ★★★★★
We have a chain of twelve stores through Taiwan, selling various sportswear and shoes.
我們在台灣各地有十二家連鎖商店，販售各式運動服裝及鞋子。

2877 vary ['vɛrɪ]   **v.** 變化   **4th** ★★★★★
The lunch menu is very short. It's less varied than the dinner menu.
午餐菜單很短，和晚餐比起來選擇比較少。

156

2878 vase [ves]　　　　　　　　　n.　花瓶　　　5th ★★★★★
My grandmother made a ceramic vase for me.
我祖母做了一個陶瓷花瓶給我。

2879 vast [væst]　　　　　　　　adj.　龐大的　　　5th ★★★★★
The company lost a vast sum of money this quarter.
公司在本季度損失了一大筆資金。

2880 vegetable ['vɛdʒətəbl]　　　n.　蔬菜　　　5th ★★★★★
People who live in this village grow fruit and vegetables by themselves; they provide for their own needs without outside help.
住在鄉村的居民自己種植蔬果，他們自給自足不靠外界的幫忙。

2881 vegetarian [ˌvɛdʒə'tɛrɪən]　　n.　素食主義者　　5th ★★★★★
The salesperson chatted over tea with his client in a vegetarian restaurant.
這位推銷員和他的客戶在一間素食餐廳喝茶聊天。

2882 vigorously ['vɪgərəslɪ]　　　adv.　用力地　　　3rd ★★★★★
A dog with fleas will often scratch itself so vigorously that the bites on its skin become worse.
身上有跳蚤的狗常會用力抓自己，使皮膚上的咬傷變得更糟。

2883 vehicle ['viɪkl]　　　　　　n.　車輛　　　4th ★★★★★
Many countries have regulations which help control exhaust emission from motor vehicles.
許多國家對汽機車的廢氣排放量有管制的法令。

2884 vendor ['vɛndə]　　　　　　n.　小販　　　5th ★★★★★
The old man is a vendor. He sells food and drinks around the temple every day.
這個老人是個小販，他每天在寺廟附近賣食物和飲料。

2885 ventilation [ˌvɛnt'eʃən]　　　n.　通風　　　3rd ★★★★★
The apartment with bad ventilation cost less than others in the building.
這間通風不良的公寓價格比大樓裡其他間還低。

2886 venture ['vɛntʃə]　　　　　v.　冒險從事　　　4th ★★★★★
When a company ventures into new markets, it will need to face various problems.
當一家公司冒險進入新的市場時，將會面臨許多問題。

2887 venue ['vɛnju]　　　　　　n.　犯罪地點　　　3rd ★★★★★

The police searched for the murderer's knife around the venue.
警方在犯罪現場周圍搜尋兇刀。

2888 verbal ['vɜbl̩]　　　　**adj.** 語言的　　**4th** ★★★★★
When we talk about communication, most of us probably think about verbal communication—that is, the words we use when talking.
當我們講到溝通，大部分的人可能會想到語言溝通，也就是我們說話時所用到的文字。

2889 verdict ['vɜdɪkt]　　　　**n.** 判決　　**3rd** ★★★★★
The jury reached a verdict of "Not guilty."
陪審團判決的結論是「無罪」。

2890 verify ['vɛrə,faɪ]　　　　**v.** 證實　　**4th** ★★★★★
My lawyer has verified that I am entitled to the heritage.
我的律師已經證實我有資格繼承遺產。

2891 version ['vɜʒən]　　　　**n.** 版本　　**4th** ★★★★★
An e-book, known as a digital book, is an electronic version of a printed book.
電子書，又稱為數位圖書，是印刷書的電子版本。

2892 vessel ['vɛsl̩]　　　　**n.** 商船　　**4th** ★★★★★
The vessel is due to arrive in Shanghai three days before Christmas.
船艦預訂於聖誕節前三天抵達上海。

2893 veteran ['vɛtərən]　　　　**adj.** 老練的　　**4th** ★★★★★
A veteran traveler knows that a hastily planned trip often ends up being tiring and nerve-racking rather than restful and enjoyable.
老練的旅行家知道匆忙成行的旅遊往往無法使人休息和享受，而是落得累人又神經緊繃。

2894 vibrant ['vaɪbrənt]　　　　**adj.** 活躍的　　**3rd** ★★★★★
In Africa, some democratic countries have vibrant political scenes, while other countries go through the routine of election but governance does not seem to improve.
在非洲，有些民主國家的政治局勢活絡，而有些國家則通過常規選舉，但治理上似乎都沒有改善。

2895 vibrate ['vaɪbret]　　　　**v.** 震動　　**4th** ★★★★★
The ground vibrated when the earthquake happened.
地震時地面震動。

157

2896 vicious [ˈvɪʃəs]   adj. 惡毒的   4th ★★★★★
Nobody wants to listen to such vicious remarks.
沒有人願意聽到如此惡意的批評。

2897 victim [ˈvɪktɪm]   n. 受害者   3rd ★★★★★
The paramedics checked to see if the victim of the accident was still alive.
醫務人員檢查意外事故的受害者是否都還活著。

2898 victory [ˈvɪktərɪ]   n. 勝利   4th ★★★★★
The victory of the home team overjoyed the people and they danced and sang on the streets for hours.
地主隊的勝利使大家欣喜若狂，他們在街上又跳又唱好幾小時。

2899 video [ˈvɪdɪˌo]   n. 錄影帶   5th ★★★★★
Break dancing was most popular during the 1980s, and during this time stars such as Michael Jackson performed this style of dancing in music videos.
霹靂舞是一九八零年代最流行的舞步，這個時期許多明星像是麥克傑克遜都在音樂錄影帶裡表演這種舞步。

2900 view [vju]   n. 視野   4th ★★★★★
This room is very comfortable. It's quite big, and it has a great view of the park.
這個房間非常舒服，空間很大，而且有絕佳的視野可以看見公園。

2901 village [ˈvɪlɪdʒ]   n. 村落   4th ★★★★★
My hometown used to be a quiet country village, but now it is noisy and crowded.
我的家鄉以前是個寧靜的鄉下村落，但現在已經變得又吵又擠。

2902 violate [ˈvaɪəˌlet]   v. 違反   4th ★★★★★
The gangster was charged with violating social order maintenance law.
歹徒被控違反社會秩序維護法。

2903 violation [ˌvaɪəˈleʃən]   n. 侵犯   4th ★★★★★
Tibet's government-in-exile demanded that the U.N. intervene to halt the severe human rights violations by China.
西藏流亡政府要求聯合國進行干預，制止嚴重侵犯人權的中國。

2904 violent [ˈvaɪələnt]   adj. 激烈的   4th ★★★★★
Violent sports are often quite popular.
激烈的運動經常廣受歡迎。

2905 violently ['vaɪələntlɪ]　　　**adv.** 暴力地　　4th ★★★★★
The angry man started hitting people around him violently.
生氣的男子開始暴力毆打他周遭的人。

2906 virtual ['vɜtʃuəl]　　　**adj.** 虛擬的　　4th ★★★★★
The university has developed a "virtual patient," created by a computer, to help train the pharmacists of the future.
大學開發了一種由電腦創造出來的「虛擬病人」，幫助訓練未來的藥劑師。

2907 virtue ['vɜtʃu]　　　**n.** 優點　　4th ★★★★★
Courage is the virtue which moves men to perform noble deeds in times of peril.
勇氣是一項優點，讓人們在危急時刻做出高尚的行為。

2908 virus ['vaɪrəs]　　　**n.** 病毒　　4th ★★★★★
Don't click everything that pops up on the Internet or you will get a virus.
不要點擊網路上突然彈出的東西，否則你的電腦會中毒。

2909 visa ['vizə]　　　**n.** 簽證　　5th ★★★★★
The foreigner came to Taiwan on a tourist visa.
這個外國人用旅遊簽證來台。

2910 visibility [ˌvɪzə'bɪlətɪ]　　　**n.** 能見度　　4th ★★★★★
The accident happened for the sake of the poor visibility.
發生這起事故的原因是由於能見度低。

2911 visible ['vɪzəbl]　　　**adj.** 看得見的　　4th ★★★★★
The street sign is barely visible through the thick fog.
因為濃霧太厚，幾乎看不見街上的標示。

2912 vision ['vɪʒən]　　　**n.** 遠見　　4th ★★★★★
A good leader needs to provide a clear-cut vision for the followers. So they know what they are striving for.
一位好的領導者必須提供追隨者明確的視野，這樣他們才知道是為了什麼奮鬥。

2913 visit ['vɪzɪt]　　　**v.** 訪問　　5th ★★★★★
Debra's uncle always pinches her cheek when he visits.
黛布拉來訪時，她舅舅總會捏她臉頰。

2914 visitor ['vɪzɪtə]　　　**n.** 訪客　　5th ★★★★★
To enter the museum, visitors must pay for the admission fee.
為了進入博物館，訪客必須支付門票。

2915 visualize ['vɪʒuə,laɪz]　　　**v.**　使顯現　　4th　★★★★★
Though Dr. Wang has been away from his hometown for over ten years, he can still visualize his old house clearly.
即使王博士離開家鄉超過十年，他的舊房子依然清楚浮現在他腦海中。

2916 vital ['vaɪtḷ]　　　**adj.**　重要的　　4th　★★★★★
Social life is vital to the existence of humans.
社交生活對人類的生存很重要。

2917 vitamin ['vaɪtəmɪn]　　　**n.**　維他命　　5th　★★★★★
Eating fruit and vegetables does people good because such food is rich in vitamin C.
吃蔬菜水果對人體健康很好，因為這些食物富含維他命C。

2918 vivid ['vɪvɪd]　　　**adj.**　生動的　　4th　★★★★★
Stella gave a vivid description of her trip in Paris.
史黛拉把她去巴黎的旅行描述的栩栩如生。

2919 vocabulary [və'kæbjə,lɛrɪ]　　　**n.**　字彙　　4th　★★★★★
Small vocabulary size usually prevents readers from fully understanding the text they read.
缺乏字彙量會讓讀者無法全盤了解他們所讀的文本。

2920 vocational [vo'keʃənḷ]　　　**adj.**　職業的　　4th　★★★★★
Vocational high school students should have greater influence in themselves in order to learn English well.
職校生為了學好英文，應讓英文對自己產生更大的影響力。

2921 voice [vɔɪs]　　　**n.**　聲音　　5th　★★★★★
The famous singer's wonderful voice made a deep impression on the audience.
名歌手美妙的聲音為觀眾留下了深刻的印象。

2922 volcanic [vɑl'kænɪk]　　　**adj.**　火山的　　4th　★★★★★
The island is, in fact, one of the many little volcanic islands in the northern Pacific Ocean.
這座島實際上是北太平洋上許多火山群島中的一個。

2923 voluntary ['vɑlən,tɛrɪ]　　　**adj.**　自願的　　4th　★★★★★
Those college students work at the orphanage on a voluntary basis, helping the children with their studies without receiving any pay.
那些大學生在孤兒院做志工，幫助孩子的學業不收半毛錢。

2924 volunteer [ˌvɑlən'tɪr]　v.　自願　4th ★★★★★
We enjoy working with Canny because she always volunteers to help.
我們喜歡和坎尼一起工作，因為她總是自願幫忙。

2925 vote [vot]　v.　投票　4th ★★★★★
The mayor's eloquent appeal for support after the city was devastated by earthquakes was voted the most influential speech of the year.
城市遭地震破壞之後，市長那憾動人心的請願被票選為年度最有影響力的演說。

2926 voucher ['vautʃə]　n.　票券　4th ★★★★★
The shopping voucher policy aimed to stimulate consumption in order to boost up droopy economy.
消費券的目的是為了刺激消費，好挽救低迷的經濟。

2927 vulnerable ['vʌlnərəbl]　adj.　脆弱的　3rd ★★★★★
Deforestation, soil pollution, and the introduction of non-native species render many species of animals vulnerable, if not extinct.
砍伐森林、土壤汙染及引進非原生種生物儘管沒有導致許多動物的絕種，也會讓牠們變得脆弱。

2928 wage [wedʒ]　n.　工資　4th ★★★★★
It seems that rising prices of commodities and products tend to neutralize workers' increased wages.
商品價格的提升和工人增加的工資似乎剛好抵銷掉了。

2929 wait [wet]　v.　等待　5th ★★★★★
Owen stirred his soup while he waited for it to cool down.
歐文一邊攪拌著湯，一邊等著湯變涼。

2930 wallet ['wɑlɪt]　n.　皮包　5th ★★★★★
On a crowded bus, you should beware of your wallet.
在擁擠的公車上，你要注意你的錢包。

2931 wander ['wɑndə]　v.　漫遊　4th ★★★★★
Carl's mind wandered and he dozed off soon after the speech started.
演講才開始沒有多久，卡爾的心思就飄到九霄雲外，還打起瞌睡來。

2932 want [wɑnt]　v.　想要　5th ★★★★★
Mr. Johnson decided to decorate his house on a tight budget. He did not want to spend much money.
強生先生決定用有限的預算來裝潢他的房子，他不想花太多錢。

159

2933 war [wɔr]   **n.** 戰爭   5th ★★★★★

War is never supposed to be a deliberate way to decide quarrels between countries.
戰爭不該是國與國之間解決糾紛的辦法，那只是未經深思熟慮下做的決定。

2934 warehouse ['wɛr,haus]   **n.** 批發店   4th ★★★★★

The bed bought from a big furniture warehouse cost less than that in a store.
家具批發店買的床比在一般家具行還便宜。

2935 warm [wɔrm]   **adj.** 溫暖的   5th ★★★★★

Most plants need a lot of water and a warm, sunny environment so as to grow well.
大多數植物需要充足的水分和溫暖有陽光的環境讓它們好好成長。

2936 warn [wɔrn]   **v.** 警告   4th ★★★★★

The UN has promised providing a tsunami warning system to be established in the Indian Ocean.
聯合國承諾要在印度洋建立一個海嘯警告系統。

2937 warranty ['wɔrəntɪ]   **n.** 保證書   4th ★★★★★

The car dealer who sold me my car gave me an excellent price and a three-year warranty.
賣我車的車商給我一個很棒的價格外加三年的保固。

2938 waste [west]   **v.** 浪費   5th ★★★★★

The man is too generous a boss to waste his money on such a hopeless project.
那位老闆太慷慨大方了，才會浪費那麼多錢在一項無望的企劃上。

2939 wasteland ['west,lænd]   **n.** 荒地   4th ★★★★★

There are groups of stray dogs moving around in the wasteland.
有一群流浪狗在荒地裡走來走去。

2940 waterfall ['wɔtɚ,fɔl]   **n.** 瀑布   5th ★★★★★

As we walked away from the waterfall, the fizzle slowly became quieter.
我們離開瀑布後，瀑布的水流聲就慢慢變小了。

2941 wave [wev]   **n.** 揮手   5th ★★★★★

He gave us a wave as the bus drove off.
公車開走的時候，他向我們揮揮手。

2942 weak [wik]   **adj.** 虛弱的   **5th** ★★★★★
The bodybuilder was weakened by a fever.
這位健美運動家由於發燒，身體變得虛弱。

2943 weapon ['wɛpən]   **n.** 武器   **5th** ★★★★★
Knives and guns are dangerous weapons that can kill people.
刀和槍都是可以致人於死的危險武器。

2944 wear [wɛr]   **v.** 穿戴   **5th** ★★★★★
I have to ticket you for not wearing a safety helmet.
你沒有戴安全帽，我必須要開你一張罰單。

2945 weary ['wɪrɪ]   **adj.** 疲倦的   **4th** ★★★★★
The engineers working in the high-tech company feel weary in body and mind.
在高科技公司工作的工程師，感到身心俱疲。

2946 weather ['wɛðɚ]   **n.** 天氣   **5th** ★★★★★
Nothing is more attractive to birds during hot weather than drinking and bathing places.
在炎熱的天氣裡，到處找水喝和還有洗澡是鳥類最喜歡做的事。

2947 weave [wiv]   **v.** 編織   **5th** ★★★★★
It takes great skill to weave a bamboo hat by hand.
手工編織斗笠需要很高的技巧。

2948 website ['wɛb,saɪt]   **n.** 網站   **5th** ★★★★★
On the subject of physical and medical research, there are thousands of amazing websites where people can get information.
人們可以從上千個很棒的網站找到有關生理及醫學的研究。

2949 weight [wet]   **n.** 體重   **5th** ★★★★★
Individuals suffering from anorexia have extreme weight loss, which is usually 15% below the person's normal body weight.
患有厭食症的人體重會大幅減輕，通常比一般正常人的體重低個百分之十五。

2950 welfare ['wɛl,fɛr]   **n.** 福利   **4th** ★★★★★
The government needs to increase welfare spending.
政府必須要增加社會福利經費。

2951 well-known ['wɛl'non]   **adj.** 出名的   **4th** ★★★★★

160

The company is well-known for caring about protecting human rights, the environment, and being against animal testing.
這間公司因為關懷人權、保護環境以及抵制動物實驗而十分出名。

2952 west [wɛst]　　　　　n.　西方　　5th　★★★★★
Some anthropologists believed that romantic love spread from the west to other cultures only recently.
一些人類學家認為，浪漫愛情是最近才從西方擴展到其他文化。

2953 westerner ['wɛstənə]　　　n.　西方人　　5th　★★★★★
An American may have great difficulty distinguishing a Chinese from Japanese. To westerners, they are both Asians.
美國人很難區別出中國人和日本人，對西方人而言，他們都是亞洲人。

2954 wet [wɛt]　　　　　adj.　溼的　　5th　★★★★★
The pitcher put some powder in his hands so that they wouldn't be so wet.
投手放些粉末在他手中，這樣他的手才不會太濕滑。

2955 whatever [hwɑt'ɛvə]　　adj.　什麼也　　3rd　★★★★★
She told herself that she would be satisfied with whatever she could get.
她告訴自己無論得到什麼都會心滿意足。

2956 whole [hol]　　　　　adj.　全部的　　4th　★★★★★
You have worked so hard for a whole year. You should consider taking a break.
你已經如此努力工作一整年了，你應該考慮放個假。

2957 wide [waɪd]　　　　　adj.　張大的　　5th　★★★★★
The man stared with wide eyes at the luxurious car.
這位先生瞪大雙眼盯著這輛豪華轎車。

2958 widely ['waɪdlɪ]　　　　adv.　廣泛地　　5th　★★★★★
As computers are getting less expensive, they are widely used in schools and offices today.
隨著電腦的價格越來越便宜，現在已經廣泛為學校和公司所使用。

2959 widespread ['waɪd,sprɛd]　adj.　普及的　　4th　★★★★★
It's necessary to learn English because it is a widespread language.
學英文是必要的，因為英文是全球性的語言。

2960 wilderness ['wɪldənɪs]　　n.　荒地　　5th　★★★★★
There are no buildings and no farm lands between us and the sea. It's all

wildernesses.
從我們這裡到海岸邊沒有任何的建築物和農地，全是一片荒地。

2961 willing ['wɪlɪŋ]   **adj.** 願意的   **4th** ★★★★★
Leo is so devoted to his work that he is willing to risk his life.
李歐對他的工作相當熱衷，他甚至願意拿自己的生命冒險。

2962 wipe [waɪp]   **v.** 擦拭   **5th** ★★★★★
To keep the glass clean, you need to wipe your mouth with the napkin before drinking the wine.
為維持玻璃杯清潔，你要在飲酒前先用餐巾擦拭嘴巴。

2963 windshield ['wɪnd‚ʃild]   **n.** 擋風玻璃   **3rd** ★★★★★
Windshield wipers of a car were invented by Mary Anderson on a trip in New York City in 1903.
車子的雨刷是瑪麗‧安德森在一九零三年去紐約旅行時發明的。

2964 wine [waɪn]   **n.** 酒   **5th** ★★★★★
Plums are used to make wine more often than they are in the USA.
在美國，梅子較常被用來釀酒，而不是直接食用。

2965 wink [wɪŋk]   **n.** 眨眼   **4th** ★★★★★
Jeffery gave me a wink to let me know that he was kidding.
傑佛瑞向我使了一個眼色讓我知道他是在開玩笑。

2966 wire [waɪr]   **n.** 電線   **5th** ★★★★★
The Internet is a bunch of wires and cables that collect millions of computers around the world.
網路就是用一大捆的電線和電纜將全世界所有的電腦連接起來。

2967 wise [waɪz]   **adj.** 智慧的   **5th** ★★★★★
Taking into account all the circumstances, John thought it wise not to say anything further.
約翰考慮到所有情況，他認為聰明的話最好不要再繼續多說了。

2968 witch [wɪtʃ]   **n.** 女巫   **5th** ★★★★★
There is a witch action figure hung on the Halloween mask.
有一個女巫小模型掛在萬聖節面具上。

2969 withdraw [wɪð'drɔ]   **v.** 提取   **4th** ★★★★★
Mrs. Liu withdrew all her savings from the bank for her son's tuition.
劉太太為了兒子的學費，從銀行提領出所有的存款。

161

2970 wither ['wɪðɚ]　　　　**v.** 枯萎　　**3rd** ★★★★★
The heat of July has withered most of the grass on the hill.
七月酷暑已經使山上大部分的草地乾枯了。

2971 within [wɪ'ðɪn]　　　　**prep.** 在⋯裡面　　**5th** ★★★★★
When I asked about advancement within the new organization, the interviewee responded, "The sky's the limit!"
當我問起新機構的前景時，受訪者答道：「前途無量。」

2972 witness ['wɪtnɪs]　　　　**v.** 目擊　　**4th** ★★★★★
Today at least half a million people will witness Carol and Jeffrey's second wedding.
今天至少有五十萬人見證卡羅和傑佛瑞的再婚。

2973 wonder ['wʌndɚ]　　　　**n.** 奇蹟　　**5th** ★★★★★
The universe is full of wonders. Throughout history, people have been fascinated by the mystery of what lies beyond our planet.
宇宙充滿著奇蹟。從古至今，大家都十分嚮往地球之外的秘密。

2974 word [wɝd]　　　　**n.** 文字　　**5th** ★★★★★
Anyone who can use word documents would be able to create their own blogs.
任何會使用Word文字檔的人，都可以創作自己的部落格。

2975 world [wɝld]　　　　**n.** 世界　　**5th** ★★★★★
Chicago is a world-renowned center of landmark buildings, a place to which famous architects were drawn to invent new spaces.
芝加哥是世界著名的指標建築中心，知名建築師都受吸引來這裡開發新的生活空間。

2976 worldwide ['wɝld,waɪd]　　　　**adj.** 全世界的　　**5th** ★★★★★
Even as economic recovery spreads worldwide, workers are finding themselves not saving more money.
即便經濟復甦已經蔓延到全世界，員工發現自己還是存不了什麼錢。

2977 workplace ['wɝk,ples]　　　　**n.** 工作場所　　**4th** ★★★★★
There are lots of issues that can affect our health in the workplace.
工作場所有許多會影響到我們健康的問題。

2978 worried ['wɝɪd]　　　　**adj.** 擔心的　　**5th** ★★★★★
The mayor is worried about gangs in the city.
市長擔心城市的幫派問題。

一考就上！考公職一定要會的3000單字

2979 worse [wɜs]   **adj.** 更糟的   5th ★★★★★

The professor expects that the domestic economic situation will get from worse to worst these years.
教授預估國內的經濟情勢將在這幾年間跌落谷底。

2980 worship [ˈwɜʃɪp]   **v.** 崇拜   4th ★★★★★

Taiwanese people tend to worship some local gods.
台灣人民往往崇拜地方神祇。

2981 worthwhile [ˈwɜθˈhwaɪl]   **adj.** 值得的   4th ★★★★★

Students should spend their time on some worthwhile learning.
學生應該把時間花在一些值得學習的事情上。

2982 worthless [ˈwɜθlɪs]   **adj.** 無價值的   4th ★★★★★

Maria's diamond necklace is actually fake and worthless.
瑪利亞的鑽石項鍊其實是假的而且毫無價值。

2983 wound [wund]   **n.** 傷口   4th ★★★★★

Gun wounds can be divided into four broad categories, depending on the range from the muzzle to the target.
槍傷可概分為四大類，依槍口到目標物的範圍而定。

2984 wrap [ræp]   **v.** 纏繞   5th ★★★★★

Bridget thinks it's funny to wrap a scarf around the snowman's neck.
布麗姬覺得把圍巾繞在雪人的脖子上很好玩。

2985 wrinkle [ˈrɪŋkl]   **n.** 皺紋   4th ★★★★★

Besides lung cancer, another consequence of smoking is wrinkles, a premature sign of aging.
吸煙除了會得到肺癌，還會產生皺紋，這是提早老化的徵兆。

2986 yacht [jɑt]   **n.** 遊艇   5th ★★★★★

The tour group sailed on a yacht around Sun Moon Lake.
旅行團到日月潭搭乘快艇遊湖。

2987 yard [jɑrd]   **n.** 庭院   5th ★★★★★

You can play outside, but you must not leave the yard.
你可以到外面玩，但絕對不可以離開庭院。

2988 yawn [jɔn]   **v.** 打呵欠   4th ★★★★★

162

Eddie couldn't help but yawn during the boring speech.
乏味的演講不禁讓艾迪打起呵欠。

2989 yearly [ˈjɪrlɪ]　　　　　　　**adj.**　每年的　　5th　★★★★★
The firm's yearly income has been increasing in the past five years.
這間公司的年收入在過去五年間持續攀升。

2990 yearn [jɜn]　　　　　　　**v.**　渴望　　3rd　★★★★★
The exchange student yearned for his hometown whenever he heard the romantic song.
每當這位交換學生聽到浪漫抒情歌時，就會懷念起他的故鄉。

2991 yell [jɛl]　　　　　　　**v.**　喊叫　　5th　★★★★★
The little girl yelled out fright when the stray dog came up to her.
當流浪狗靠進小女孩時，她嚇得大叫。

2992 yogurt [ˈjogət]　　　　　　　**n.**　優格　　5th　★★★★★
Linda likes to eat bread with yogurt for breakfast.
琳達早餐喜歡吃麵包配優格。

2993 yolk [jok]　　　　　　　**n.**　蛋黃　　5th　★★★★★
Brian is allergic to the yolk of an egg.
布萊恩對蛋黃過敏。

2994 youth [juθ]　　　　　　　**n.**　少年　　5th　★★★★★
Youth organizations, like the Boy Scouts and YMCA, are known for having lots of summer camps.
像是童子軍和基督教青年協會這類的青年團體，以舉辦夏令營聞名。

2995 zeal [zil]　　　　　　　**n.**　熱忱　　4th　★★★★★
Zeal without knowledge is a runaway horse.
志大才疏，一生庸碌。

2996 zebra crossing　　　　　　　**n.**　斑馬線　　5th　★★★★★
Vehicles are supposed to stop so that people can walk across the zebra crossing.
車輛都應該停止，以便人們能走過斑馬線。

2997 zenith [ˈzinɪθ]　　　　　　　**n.**　頂點　　3rd　★★★★★
The president is at the zenith of his fame.
總統的聲勢現在如日中天。

2998 zero [ˈzɪro]　　　　　　　**n.** 零　　　**5th** ★★★★★

My favorite team won the game with a score of two to zero.
我支持的球隊以二比零贏得比賽。

2999 zip [zɪp]　　　　　　　　**v.** 拉拉鍊　　**4th** ★★★★★

Don't forget to zip your jacket when you ride a motorcycle.
你騎機車的時候不要忘了把外套拉鍊拉上。

3000 zip code　　　　　　　　**n.** 郵遞區號　**4th** ★★★★★

Writing down precise zip codes is essential to mail a letter.
寄信時，務必寫下正確的郵遞區號。

3001 zone [zon]　　　　　　　**n.** 地區　　**4th** ★★★★★

Jet lag, caused by traveling between time zones, is becoming a common problem for frequent travelers.
因旅行於不同時區所產生的時差，對經常旅行的人來說是很普遍的問題。

3002 zoo [zu]　　　　　　　　**n.** 動物園　**3rd** ★★★★★

These lions were born in the zoo.
這些獅子是在動物園出生的。

我們改寫了書的定義

創辦人暨名譽董事長　王擎天
董事長　王寶玲
總經理　歐綾纖　　　　印製者　絃億印刷公司
出版總監　王寶玲

法人股東　華鴻創投、華利創投、和通國際、利通創投、創意創投、
　　　　　中國電視、中租迪和、仁寶電腦、台北富邦銀行、台灣工業
　　　　　銀行、國寶人壽、東元電機、凌陽科技（創投）、力麗集團、
　　　　　東捷資訊

策略聯盟　采舍國際‧創智行銷‧凱立國際資訊‧玉山銀行
　　　　　凱旋資訊‧知遠文化‧均洋印刷‧僑大圖書
　　　　　交通部郵政總局‧數位聯合（seednet）
　　　　　全球八達網‧全球線上‧優碩資訊‧矽緯資訊
　　　　　（歡迎出版同業加入，共襄盛舉）

◆台灣出版事業群　　新北市中和區中山路2段366巷10號10樓
　　　　　　　　　　TEL：2248-7896
　　　　　　　　　　FAX：2248-7758

◆北京出版事業群　　北京 市東城區東直門東中街40號元嘉國際公寓A座820
　　　　　　　　　　TEL：86-10-64172733
　　　　　　　　　　FAX：86-10-64173011

◆北美出版事業群　　4th Floor Harbour Centre P.O.Box613
　　　　　　　　　　GT George Town, Grand Cayman,
　　　　　　　　　　Cayman Island

◆倉儲及物流中心　　新北市中和區中山路2段366巷10號3樓
　　　　　　　　　　TEL：02-2226-7768
　　　　　　　　　　FAX：02-8226-7496

www.book4u.com.tw

www.book4u.com.tw

國家圖書館出版品預行編目資料

一考就上！考公職一定要會的3000單字　/ 蘇秦著.
—初版.—新北市：華文網, 2011.01
面；公分· — (Excellent；37)
ISBN 978-986-271-049-4(平裝)

1.英語 2.詞彙

805.12　　　　　　　　　　　100000317

知識工場‧Excellent 37

一考就上！
考公職一定要會的3000單字

出版者／全球華文聯合出版平台‧知識工場
作　者／蘇秦　　　　　印行者／知識工場
出版總監／王寶玲　　　文字編輯／丁翊倫
總 編 輯 ／歐綾纖　　　美術設計／蔡瑪麗

郵撥帳號／50017206 采舍國際有限公司（郵撥購買，請另付 一成郵資）
台灣出版中心／新北市中和區中山路2段366巷10號10樓
電話／（02）2248-7896
傳真／（02）2248-7758
ISBN-13／978-986-271-049-4
出版日期／2019年1月三版十五刷

全球華文市場總代理／采舍國際
地址／新北市中和區中山路2段366巷10號3樓
電話／（02）8245-8786
傳真／（02）8245-8718

全系列書系特約展示門市
橋大書局　　　　　　　　　　新絲路網路書店
地址／台北市南陽街7號2樓　　地址／新北市中和區中山路2段366巷10號10樓
電話／（02）2331-0234　　　電話／（02）8245-9896
傳真／（02）2331-1073　　　網址／www.silkbook.com

線上pbook&ebook總代理／全球華文聯合出版平台
地址／新北市中和區中山路2段366巷10號10樓
主題討論區／http://www.silkbook.com/bookclub　◆新絲路讀書會
紙本書平台／http://www.book4u.com.tw　　　　◆華文網網路書店
瀏覽電子書／http://www.book4u.com.tw　　　　◆華文電子書中心
電子書下載／http://www.book4u.com.tw　　　　◆電子書中心(Acrobat Reader)

本書採減碳印製流程並使用優質中性紙（Acid & Alkali Free）通過綠色印刷認證，最符環保要求。

本書為蘇秦名師及出版社編輯小組精心編著覆核，如仍有疏漏，請各位先進不吝指正。來函請寄
mujung@mail.book4u.com.tw，若經查證無誤，我們將有精美小禮物贈送！